DARK MIND

FALL OF MAGIC BOOK TWO

VAL NEIL

Living Relic Press

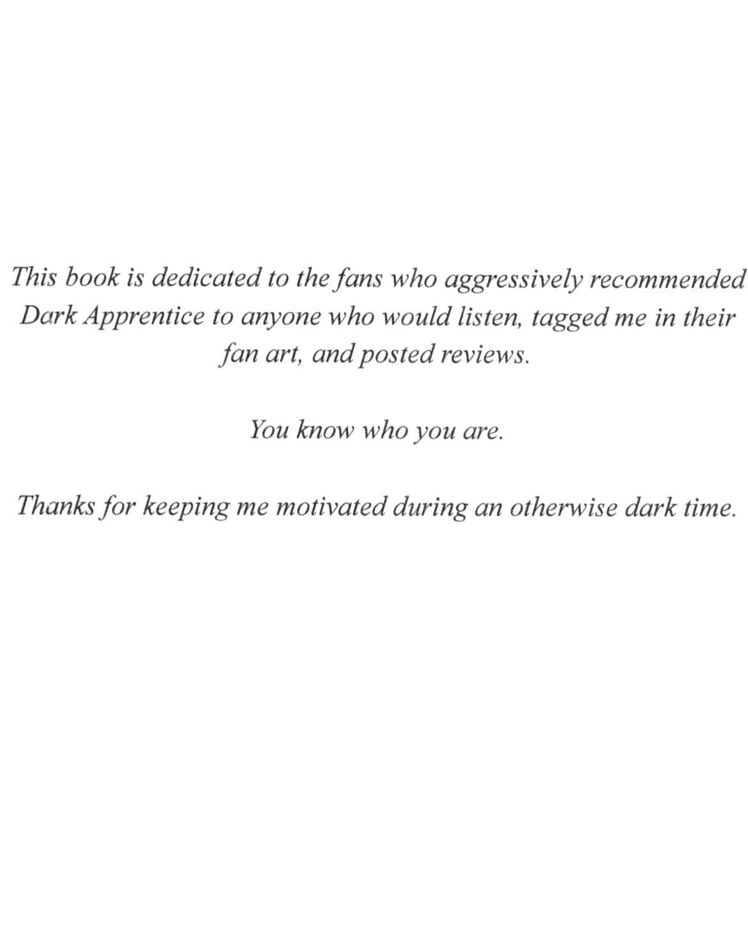

This book is dedicated to the fans who aggressively recommended Dark Apprentice to anyone who would listen, tagged me in their fan art, and posted reviews.

You know who you are.

Thanks for keeping me motivated during an otherwise dark time.

CONTENTS

OBLIGATORY REMINDERS

The Major Players

Nikolai: Psychopathic wannabe dark wizard, natural-born telepath, too horny for his own good. Medea's apprentice. Reasonably accurate portrayal of Antisocial Personality Disorder (psychopathy) confirmed by psychologist and multiple people with ASPD.

Medea: Immortal autistic bookworm with a special interest in magic and kicking ass. At home in her element and a hot mess everywhere else. Currently training Nikolai. Accurate portrayal of autism because the author is autistic.

Yoxtl: Furloughed trickster spirit, will work for souls. Pronouns are yit/yitself when inside its point of view. Has the ability to teleport to known locations (or people, via a blood link). Can choose who sees and hears it, and whether to be corporeal.

The Magic

Spells take three things to cast: mana, will, and focus.

Mana is like magical energy, and the amount of mana a spell takes is directly proportional to the amount of energy expended. (Except when it's not. Don't come at me with numbers. I didn't enjoy physics in college, and I'll be damned if I'm going to do the math for every spell now. Just understand this isn't *Star Wars*—the size of the object moved *does* matter.)

Will is the caster's commitment to action.

Focus is the caster's ability to concentrate and see precisely what they wish to happen.

Magi are people born with enough inherent mana to cast spells. They can increase their natural mana pool by casting spells, just as an athlete can increase stamina or strength through training.

Mundanes are people born below this threshold. Most are unaware magic exists.

Witches are people who get their mana from a spirit in exchange for their soul (upon death). However, Mundanes often apply this term to anyone who uses magic.

Spirits are conscious beings made of magic.

Gateways are magical portals connecting distant places together. Medea has a hub of them on her island.

There is much more, but Medea goes into great detail in *Dark Apprentice* and I'm not going to repeat everything here.

The Story Thus Far

    Reminders of major events in *Dark Apprentice* take place

within the book itself, in the form of mini-flashbacks (you know, those paragraphs you skim over if you're binging). I'm planning on this being a long series, though, so I will probably end up using this place for more detailed recaps in later books.

If you missed the bonus epilogue for *Dark Apprentice*, you can grab it on my website under Bonus Content (valneil.com/bonus-content/).

AUTHOR NOTES

Yes, there are author notes at the beginning *and* the end now.

This book nearly broke me. Both because I had to split it and because it covers heavy topics like racism and mental health treatment (or what passed for it) in 1957. While not historical fiction, the series is based in the real world, which is an objectively shitty place to live depending on who you are. To say this book strained my own mental health is putting it mildly. I had to stop many times during my research because it was so upsetting. I will never cease to be devastated at the casual horrors humans inflict on one another. It didn't help that I was doing revisions during a global pandemic or that certain news stories mirrored scenes I'd written —things that shouldn't still be happening today but most decidedly are.

I've always intended for the series to overlap with historical social issues, so I got a little concerned when readers praised *Dark Apprentice* for not taking itself too seriously. Don't get me wrong, there's a lot of humor in *Dark Mind*, but it *is* dark fantasy and certain parts are intentionally uncomfortable. There are the things you expect: swearing, violence, murder, gore, and body horror. But there is also sexism, racism, homophobia, and ableism (as usual, written to be accurate). Perhaps someday I will write cozy fantasy, but today is not that day.

Special thanks to all my beta readers, but particularly Kakwasi, who generously donated her time to help ensure that my portrayals of Black characters and their experiences in the 1950s were accurate, and to Jem for doing the same with regard to the Black disabled autistic experience.

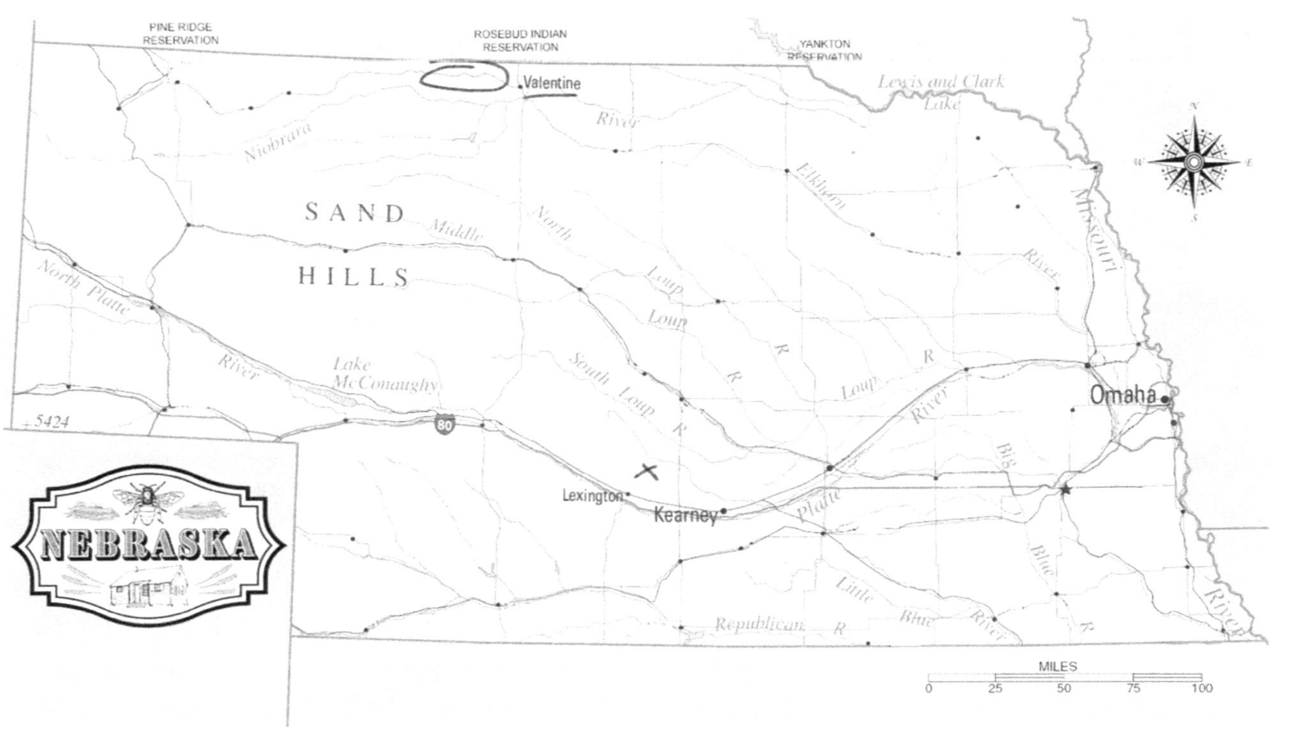

PINE RIDGE RESERVATION
ROSEBUD INDIAN RESERVATION
YANKTON RESERVATION
Valentine
Lewis and Clark Lake
Niobrara
SAND HILLS
Middle
North
Elkhorn
Loup
Loup
R
R
Loup
River
North Platte
River
Lake McConaughy
South Loup R
Platte
River
Big
Blue
Little Blue River
Republican R
Missouri River
Omaha
Lexington
Kearney
80
5424
NEBRASKA
MILES
0 25 50 75 100

1

HEAT

Nikolai landed hard on the smoldering ground. Something burned, but it wasn't the grass. A tendril of flame snaked up his lapel. He smothered it with his hand and discarded the coat.

"Why must you overdress for everything?" Medea stood a ways away, a ball of fire dancing from one hand to the other.

"This is perfectly acceptable casual wear. See? No tie. If it offends you, I can take everything off."

A fireball winged toward him. He rolled away, then sprang to his feet and replaced his shield. It was barely up before the next bolt hit. Even with his heels dug in, the force pushed him back several inches.

Heat radiated through the shield. Water. He needed water. Medea had intentionally chosen a location far from lakes and streams to practice combating pyromancy. At first, he'd tried to summon water, as he did with food, but Medea had tsked and told him to try something else. Lately she'd doubled down on insisting he be more creative in solving problems, discarding his first and sometimes his second ideas.

Conjuring water hadn't yielded nearly enough. His meager

attempts turned to steam and dissipated. Conjuring, unlike summoning, made use of whatever was in the vicinity, and the air was simply too dry.

He shot a spell from behind his shield, not really aiming, just trying to buy himself time to look around. A fine layer of white gravel covered the dry earth, reflecting the intense midday sun. What little vegetation dotted the landscape was yellow and parched. No water there. A small grove of trees stood in the distance. Would they hold enough moisture?

Fire kissed his toes. He yelped and danced backward. It had been two years since he began training with Medea, and he still couldn't launch projectile spells from any point other than his own body. She'd told him to keep practicing, that it would come, but in the meantime, he was forced to use a partial shield, one that left several body parts exposed, a weakness Medea consistently exploited.

"It's not good to stay in one spot for too long!" she called out, conjuring a flaming lasso and sending it hurtling in his direction.

He tried to move, but he was too late. The lasso encircled him, shield and all. Pain seared his unprotected back. He slashed apart the lasso and bolted for the grove.

Blood pounded in his ears. As soon as he reached the trees, he started drawing water from the foliage into the space between his hands. Leaves browned and fell like rain. When all the leaves had been drained, he had an orb with enough water to counter a single fireball. It wouldn't make a difference in the onslaught he knew was coming.

Medea strolled toward the grove at a leisurely pace, as if she were simply enjoying the countryside. When she reached the trees, her eyes fell to the ankle-deep mass of leaves.

She shook her head. "That was a mistake." With a flick of her wrist, the carpet of dried leaves burst into flame.

He spun the orb about himself, encasing his body in a thin

film of water, and tore from the grove, flames licking at his heels. He crested a small hill and flung himself down the opposite side, out of Medea's line of sight.

He was missing something. Medea was forever lecturing him about tackling problems from a new angle. Water was the obvious counter to fire. What was less obvious?

Regular fire needed fuel to burn, but magical flames could be conjured at will and hurled through the air. Magical fire might not need fuel, but it was a fair bet it still required oxygen.

Back over the hill, Medea had just left the inferno. Ash and embers swirled around her. Already her palms were filling with fire. A year ago, he wouldn't have recognized it for what it was— pure spectacle, a handicapping of her abilities for his benefit, as he'd once done for his sparring partners. She could unleash fire instantaneously, but then he'd never be able to dodge or block, and he'd never learn.

He focused on the air in front of him, willing out the oxygen. The fireball would extinguish before hitting. Sweat beaded his brow. The necessary focus was like nothing he'd ever experienced before. His chest hurt with the effort.

As the first fireball hit the oxygen-free zone, it winked out. The pain in his chest was excruciating now. He ignored it, holding his focus as the second fireball approached. Instead of winking out, the fireball grew dim. Everything was getting dim. He had to focus just a little longer! The fireball extinguished, and the world went black.

———

"... Nikolai ... Nikolai!"

Someone called his name from far away. His head pounded. A hazy red shape hovered above him—Medea?

He sat up and the world spun. A firm hand pushed him back down.

"Not yet." Medea knelt beside him. Christ, how many times had he been unconscious around her?

"What happened?" He rubbed his eyes with his palms, stars adding chaos to his vision. Memories came back slowly—pyromancy . . . trees . . . he had tried to stop a fireball.

"You blacked out. When you suffocate fire, take better care not to suffocate yourself as well." She sounded amused.

He groaned. So that's why his chest had hurt. He should've left a small region of oxygen near his face. He'd been so focused on pushing it all away that he hadn't realized his error.

"Didn't you feel it?" she asked. "You almost drowned twice. I should think you'd be used to the sensation."

"I felt it. I just ignored it."

"Pain is the body's way of saying—"

"—that something is wrong. I know, I know."

Medea helped him sit up. "Heal yourself."

He turned his focus inward and urged his body to heal. She'd taught him little else the past year. He could now heal surface wounds with minimal scarring, mend bones, even regrow limbs, though the latter took far too long to be practical in combat. Grievous injuries were still a challenge, especially if they involved internal organs—he was no good with those—and the small details, what Medea called "fine work," eluded him completely. She could glance at someone and instantly know their ailments but couldn't adequately describe half the things she did, working from some intuition he lacked. The body simply spoke to her in a way he couldn't perceive. When he failed to grasp the fine work, she'd been unable to hide her disappointment.

"I'm not sure my healing is doing anything."

"It's not. Here."

The world came into sharp focus.

"Can you stand?"

He tried his legs and nodded. Getting up proved harder than anticipated. Once on his feet, he felt like a gentle breeze might knock him over.

"Come on. I'll support you."

He began to walk, and a magical force steadied him. Medea never did by hand anything that could be done with magic. Even if that weren't the case, an arm around him would have been too familiar. She set a brisk pace toward the gateway, the force nudging him along as she lectured.

"You did quite well at the end there, despite your blunder. However, you missed a very bountiful resource at your disposal—earth. It can be used to smother fire, blind your opponent, block attacks. Even if you have nothing else at your disposal, remember you always have that."

They arrived at the gateway—a space between two massive boulders. Medea, with her slight frame and short stature, slid through easily. Nikolai ducked his head and turned sideways to shimmy through the opening but got stuck.

"Why must you hide your gateways in the most enclosed spaces?"

"Why must you keep complaining about it?"

He sucked in his stomach and pushed against the rough granite, nearly tumbling into the gateway room. He grasped the center table to steady himself, then reached back and yanked out the peg marking their location, depositing it in the box.

"You going up to your room to juggle oranges?" he asked.

Every afternoon she retired to her room. When he'd begun his apprenticeship, he'd imagined she was doing all sorts of sordid things up there, most involving black magic and draining his youth to keep herself young. That hadn't turned out to be the case, and while he now knew he could just ask and get an answer, it was far more entertaining to postulate increasingly outlandish theories. Sometimes he got a laugh from Medea. Today she rolled her eyes.

"No oranges. I did want to talk to you before retiring though." Medea took a steadying breath, as she always did before saying something important or launching into a lecture. "I've decided you're ready to begin telepathy training."

Yes! He kept his face impassive. He'd spent a year boiling water and stacking stones and getting his ass kicked in sparring sessions. All Useful, but not what he craved. Telepathy though—that was a talent he was born with. Medea's library was filled with books written by mages trying to acquire a tenth of the power he naturally possessed. With Medea's aid, he could become the most powerful telepath who'd ever lived.

"We will be training in America, so I'd like you to take a few days to adjust to the time difference."

"I'll be fine," he said hurriedly. "We can start tomorrow."

Medea balked at the suggestion. "Well, *I* need to adjust."

"It's okay, no need to apologize. I know at your *advanced age* you probably need lots of rest and—*ow!*" He rubbed his arm. "Must you attack me?"

"When you're running your mouth, yes. Unless you want me to seal it again." Her smile crumpled at his chilly expression. "I, uh . . ."

He stepped forward. Medea was so short that he loomed over her. "No, please continue. What about my face?"

During the first year of his apprenticeship, he'd been opposed to learning any magic outside of what he considered "dark." To make a point, Medea bested him in a sparring match using only healing magic. She hit him in the face with a spell designed to heal damaged tissue. His mouth and nose had sealed shut. He'd had to cut open his own face to breathe, but the wound had rapidly closed again. Subsequent injuries, no matter how small, caused the tissue to swell out of control. A single nick while shaving could wipe out weeks of facial reconstruction. He'd resigned himself to wearing a beard for months, though it made repairs even more difficult, until at last he was able to remove the spell.

With the spell gone, the skin no longer regrew when damaged, but he wasn't good enough at healing to restore his once-perfect face. He'd hoped that by learning healing, Medea would consent to return his face to normal. She hadn't. And now she had the gall to make cracks about his scars.

Medea met his gaze with stony eyes. "I stand by my decision. If you practice, eventually you should be able to—"

"I've been practicing for a year!"

"Then practice for another. Or ten. I'll not do it for you. Take two days off. Friday, we go to America." She spun and exited, leaving him alone with his desire to strangle her.

He gave her a minute to cross the common room before proceeding to his own. He pulled off his shirt—scuffed and scorched—and threw it into the wastebasket. He'd get another in London tomorrow. Harper was due for a visit anyway. He'd let most of his other relationships lie fallow the past two years. Medea's training schedule didn't leave him with much recreational time.

The gilded mirror above his desk beckoned. Try as he might, he couldn't avoid locking eyes with the image. Once handsome and impeccably chiseled, his ruined face still bore evidence of Medea's attack. He'd returned his nose to its proper shape and smoothed out his skin, but like a wax figure, it was indescribably wrong. Replicating the details that made the face human was beyond his capabilities. If not for the illusion Harper had constructed to hide the damage, he'd never be able to show his face in public.

And yet there were those who could see through the illusion. Yoxtl had. Medea probably could. Would more powerful allies spurn him because of his face? If he cultivated others and raised them to power, would they one day gasp in shock at the revelation of his true form?

Unacceptable. He'd find a way around it one way or another, and telepathy just might be the key.

2

AMERICA

Loud knocking jogged Nikolai awake.

"Mmpf?"

"Get up," said Medea through the door. She never set foot in his room if she could help it. "We leave in thirty minutes."

Nikolai rose and stretched. Back in Haven, he'd chosen decor with an eye for what would appeal to others, particularly women—tasteful paintings, silk sheets, even a picture of his "mother." Lacking someone to impress, he'd begun decorating more to his style. There were subtle touches of opulence—a golden mirror, cancelabra, and inkwell. Furs adorned the bed. At the front of the room hung a painting of a tormented man being attacked by a serpent. Further back and slightly out of view of the door, a second painting depicted a nude woman reclining on a bed.

Out of habit, he opened the curtains over his "window," a projected image from the coastline of the island, created by Medea at his request. Pale moonlight tipped the waves in silver as they crashed silently onto the rocks. Right—they'd be traveling to a different time zone.

He donned his robe and made his way through the common

area to the bathroom. Something black and silver darted between his legs. His arms spun, and he caught the wall. He glared at Yoxtl. The spirit's normally incorporeal form—a cross between a fox and a cat—stood solidly in his path. Amber eyes greeted his with a glint of mischief.

"Well?" he asked it, though he already knew. A year ago he'd agreed to build Yoxtl a following in exchange for certain information. He'd done so offhandedly, without a second thought, but spirits considered such things binding. While Yoxtl was too weak to enforce the agreement, the spirit had been relentless in its reminders.

"I hear you're going to America today," it said.

"And?"

"And you still owe me. You've been putting me off for a year, claiming you're too busy—"

"I *am* busy. Water boiling, potions, practical lessons, Latin, more practical lessons, reading assignments—when do you expect me to fit in building you a following?"

"Your days off."

"I only get one a week. I have better things—and people —to do."

The spirit smirked. "You wouldn't be 'doing' anyone, if not for me."

"I haven't forgotten. I *will* get to it. Right now I need to focus on my studies. The more powerful I am, the better I'll be able to aid you. Stop pestering me. I promise to keep my eyes open for conversion opportunities in America, but for now, my apprenticeship takes priority."

Yoxtl's tail swished irritably. "Fine. But don't think of crossing me, mortal. I may not be as powerful as I once was, but I can still make your life a living hell."

"Not without breaking the geas you can't."

When Yoxtl had first arrived on Medea's island, she'd placed a spell on the spirit to prevent it from interfering with her training. The geas attached to the soul, and if its conditions were violated, it tore the soul apart. How she'd cast a geas on a soulless spirit was a mystery, but Yoxtl wasn't about to put it to the test.

The spirit's eyes narrowed. "Once your apprenticeship is over, the geas will no longer apply. If you don't help me then, you *will* pay."

"Understood. Now, mind moving your furry butt so I can shower?"

Yoxtl slunk away and Nikolai entered his bathroom. He leaned against the wall and focused his will on the water tank Medea had installed. After a year of practice, he still couldn't bring it to a boil, though he could now get it lukewarm if he focused for an hour. Lacking the time today, he practiced for ten minutes before stepping into yet another cold shower.

Medea was already in the gateway room when he arrived. Colored lights twinkled from the maps plastered on the circular walls—green for gardens, red for hazardous, white for safe, and blinking yellow for intruder. As usual, Medea didn't look up before addressing him.

"You're late."

"Yoxtl accosted me."

Medea tensed. She'd been chilly with the spirit ever since it rescued Nikolai from the ocean nearly a year ago. Both parties had been evasive when questioned, stating only that they'd had a disagreement. Yet Medea allowed Yoxtl to remain on the island. Perhaps the bargain he'd struck with the spirit allowed it to remain close.

"And I had to do my boiling exercise," he added. She couldn't be mad about that.

Medea relaxed and nodded, satisfied at the academic reason for his tardiness. "Be careful today. America has no magical oversight. There are no Enforcers, and no old guard like you see in many Magi towns outside the Collective. It is important that your magic remain discreet. *Do not draw attention to yourself.*"

Wouldn't the lack of Enforcers mean they could be more relaxed? He was about to ask when Medea inserted the peg into the hole that marked their destination—California.

Hollywood! Sun! Beaches! He could meet movie stars and fuck Marilyn Monroe. Excellent choice.

He followed her through the gateway, exchanging excitement for the pang of loss, amplified by the sparse brown bushes and gloomy skies that greeted him on the other side. He used to think the denuded feeling was a spell to discourage apprentices from leaving. The reality was far worse. Magic was dying out. Medea warded her island to retain ambient magic, and with it came a sense of completeness he experienced nowhere else. Here in California, as in most places around the world, magic was so scarce it was physically sickening. A great void opened in his chest, one that would never be filled.

"Deep breaths help." Medea closed her eyes, inhaled through her nose, and let out a long breath. When their bodies had adjusted, she led them down a narrow game trail. "Since we're going to be working in America for a while, I'd like to start performing experiments. See if we can't pinpoint the cause of magical decline."

"Absolutely." The world wasn't meant to feel like this.

As they made their way toward town, Medea lectured on telepathy, occasionally interrupting herself whenever she spotted an interesting plant. Novices could block telepathic probes and send messages to others. Some might be able to skim surface thoughts or feelings, though these were often unclear. Journeymen could read thoughts, though it usually required all of their concentration to do so. Masters could read deep thoughts, including the subconscious and—here Nikolai's ears perked up— implant temporary thoughts, make suggestions, and delve into memories. Grand masters could do all kinds of fun things like change memories or remove them completely, alter consciousness, even perform mind control. He'd chosen a damn good specialty and, judging from Medea's descriptions, he was already a journeyman.

"What about avoiding detection?" he asked. "I can read Mundanes fine, but Magi always know."

"We can work on that. Today I want to get a feel for where you are."

They arrived at the outskirts of a town. Citizens walked by wrapped in heavy coats as if it were freezing. If California was normally sunny and warm, maybe they were.

When Nikolai stopped a man to inquire about Hollywood, he was laughingly educated about the size of the state, dashing his hopes for a celebrity tryst. Apparently Stockton was nowhere near Los Angeles.

A light drizzle began to fall, and then it began to rain in earnest. Medea conjured an invisible shield over their heads. So much for discretion. They passed a couple too focused on sharing an umbrella to notice. A man approached from the opposite direction. His eyes ran the length of Medea, paying particular attention to her breasts. He did a double take as they passed, finally catching sight of rain pelting off seemingly nothing, and almost walked into a sign.

Nikolai bent and whispered, "You might want to—"

Medea jumped and rubbed her ear. "Don't do that!"

"What? Talk into your ear?"

"Yes. Now what were you saying?"

He nodded at the shielded area above her head. "You need an illusion. People are starting to notice."

Medea glanced up, then shrugged. "If it bothers you, why don't you do it?"

"Illusions were never my forte."

She laughed and nodded to the illusion concealing his scars. "What about that?"

"This is Harper's work."

"But the inscription in your illusion book said it was your favorite subject."

Illusion book? What illusion—oh, right. He'd given her his old textbooks from the Academy. How the hell had she remembered something she read two years ago?

"Harper wrote that, and he was being sarcastic. I only learned enough of illusions to graduate, and thankfully that wasn't much."

"You're serious? You lie *all the time*, but you never bothered to learn illusions? Usually your type—"

"Where are we headed? We've been walking for nearly twenty minutes."

"I'm looking for a restaurant of some sort, not too crowded."

"I see one up the street." He crossed without her, rain pattering his coat and hat as he left the protection of the shield. Behind him, Medea's bare feet slapped the wet pavement as she hurried to catch up.

"There's no shame if you have trouble with illusions. We can work on it."

"I don't have trouble with illusions, I just don't like them." *Despise* was a better word, but that would invite questions. He walked faster, his longer stride eating the distance to the diner, and soon Medea lagged far behind. By the time she arrived, he had already given his name and the hostess was ready to seat them.

Medea wrinkled her nose when she entered. "This place is too crowded."

"Any place you can get seated right away isn't 'too crowded.' Besides, it's all young couples. We'll fit right in."

The hostess stood politely, pretending not to hear. Her eyes took in Medea's strange attire. "Uh, ma'am?" she ventured, "I'm so sorry, but we require shoes."

"I'm wearing shoes." Medea stuck out a foot. Sure enough, it bore a thin leather sandal with straps that crisscrossed and encircled her ankle.

"Oh! I could have sworn . . . never mind. Right this way." The hostess directed them to a table by the kitchen.

Medea sat, then jerked up again as if she'd landed on a tack. "Not here. There, that spot in the corner." Before they could argue, she marched to an empty booth.

Nikolai exchanged a look with the hostess. "Uh, sorry about her. She's a bit . . . odd."

They followed Medea to the booth, where she sat with her back to the wall, glaring imperiously at the lights overhead. After the hostess had given them menus and departed, Nikolai leaned across the table.

"They don't like that, you know. Each waitress has certain tables they service—"

"They can service us just as well over here. Now, silence a moment. There's something I need to attend to." Magic rippled overhead. The lights flickered. Several patrons glanced up, but the light stabilized and they soon lost interest. The voices around them abruptly muted—that would be her sound shield. Medea picked up a menu and scanned it, frowning like it had done her personal harm.

"What's up with you?" he asked.

"I don't like this place. I told you that, but it's fine. I've made the necessary adjustments."

"What did you do to the lights?"

"I severed the power cords and cast a light spell so no one would notice."

"Why?"

Her face said it was the stupidest question he'd ever asked. "Because they were bright and flickering and it was annoying."

"I didn't see them flicker until you started messing with them. What about the other table?"

"There was a disturbance from the machines in the kitchen." She slapped the menu on the table. "Nothing good. I shall have to summon my own food."

"A disturbance?"

"Like a low hum, or a vibration."

"And here I thought you were too powerful to be affected by Mundane technology. If even you're affected, that doesn't bode well for the rest of us."

She pierced him with her gaze. "It doesn't affect my ability to cast spells."

Nikolai dropped his eyes to his menu, trying to appear subservient. He'd worked hard to regain a modicum of trust. Killing her no longer interested him, but it was difficult to convince her, given that most of her apprentices had tried.

"Look, all I'm saying is that Mundane technology affects Magi. That's why Haven doesn't allow cars or phones or electricity. It's why only witches live in big cities. That the most powerful of us—you—can be affected by a few fluorescent lights is worrisome." He stole a glance. Her body had relaxed. Good.

"You think Mundane technology is responsible for magic dying out?"

"What else would it be?"

Medea opened her mouth to respond, but a pretty waitress in blue arrived with glasses of water. She set them on the table and pulled out a notepad to take their order. Nikolai ordered porterhouse steak, while Medea aggressively asked about the mashed potatoes. Did they have lumps? Any lumps at all? The waitress, thrown by the fervor in Medea's voice, couldn't give her a satisfactory answer. Medea ordered them regardless, but her tone made it clear she expected to be disappointed.

The waitress moved away, tight blue skirt hugging her ass nicely. Medea kicked him under the table.

"Focus! We're here for your telepathy lessons." She indicated a girl at the counter nursing a milkshake. "There's your first target. Expand your senses. Feel yourself reach toward her mind. Deciphering what you find is not always straightforward. People tend to focus on different things."

"I've done this before, you know."

"Then it should be easy for you."

He skimmed the girl's mind. "She's on a date with the boy next to her. The guy she met last week was better. This one won't shut up about fishing. She hopes the date is quick."

Medea shook her head. "I expected you to take this more seriously. You didn't even look at her. If you're just going to make things up—"

"Why would I need to look at her? You don't look at me half the time when we're talking, and you hear me just fine. And in any case, why didn't you just check for yourself?"

"True enough. I suppose it's a difference between natural-born and trained telepathy."

Had she not heard his question, or was she avoiding it? Her hand made idle flicking motions, causing a fork to spin of its own accord. He placed a thumb on top to still it, and she muttered, "Oops."

"Maybe it would help if you told me a bit about your own process."

She took a breath and began reciting nearly verbatim from a scroll he'd seen in the library, almost like she didn't actually know telepathy.

He plastered on his most deferential, studious face. "Pardon me, but could you explain it in your own words? I've read the texts. Firsthand experience is so much better."

"I, uh, certainly." She shifted in her seat. "Well, you look at your target and picture hovering over them and sort of . . ." She mimed yanking up things with her hand.

She didn't know. How could she *not know*? Medea. The most powerful mage in the world. He could have sworn she'd used telepathy on him before, despite her protests to the contrary, but she clearly didn't know what the fuck she was talking about. She couldn't train him, but at least he was superior in one school of magic.

He leaned back with a smug smile. "You don't actually *know* telepathy, do you?"

Her body tensed. "I know enough to know I don't like it."

"So you can't teach me anything. You can't even verify that my mind readings are accurate."

"If that's what you found, I'm sure it's correct."

"That's not the point." He leaned forward, jabbing the table as he spoke. "I did everything you asked. I put all my own studies on hold, confident that when the time came, you'd be able to teach me. And now I find out that I've wasted two years—"

"*One.* That first year was your own damned fault. And the past year has *not* been a waste—you've done your exercises, learned a reasonable amount of Latin, and have become marginally competent in healing. And I *can* teach you. I just . . . telepathy makes me extremely uncomfortable."

"Why?"

"You wouldn't understand. Men's—I mean, minds are . . . I don't like what I find."

"Fair enough. Is that all?"

Her expression soured, as if she were holding back.

"Medea?"

She rubbed her face and picked up her glass, taking her time drinking before setting it back down. "Out of all the magical schools, telepathy has the most potential for abuse."

He scoffed. "You teach dark magic and have a dungeon, yet you've suddenly grown a conscience?"

"I've always had a conscience. But I believe—truly believe—that knowledge is meant to be shared. It is not up to me to decide who will learn and what they learn, only that they learn. What a person does with that knowledge is up to them. And so I will teach you, to the best of my abilities, a school of magic I personally find abhorrent. Is that acceptable?" She'd been staring at the table but glanced up for his response.

"Yes. But—and I hope you don't mind my asking—what can you do? Because what you described was, to put it bluntly, extremely lacking."

"I appreciate your candor. Most of my studies have focused on repelling telepathic attacks, not making them. That's not to say I can't read minds. I can. I'm just not subtle about it. You'd definitely know I was there. But I have read all the texts. I've spent the last year rereading them in preparation for training you. While I may not have practical experience for everything, I am well versed in the theory."

"How many of those texts were written by natural telepaths?"

She winced. "Very few. Either natural telepaths did not feel the need to share their methods, or else they were killed before they had a chance. I don't know if you've experienced it, but there's a certain stigma attached to telepathy."

"I'm well aware." His gift had made him an outcast for the first few years at the Academy.

"Here we are!" The pretty waitress slid their dishes onto the table. Medea took her mashed potatoes without a word and began stabbing them suspiciously with a fork.

He flashed the waitress a winning smile and affected an American accent. "Thank you, Nancy."

She smiled and flounced away. He surreptitiously tracked her across the diner until she vanished into the kitchen.

"And what is that one thinking?" Medea studied the mashed potatoes on her fork and took a cautious bite.

"Nothing about me, sadly. Not yet. They have a rush of customers and her feet hurt. Mundanes are easy. I don't have to *look* at them, I just have to know they're there. It's not like hovering over them, plucking up thoughts or whatever you were trying to pantomime."

"What is it like then?" Medea's fork paused, her attention rapt. He could almost see her itching to take notes. As the library lacked accounts from natural telepaths, whatever he told her would be written down for posterity.

One didn't give away trade secrets. Then again, she'd drilled into him time and again that she couldn't properly train him if he wasn't forthcoming. But what good would it do if she didn't know telepathy? He stamped the thought down. That was first-year Nikolai talk. Besides, she was only asking for a description of how it felt—a telepath would already know and a non-telepath wouldn't benefit.

"It's like . . . walking down a street with shops and peering into windows. Sometimes the glass isn't clear, but you can still make out what's inside. With Mundanes, their wares are on full display. You can tell there are objects farther back in the shop, but it's too dim to make out what they are. With Magi, there are shutters in the way. I can pull them back easily enough, but they notice."

"Interesting. I'd like you to document your experiences for the library. The next telepath should have more to go on than what I have now."

He would do nothing of the sort. "If you get any, send them to me with their questions."

"I prefer to have a permanent record."

There it was, the unspoken assumption that he would die. She was wrong. Whatever it took, he would be immortal.

The waitress returned. "How are we doing?"

"Fine," Medea said flatly, eyes on her plate as though the waitress didn't exist.

It had taken him the better part of a year to decode Medea's expressions. Her neutral face was a frown, and nearly all of her expressions were some variation of that. He sorted them into two main categories: frowns and glares, with increasing levels of severity. Frowns were innocuous, usually demonstrating no emotion at all or else some degree of concentration. Only when you hit a #5 frown did you start to move into glare territory. At the glare level, a #1 was only mild irritation, while #3 was angry but holding back. Things didn't get dangerous until you hit #4. He'd only seen a #5 a few times, most notably when he'd used telepathy against Medea on the day she'd scarred his face.

The waitress, unable to recognize Medea's seemingly murderous expression for polite disinterest, struggled internally to figure out what she'd done wrong.

Nikolai smiled at her. "We're well, Nancy, and you? I hope the rush of customers isn't keeping you too busy." His thumb gently caressed the lip of his mug.

She blushed and glanced nervously at Medea. He skimmed her head. Damn, she was attracted to him but conflicted. What kind of ass showed interest in a waitress in front of his date? No wonder his date was mad.

"I'm well, sir." She refilled his water and fled.

He waited until she was out of earshot. "Can you *not* stare daggers at our waitress?"

"This is how I look." Medea's words came out muffled by potato.

"*I* know that. *She* doesn't. You scared her."

Medea shrugged. "What do I care what she thinks of me? She's only Mundane anyway. Let's get back to telepathy—"

"Yes, let's. If you used it, you might not be so abrasive. Thanks to you, she thinks you're on the world's worst date. With *me*."

"And?"

"And she's pretty, so I want to start laying the groundwork."

Medea paused for a moment, chewing. "If you mean sex, we're not here for that."

"*You're* not here for that. I, on the other hand, am *always* up for it. At least pretend you're not miserable sitting here with me. Smile once in a while."

"Is this better?" Her mouth became a rictus. She widened her eyes, worsening the effect.

"No! Look, I'll just tell her you're my sister."

"I'm not lying."

"You don't have to lie—just don't contradict me."

"No promises." Her amused smile was genuine. "Back to the lesson. What you described were surface-level thoughts. As you haven't learned to delve deeper on your own yet, I thought we'd try something else—influencing the mind. I want you to give the woman at the counter an itch on her nose."

He glanced at the woman and focused on her nose. Medea magically swatted him away.

"No, not like that. You're breaking your own rules, looking at her and attempting to reach her not with telepathy, but with telekinesis. You need to create a thought—in this case, the sensation of an itch—then push the thought into her mind."

Easy enough to imagine. Every time he went back into the jungle, the bug bites were horrendous. He focused on the memory, on the desperate urge to scratch until the bumps bled. He packaged the urge into a bundle and flung it at the woman.

The effect was instantaneous. She absently scratched at her

arms, then her neck, and finally her face. It got so bad she excused herself and dashed to the restroom.

"You overshot, but it was a decent first try. Do the man now. This time, focus only on the sensation and the precise body part."

The second time was better, though the man scratched far more forcefully than was necessary. By the fourth time, he had it.

"Well done." Medea pushed back her empty plate with a loud belch, earning looks of reproach from several nearby patrons. "I'm off for the evening. Stay and practice if you like." She dug around her hip pouch for something and made a frustrated noise. "How much did our meal cost?"

"Uh . . . three dollars for the steak. Yours would have been a lot less." He'd ordered based on price, counting on her to pay. If she was out of money . . .

She swiped a napkin and hid it under the table. When her hand came back, it held a ten-dollar bill.

He feigned a gasp. "Are you paying with an *illusion*? That's so dishonest!"

"Shut up. I only carry gold, but most places don't accept unminted coins anymore. I can't be expected to keep track of all these paper monies!"

He snatched the bill off the table and tucked it in his pocket.

"What are you doing?"

"Saving it to pay. Do you have any idea how good I'll look telling the waitress to keep the change on a ten?"

She rolled her eyes and stood just as the waitress returned.

"Can I get you two anything else? Pie maybe?"

"The bill. Oh, there's one other thing." Medea gestured to him. "This is my apprentice. We're not romantically involved. Should you choose to bed him, I promise I won't feel the slightest animosity, though I'd find your decision odd, to say the least."

Medea strode from the diner, either oblivious or apathetic to the havoc she'd created.

3

CONFIRMATION BIAS

"I am *so* sorry about my sister. She's a little"—Nikolai made a wavy motion next to his head—"you know."

The waitress' brow furrowed. "That was your sister? She doesn't look like you."

"She doesn't, does she?" He glanced to the side as though fearful someone was listening and leaned forward, speaking at a lower volume. "Personally, I think she was adopted, but our parents passed on a few years ago and I was never able to ask. I'm all she has left. I try to meet her once a week, make sure she's doing okay."

"That's so sweet of you," the waitress cooed.

He shrugged as though it were of no consequence. "I do what I can. Family is important." Despite Medea's faux pas, this was going well.

An unearthly scream broke the still night. The din of the restaurant ceased and a few people looked about worriedly.

"What was that?" The waitress leaned across the table to peer out the window, unintentionally giving him a closer look at her breasts.

"Do you see anything?" he asked, eager to retain the view.

"No, it's too dark." She straightened up.

Damn. No matter, she'd show them to him later. "So, Nancy—"

Shouts interrupted, inhuman and angry. Now she wasn't the only one looking out the window. Diner patrons nervously pressed their faces against the glass. The distraction was getting annoying, having driven all thoughts of him from the waitress' mind.

"Shouldn't someone go check?" asked a girl at the bar.

He scanned the room. Everyone was curious about the noise but unwilling to risk themselves. Bunch of pussies.

"I'll do it." He stood and buttoned his coat. Whatever the fuck was screaming, it was screwing with his plans for the evening.

The waitress put a hand on his arm. "Be careful out there."

Oh good, dealing with the perceived threat had won him points. "I'll be fine." He gave her hand a squeeze.

Nikolai stepped into the moist night air. Night had not yet fallen, but storm clouds blanketed the sky in ominous shadow. The shouting had stopped. He strained to hear anything through the silence. There. Scuffling and a voice.

Medea stood at the edge of the building, her hand bloody. A man was doubled over in the alley, jabbering and clasping his hands to his mouth.

"You misuse it, I get to keep it." Medea held up her palm, upon which rested the man's tongue. It burst into flame, curling and shriveling. When the tongue was no more than a charred nugget, Medea let it slip from her fingers.

The stupid man charged her, making no more than a few steps before collapsing to the ground. The skin on his arms blackened and sloughed off in patches.

Nikolai leaned against the building. "I love it when you hurt people who aren't me."

"He should've stopped with the tongue. Weren't you courting the waitress?"

"This is more entertaining."

Blood trickled from the man's nose. Still he reached for Medea, his hand an open claw of defiance. When the light began to fade from his eyes, Medea stretched out her hand, yanking it back into a fist. Nikolai sensed something flowing from the man's body.

"What is that? What are you doing?"

"I'm taking his soul."

It was the sexiest thing he'd ever heard.

"Don't look at me like that," she said, misinterpreting his look. "He's dying, it's not like he needs it anymore."

"What are you going to do with it?"

She smiled. "Would you like to see?"

Hell yes. "Absolutely."

They walked through the darkness back to the gateway. At the edge of town, Medea conjured a light in one hand. The other hand rested at her side, fist still closed tight. When they reached the narrow game trail, Nikolai fell into step behind her and conjured his own light, admiring the figure before him. A bit slender for his taste, but quite nice.

Medea was already beautiful, and the power she wielded made her all the more attractive. His efforts the past year had focused on building trust. Seducing her was long overdue. It wasn't merely about sex, although that was reason enough for his pursuit—there would be a certain glory in having the world's most powerful mage beg for your cock. What he really wanted was influence over who she trained and how she used her powers.

Petrov's old warning came back—*whatever you do, don't flirt with her.* For a time, Nikolai had considered Medea off-limits. After all, she'd shown no interest in men. If she preferred women, there wasn't anything he could do to change that, putting her forever out of reach.

But the day she'd scarred his face, he'd trespassed into her mind and discovered not only that she had feelings for a previous apprentice, Thomas, but that she'd taught him immortality as some sort of placating gesture. When Nikolai accused her of sleeping with Thomas, she became distraught but didn't deny it. At least one man had succeeded, which meant he had a chance.

Well, if she thought Thomas' stuffy Puritan sex was sufficient, she'd be amazed at his prowess. He'd yet to leave a woman unsatisfied. Once she'd had a taste of him, he could use sex as a bargaining chip, convincing her to fix his face and teach him immortality. Women were always willing to do more for men they loved, and sex was a surefire way to get Medea addicted to him.

They reached the gateway and stepped through into darkness. Completeness washed over Nikolai as the ambient magic permeated his body. It took a moment to register the gentle rhythm of waves. Medea's gateway system was heavily warded. If someone unauthorized managed to pass through, they arrived not inside the hovel, but on the beach. He spun, half expecting to find an intruder.

"Why did the gateway take us here?"

Medea held up her fist. "If I had absorbed the soul into my own, the wards would not detect it, but as it's still considered a separate entity . . ." She smiled and opened her hand.

"Did you just let it go? Why bring the soul all the way here then?"

"It adds to the ambient magic of the island. That's all souls are —magic." She started up the hill toward the hovel and Nikolai followed.

"I take it he can't haunt the place?"

"Retaining a sense of self upon death requires extreme willpower or at least some magical skill. Mundanes usually dissipate into the world, a drop in a vast ocean. Will you be returning to the diner?"

"Can't wait to get rid of me?" he teased.

"I—no, of course not."

"It's alright. I know you 'retire early' to . . . count your tongue collection."

The jest won a smile. "Not even close. The only tongues I have are in the lab, and those belonged to oxen." She knew he was joking, yet something always compelled her to respond literally.

As tempting as it was to go back to the diner and regale the waitress with a thrilling lie, he was making progress with Medea, and one didn't bail while making progress. "I was hoping we could discuss what you'd mentioned earlier. About conducting experiments to see why magic is dying out. You said I needed to do some reading?"

Medea might prefer to retire early, but if there was anything that could prevent her from doing so, it was the chance to lecture and share a book or ten. Even in the early morning darkness, he could see the internal struggle play out across her face.

"That's a long discussion," she said at last. "But I suppose I could give you the reading now. Get you started."

Nikolai smiled. "I would love that."

Medea quickened her pace to the library. Nikolai's attention was fickle. She had to make use of it while she could. The boy had performed admirably the past year, throwing himself fully into his studies, yet his natural inclination was to take the quickest, laziest route to accomplish his goals.

The day she'd scarred his face, he'd insisted on making a wager. If he won, she'd teach him immortality. If she won, he would become a master healer. She didn't like making wagers, but given the two outcomes were virtually identical, she'd agreed. He lost, of course, and after much figurative kicking and screaming, he dove headlong into her healing books and learned all he could.

Six months later, it was apparent he wasn't cut out for healing. He could close wounds easily enough, even regrow a limb if he had all day, but the fine-tuning, the intricate workings of the human body—those remained beyond his reach. Nikolai saw the big picture, looking at the whole and assessing how best to make use of it. The minutia was simply not his forte. His natural inclination was to use knowledge gleaned from their lessons to attack more intelligently. Not that there was anything wrong with that— it was one of the many benefits of learning anatomy and physiology. If he worked diligently for the next twenty years, he *might* make it to master rank. He'd just never *excel*.

Which meant he would never be immortal, at least not via that route. The realization was upsetting. Despite their rocky start, she'd grown fond of him. The idea of losing another apprentice— particularly a capable one—to the effects of aging was almost unbearable. Yes, she'd lost apprentices before, but things were different now. Magic was fading from the world, and unless they found a way to stop it, there would be no more like him. Not one with remotely decent talent. Each successive generation of Magi would dwindle in power, until only the Mundane were left, and then she would be truly alone.

And so she'd kicked him off the island for a week, spiked her tea with ergot, and spent the days hallucinating, which was better than facing reality and crying. No point in divulging her revelations to Nikolai, not after how hard it had been to convince him that healing was worth studying, but there was no longer any reason to keep it the sole focus of his studies. Far better to work on his natural abilities concurrently, which meant telepathy.

When Nikolai returned after his week away, she was herself again, and he none the wiser about her emotional turmoil. There were other methods to immortality. Perhaps he'd find one of them. He was in what, his mid-twenties? Plenty of time.

Plenty of time . . .

The library always smelled wonderful. Apprentices might come and go, but books were forever. She'd have to pester Nikolai about writing down his telepathy experiences. He might have agreed, but his heart hadn't seemed in it.

She made her way to the fifth alcove and her master grimoire. Nikolai plopped down in an armchair, leaned back with his hands laced behind his head, and rested one ankle on the opposite knee. He was grinning for some reason.

"What are you smiling about?"

"I just enjoy spending time with you."

Odd thing to say. "You're with me all day every day." She scribbled authors into the grimoire. Aristotle. Couldn't forget Aristotle. Descartes. Should she do Descartes? His logic was faulty, but the man had tried. No. Nikolai's attention span was short enough. Better to give him three solid books, increasing the odds of him actually reading them, than twelve he'd never touch.

"You look irritated."

"I'm thinking!" Few things were more irritating that being called irritated when you weren't. Her pen hovered over the page. Fuck it. She'd have to pull them all out so she could visualize what she had, then make assignments as necessary. Six more titles were added to the list, then she placed a palm flat on the page, summoning the books.

As the first text rounded the corner and came into view, Nikolai remarked, "When did you add that spell?"

"Recently. I got tired of walking to the far end of the library. It only works for the bound books. Scrolls and loose papers are too fragile. I really need to make copies of everything." Yet another thing for her to-do list. Cataloging and magically tagging the books was at least going faster these days, now that Nikolai was here to help. He only chose sections of interest to himself, but it was better than nothing.

"Here we go." She snatched books from the air and spread them out on the table. Definitely Aristotle. Ibn al-Haytham, Francis Bacon . . .

"Uh, Medea . . . these are all Mundanes." *Novum Organum* lay open in Nikolai's lap.

"What else would they be?" Newton or Galileo? Roger Bacon? Which texts would benefit Nikolai most?

"I thought we were going to find out why magic is dying?"

Why must he always interrupt her train of thought? "We are. To discover the cause, we must create experiments, gather data, and analyze it to the best of our abilities. And to do that, you need to understand science."

People were hard to read, especially in the moment. Sometimes it wasn't until after a conversation was over, when she'd had a chance to dissect it, that she was able to postulate what they'd been trying to convey. Time together certainly helped. After a year, she could recognize a few of Nikolai's expressions. The carefully blank face he wore now meant he disagreed with her, but for some unfathomable reason, avoided saying so.

Her voice was a whip crack. "State your objection."

"Shouldn't we be using *magic* to find out why *magic* is dying out?"

Didn't he realize magic and science were intertwined? Apparently not. Everything was so separate these days.

"When I was younger, the terms 'wizard' and 'scientist' were used interchangeably. Both sought to make sense of the world, and many of the subjects that scientists studied were considered magic." She grabbed *Opus Majus* and brandished it at him. "Roger Bacon was considered a wizard in his time. Mundane scientists have far more in common with wizards of old than today's Magi."

Oh god, he had that overly patient expression now, the one he got whenever he tried to explain something he thought he understood better than she.

"Magic can do things that science can't. It's *better*."

"What did you say the first time I told you to wash your hands?"

"What? Oh, uh . . . that everyone knows to wash their hands."

"But not everyone does. Our kind have been avoiding illness for centuries by washing hands and boiling water. Mundanes didn't figure it out until the mid-nineteenth century, and even now it's not practiced everywhere."

"I don't follow. There's nothing magical about hand washing."

"Two centuries ago it was an arcane ritual, one with no logical explanation. We knew it worked, but not why. Magic is that which we cannot explain. Science gives us the explanation. They are two sides of the same coin."

"That's not . . ." Nikolai pressed his hand to his temple and shook his head.

Why was he trying so hard not to argue? Verbal sparring was the only type of sparring he could possibly win with her, and it seemed his favorite pastime. Yet today he was holding back. Why? For fear of offending her? She had to get him going again. Especially if they were to do experiments together, they needed open communication, honesty. They needed to be able to point out each other's blind spots.

"How would you define magic?" she asked.

"Mana. You said it yourself—magic requires focus, will, and mana."

"Witches have no mana."

He leaned forward, thoroughly engaged now. "But their spells use mana. They just get it from spirits."

"The Mundane draw power from electricity."

"It's not the same thing!"

"They are both forms of energy. It's important you understand this." She sat across from him, idly tapping the collected works of Isaac Newton. "If you cast a spell at an opponent, that spell requires mana. Your opponent requires an equal amount of mana to block it. In many ways, mana works the same as other forms of energy."

"Ah, I see. Because they're both forms of energy, electricity interferes with mana. Electricity is to blame for all of this." Nikolai gestured around the room.

"No. That is *not* what I'm saying. You're leapfrogging to a conclusion without any evidence. It's exactly what I'm trying to prevent. When you decide on the answer before even asking the question, your data collection will be biased."

"But we have evidence. Look at where Magi cities are built— far from large Mundane cities. Witches are the only casters that routinely make their homes among the Mundane."

She slapped the table. "This is what I'm talking about! The idea that Mundane technology interferes with magic is a *hypothesis*. When you decide that it is true, you cherry-pick information to support what you've already decided."

"No, I haven't."

"Oh really? Then tell me this—does telepathy require mana?"

He frowned. "No. At least I don't think so."

"There's a place to start—we bring you to the point of mana exhaustion, then see if you can use telepathy."

"If it doesn't require mana, that could be the reason it still works around the Mundane." He cocked his head at her. "Do potions use mana?"

"Now you're asking the right questions. I don't know. I suspect not, but it's easy enough to test."

"Yeah. Yeah, it is." He propped his chin on his hand. "If the only magic that works around the Mundane doesn't use mana, then we know the two are connected."

"No. NO. Correlation doesn't equal causation." Medea sank back in her chair and rubbed her eyes. He still wasn't getting it.

"I'm sorry." He genuinely looked it.

"It's not your fault. No one trained you to think otherwise." Medea sighed and pinched the tip of each finger in sequence, the calming pressure a balm. "I have it. Let's say there's a woman. She has six children and works all day to take care of them. Her back begins to hurt. She's always tired and out of breath, and sometimes she has cramps. If you were a healer, what would you do?"

"If she's married, I'd suspect she was pregnant. If that's not the case, I would tell her to get some rest. Make her husband help out more. The stress of raising so many children is taking its toll."

"Did you perform a physical examination?"

"I checked for pregnancy."

Medea smiled. "All perfectly logical actions and recommendations, considering the evidence. However, your hypothesis was wrong, and within a week she's dead."

"How the hell could she be dead? From what?"

"A heart attack. Those are all symptoms of a heart attack in women. However, because you *assumed* her symptoms were caused by something else . . ."

"I didn't bother to check for other things." He leaned back and shook his head. Finally, he'd gotten it.

"When you decide on a cause, you rule out all other possibilities, and when you do that, *you can't fix the problem*. Assumptions allow us to make snap decisions in life-or-death scenarios. They have their place. But not here. If you're going to help me with this, you need to look past your preconceived notions. Can you do that?"

"I can try."

"Good." She stood and considered the books. "Start with these three. I know it's dense reading, but pay considerable attention to logic, deduction, and how experiments are conducted. Make a list of all possible reasons magic could be dying out, *besides* technological interference. I shall do the same, and I'll start designing experiments we can run concurrent with your lessons. Are you alright? You look a little . . ." Dazed? It was hard to tell.

"I'm fine. Did Thomas do this kind of thing with you? Experiments, I mean."

Always competitive. At least it would spur him on. "Yes, though we mostly tested new spells."

Nikolai nodded and opened a book.

4

HYPOTHESES

For the next several weeks, Nikolai's life oscillated between the island and America for telepathy training. They bounced from city to city, ostensibly to give him a variety of targets to practice on. Before entering the gateway, Medea always paused to remind him not to cast spells in front of the Mundane or draw attention to himself. Tired of hearing the same old lecture, he began reciting it along with her one day. She paused mid-sentence, eyes narrowing.

"That's not funny."

"Yes, it is. You give the same lecture every time. I *know*. And if I didn't, saying it again wouldn't help."

She pursed her lips, then grabbed the control peg and jammed it a little too forcefully into the map.

"You know, you're going to break the shaft if you do that too hard."

She shot him a glare before entering the gateway.

Ridiculous. It wasn't like she followed the rule herself. Her dress drew stares wherever they went. A simple Glamor spell would have disguised it, but she refused to cast one. At least a dozen times he saw objects fly into her outstretched hand. She kept a sound shield up constantly, confusing the hell out of any Mundanes that happened to pass through. They'd halt mid-stride and rub their ears, confused by the sudden lack of noise.

If he slipped and used magic in public, Medea would telekinetically rap his knuckles and chastise him. When he pointed out the irony of punishing him for using magic in public by using magic in public, she waved him off with a "do as I say, not as I do."

But the most flagrant disregard for her own rule was when she attacked the Mundane. After the tongue incident, there was Philadelphia. He entered a store. Medea, complaining of the smell, chose to wait outside. He emerged to find her staring down two laughing men. She flashed them a wicked smile, then detached a large overhead sign. It crushed one man's skull and pinned the other to the sidewalk by his legs.

Once, in Syracuse, he stopped to ask for directions and Medea wandered ahead. When he caught up to her, she'd taken another tongue, though not a soul. When questioned, she responded vaguely that the man had been bothering her. The incidents always occurred when he wasn't around. What was she hiding? He stamped down the old distrust. Whatever it was, it was nothing to do with him.

The gateways were usually located in older cities that had been established along rivers and trade ports earlier in the nation's history. *Old* was a relative term, given the United States hadn't been around that long, and he was able to get a laugh out of Medea by poking fun at a city celebrating its sesquicentennial anniversary, as if that were some great feat.

She'd opened up a bit after the joke, talking at length about how things looked back when she first made the gateway. There used to be a blacksmith, and there a tanner. This building was an original, though the interior had much changed. One of her favorite bookstores used to be here. She soon grew pensive.

"It all grows too big too fast these days."

Maybe that was what drove her to leave the larger cities behind. Upon arriving, she always had him hail a cab and convince the driver to take them to a smaller, neighboring town. She rarely chose the same gateway twice—they could be in Boston one day and Albuquerque the next—but it was always restaurants, restaurants, restaurants. And not good places. No, she always chose the cheapest place she could find with a bland menu to match her taste.

"I'm not saying I want you to go hungry," he said one day at yet another sleepy diner in the Midwest, "but maybe once in a while you could summon a snack beforehand so we can eat someplace nice."

Across the table, Medea carefully dissected her cheese sandwich. They'd included lettuce despite her instructions. She wrinkled her nose and set the lettuce aside, covering it with a napkin as if the very sight was unbearably offensive. The cheese was also set aside, but for a different reason—she'd eat that last. She picked up the plain, untoasted white bread and took a bite.

"You don't think this place is nice?" She spoke loudly to compensate for her mouthful of food, drawing more than a few irritated looks from the staff. "What's wrong with it?"

"Nothing. *Nothing.*" He flashed a smile at their waitress, who eyed them stiffly as she poured coffee at a neighboring table. He waited until she moved on before leaning forward and speaking in a hushed tone. "I'm just saying, we should try something new once in a while."

"Why? I know I like this." Medea wiggled her bread.

"Fine dining would expand the repertoire of foods I can summon."

"Pfft. You can do that on your days off."

He stared at her in silence a moment. "Medea, if I have to eat one more egg salad sandwich or overcooked hamburger, I'm going to stab someone."

She rolled her eyes. "So melodramatic. Fine. I suppose we can alternate selections. The food is irrelevant. I only order because it would seem odd if I didn't."

"Great! We can stop going to restaurants altogether."

Medea was shaking her head before he'd even finished. "They provide a place for us to sit and give you a variety of targets."

"A variety? There's like six people here, including staff."

She shrugged as though it was of no great consequence. He gripped the underside of the table. She couldn't help being so obstinate. Old people were just like that. Stuck in their ways.

"I'd have a lot more targets in a place like Hollywood Boulevard or Times Square," he pressed.

"Out of the question. Too crowded and noisy."

"Crowded is good. More targets."

"You're welcome to go on your own time."

Medea would never admit it, but the prevalence of Mundane technology affected her. She was forever cutting power to lights and disabling machines she deemed "too loud." If he asked to explore a city for a bit she might allow it, but she'd grow increasingly restless and agitated the longer they stayed. When she began snapping at him over every minor thing, it was time to leave. Once safely ensconced in a cab, she'd draw up her legs and stare out the window in silence. Any attempt to start a conversation was fruitless, and though she usually recovered by the time they reached their destination, she bolted halfway through every meal, leaving him with vague instructions to practice his telepathy.

Though he no longer intended to kill her, he couldn't help but file away her aversion to lights and electronics under "opponent weaknesses"—a Useful thought exercise, and one she actively encouraged in their lessons. He respected her ruthless pragmatism. It made her all the more attractive.

He'd given much thought to the best way to seduce her. There'd been a promising incident during the first year of his apprenticeship. He'd exited the bathroom after a shower, wearing no more than a towel, and found her waiting at his door. Medea had blushed and sent many a furtive glance at his crotch. Had it not been for an embarrassing faux pas, things would have ended more pleasantly. She wanted him. He just had to remind her of that.

Medea had gradually shifted their schedule so that they left the island in late afternoon or early evening and arrived in time for breakfast or lunch, depending on the time zone. She always busied herself in the lab and the garden before departure and he suspected she preferred doing so in daylight. While she might not come downstairs at precisely the same time each day, her routine proceeded like clockwork once it began—ridiculously complacent for someone so paranoid about assassination, but it would make arranging "accidental" encounters easier. In preparation, he stopped drinking liquids for two days—an old trick to make the muscles stand out—then woke up early and waited inside the bathroom, cracking the door just enough to hear sounds from the common room.

Any minute now.

The creaking of metal announced Medea's descent. Once she stepped off the iron stairs she'd be inaudible, but he knew her every move. She'd ghost across the common room on bare feet, face determined, mind too focused on tasks to take note of her surroundings. A thrill shot through him—the primal pleasure of stalking prey unnoticed. If he burst out now, he'd startle her, but that wasn't his aim. He waited until the far door opened and closed, then glanced at his pocket watch and noted the time.

Fourteen minutes might not be long enough to work up a sweat, especially after going without liquid for so long. He moved to the sink and turned on the tap, staring longingly at the water.

Parched as he was, it was all he could do not to put his mouth to the stream and start guzzling. He wet his hands and ran them over his hairline. A few more flicks on his bare chest completed the illusion. When Medea exited the lab, she'd find him shirtless and glistening.

He stretched out on the common room floor and leisurely went through his normal repetitions of sit-ups and push-ups. At thirteen minutes he switched to just sit-ups at a normal speed.

At sixteen minutes he slowed. What was taking her so long? She was never more than fifteen minutes in the lab.

Seventeen minutes. His muscles began to protest despite the reduced speed.

Twenty. What the fuck?

Twenty-four. Sweat dripped off him in earnest. A wave of nausea and lightheadedness forced him to pause. Damn her. Why did she have to go off her schedule today? It was either quit and try again another day or continue for god knew how long and risk looking winded. There was one last thing he could try.

He doubled down, huffing and grunting loudly with each repetition.

Medea emptied the bag of rocks onto the laboratory counter. A hundred or so—enough to get started. With a wave of her hand, she hovered a group and sent them spinning, sanding them as they rotated. She snorted. Nikolai had made a jest about her juggling, and if he walked in now, that's exactly what she'd appear to be doing.

She left the rocks spinning and pulled a map from her pouch, spreading it on the center table. They needed a test site reasonably close to a large city, yet far enough away that it wouldn't be influenced by Mundane technology. Thankfully, despite its rapid growth, America retained large swaths of undeveloped space. She circled a few likely candidates based on what she'd gleaned so far during their visits.

If their initial hypothesis proved worthy of further investigation, their follow-up experiments could run for several years. Which meant purchasing land. The last thing she needed was to set up a seemingly abandoned location only to have the owner show up later and try to evict them. Where did one buy land these days? A bank? Local government office? How much did it cost? Could women even purchase land? What if they needed some sort of identification? Would they ask her age? They'd certainly ask her name. What if she said the wrong thing and they refused to serve her? She could threaten them with magic, but that would only draw unwanted attention. No, this had to be done the Mundane way. She sank onto the stool and stared at the map.

She'd have to scout for a suitable property (time-consuming, but simple).

Find out who held the deed (hard).

Figure out the current process for transfer of land ownership (harder).

And convince the owner to sell in a way that wouldn't compromise the site (hardest).

This would take *months* of on-site reconnaissance, and if she failed at any point she'd have to start from scratch. Aside from scouting land, every step involved going to new places and talking to people. It was draining enough being around Nikolai all day. How the hell was she going to do all this? She rubbed her face and stared at the map, willing a location to jump out and declare itself The One.

Something nudged her awareness. The first batch of rocks was now polished smooth. She set them on the counter, started another batch spinning, and pulled out a notebook. Each rock had to be magically tagged and bound to a specific page in the notebook.

With mechanical efficiency, she started working through the pile. Why couldn't all tasks be this simple?

A rhythmic sound, heard but unnoticed, crowded her thoughts again. Had she bound a rock to this page yet? She felt for a link and found none. Page seventeen had two links—how did that happen? And what the *hell* was that noise?

She set the rock down and opened the laboratory door a crack —it was counting, interspersed with grunting and heavy breathing. Nikolai's head popped into view across the room and vanished suddenly. A half second later it happened again. She tiptoed around the chairs. He lay on the floor with his knees bent, torso curling forward and backward.

"What on *earth* are you doing?"

He paused and rested his arms on his knees. "Keeping myself fit. The mage life doesn't exactly tax the body."

"That's one of the benefits." She studied him, irked but unable to ascertain why. A trickle of sweat raced down his cheek and dripped onto his bare chest. Ugh. The common room was going to reek of unwashed man. "Must you do it here?"

"My room is a bit cramped, so I thought I'd move."

"I can enlarge it if you want."

"No need to trouble yourself." He flipped over, planted his palms on the floor, and began pushing his body up and down. It looked exhausting. He switched to one arm and the loud breathing resumed.

"Can you keep it down at least?" The whole thing was completely unorthodox. The common room was for relaxation, not sweaty repetitions. "Actually, no, can you do that outside?"

"As long as the weather holds."

"You can take a gateway anywhere in the world. It's bound to be nice somewhere."

He stood and slowly began patting himself with a towel, his gaze oddly intense. "It's always nice here with you."

"Yes, and I'd like to see it remains so." She started toward the lab. Snarky Nikolai was preferable to whatever the hell this was. His mannerisms, even his tone—everything was off. Maybe he was ill. She paused at the door and did a quick scan of his body. Ah, that was it. "Drink something. You're dehydrated."

If he was going to care for his body, he should at least do it right.

Over the next few weeks Nikolai appeared outside more often, jogging by whenever she tended the garden or stopping to stretch against the wall when she did her focus exercises. His gyrations at the corner of her vision made it difficult to concentrate, and she found herself becoming increasingly curt. It wasn't uncommon for men to worry about their mortality, but this usually occurred in middle age. Nikolai, still in his twenties, hadn't even hit his prime. But telepathy training had forced both of them to change their schedules. Perhaps he'd always exercised this frequently and she'd just never seen it.

He began spending his free days on the island, studying Latin in the library or reading by the hearth wearing nothing but trunks. She checked her temperature regulation spells—still active and keeping the summer heat at bay. He was Russian though, and probably preferred it cooler. Well, he could deal with it. She wasn't changing her specifications for anyone.

When they'd first started telepathy training, she'd worried about him backsliding on his other subjects, so it was nice to see him take the initiative. He'd come a long way in the past two years. She started practicing her Russian with Tino, her second-hand familiar—languages got rusty without use, and Nikolai might appreciate a periodic break from English and Latin.

As proud as she was to see how he used his free time, he was cutting into hers. There was only so much human interaction she could take in one day, let alone several back to back. Now Nikolai was ever present. It wouldn't be so bad if he'd just shut up. He asked for help practicing Latin; she reminded him those lessons were on hold. He peppered her with questions about magic, but the conversations seemed superficial and one-sided, and if she asked about telepathy he diverted to some other topic. When she tried joining him by the hearth with a book, he inevitably felt the need to talk, as though he didn't understand the point of reading.

"What book is that?" "Is it any good?" "Can you recommend something for me?"

"A still tongue." She snapped the book shut and left. Some things *hadn't* changed in two years.

She tried giving him a second day off each week, but he only spent them on the island. Didn't he have friends or lovers to see? She found herself lingering in her room to avoid him. The situation was rapidly becoming untenable. As loath as she was to change her schedule, it might prevent her from constantly running into him. She cast a spell to wake her an hour early and tiptoed across the common room. Ridiculous having to sneak about her own house, but the alternative was telling Nikolai his excessive studying and exercising were bothersome. No way that conversation would end well. Either he'd be offended or else he'd cut back on one thing—probably studying—or both.

She exited the house and breathed a sigh of relief. The island was silent except for the murmur of waves and the gentle hum of bees. On the garden wall, a green mantis cocked its head as she passed. She inhaled the balmy air and struck off toward the beach, the earth pleasantly warm under her bare feet.

At the sloping shore she dashed down the path and thrust her feet into the sand. She wriggled her toes and sat for a time, reveling in the simple pleasure of the sensation. Part of her wanted to sit here for hours with a good book, but there was work to be done. With a sigh she stood and began her focus exercise.

YOXTL'S BARGAIN

There was no doubt about it—Medea had altered her schedule to avoid him. He'd done everything he could to draw attention to his body. It had worked before, so why wasn't it working now? Her reaction—if he got one at all—was always mild irritation. Probably warring with herself over the temptation he offered. Sleeping with an apprentice would be a conflict of interest. No doubt she'd waited until Thomas gained master rank before opening her legs. She'd fight against her attraction to him every step of the way.

It didn't take him long to figure out her new schedule, but as he'd timed his own to match, he couldn't very well change it without arousing suspicion. The encounter had to appear random. He started waking before her and waited for a hotter-than-average day. Today the summer sun blazed overhead, providing the perfect excuse to go swimming.

He kicked off his shoes and waded into the ocean. The water lapped against him, pleasantly cool. He inhaled the salty sea air and swam offshore. There he floated on his back and waited.

Medea appeared on the horizon and started down the path,

eyes on her feet. About halfway down she glanced up and noticed him. She froze, then turned to leave. Shit.

He called after her, and she reluctantly trudged down the path. When she was close enough to have a decent look at him, he submerged and rose again gracefully, dripping water accentuating his muscles. He waded ashore and she greeted him with an icy glare—a #2 on his internal scale, nothing to worry about.

"What are you doing here?" she asked.

"Swimming, obviously. It's hotter than hell today."

Her expression softened fractionally. "It takes time to adjust to a new climate. If you wish, I can alter your room's temperature or teach you to do it yourself, though it's rather mana-intensive. I'm not sure you're there yet."

"I'll be fine. Care to join me?"

"I'm hardly dressed for a swim. I'm here to do my focus exercise."

"In that case, may I join you? I haven't done mine yet today. Sand is more challenging than gravel, isn't it?"

Her jaw clenched. She wouldn't say no to a polite request from a student wanting to learn, but it was incredibly amusing to watch her try. After a moment she nodded curtly and plopped down on the sand. He moved into position across from her, leaving a sizable gap.

"Is this far enough? I don't want to impede your design."

Her posture relaxed at the courtesy. "Yes."

They worked in silence. He could now hold ten pieces of gravel in a circular formation. Sand turned out to be infinitely more challenging. Picking out a single target was maddening. Every time it seemed he had one, the onshore breeze blew it away. When he'd lost his sand for the umpteenth time, he gave up and simply watched Medea. Her design wasn't as grandiose as the one she practiced with gravel, but it seemed more intricate—some sort of cubic, tetrahedral pattern. He waited until she let the sand fall before asking what it was.

"The molecular structure of diamond." She raised several grains into a miniature of the repeating pattern. "See? This is what makes it so strong. And this"—the pattern shifted to a flat, hexagonal thing—"is graphite. Same molecules, vastly different structures and properties."

"And you got all this from reading Mundane science books?"

She smiled. "Some of it, yes. I've long been able to sense things on a small scale. Healing was the first magic I learned. While studying anatomy, I discovered I had an eye for details missed by others. Everyone else seemed to focus on the whole or on specific organs. I had no words for what I sensed, and when I tried to describe it, people thought me mad."

Sand rose between them and formed into the shape of a liver. It morphed into a blood vessel, growing larger until he could make out sandy shapes of red blood cells tumbling through the tube.

"Flesh is a symphony of moving parts, each doing a job." Her reverent voice quavered, almost as if she were near tears. More sand joined the rest, swirling into branching blood vessels, each with dancing shapes running through the center. She leaned back on her arms and stared at the moving shapes as though she looked into the face of God.

After a minute she seemed to realize he was still there. The sand swirled to form a large red blood cell, then zoomed in, making an unrecognizable squiggly structure, and again, forming a hexagonal cloud.

"The more experienced I got, the more detail I could sense, smaller and smaller. I didn't have names for any of it, but one doesn't need names to see patterns. There is beauty all around us, for those who choose to look. What seems like chaos is actually quite ordered." She took a breath and let the sand fall. "We should get going. I still have work to do before we leave for your lesson."

He stood and offered her his hand. For a wonder, she took it, though she relinquished him as soon as she was on her feet. Not that he minded—hand-holding was one of those courtship gestures he'd never quite understood. An arm around the waist was better, more possessive, with better proximity to the ass.

They walked in companionable silence, wind teasing Medea's blonde hair, which had an unnatural ability to stay out of her face. She ran a hand over the harp grass, an almost wistful smile on her face. Seems like he'd found a winning formula—bare chest plus studious nature and favorite topics equaled happy Medea. He had to keep this going.

"Do you still scan people?"

"Oh yes. In the diners, I often scan the patrons. As with focus and boiling exercises, it's important to make a habit of things that enhance your abilities. Incremental advancements add up over time. I've been doing it for so many centuries that now when I scan people, I can immediately see when things are amiss." Abruptly, she locked eyes with him. "You worry about being able to fix your face. Don't. Detail takes time. Time and practice."

Anger boiled to the surface, only to be swept away by a rising tide of anxiety. Was this why most of his efforts fell flat? The first time she'd responded to him shirtless, he'd been unscarred. Did she find him repulsive now? His traitor tongue gave voice to the question.

"When you look at me, do you see the illusion or my scars?"

"Both. I can see beyond the illusion, if that makes sense."

A pit opened up in his chest. No wonder she'd avoided him. Her irritation was revulsion in disguise. She'd never love his deformed visage.

He winced at the intrusive thoughts, knowing their source. Two years ago he'd murdered his old master, Petrov, and unknowingly released a curse upon himself. The curse, which mimicked the effects of anxiety and depression, had a habit of striking when he was doing well, hamstringing his path to success. He'd found a treatment—a rare plant known as Frog's Fancy that grew in one small grove in Mexico—but it wasn't a cure, and the effect seemed to wear off faster these days. He instinctively reached for his hip pouch, knowing damn well he'd left it in his room with the rest of his day wear when he decided to go swimming. He'd taken a dose before leaving, barely an hour ago. How could it be wearing off so soon?

They were nearly to the hovel. If he moved fast enough, held the darkness at bay, he could get to his room and take a dose. Despite what the curse told him, the conversation was going well.

"Do you ever heal the people you scan? As practice?" He threw out the question, barely listening to the response, quickening his step. The curse pushed back. He was hideous. Deformed. Medea saw not only the scar but also the immaturity that led him to think he could best her in a duel and his inability to fix the damage. Thomas had been a master healer. What was he compared to that? She probably still saw him as "the boy."

Almost there. Blessedly, the curse hadn't stolen his movement —not yet anyway. The thought alone sent him down a new anxiety spiral. Just a little bit farther, past the gardens, through the door, into the—

A black form materialized at his feet. He sprawled toward the wall bordering the garden, slamming his chin into the rock. Pain shot through his jaw. He had a brief glimpse of Yoxtl grinning beside him, then the spirit vanished.

Hot anger momentarily drove the curse aside. He got to his feet and spat blood. One of his teeth was missing. Motherfucker! It wasn't something he'd practiced regrowing. He turned to Medea. "Would you mind?"

She glared at him, arms crossed.

"Medea?"

"Is this why you've been here on your days off? Trying to find a way to get me to heal your scars?"

"I tripped!"

"Over your friend Yoxtl. And now you want me to heal your face."

"If I were going to come up with a plan, it would be a hell of a lot better than falling into a fucking *wall*." Blood spurted from his mouth. Great, just fucking great. So sexy.

She nodded toward the wall. "Your tooth is there. You should be able to reattach it." With that, she turned and entered the hovel. The curse, as though sensing his defeat, abated.

He swore and picked up his tooth.

Yoxtl appeared on the wall. "You won't get anywhere with her, so you might as well put your skills to better use."

He spun and punched the creature, swearing when his fist passed through and hit rock.

"Careful. You don't want to break your hand too." The spirit shot him a lolling grin.

"What the fuck did you do that for?"

"You don't think I see what you're doing? All the laps you run—"

"I've always run laps!"

"Not half-naked, and not on your days off. You should be using that time to build me a following."

"This is more important. If I can make Medea love me, she'll give me immortality. Then I'll have an eternity to help you."

"She won't."

"She did it for Thomas. Help me. Ask the other spirits what he was like so I can replicate it."

"Oh, I *have*." Yoxtl's eyes twinkled. "You can't possibly compete. Six foot five, built like an ox. Long, flowing locks of jet-black hair. The power of a god, cock as big as a sword—"

"Don't waste my time with lies." Despite the ridiculousness of Yoxtl's statements, he couldn't help but imagine Medea standing before the Adonis. As she unbuttoned his trousers, her mouth fell open in eager disbelief. He scowled at the thought and Yoxtl cackled.

"No more favors until you pay off your first debt, mortal." The spirit leapt from the wall. "And I *expect* my payment soon."

The geas prevented Yoxtl from interfering with training and study, but that left plenty of other opportunities for mischief. One morning, soon after the tooth incident, Nikolai awoke and found himself abnormally clumsy—stubbing his toe against a chair, throwing something to the bed and missing, going to set something on the desk and dropping it instead. Turned out the furniture had been moved an inch or so from where it normally stood, too subtle to be immediately noticeable but enough to fuck with his muscle memory.

Not long after that, his bedroom began to smell, faintly at first, but by the end of the week it reeked of something dead and bloated on the beach. He tore apart the room searching for the source, checking every place he would have hidden something—sewn into the mattress, underneath a lamp, slid between the desk and the wall. Nothing. It had to be a spell, but Magic Sight turned up nothing peculiar. Resigned to spend the night in the common room, he began gathering up his bedding but halted at the sight of the curtains unobtrusively hanging over his faux window. He pulled them aside and unscrewed the rod, tilting it toward the floor. Out slid several dead fish.

The next morning he awoke to the sound of a man's relieved sigh. He jerked upright. Instead of waves breaking over the rocks by the sea, his window held a new view—that of a man's hairy asshole. It dilated and released a long brown turd. He rose and yanked the curtains closed in disgust, though it did nothing to muffle the grunts and wet plopping sounds. Medea had to be enlisted to change the view back. She warded his room against spirits for good measure, but Yoxtl wasn't to be deterred.

The spirit began turning up anywhere Nikolai happened to be. It relentlessly tripped him whenever he ran. If he sat with Medea and pretended to read, Yoxtl appeared atop the book, flopping its body across the pages like an obnoxious cat.

After a week of this, Nikolai gave up spending his free days on the island—he wasn't gaining much ground with Medea there anyway—and made a few trips to hospitals to convert more souls. If he got enough, maybe the spirit would leave him alone.

Unfortunately, Yoxtl would not be placated. "Individual souls give me nothing. I need a new religion—*followers*."

That was another source of annoyance—Yoxtl, for all its wit and perception, didn't seem to understand how building a following worked. Nikolai was beginning to see why it never rebuilt after losing its people to the Aztecs. It wanted followers, and it wanted them *now*.

Nikolai had gathered followings twice before, once as a student at the Academy and again in Haven. It wasn't the kind of thing that happened overnight. People needed to see you every day, hear you speak, revel in the connection you made them feel. Out of sight meant out of mind. If you couldn't be present daily, there had to be constant reminders of your power and presence. Christianity had done this masterfully, weaving its tenets into everyday life—a picture of Jesus, cross on the wall, rosary in the pocket, Bible on the nightstand. Each served as a reminder of the faith. Such things required planning, infrastructure. If he was going to put that much work in, it should be for himself, not Yoxtl. The task irritated him on a level he hadn't anticipated, forcing him to confront the hidden cost of Medea's training— forfeited opportunities.

Isolation had never been his thing. You couldn't *play* in isola- tion. He missed the networks, the gossip pipelines feeding him information about rivals and allies, the grovelers who tried so hard to get him to look their way, the lieutenants he could count on to carry out any order, the dance of it all. Sex was a good one-off ego trip, but it was no substitute for that kind of power.

He visited Haven on occasion to pick up his mail—Mrs. Gallagher was nice enough to hold it for him—but it wasn't the same. The young Magi who once adored him had moved on to better things. They might nod at him in passing or join him for a pint, but he no longer *owned* them. Relationships, like any good garden, required tending. You had to pluck out the weeds, cultivate whatever gave you the most benefit, prune and graft and shape things to your will. Only then would the garden bear you fruit. He had no time for gardening now. The most he could hope for was the cheap thrill of stealing a neglected peach off someone else's tree. It chafed in a way he couldn't describe, and he looked forward to the day when he could wield that kind of power again.

6

KINDNESS AND GRACE

Medea sat under a shady tree and pulled out a notepad. She expanded her senses, allowing her consciousness to drift over the countryside, and scribbled down the addresses of potential test sites. While not as good as curling up at home with a book, it provided a reprieve from talking to people. Of course, she'd have to do that eventually, but for now she could enjoy simply being alone.

Week after week, town after town, her list expanded, and still she hadn't sought out any owners. Maybe if she searched for *just* a little longer, she'd find something ideal—a house with a FOR SALE sign and a giant bin outside labeled INSERT PAYMENT HERE would be nice. It wasn't until she accidentally went to the same town and jotted down duplicate candidates that she conceded it was probably time to search for the property owners.

She tried a town hall first.

"Oh, you want the County Clerk's office."

She was simultaneously elated that the conversation ended so fast and devastated that she'd have to go somewhere else. Having filled her socializing quota for the day, it wasn't until a few weeks later that she sought a county clerk's office. She chose one of Nikolai's days off, leaving well before he was up, so that she'd have as much energy as possible to dedicate to the task.

Digging through records at the clerk's office didn't yield any new information—now, she just had a name to use if she went knocking on the door of the house she'd targeted. She must have been making a face, for a clerk asked what was wrong. He took pity on her and brought her the business card of a real estate agent, but it only contained a phone number. What was she supposed to do with that?

"Can *you* call him for me?" She tried to smile. Men liked that sort of thing.

"Uh, sure."

But the line was busy, and the clerk had to return to his duties. She left without the number, but at least she knew what to look for.

The first real estate office she visited wanted to know where her husband was. No husband? A pretty thing like her shouldn't be making big purchases on her own. Maybe her father could come in, or her brother? The second said the same thing, though not as blatantly. The third wanted her bank account information.

"I don't have one."

"There's a savings-and-loan right up the street."

She rose and braced herself for the next location. Thank god she'd left herself the whole day. Every place she visited chipped away at her.

The bank was more than happy to hear that she wanted to open an account, but that didn't last long. She didn't have a Social Security number, or last name, or a street address, or any kind of documentation of who she was. Why did Mundanes need to make things so complicated?

"Look, I just need a bank account so I can buy a house. I have money." She dug a gold bar out of her hip pouch and set it on the man's desk with a loud clunk. Paying here and there for small things with illusions was fine, but for a purchase this large, she felt better making sure someone was fairly compensated.

The clerk's eyes fell to the gold bar, but he made no move to take it. "You can't have that."

"But I do, so please deposit it in my account."

"Miss, it's illegal to have gold bullion without a special license."

"Since *when*?"

He shrugged. "Sometime in the thirties. Blame FDR. I'll have to confiscate that." He grabbed the bar off the desk and turned to a coworker. "Jim, lock this in the vault, will you? I need to call the Feds. They'll decide whether or not to press charges."

Her chest tightened as the gold bar made its way through the lobby, turning heads and causing more than a few whispers in its wake. It's not like she couldn't make more, but that was beside the point. They'd just *taken* it. "I'm not even American."

"In that case, they'll reimburse you, though I can't say how long that will take."

"But I need to buy a house. I need an account. I gave you money . . ."

"I'm sorry." He said some other things, about identification and citizenship, but the words barely registered, and soon he was picking up the phone. When he set it back down, he gestured to the lobby. "You can wait over there, miss. They'll be right down."

"But I gave you money."

"I'm sorry, miss."

He just looked at her. This wasn't the way it was supposed to go. She'd given him money and a name. He was supposed to open an account. That's how it worked. How could they just take what was hers and turn her away? Was there some magic phrase she'd failed to use? She'd seen it often enough—she'd hit a wall with a person, then someone else would walk up, say some nonsense, and CLICK they'd open, like an invisible keyhole had been found. She'd stare at the bent key in her hand and wonder why it hadn't worked. What the hell was she supposed to do now? She had no contingency plan for this.

"Miss, I need you to take a seat in the lobby."

"Help me." She tried to keep her words from wavering. "I just need an account. *Please*."

He gave her a kindly look. "I know this must be hard for you. Do you have a husband who could come down and talk to us? Or perhaps a fath—"

She slammed her fist on the desk, overturning a cup of pencils, and shot to her feet. "I am Medea. I lived countless lifetimes before you were even *born*. Before your *grandparents* were even born. I traveled the globe, learned magic you couldn't even *dream*, and I did it all without the Need. For. A. Husband." The last few words were punctuated with the snapping of pencils. He should be glad it wasn't his fingers. Good-for-nothing Mundane. He wouldn't be refusing her if he knew what she could do. Her body shook as she spoke through gritted teeth. "Open an account." Fuck keyholes when you could break down doors.

"Miss, why don't you take a seat? The police will be here soon and they'll sort this all out. I'll have Jim bring you some water."

"Water? Water?!" In an instant, she'd drawn moisture from the air into her hand and flung it at his face.

He sputtered. "Did you just spit on me?"

"Do people normally spit with their hands? Open my account!"

Several employees converged on her position.

"Why can't you people *help me*? All I want is an account!

YOU STOLE MY MONEY AND YOU WON'T EVEN GIVE ME AN ACCOUNT. I JUST NEED AN ACCOUNT."

"Please lower your voice, miss. There's no need to shout."

"I'M NOT SHOUTING!" If she were, they'd be able to hear her words, but they just stared at her with deaf ears and faces made of stone. Her breath came hot and fast as the pressure built in her chest. She was losing it. Soon she'd spin out of control and there'd be no coming back. She clenched her fists and stormed for the exit.

A clerk made a grab for her arm and she sent him flying. How *dare* they try to restrain her! She glared around the lobby, power thrumming through her hands. The place had no right to exist if it couldn't do its job. A proper burning required scanning the building for flammable materials and starting there, but she was in no mood for finesse, not when she had the mana and the will to melt everything.

A siren wailed in the distance, grating on her already frayed nerves. Reluctantly, she turned heel and ran, out the door, down the street, running until a stitch in her side forced her to turn down an alley. She collapsed against the wall, fists pounding futilely at the red brick.

Denied. For the most arbitrary reasons. Her magic could do anything—raze cities, teleport her across the globe, heal any injury—yet it couldn't get her a damned bank account. Oh, she could hold their feet to the fire and *make* them do it, but this whole transaction was supposed to be aboveboard, not draw attention to the fact that she was a mage. She'd certainly failed at that.

Medea buried her head in her hands, hot angry tears stinging her eyes.

"Miss, are you alright?"

Medea's head jerked up. A man stood at the mouth of the alley. She turned aside and dragged her sleeve across her face. No one could see her like this. "I'm fine. Fine."

"I was in the bank there, and uh, well, I don't mean to be nosy, but I wanted to make sure you were okay. It wasn't fair, them taking your gold an' all."

"No, it wasn't. Not that it matters. I have more."

"You do?"

She opened her hip pouch. "Three—no, four."

He whistled. "How do you fit all that in a tiny purse?"

"Magic."

He laughed and offered her a hand up. "Are you parked in front of the bank? If so, I'd wait a while before heading back. The cops are looking for you."

"I walked. Before that I took a cab."

"I can give you a lift home if you want."

"I would appreciate that."

The Samaritan led her to his vehicle. She slid gratefully into the front seat and gave vague directions toward the gateway. All these towns and streets—it was impossible to keep track of specifics. The car rumbled and gospel music blared to life on the radio. Samaritan clicked it off and pulled away from the curb.

"What do you plan on doing with all that gold anyway? I heard something about a house?"

She was in no mood to talk, but it seemed rude not to answer. "I'm looking for a place far outside of town, no close neighbors, no chance of nearby developments. Farmland would be perfect, but there needs to be a house."

"You know, I have a friend with a place like that. He's been thinking about selling. If you're paying in gold, I'm sure he'd be happy to take it."

"Really?"

He smiled. "Sure thing. If you want, I can swing by now and see if he's available."

"Yes!" Finally, something good about this day.

He drove to a neighborhood of oddly similar houses. She counted a few different styles. Some were mirror images of one another; while they varied in color, they used the same palette. Only the adornments varied—a flag here, a bicycle there, a couple of lawn chairs on what passed for a front porch.

Samaritan parked in front of a yellow house. "I'll be just a minute." He jogged up to the door and knocked. She rummaged through her pouch and pulled out a hefty tome on telepathy, settling it onto her lap. She'd gotten a few pages in before Samaritan returned with not one but two men. "This here is Robert and his son, Earl."

The first looked to be in his fifties, with salt-and-pepper hair and a well-groomed mustache. The other had that shit-eating grin young men often got when they met her, and he not-so-subtly looked at her breasts. Ugh. Thank god she was sitting up front.

Mustache reached out to shake her hand. "Hope you don't mind me bringing my son. He's old enough to see how these things are done."

She shrugged noncommittally. Not like she could afford to miss this opportunity.

No sooner had they settled into the back seat than Sonny leaned forward and whistled near her shoulder. "That is a *big* book. What language is it?"

"Arabic." There were excerpts from older works in Sumerian as well, but elaborating would only lead to more questions.

"And what's a pretty girl like you doing learning Arabic?"

"I'm not *learning* Arabic, I'm *reading* Arabic."

"You one of them college girls?"

"No. Though you could say I'm a professor of sorts." That earned her a round of chuckling. "I'm older than I look." More chuckling. With a pang of regret, she slid the book back into her pouch and turned to the father. "Tell me about your property."

"It's seen better days, but Howard here says it's exactly what you're looking for."

Sonny leaned forward even more. "He also said you're paying in gold bars." His father jabbed him and he sat back.

"That's not a problem, is it?"

"Not at all—assuming you got them legally," Mustache said.

"I didn't steal them if that's what you're asking. Is there anyone else living nearby? Privacy is paramount."

Sonny smirked. "You could run hollering out the front door and no one would ever hear you."

Mustache shot him a withering gaze. "It's a big lot—plenty of acreage—and no neighbors for miles."

"Excellent."

They drove for nearly thirty minutes, though it felt like hours with Sonny's numerous attempts at conversation. She wanted nothing more than to read, but people found that impolite so she resigned herself to staring out the window. City streets gave way to farmland until at last they turned off the highway. She braced herself as the car jostled along the dirt road to a house with faded blue paint.

A solitary tree provided some shade, and though the surrounding land appeared fallow, there were several garden beds. Not that she needed any of that. There wasn't another house as far as the eye could see. But did it have water? She expanded her senses and found a well out back.

"I'll take it. Let's go." She looked expectantly at Samaritan, who glanced at his cohorts.

"Uh, don't you want to see it?" asked Mustache.

"I have. It suits my needs perfectly. I'd like to get back so we can sign the paperwork." Not something she was looking forward to, but gone were the days when you could make a verbal agreement and have it stand.

"No offense, miss, but I wouldn't feel right taking your money when you haven't seen it properly. I'd hate to have you go in there and find something that makes you change your mind."

"I doubt there's anything in there that could make me change my mind."

"Even so, I insist you inspect it first." He stepped out, followed by the others.

She closed her eyes and thudded her head against the window. Just a little longer. Just a quick tour, then she could pay the man and put this whole ordeal behind her. No more real estate agents or banks. She took a breath and opened the door.

Sonny had lingered by the car. He tried to walk beside her, glancing at her breasts again with that stupid grin. She quickened her pace. At least Mustache was courteous. He waited at the door and gestured her inside. She followed him through the house as he turned on faucets and flipped light switches to prove they worked.

"As you can see, it hasn't been lived in for a while, but we keep it clean. Here's the bathroom. Howard said he had to use it so we'll just skip that for now. This here is a closet . . ."

It was all a blur. The day had gone on entirely too long, and they still had paperwork to do. She needed to get back home and rest. "Fine. It's all fine. Can we head back now?"

"Not yet, miss. There's still the basement."

"I'm sure it's perfectly adequate."

"I insist." He opened a door and tugged a thin chain. A light bulb snicked on, illuminating the stairs in a faint glow that dissipated halfway down. "Blast it. The other bulb must've burned out. Earl, be a good lad and go get the flashlight."

"Really now, it's fine." She turned to leave but the man's girth blocked the door. He smiled pleasantly and gestured that she should go first.

She took a breath and descended, whirling around as soon as she touched the bottom. "Alright, I've seen it."

Blinding light hit her from the top of the stairs and her shields automatically expanded in anticipation of an attack. Something slammed into them and bounced off.

Disappointment washed over her. So that's why they'd been so nice. She should've known better, should've seen it coming. In retrospect it was obvious, but she was tired, frazzled even, and wanted desperately for these men to be the solution to her problem. Her whole day—the work she'd put in, the things she'd endured—all would have been worth it if only she'd secured a place. Now she was back to square one.

They were enemies, but it remained to be seen what kind. Robbers? Rapists?

She conjured a ball of light and tossed it toward the ceiling. It stuck there, casting a blue glow over the basement. In the corner of the room was a stained metal chair. Something shifted beside her, and Samaritan rose to his feet from where he'd fallen, hands clasping a pair of iron manacles. Betrayer. At the top of the stairs, Sonny trained a rifle on her. His father stood halfway down—on high ground, blocking the exit, yet out of reach.

"On your knees." Mustache's voice was no longer pleasant. None of them looked the least bit surprised she'd used magic.

"I don't think this property will work for me after all. It's infested with witch hunters."

"Shut up. Howard, bind her."

"I tried, something blocked me."

"Well, try again!"

The Betrayer lunged. At her will, the manacles snapped about his wrists and dragged him backward.

"You know, it's a myth that iron interferes with magic. Any binding that prevents gesticulation will do, but only for casters who rely on such things." She slammed him into the wall and pinned him there. "Not me, obviously."

"Get your hands up!" This from Sonny.

"I *just* said I don't need to gesticulate."

"Now!" He took aim.

"You really don't want to do that."

"Wait," cried Betrayer. "She's got some sort of force fiel—"

A deafening blast—she *hated* how loud guns were—and the bullet ricocheted into the ceiling. Young men, always so trigger-happy. She yanked the rifle from his hands, bent the barrel, and cracked it against his jaw. He toppled over the side of the stairs, landing on the hard-packed earthen floor.

"It's called a shield. Not terribly common here, I know, but common enough where I'm from." There was a thought—America had a serious witch hunter problem. In Europe it was assumed that Collective Enforcers kept the population in check, but maybe European casters simply had better spells at their disposal. American casters were more spread out, with little to no transfer of knowledge between groups. If not many knew of shields, they'd be at higher risk. Correlation didn't mean causation, but there was definitely an inverse relationship there, and a potential for further testing. She dug through her hip pouch for her notebook so she could write down the idea before she forgot it.

Mustache's fist cracked into her shield, scattering her thoughts. She glared at him. "You made me forget what I was thinking."

He ignored her and called up the stairs. "Earl, go get the sledge." Sonny vanished and reappeared a moment later with a sledgehammer.

She snorted. "You really think that will help?"

"See, I will make you into a threshing sledge," Mustache

intoned, "new and sharp, with many teeth. You will thresh the mountains and crush them, and reduce the hills to chaff."

Technically it *could* work. Shields only lasted as long as you had mana, and every impact would cost mana to absorb. Even if her mana regeneration didn't exceed the rate at which they applied force—and it most certainly did—they'd have to whale on her for centuries before she ran out. It seemed an odd hypothesis for them to check, given they didn't even know how shields worked.

Mustache waited until Sonny was in a position to guard her, then made his way to a makeshift bookcase of milk crates. She scanned the titles—always interesting to see other people's taste—but they were all religious texts. Mustache returned with a Bible and a flask. He uncapped it and doused the sledgehammer with clear liquid—probably holy water. It wouldn't do anything, but it made their hypothesis slightly less illogical. Mustache opened the Bible and began to recite. Witch hunters preferred to exorcise or convert their victims before killing. Sonny raised the hammer to strike.

"No." She snapped their necks and they crumpled to the floor. Slow, painful deaths were preferable for witch hunters, but they'd already wasted enough of her time.

"You'll burn in hell for that! And all for your other sins!" The Betrayer tried to wrench free from his manacles, but her will held them firmly against the wall. For him, at least, she could spare a moment.

She clasped her hands behind her back and sauntered over. "You may be a betrayer, but it is you who have been betrayed. Hell doesn't exist, nor heaven. I know you don't believe me. If you did, you'd have to admit to yourself that all your killings have been for naught, but I want you to go to your grave knowing the truth—that nothing awaits you on the other side." She began compressing his kidneys, watching his face intently for the pain to register.

He gritted his teeth and glared down at her. "You're right, I don't believe you, but even if I did, it wouldn't make a difference. Your kind deserve to die, whether God wills it or not."

That gave her pause, and she released the pressure. Perhaps that was his goal, but she had to know. "Why?"

"You think I didn't see what went on in the bank, how you attacked that man, how close you were to losing it?"

Her cheeks burned. "They refused to help me!"

"And you didn't take that very well, did you? They were just doing their jobs. Normal person gets mad, there's not much they can do. But your kind—you're dangerous. *Especially* women. So emotional. I saw it in my sister. She used to get hysterical, and instead of biting her tongue and sulking in her room like a good girl ought to do, she raged, her magic destroying whatever it happened to touch. It was a disgrace, having one in the family. That was my first kill. Father showed me how to do it. 'If you can take care of your own sister, you can handle anything you come across.' Mother was upset—we all were—but that's how it had to be. We all saw the danger, knew what she would've become had she been allowed to exist. There's a reason God tells us not to suffer a witch to live, and it has everything to do with protecting one another. Power like that is for God alone."

She stared at him in silence. What does one say to a person who killed their own sister because she had magic? It's not like you could logically argue with someone like that. "You're wrong."

"I've lived a life of kindness and grace. Took care of my family, been a good father to my children, volunteered at church, always available to help a friend in need—for a lift, another pair of arms, a bite to eat, a comforting word. These are the actions that enrich our lives and the lives of others. What have you done? What goodness have you brought others?"

"I've catalogued millions of spells, built the world's most comprehensive magical library, shared my knowledge with others—"

"But what *good* have you done? All that magic, and what have you done with it besides terrorize bank tellers?"

"That's not all I've done! I . . ." Saved a village from drought. But her magical fountain only made the village a target for the local warlord. So she'd killed him, but that created a power vacuum. More and more people sought control of the fountain. By the time she destroyed it, the whole region was in chaos.

She'd assassinated a dark wizard—a truly loathsome man. But then she found out the assassination contract was from someone even worse who stood to benefit from the loss of a rival. And it wasn't the only time. More than once, Mundane men had begged her for assistance, citing abhorrent grievances to legitimize their military campaigns. She'd slain entire armies, reveling in what looked like justice, only to find out she'd been used.

And of course there was Valerio. She'd paid dearly for her meddling, losing a friend simply because she'd helped him the wrong way. All that remained of Valerio now was a facsimile voice in a gecko familiar.

She didn't help people anymore. Sometimes things ended badly regardless. When she traded magic with the natives of the New World, she'd hoped they'd be able to stand up against the tide she knew was coming, but she wasn't optimistic. Nor was she surprised when she returned to find them gone or slaughtered. It wasn't her problem, though. She couldn't be everywhere at once, and *someone* had to catalogue all their magic before it was lost. Who knew how much worse things would have been if she'd intervened?

When you moved in your own little bubble, it was better not

to touch things outside of it. Ignorance of the specifics only made things worse, like a toddler bumbling into a chess match and moving pieces at random. She was woman enough to admit she didn't have the knowledge, patience, or expertise to meddle in the affairs of mortals. Noninterference *was* her way of helping. It gave people agency.

She straightened her shoulders. "I allow people to help themselves."

He laughed in her face, long and hard. "You do nothing and you stand for nothing. Go on, kill me then. My conscience is clear."

She balked at being told to do something she'd planned on doing anyway. For a moment she wondered if she could punish him without killing him. She had enough curses in her arsenal to make it really nasty, but no, he deserved death, regardless of how he felt. He was a danger to others.

As was she.

She shoved the thought aside. He was wrong. She was only dangerous when she chose to be, not because she lost control. Had she burned the bank? No, despite how much she wanted to. Of course, she'd hadn't done it for any philanthropic reason—she had been trying to be discreet. But she'd have been perfectly within her rights after how they'd treated her. It's not like she went out of her way to kill people, and what did it matter if mortals got hurt? They lived and died so fast anyway. Compared to others with her power, she was doing quite well, thank you very much. This man, this *Mundane*, had no right to judge her. What the hell did he know of the suffering of the world? Of the evils men enacted on one another? Nothing. He was a simple man from a simple town killing the few people who had a chance at something greater, including his own sister.

She looked into his eyes as she killed him, willing him to scream out in pain, but he watched her with a knowing smile, and his death left her wholly unsatisfied. She let the body fall and glanced about the basement.

Could she salvage this place? No, even if no one came looking for the bodies, eventually the men would be declared dead and their property would pass on to someone else. And as a site where several Magi had likely died, there was bound to be magical residue left behind. The test site needed to be legally hers and free of magical contamination.

She burned the building down, erasing all evidence of the men, though she couldn't erase the witch hunter's words.

7

PERSISTENCE

Nikolai stood beside the cab, trying to hold back his irritation at being made to wait in the hot sun. Medea stood in the alley between two drab buildings and fiddled with her hip pouch, pen clenched between her teeth. She'd been doing this a lot lately—extracting something, making a notation in a notebook, then discarding whatever it was before he could see. He swore it looked like a rock.

Out it came, obscured by her hand, along with a notebook. She tucked the thing under her armpit and hastily flipped pages, mouthing silently, and wrote something down. She stuffed the pen between the pages to hold her place and tossed the thing—he swore it looked like a rock—underhanded into the alley behind her. Then she rushed to join him, stepping into the cab without a word. He shook his head and slid in after her.

"Where to?" said the driver, looking to Nikolai.

"Out of town," said Medea, plopping the notebook in her lap. "Preferably someplace at least twenty miles away that has a diner."

"Twenty miles!"

"I have money." She pulled out a stack of illusioned paper and shoved it toward him. He counted it with a frown.

"I can take you as far as Franklin. That okay?"

"Is it at least twenty miles and does it have a diner?" Her tone screamed he was an idiot for asking.

"I believe it's twenty-seven miles. For diners, you've got Susanne's Place over on Main Street, then there's Cha—"

"That's fine." She turned her attention to the window.

The driver made a disgruntled face but pulled onto the street. A half mile later, he glanced at them in the mirror. "So, what brings you two—"

"That won't be necessary." Medea hadn't bothered looking up.

Nikolai caught the driver's eye and mouthed, "Sorry."

When they were out of the city, Medea started rummaging through her pouch again. She extracted a stone and plopped it on the seat next to her before recommencing her digging. It appeared to be a river stone, worn smooth by the passing of water, but when he cast Magic Sight, a forest of orange tendrils materialized on the surface.

"What's that?"

"Huh?" Her search became frantic. "Where the *hell* is my notebook?"

"In your lap."

"Oh. Right." She gave her head a shake and opened it to a table with several columns already filled.

"What's that?"

"Notes."

"Not that. *This*." He tapped the rock.

She looked at him pointedly. "Did you read the science books I gave you?"

Aside from the times he'd taken them out and pretended to read, the books had sat untouched on a shelf in his bedroom.

Dense reading, she'd called them. *A cure for insomnia* was a more accurate description. Oh, he skimmed here and there, just enough to pick up key vocabulary words in case she tested him. Medea loved clarifying. If his knowledge seemed incomplete rather than absent, she'd willingly vomit up whatever she thought he needed to know. It was a far more efficient use of his time. "Of course."

"Good. Did you come up with a list of hypotheses for why magic is dying?"

The driver gave her a curious look in the rearview mirror.

He hadn't, but it was easy enough to wing if he stalled for a moment. "Forgive me," he said, switching to Russian so the driver wouldn't understand. "I didn't bring the list, so I'm doing my best to remember. The collective wisdom is that Mundane technology interferes with magic. There may be some truth to that. I know it's only anecdotal evidence, but highly developed areas *feel* like they have less ambient magic. I tried to think of what else might cause this effect. We need to look at what's there and what isn't. Technology is there, but also people. Maybe having that many Mundanes in one area is somehow displacing magic."

Medea pursed her lips, then responded in English. "I don't like the implications of that."

He continued in Russian, hoping she'd take the hint. "Nor do I, but we also need to look at what's missing, and that's obvious enough—nature. Your gardens, particularly the old-growth areas far from civilization, seem to have an abundance of ambient magic. Just look at the Aztec temple. It's deserted now, but presumably it once held a large number of people, and it still retains magic. Why? Maybe because of where it is—right in the middle of the jungle."

"So you hypothesize that the displacement of nature might be to blame." Medea sat back and steepled her hands before her mouth. "I'd never considered that. Thank you. I've been at this for so long on my own. It's good to finally have someone else to lend a fresh perspective." She offered him a rare smile, quickly replaced with her #2 frown. "Unfortunately, I don't yet see how those hypotheses connect with some of the other things I've noticed. Each successive generation is born with less magic. Someone with your strength is an anomaly. If it were simply a matter of nature being displaced, we'd see more Magi born in less-developed areas. Tell me, where were you born?"

"In a large city." He'd offer no more than that. She might be oblivious to what the Soviet people endured during the war, but he didn't need her blabbing his personal history. *This is my apprentice . . . should you choose to bed him . . .* Honestly, what the fuck was wrong with her?

Light frown, #2 bordering on #3. "Obviously you wouldn't have been cognizant of your birth, but did any adults ever mention strange circumstances around it?"

"No."

"Do you have any siblings?"

He contemplated lying but decided against it. They needed to share information if a solution was to be found. If she got too close to something he'd rather not discuss, he'd just tell her flat out. "I was the eldest of five boys. Two were twins, if that makes a difference."

Medea winced. "Your poor mother. Were any of your brothers Magi?"

He started to say no, then paused. "I've always thought of them as Mundane, but they died so young I couldn't be certain. My parents weren't Magi. Does it run in families?"

She cocked her head to the side and grimaced. "Eh, it's never been formally studied, but I don't believe so. In the old days, anyone could apprentice in magic. Some are naturally more talented than others, or born with more mana to start, but training and study make a huge difference. Saying certain bloodlines are inherently more magical is like saying people raised in a family of bakers are inherently better at making bread. It only looks that way because they grew up in the trade. We could check mana levels in infants, see if there's a correlation between inherent magic and birth location, but it requires me to be on-site and look at each individually. Not very scalable."

It was something Yoxtl could easily help with—the creature could sense the strength of mortal souls and teleport to any known location—but bringing up Yoxtl would only irritate her.

The cabbie tilted his head. The rigid set of his body and the intensity of his focus screamed of a man trying to appear as though he weren't listening.

Medea continued, oblivious to their eavesdropping driver. "But back to your hypotheses, I don't yet see how they could account for the increase in dead spells."

A memory percolated to the surface—the first day he'd met her, when she'd come to Petrov's shop to identify their unknown wares. She'd moved down a table, pointing to a dagger, a necklace, a ring, and without so much as touching them, told him their enchantments.

At a pendant she'd paused. "Luck, but it's a dead spell. It'll need to be enchanted with something else."

He'd started to ask what she meant, but she'd sternly reminded him to wait until she'd finished. Except he hadn't remembered, not until now.

"What's a dead spell? You mentioned once that Luck was dead. And please stop talking about magic in English. You're making the driver nervous."

She glanced at the driver with a "So?" expression but switched to Russian. "A spell is dead if it doesn't work anymore. At first I didn't know that's what was happening. I'd try to cast a spell from a book or my notes, only to have it fail. I thought they were bad translations. Maybe I'd written them down wrong or mispronounced a word." She laughed sadly and shook her head. "I've encountered more of them of late, even with spells I've been casting for hundreds of years. Some have gotten weaker or only work intermittently. Others, like Luck"—she shrugged— "nothing."

Her Russian was surprisingly fluent, though badly accented. She'd never responded well to his compliments on her magic, but then she considered him an inferior caster and thus an inadequate judge of her abilities. But now the situation was reversed. Perhaps he could earn some good will with genuine acknowledgment.

"Is there any commonality between dead spells? By the way, your Russian is excellent."

"I've been practicing." She spoke matter-of-factly and continued without pause, but it gave him new insight—she'd specifically set aside time to relearn his mother tongue. "Most are standard spells using invocations—yet another reason why I suggest using custom, nonverbal magic—but there may come a time when that doesn't work either."

An uncomfortable feeling settled in his chest. He could spend a decade learning magic only to have it ripped away.

Magical interference didn't account for fewer Magi being born, but it *could* account for dead spells. Perhaps some spells were more susceptible than others. "I think the real question is whether magic is becoming scarce, or if something is interfering."

"I'm inclined to agree. We need information first—where magic is decreasing, at what rate. That's why I created these." She handed him the rock, finally arriving at her point.

The cabbie stole a glance at them in the rearview mirror. What was the guy's problem? Did he speak Russian too? A peek into his mind revealed he thought they were Communist spies. Apparently the United States was in some sort of clandestine war with the Soviet Union. All this talk of magic was obviously code for something.

He returned his attention to Medea, who hadn't stopped talking. "Sorry, repeat that last part. The rocks do what?"

"They measure the amount of ambient magic nearby. The plan is to drop them inside major cities and then the surrounding country to see if there's a difference. Once a day, they send their data to a notebook I have in the lab, which records the number."

"Number of what? How are you quantifying this?"

"You *did* read the books." She smiled like he'd surprised her with flowers on an anniversary he usually forgot.

"I don't claim to have a perfect understanding, but I did my best."

She scooted closer. "I created a new unit of measurement for ambient magic."

Medea usually maintained a distance between herself and others. Now he could feel the pressure she exerted on the seat, the warmth of her breath, the tickle of her dress brushing against his calf. She smelled earthy, with a hint of the meadow grass and a dash of ocean breeze. Her smaller stature unintentionally afforded him a better-than-average view of her chest. The trick to not getting caught was to look only when their gaze was somewhere else, and to memorize as much as you could in an instant. Medea didn't often make eye contact, affording more opportunities, but never this close before. No bra that he could see. Either she had naturally perky tits or she used magic to hold them up. It was a mystery he longed to solve. Careful to maintain his attentive face, he slid his eyes back to the stone.

"It's similar to how I measure mana," she continued, "based on how long it takes to bring a set amount of water to boil. If you're interested, I can show you my calculations in the lab."

Dear god no. "That would be lovely."

She reached out and caressed the air above the rock in his lap, as though petting the orange tendrils. He moved one arm to hide his growing bulge, but she grabbed his hand and put it over the rock. "Feel that?"

"No, but I see it. It looks like an orange wig."

"Magic Sight forces your brain to sense magic visually, but it's important you learn to sense individual spells without aid. You recall in the forest when you sensed my plant attacks?"

An echo of pain rippled through his feet. "How could I forget?"

"This is no different. Cancel the spell and try again."

He did, but the rock now seemed like just a rock. "I don't sense anything. Maybe because it's not moving?"

"Close your eyes." She plucked the stone from his lap and her scent retreated. "I've put the rock on the seat. See if you can find it by sense alone. Analyze the shape of the spells and tell me how many there are."

He focused on the area beside him. There *was* something—a warmth or a breath of promise, like the ambient magic he felt on the island, only smaller and more seductive. He reached for it and his perception sharpened. A bouquet of spells! Individually they were nothing, but together they radiated a power so tantalizing he could taste it. He wanted to grasp the power and absorb it into himself. His fingers closed over it, soft and warm, and it jerked away. Shit.

"I suppose I shouldn't be surprised." Medea rubbed her hand with a bemused expression. "I've got quite a few enchantments on my person. You felt nothing else, nothing at all?"

"No." Now that she'd called attention to it, he couldn't ignore the sense of magic emanating from her body like the world's strongest aphrodisiac. Magical desire combined with physical to create a carnal longing like nothing he'd ever experienced. Whatever it took, he would convince her he was worthy of her affections.

"With practice you should be able to feel individual spells. Incidentally, how did you sense it?" She looked at him with interest.

He crossed his legs and adjusted his coat to hide his lap. "Meaning what, exactly?"

"Everyone senses magic differently. Some experience it as a change in pressure or temperature. Others can hear it resonate. I've even met people who claimed they could smell magic. What did you feel when you reached for my hand?"

Desire.

"I'm not sure. It's difficult to put into words."

"If you figure it out, let me know. I keep a catalog of all the ways magic can be experienced." She glanced out the window. "I think we're far enough away from the city now." She grabbed the rock and reached for the window crank.

"What're you doing there?" the cabbie asked as she rolled it down.

"Tossing a rock out the window."

"A rock, eh? Let me see it."

Medea shot him a puzzled #3 frown. "No."

"He thinks we're Russian spies. Sorry. I didn't realize it wasn't the best language to use."

"Speak English!" barked the cabbie. "And you, put down the rock."

Medea exchanged a look with Nikolai, then chucked the stone out the window.

"Hey!" The cab screeched to a halt. "Out!"

"Really now, you're being preposterous." Despite her protest, Medea exited the cab.

Perhaps he could salvage this. *We're not spies.* "Don't mind my sister, she's a bit funny in the head you know, and—"

"I don't care what she is. I've had enough of her. Now, out!" Foremost in the man's mind was Medea's earlier bluntness, how cold and dismissive she'd seemed. His mind replayed it, with added emphasis on how it made him feel. She'd predisposed the man to dislike her, so it was easier for him to believe she was a spy.

Nikolai leaned across the seat. "Look, I'm sorry about all this. I just brought my sister over from the Ukraine and I know she's a bit"—he chuckled—"well, you've seen how she is. What can I do to make it up to you? Double your fare?"

"You can get out of my cab." The driver didn't even wait for the door to close before peeling away, leaving them on the side of the road in a cloud of dust.

Medea coughed and waved a hand in front of her face, magically swirling the dust aside. "Well, that was rude."

They walked until they came to a bus stop. There wasn't anything nearby, not a single tree for shade or even a bench, just wide-open fields of some crop or another planted in tidy rows. Medea plopped down on the dirt and began to read. In an effort to appear equally constructive, Nikolai practiced his focus exercise with pebbles. When that grew tiresome, he kicked the top off an ant mount and ignited the fleeing insects—much more fun. It took ages for a bus to show up and when it did, it was headed in the wrong direction. Medea was too intent on her book to notice and he didn't bother to tell her.

The bus was packed with commuters. Still staring at her book, Medea groped along the aisle and took the first available seat. The only seat left was next to two children. Great. No chance of decent conversation there. He sat and the bus pulled away. Medea didn't look up. Hopefully she wouldn't notice where they were headed until they reached the city.

As they rode, he slipped in and out of minds. It was always the same thing—worries over money, worries about love, anticipation of some upcoming event or trip, rumination on tasks to be done. Then there was the odd scratcher—they'd flinch and scratch the back of their head, not unlike how Magi reacted, but these were Mundanes. They weren't common, but there was one now, seated across the aisle. He flinched at the probe and whipped his head around, as though expecting to see someone standing just over his shoulder. That part wasn't like Magi. Magi knew. Every goddamned time, even as children. It was always "Get out of my head!" or "What the hell do you think you're doing?" or "Nikolai!"

Not this guy. This guy frowned at the lack of an assailant and turned his gaze toward the passengers seated behind him, their faces covered by matching newspapers. He watched them for a moment, daring one to flip the paper down and laugh, but neither took notice. He faced forward again, back rigid, mind full of discomfort, and absently rubbed the back of his skull. Hold the mind long enough and he'd start to get *really* paranoid. It would certainly make the ride more interesting.

"Hey, beautiful. Whatcha reading?"

Nikolai snapped his attention back to Medea—still reading her book. The man beside her was late middle-aged, just starting to go grey. He eyed her with interest, the slow, crawling rake of a man who didn't care if she noticed, who, perhaps, wanted her to notice. Men used to stare at Mother like that, give her ass a squeeze as she walked by. She'd arm herself with a smile and a *good day*, tightening her grip on his small hand and pulling him along, so fast it was hard for his shorter legs to keep up. Her face turned to stone as soon as the men were behind her, and when they were out of earshot, she'd lean over and speak to him in hushed Turkish, "Don't ever do that, Kolya. Look if you must, but *don't ever let her see it*, and don't touch what doesn't belong to you." He'd asked if she belonged to Father. "We belong to each other," she'd said with a smile.

Mother hadn't had power, though. Unlike Medea.

"You sure are a pretty thing. What's your name?"

Medea stared resolutely at her book. Hadn't she heard him? She often became engrossed to the point of obliviousness. Or perhaps it was her sound shield. No, her jaw was clenched and she'd stopped scanning the page.

"Hey. I'm talking to you. Don't be like that. I just want your name. What's your name, pretty girl?" The man put an arm over the back of the seat and leaned into her personal space. "Oh, I see. You think you're too good for me. Stuck-up bitch. What you need is a good spanking." He slapped his knee and guffawed.

A few people nearby shifted uncomfortably and looked in the opposite direction. If it had been any other woman he would have intervened—one man's faux pas was another man's gain—but Medea was perfectly capable of handling it herself. Hell, she'd probably yell at him for butting in. Why was she just sitting there? It made no sense. Mundane women might have something to fear, but this was Medea, the woman who magically slapped him for the slightest infraction. Her glare was already at #3, though it was still directed at her book.

The man slid his hand behind her back. He eased it down, lower and lower, until he reached her buttocks. Medea's glare jumped to #4 and the man yanked his hand back with a hiss, clutching it as though it had been burned. He began to cough— here and there at first, then more violently, until he doubled over hacking. Nearby commuters leaned away.

Medea stared off into space for the rest of the ride, her book open but ignored. When the bus arrived at their stop, she closed it with a snap and turned to her groper with a saccharine smile. "You die tonight."

The man goggled after her, then fell into another coughing spasm.

Nikolai joined her on the sidewalk. Downtown was bustling, but she didn't seem at all surprised by the location. She squinted down the street. "I see some restaurants down this way. I suppose I should let you choose where we dine, now that we have a selection."

"So you *did* realize we were headed back."

"Yes, but you're still an asshole for not telling me."

He shrugged. "You'd already dropped your rock. What curse did you use on that guy?"

"Spontaneous Combustion. I must say, I miss the earlier part of this century. Women had long hat pins and didn't hesitate to use them."

"Excellent. Why didn't you tell him you weren't interested?"

She threw up her hands with exaggerated shock. "Why didn't *I* think of that? To think, all these centuries I could have *asked* them to go away and had them done so."

"You know what I mean. If you'd told him to fuck off—"

She spun to face him. "Did *you* go away that first day in the Hanged Man?"

"Of course. I went and spoke with the bartender."

"And then you came back."

"That was different. I wanted lessons."

"And he wanted sex. Whether or not I was interested didn't factor into his—or your—decision to continue, and engagement only increases persistence."

The parallel was irksome. He wasn't like that. Didn't she realize he wasn't like that? He wouldn't apologize for pursuing an apprenticeship. How else would he have gotten it? There were some things you didn't give up on, and yet being thrown into the same category as that man . . .

She watched him with quiet intensity. When he didn't

respond, she shook her head. "This is how it is for women. I'd like to say it's gotten better over time, but it hasn't. It's always been this way."

"The man in the alley—the one whose tongue you stole—and those guys you smashed with the sign—are you telling me that every time, they made a pass at you?"

She nodded. "At least it doesn't happen as much when you're around. I expect it's because they think we're together. Men respect another man's 'property' in a way they don't respect me."

He chuckled. "If they only knew what you could do."

"They shouldn't have to. And what of girls like that redhead you saved back in Haven? Should *she* be a target by virtue of her sex, simply because she is weak?"

Yes. No. "Of course not!"

Why did Medea have to use that word? Weakness demanded exploitation. The strong controlled the weak—that's all there was to it. And yet for some reason, he couldn't agree with exploiting girls like Kate. The conversation had gone from bad to worse.

"I see a restaurant ahead. Let's have a look at the menu." He strode to the front and pretended to read the posting.

Medea's comparison of him to the crass man on the bus—was this her way of signaling disinterest? No, she was more up-front than that. But then she hadn't told the man on the bus to fuck off either. *Engagement only increases persistence.* Was she intentionally ignoring his seduction attempts, not because she feared the consequences of her attraction but because she wasn't attracted at all? Was her irritation because he wouldn't leave her alone? She *had* changed her entire schedule to avoid him . . .

A subtle shift in magic announced Medea's arrival at his side. Now that he was aware of how her power radiated, it was difficult to ignore. Her face tilted toward his, menu unconsidered, for once favoring a person over the written word. "It's a myth that truth is painful. Truth is simply knowledge. The pain comes from within us." She entered the restaurant, leaving him alone with his thoughts.

He pulled back in the weeks that followed, though it didn't seem to help. Medea was increasingly distracted of late. She stopped inquiring about his telepathy progress and made no effort to expand on his training. Instead, she left their meals earlier and earlier, sometimes before the food even arrived. It's not like he needed her anyway. She always gave the same boring instructions —make them scratch, play with their hair, order the soup. Why stop at itches when there were far more entertaining subliminal commands?

Boy too nervous to tell his date how he felt? *Stand up and sing it.*

Two men spoiling for a fight? *He called you a jackass.*

Well-dressed man bragging about his new Jaguar? *Take a cab. Pass me your keys on the way out.*

Woman looking for a good time? *I'm free tonight, and I have a new Jag.*

He saw no reason to tell Medea how much fun he was having watching people dance to his tune. The woman was entirely too sensitive about telepathy—too sensitive about everything, really —and she seemed mentally checked out of late. Why shouldn't he take the opportunity to amuse himself? Waitresses and sometimes patrons marked Medea's rapid and seemingly sour departure. It became a fun challenge to concoct elaborate stories as to why they'd been dining together.

Medea was his mentally unstable sister. He was only trying to convince her that she needed help. But she wouldn't listen. She never listened!

He was an undercover operative (they must never tell anyone!) tasked with getting close to Medea. He dazzled them with his knowledge of Europe and fluency in multiple languages.

Medea was his high school sweetheart. They were destined to

marry, or so he'd thought. He'd spent a year abroad, working tirelessly for a callous boss to earn enough to buy her dream home, but he'd returned to find her engaged to his best friend. How could they betray him so?

It was all very entertaining. Waitresses were his favorite target, at least until he discovered the untapped resource of American housewives. Talk about starved for attention! The ladies worked hard to maintain their appearance and keep a home, just so their schmuck husbands could roll around on top of them for a couple minutes at the end of the day. A few of them told their friends, and soon he was making regular visits to certain neighborhoods a few times a week. The ego boost was incredible. He was a goddamned hero, bringing neglected women to new heights they'd never experienced before. The rest of summer passed in a blur of parties and panties. Medea had no idea what she was missing.

8

SENSITIVITY

I f she had to hear the phrase "why don't you come back with your husband" one more time, Medea swore she was going to start exploding heads. At least she'd solved the money problem, gradually pawning gold and gemstones until she had a small hoard of Mundane cash. The exchange rate was no doubt terrible, but there were far fewer questions. Her new plan was to bypass the bank and make her offer directly to owners—cash for a deed. Someone had to bite eventually.

Confident the matter would soon be settled, she turned her attention back to training. Nikolai's progress had plateaued and she had no one to blame but herself. She'd been distracted, yes, but also ill prepared. Nikolai tore through her library's meager telepathy section and declared most of it useless. He almost seemed pleased.

"It's a *shame* you didn't bother to get primary sources for telepathy. Can you imagine if your healing section looked like this? But I know that's your favorite. It's only *natural* you'd want to do a better job there."

She seethed at the insinuation, but he had a point. What if her bias had influenced her collection? She tried to think back. Had she overlooked purchasing a text? Failed to interview a telepath? Catalog a method? Most of what she had was pieced together through the centuries. It's not like there was an abundance of telepaths to begin with, and most refused to identify themselves. Anyone claiming to be a mind reader was typically a fraud.

The last legitimate telepath she could remember was an assassination job, back when she still took assassination jobs. That had been a hard-won duel—thankfully information on blocking telepathy was more common, otherwise she might not have survived. The man's journal entries and assorted notes, though extensive, had contained nothing on his gift. Could she have kept him alive long enough to question him? She'd learned the hard way never to leave true enemies alive. This man was particularly powerful and never would have answered her anyway, but there was still that nagging doubt—had her fear caused her to miss an opportunity to learn more? If she'd learned more, she might not have to fear telepathy at all, and she wouldn't be so woefully unequipped to instruct Nikolai.

There was one person—*entity*—who could probably help him, but she dared not go down that road.

After rescuing Nikolai from the boiling ocean, Yoxtl had reached across the ether, *directly into her mind*, to beckon her home. It should have been impossible. Her mind barrier was constructed to allow view of incoming attacks without compromising strength, yet the spirit bypassed her defenses without so much as a whisper. Naturally she'd asked Yoxtl how it was done. If the usual mind barriers didn't work on spirits, she'd have to engineer a method that did. She would *not* leave herself open to attack.

The spirit denied having called her at all. Refusing to share the information was one thing—spirits were notoriously tight-lipped about their abilities—but *lying*? Especially when they both knew it to be true? She seethed just thinking about it. She'd demanded it leave the island; Yoxtl threatened to tell Nikolai why. It hadn't taught Nikolai its method yet, and they blessedly seemed to be at odds of late, but the sword of Damocles remained over her head. She would not give Nikolai a reason to think Yoxtl could help with telepathy. He'd just have to figure out how to progress on his own.

It would help if he actually *applied* himself, though. They were at yet another diner, and once again he was spending more time observing pretty girls than focusing on his lesson.

She gave him a stern kick under the table. "Stop that."

He blinked and shifted his attention back to her. "Stop what? I swear, it's as though you think I can *read minds*."

"You've been staring at the hostess for the past five minutes."

There it was again—that subtle shift in body language she'd yet to decipher. "Really? It's never bothered you before."

"You're supposed to be practicing, not wasting your time on frivolous pursuits." She slathered butter on her bread and took a bite.

He leaned forward with a grin. "Oh, I've been practicing. Telepathy has always ensured I knew what my partner wanted, but I'm no longer limited by what my hands and mouth can do. Every *kiss*"—his tongue seemed to caress the word, making it obscene—"every *lick* and *pinch* and *squeeze* can be amplified and—"

She nearly choked on her bread. "Enough!" she said between coughs. "I don't need to know the details of your . . . your *escapades*."

"Are you *sure*? I thought you wanted more information about how telepathy worked. I've been practicing quite diligently."

"No. *No*." She shuddered and looked away, heat rising in her cheeks. "It's enough that you practice. I'd feared you'd plateaued. I know I haven't been very . . ." She shook her head. "Why haven't you said anything until now?"

He shrugged. "You seemed preoccupied. Besides, it's not like you can help me anyway." It was true, but it stung to hear him say it.

She laced her hands together on the table and steeled herself for more unintentional rebukes. "Please update me on your progress. What can you do?"

"It's easier if I show you." His glance flicked over her shoulder, but then he was back to cutting his food, pushing a portion of each item neatly to the side.

"Well?"

"Christ, woman, have some patience."

She scoffed. "I'm the epitome of patience."

"Just give it a minute. And act normal for once."

She was about to ask what he meant when a well-dressed man approached the table and stared at Nikolai in awe.

"Is it really you?" the man said.

Nikolai dabbed the corner of his mouth with a napkin and shot her a knowing grin. "It is."

"It's an honor to meet you, sir!" The man extended his hand and Nikolai shook it. "You've done so much . . . the missus and I, so very grateful." He continued to fuss over Nikolai, rambling about how great he was, how caring and wonderful and *generous*. "Please allow me to make a donation to your cause." The man took out his billfold and extracted a five, setting it on the table.

"I'm very much obliged. Thank you, sir."

"No, thank *you*." He clapped Nikolai on the back and returned to his table, conferring with his wife in hushed whispers.

Medea sat back. "What the hell was that?"

"*Language*, my dear woman. We're in public."

"Oh, I'm sorry. What the *fuck* was that?"

He suppressed a smile. "I gave him the impression that I'm a famous philanthropist and that he'd get lots of social credit by saying he'd met me and"—he snapped the five—"made a donation."

"I see. That seems rather advanced." Frighteningly advanced. No wonder he hadn't seemed attentive during telepathy lessons. Here she was reading a primer to someone who'd already mastered the language. She pinched the tips of her fingers. "I'm not sure where to go from here. I feel . . . inadequately equipped to teach you telepathy."

He smiled—a brief flash and it was gone. They both knew he was better at this. She felt a rush of gratitude that he wasn't rubbing it in, immediately overshadowed by stark reality. Magic had always kept her enemies at bay, and not just magic, but being better at it than everyone else. This was a precarious position to be in, especially with a man like Nikolai.

"I didn't choose to train with you because you're better at telepathy. I chose you because you know more about magic than anyone. And you can make connections I can't." Consciously or unconsciously, he touched his chin, the very place where she'd scarred him with a rudimentary healing spell. Good to see he hadn't forgotten that lesson.

She straightened. "Are you struggling with anything? Do you have any questions?"

"It's not a question so much as an observation."

"Sir?" A demure brunette appeared at Nikolai's side. "I just wanted to thank you ever so much for all your charity work . . ." The woman fawned over Nikolai, who seemed to revel in the attention and did nothing to get her to leave.

Medea drummed her fingers and waited. Eventually the woman pressed a coin into Nikolai's hand and joined her friends in leaving the restaurant.

"Sorry about that. As I was saying, I've noticed something odd. Sometimes when I touch a mind, the person acts strange.

They look around wildly, or flinch and rub the back of their head. I've seen Magi react like that, but these have all been Mundanes."

"Are there any here now?"

He nodded toward a booth at the back. "There in the corner, the bald guy."

Back when ambient magic was strong in the world, it was difficult to pick out individual Magi unless they were fairly strong. Now they contrasted sharply against the backdrop of nothingness, though they felt dim, like oil lamps turned low. The bald man wavered somewhere in between, a candle ready to be snuffed out. "He has enough mana to make him aware of your intrusions, but not enough to cast spells."

"I don't understand. If he's Mundane, how can he have mana at all?"

"It's a gradient. Some people are born with more, others with less. One of the first things I noticed when we met was that your inherent magic was far greater than most Magi these days."

"Really?" He didn't sound the least bit surprised. "Why didn't you tell me?"

"Your head was big enough already. Speaking of which . . ." She rolled her eyes as a couple stopped to praise him and hand over their money. When they'd left, she shook her head. "You know, that's less impressive the more often you do it."

"Sorry about that. Please continue."

"Spells require a minimum threshold of mana to cast. If you're not born with it, you can borrow from a patron spirit, but you can also tap into ambient magic. It's harder, of course, taking a good deal of will, but with enough practice you can increase your mana pool enough to cast spells on your own."

"So you could be born Mundane and become Magi?" He looked incredulous. No doubt they'd taught him otherwise at the Academy.

"Through dedication and practice, yes. Magical sites make it easier—places like the temple in Mexico. They're imbued with magic, allowing practitioners to perform spells beyond their normal abilities. Mundanes often view these places as holy and battle to maintain control over them, not understanding their true significance. But if a Mundane were to live and train there for many years, they could eventually become Magi. That's the wonderful thing about being human. So long as you exercise your mana pool—even if it is minuscule—it will increase. But now . . . No wonder there are so few of us."

She studied her plate. Always she'd thought of how the decline in ambient magic made each generation of Magi weaker. She hadn't considered that it also cut off the most accessible route to magic. Magical sites remained, but Mundanes didn't know how to use them, and even the spirits to which they could pledge their souls in exchange for power were growing weak. What options did that leave?

"Excuse me," said a slender man, "are you . . . ?" He faltered at Nikolai's withering expression, a mouse who'd inadvertently caught the attention of a cat.

"You were supposed to be here ages ago," said Nikolai. "I told you not to bother coming."

"I— What?"

"Can't you see we're in the middle of a conversation? Just leave it on the table and go."

The man fumbled in his pocket. "So sorry to interrupt." He set a few coins on the table and scurried away.

Nikolai swept the change into his palm. "My apologies, he was the last one."

She studied the man as he moved across the diner, headed for the exit. Middle aged. Average height and dress, nervous disposition. Forgettable. Unaware that magic existed. In a few decades he'd be just another corpse in the ground. "What do you think of Mundanes? You're usually nicer to them."

"I usually want something from them." He nodded to the man. "That one let me down. Never pick a coward for a timely job."

"That's not what I mean." She frowned. What *did* she mean? There was something here, some niggling idea she couldn't quite grasp. "What do you think of them . . . compared to Magi?"

He shrugged. "When you view people the way I do, it makes no difference whether they're Mundane or Magi."

"I've never cared much for Mundanes. I have at least a begrudging respect for Magi, even the bad ones. But Mundanes just seem so . . . *mundane*. Maybe it's gotten worse with age. They live and die so fast and they're so interchangeable with one another, but it's always bothered me how they can look around the world, see all the magic inherent there, and say 'that's not for me.'"

"Like they snubbed something you cared about."

"Yes! Exactly like that. But worse. It's like people who say they can't read. So learn! It's not difficult! I cannot abide willful ignorance." Just thinking about it made her angry. How many times had she repeated the master's words in her mind as he read aloud? How many times had she pilfered his scrolls and hidden among the hay, studying the words and tracing her own in the dust? None of the other children had her interest in letters, preferring to chase each other around with sticks, and look where that got them—dead in other people's wars, dead from disease, dead during childbirth—while she'd vanquished her enemies and made herself immortal. With magic, you could do *anything*.

Except now there was no ambient magic.

People could still be educated, but they couldn't be Magi, not unless they were fortunate enough to be born into a family that practiced magic, not unless they were identified by the Collective and shipped off to the Academy, as Nikolai probably had been. Thanks to the Collective, most Mundanes didn't even think magic *existed* anymore. Oh, they wanted it to, but without seeing it on a daily basis, what else were they to believe?

Suddenly the circumstances of her childhood, horrible as they were, seemed a lot more fortunate. She'd *had* a learned master. She'd *had* access to his scrolls. She'd grown up at a time when magic was prevalent. What would she be if she'd been born now? Against her will, she scanned the diner for women her physical age—all she saw were young women out on dates, as she appeared to be. The others were probably married, trapped at home cooking for their husbands and tending to their numerous children. She could think of few worse fates.

Nikolai placed a copper coin on the table and slid it toward her. "Penny for your thoughts."

She took it, running her thumb along the edge. "My childhood wasn't pleasant. I worked very hard to get out of the situation I was in. Perhaps I was born with a predisposition for magic, perhaps not—I have no way of knowing—but the fact of the matter is that I used it to gain my freedom. And when I've come across Mundanes in similar situations, even when I've helped them, even when I've felt sorry for them, I couldn't help but think if only they committed themselves to learning magic, if only they tried harder, they wouldn't be where they were. Yes, those who kept them in thrall were to blame, but it was just as much their own fault for not escaping. The answer was right before them. They just lacked the mental fortitude to take it. And now . . . now I don't know what to think."

Another patron approached and tentatively laid a coin on the corner of the table next to Nikolai.

As soon as he walked away, Medea hissed, "You said you were done!"

"That wasn't me. Notice how he didn't say anything? He just saw others giving me money and decided it was the thing to do." He reached for the coin, then smirked and left it on the table.

"Anyway, you're right. If magic was that common in the old days, then anyone who didn't use it got what they deserved."

Her stomach knotted. The validation felt tainted coming from a man like Nikolai, who cared for no one but himself. Maybe she was more wrong than she'd thought. "But some people are just bad at magic. For all I know, Mundanes might have tried it and given up. And what of me? What if I'd been born now? What if I'd been unskilled despite my best efforts? What if I tried to free myself and failed?" God, where would she have been then? Her mind shuddered away from the thought.

"You would have found another way." He said it with such certainty, but how could he know? How could she?

She twisted her hands under the table. "Have you ever been at the mercy of someone else? Totally and completely?"

"Person, no. Circumstance, yes."

"Then you know what it is to feel helpless. To have no choice."

Another couple passed by. The man tipped his hat at Nikolai and set a handful of coins on the corner of the table.

"Thank you, sir." Nikolai leaned forward with a grin. "Everyone has a choice. *Everyone.* Even if that choice is to give up. When things get bad, only the strongest survive. You said you worked hard to get out of your position—that was a choice you made. You know I'm right. Determined people claw their way out no matter what. Pretend for a second that magic doesn't exist. What would you have done?"

Unfathomable to think of it. Magic was her power, how she protected herself, but Nikolai was right. She wasn't the type to roll over and die, no matter how weak she was at the start. Her vengeance was patient. She'd practiced in secret for years, biding her time until she knew she could win. "I would have learned the blade. Or poison, or . . . I don't know." Stabbed the motherfucker and burned the place to the ground. In hindsight, it would have eliminated many of the repercussions that followed.

Nikolai wore a smile. Not his usual smirk, but something else, something like pride. Two more people walked by and left money on the table. He didn't spare them a glance. "You would have found a way. Not everyone has the will to make the hard decisions."

She thought of those who'd taken her place, when she'd grown too old to be of interest. She hadn't killed for them, only for herself, but that didn't lessen their suffering or make it any more deserving. "Maybe not, but lacking will doesn't make people worthy of their fate."

"Yes it does." He leaned forward with an almost manic energy. "I'll tell you the real reason for your noninterference policy. Because deep down, you know that even if you put everything to rights for other people, without constant intervention they'll just go back to where they started. People *like* their cages. They *like* being controlled. It gives them the ability to abdicate responsibility. That way, when their life is hard, they can point the finger at someone else and say, 'It's not my fault.'"

His words echoed far too closely with her own thoughts at the witch hunter's accusations. It was one thing to be a cynic; it was another to have someone agree with that cynicism wholeheartedly, especially when you wanted to believe in something more, despite all evidence to the contrary. Nikolai was still in his twenties. Easy to be a philosopher at his age, before you'd had much life experience.

"Not everyone is like that," she said without conviction.

"Just most people." He nodded to the growing stack of change. "Look at how easily they copy others, without even knowing why. You're focusing on the wrong thing. Magi or Mundane—it makes no difference. There are those who accept fate and those who craft their own destiny. You're either one or the other. Do circumstances make it harder? Absolutely. But those of us with the proper constitution will always rise above."

As if to emphasize his point, a man with an air of authority approached the table and introduced himself as the manager. He pretended to know all about Nikolai's charity work and said their meal would be on the house. When he left, Nikolai shot her a knowing grin. "That wasn't me either. By and large, people are sheep. And there's only one use a wolf has for sheep."

<hr>

Nikolai leaned back in his chair. Medea would never admit it, but she was more like him than she realized. Why did she fight it so hard? When he'd asked her to imagine what she'd do if magic didn't exist, the color had drained from her face and she'd begun to wring her hands. For a second he thought he'd misjudged her, but then her lip curled into a snarl and she spoke of blades and poison with beautiful contempt. Medea might be many things, but weak wasn't one of them.

She'd continued to debate him—perhaps she simply enjoyed playing devil's advocate—but he suspected there was more to it than that. He knew he'd won when she abruptly changed the subject back to the bald man who'd felt his telepathic intrusions, her body relaxing as she fell back into lecturing.

"Let's call them magically sensitive Mundanes. As I was saying, the ambient magic is too low to supplement their lack of mana. When you probe their minds, they can feel *something* but have no means of identifying what, and so their brain probably makes sense of it in other ways—hair standing up on the back of the neck, skin crawling, the feeling of being watched, the perception of someone standing just outside of view."

"Should I avoid using telepathy on them then?"

"Not at all. I've been wondering how to tackle the problem of you learning to read Magi without detection. It's not like you can just practice in a Magi town. I mean you *can*, but you'd be arrested or driven out before you'd made sufficient progress. These magically sensitive Mundanes could be the bridge you need. It's not like they can report you. When you can consistently enter them without adverse reactions, we will try your hand at Magi."

And so he practiced. The more he tried, the more distracted or agitated his targets became. If alone, they often finished their meal and left in a hurry, with many a nervous glance over their shoulder. If they dined with others, they would flee to the bathroom, or feign illness as an excuse to leave the restaurant. It's not like targets were easy to come by either. He checked minds all the way to the restaurant and back, and on some trips they still found none.

Summer gave way to autumn, and still the magically sensitive Mundanes felt his intrusions. Medea was no help, reciting passages from the library about approaching targets gently but unable to offer practical advice. He found himself getting testy. It's not like he'd managed to make any progress with her either.

"You're supposed to be the best!" he snapped one day in the library. "How can you claim to be the most powerful mage in the world if you don't know a bit of telepathy? Why, out of all the magical schools, did you neglect this one?"

"I've told you why, and I'm trying my utmost to help you. Sooner or later we'll figure it out."

"I don't want *us* to figure it out. You're supposed to *know*. That's why I came to you, the great and powerful Medea, knower of every-goddamned-thing-to-do-with-magic!"

She tensed. A small part of his brain whispered that he was supposed to be getting close to her, but the sign of weakness only spurred him on.

"Centuries traveling the globe, and *this* is all the information on telepathy you could find? I don't believe it. Where are you hiding the rest?"

"You know I don't hide information."

He approached her, voice deadly. "Except your track record isn't exactly pristine, is it? You blocked off half the library from me that first year."

She took a step back. "That was a mistake. You know I don't normally—"

"You know what *I* think? You didn't even *try*. You don't like telepathy, and so you spent your time collecting stuff on healing and plants, to the point of *obsession*—how many copies of *Hekate's Herbal Healing* do you need, by the way?—and you neglected the one magic that didn't interest you. What the hell good is your library if it doesn't have what I need? What are *you* good for, Medea? Because right now, I'd be better off asking a Mundane for help."

"Then why don't you?" Her voice quavered, but it was unequivocally cold. She jammed several texts onto the shelf in front of her, heedless that they belonged elsewhere, and stalked to the edge of the alcove. "I'll have you know those copies of *Hekate's Herbal Healing* are different editions."

"Well thank fucking god for that. Not like we'd need to throw out the old edition whenever the information was updated."

She clenched a fist and stormed from the library.

9

PUPPETS

Nikolai's anger fled almost as swiftly as Medea, and he woke the next day mired in guilt. How could he have done that to her? She was only trying to help. He was the one with the problem. If he wasn't so stupid, he would have figured it out by now. He'd never be a master telepath. Such skill was beyond his reach.

In his sleepy stupor, it took several minutes to realize the source of the thoughts. He lurched to his feet and stumbled to the chest of drawers, yanking the top drawer open. His supply of Frog's Fancy, the plant that kept his curse in check, had dwindled significantly over the past year. Every month he checked on the grove where the plants grew. The charred trees hadn't recovered from his fire, and though he found new Frog's Fancy plants sprouting on adjacent trees, they grew exceptionally slowly. Growth spells only caused the plants to soften and disintegrate. Medea, adamant in her position that she wouldn't interfere with another's magic, offered no solutions, save to say that accelerated growth spells worked best on plants with a fast life cycle.

He fumbled for a bottle of Frog's Fancy but wrenched the lid too hard and sent it flying. The bottle seemed to fall in slow motion. He watched impassively as it struck the stone floor and broke into shards.

Half the bottle remained intact, slowly dripping fluid. He ought to care about this, but nothing mattered, so why bother?

Drip, drip.

He should probably pick it up.

Drip, drip. The antidote vanished into the crack between the stones. He really ought to do something.

He slowly knelt and stared at the broken bottle for a minute before gingerly picking it up. He dipped his finger in the solution and rubbed it over his tongue, the minty taste filling his mouth.

FUCK FUCK FUCK!

Towel! *Where* was a towel? If he could soak up some of the solution, he might be able to use it. No towels. He grabbed yesterday's shirt from the hamper and mopped up what he could. If worst came to worst, he could soak it in water and try to make a dilute solution from the fibers. He lay on the floor and expanded his sense between the stones. Where he hoped to find a pool of liquid, there was only the dust and grime of centuries.

He rose and pressed his fists against the wall, head bowed. Magic burned from his arms to his hands. Another bottle down. How would he last the next few years, let alone centuries? It was all Medea's fault! If she'd told him the significance of the plants from the outset, he never would have burned the grove. Now he was looking at sucking residue out of a dirty shirt. Smoke curled beneath his fists, bringing with it the scent of singed wood and the memory of that day.

He yanked his fists away from the wall, leaving two scorch marks behind. *No.* This was the same thought process that got him here. Medea *had* told him—albeit in a stupid, roundabout way that assuaged her conscience—but he'd chosen not to listen. And it didn't matter that he hadn't known what the plants were at the time. What mattered was that the outburst had cost him. Just as yesterday would cost him. He was supposed to be getting close to Medea, not driving her away. Guilt trips were wonderful tools when used well, but he'd laid it on without any reason beyond causing hurt. The brief satisfaction served no long-term purpose and was ultimately damaging. He had to work on that.

So, first thing—apologize to Medea. He might be right, but he could be magnanimous. She might even try to make it up to him.

Second—ensure the safety of his current stock of Frog's Fancy. Glass bottles were too fragile. He'd have to switch to metal flasks. Medea was bound to have some in the lab. If not, they were easily purchased. Problem solved. It didn't fix the supply issue, but he could tackle that later.

He dressed quickly and went to the lab in hopes of finding her. Medea stood at the back counter with a notebook, enchanting and cataloging more rocks. She didn't turn or acknowledge his entrance, and he knew better than to interrupt her. He collected his ingredients and began brewing mana potions. They weren't needed during telepathy training, but it was a convenient excuse to stay.

He waited until she'd finished stuffing the rocks into her pouch before speaking. "I want to apologize—"

"Today I thought we'd—" She'd spoken at the same time.

"Sorry. You go ahead."

"You first."

"I want to apologize about yesterday. I took my frustration out on you and that wasn't fair."

"I know, but thank you for saying so. It's understandable that you're frustrated. *I'm* frustrated." She crossed her arms and leaned against the counter. "That's what I wanted to talk to you about. I know you're stuck, and sometimes when you're stuck, it's good to try something else for a while. It allows your brain time to work on the problem, while simultaneously giving you a different goal to work toward, which—if you succeed—gives you a mental boost."

He couldn't hide his disappointment. "So you're putting telepathy training on hold?"

"Not at all." A slight smile graced her normally dour face. "I thought we'd put your current abilities to the test."

Patrick opened his eyes and struggled to make sense of what he saw. Pale light emanated from odd rectangular stones in the ceiling. Metal doors embedded in the wall in front of him reflected the dim light. He sat up, expecting a bench, and found he'd been lying on a long metal slab.

Where was he? How drunk had he gotten last night? He'd had a lot of wild nights at the Spotted Sow but never before woken up somewhere he didn't recognize.

"Hello? Eddie? Flynn?" His own voice echoed back.

Patrick slid to his feet and groped along the wall, blinking his eyes against the weird blur of his surroundings. He shouldn't look to the left. Bad things would happen if he looked left. The thought sat in his mind like an elephant and was just as hard to ignore. Surely a quick peek wouldn't hurt. He glanced to the side.

On his left squatted a malevolent-looking stone table, clearly sized to hold a human. Restraints dangled from the sides as though awaiting their next victim. Something sharp pricked his hand, and Patrick yanked it back with a yelp. He spun, expecting an attacker. What he saw was little better—cruel instruments of death hanging neatly on a rack. He armed himself with one of the long knives, the weight of it lending him courage.

A open doorway beckoned ahead. Stairs! He started toward them, pausing at the sound of a foot scuffing on stone.

"Who's there?" He waited but only heard the thudding of his heart. "This isn't funny."

Something moved out of the corner of his eye. He spun, knife at the ready. Vague shapes shifted on the far side of the room. He edged forward and the lights seemed to dim in protest.

The shapes resolved into ragged men in cages. A few gestured at him wordlessly; one even appeared to be shouting and pointing behind him, but no sound escaped.

"Hello? Can you hear me? Where am I?"

He stuck a finger in his ear and twisted. Why couldn't he hear them? Had he died and gone to hell? In a moment of panic, he patted his face and body. Stupid. If he was dead, how could he hold a knife? He didn't know how he'd gotten here, but he had to get out.

Patrick left the prisoners behind and stumbled up the darkened stairs, breath coming hot and fast as he groped along the wall. Around and around he went, unable to tell if he made any progress. Up and out—that's all he knew.

A sliver of light appeared at the top of the stairs. He dashed toward it. The room at the top was empty—some sort of laboratory with shelves of jars and glass instruments.

A faint whisper raised the hairs on the back of his neck.

"Who's there?" He spun in a circle, knife out, but saw no one. There were several doors. He rushed to one and grabbed the handle, jerking it desperately, then moved to the next—also locked. He strode toward the third door.

". . . that way . . ." Another whisper.

He froze. Was someone watching him? Was this place haunted? Several cabinets were large enough to hide a person. Patrick yanked them open—nothing but junk. Another snatch of conversation on his right. He made a grab at the empty air, hand coming away with nothing, though a nearby flask on the counter wobbled and then abruptly stilled.

Nikolai put a hand on the flask and shot a glare at Medea. "Stop knocking things over."

"He almost touched me!" She lurched away with a look of distaste as the prisoner made another blind grab. "What exactly are you trying to do? What are you showing him?"

"I'm *trying* to block out our sight and sound. Can you please stop talking? You're making this harder."

"Your learning experiences should be sufficiently challenging."

He clenched his jaw and tried again. It was taking all his focus to hide them from the prisoner, or Expendable Subject Three, as Medea called him. Nikolai had first encountered the prisoner and his mates back in Haven, when they'd harassed the local barkeeper's daughter. He'd laid all three of them out, a punishment Medea found insufficient, and had later discovered them in the morgue-like drawers in her dungeon.

The prisoner inched closer, forcing them to move around the center laboratory table.

Don't look over here. There's nothing over here. Don't look over here. Take the door over there.

This time the man listened. He exited to the common room, where there were even more doors to hide—library, kitchen, bathroom, his room, the stairs to Medea's room. He tried to make the man ignore all but the exit. The prisoner froze near the hearth, squinting around the room.

THE DOOR RIGHT THERE. GO OVER THERE.

It took entirely too long for him to cross the room and exit through the antechamber. He paused again outside, looking wildly about.

"Which way?" Nikolai whispered to Medea.

"Take him to the edge of the cliffs."

You hear a sound up ahead. Your mates are calling.

The prisoner set out at a brisk pace toward the cliffs, though he wobbled slightly.

"Is he still drunk?"

Medea gave a half shrug. "Probably. The drawers hold them in perpetual stasis. Don't get any ideas—whenever my apprentices hear that they immediately think immortality, but stasis doesn't allow you to do anything but stay locked in the moment. That's not living."

Damn, that had been his exact thought. Even with her explanation, he couldn't help but wonder if a version could be crafted that allowed for movement and consciousness.

"It can't be done. I've run the experiments and the body always breaks down eventually."

He tossed her a smile. "See, it's that kind of thing that makes you look like a telepath."

"It's not telepathy to recognize a personality type and make predictions based on past experience."

There she went, lumping him in with every other dark mage she'd ever trained—someone who'd eventually die and become yet another nameless apprentice by which she judged future students. He could let it fester . . . or he could use it to his advantage. "I take it Thomas never fell into the predictable category."

Medea rolled her eyes. "Don't you ever get tired of comparing yourself to him?"

"Not really. I like to set my goals high."

The prisoner arrived at the cliffs. They stopped twenty paces back, Nikolai working to conceal their presence as the prisoner paced along the edge, calling frantically for his friends.

"So what was Thomas like? As a person I mean, not a caster."

Medea pursed her lips, as if disentangling the man from his magic were a difficult task. "Shy, reserved. Loved to read. Loved to read *poetry* of all things, and philosophy. There was a quiet competence about him, but you could always tell he was listening." She smiled wistfully. "I once mentioned how much I enjoyed the smell of orange blossoms. A few weeks later, I came into the lab to find them strewn over every surface. It was impractical and annoying to clean up, but he meant well." She chuckled and shook her head. "I told him next time just get me a tree."

Ugh. He was competing against one of *those*. Yoxtl's description of Thomas—tall and handsome—came unbidden to his mind. Thomas splayed out with Medea on the floor of the library, surrounded by orange blossoms and poetry books, fucking her with his massive cock.

"Where am I? Who are you?" The prisoner's voice tore him from his thoughts.

Medea shot Nikolai a sidelong glance and shook her head. "You lost your focus."

The prisoner squinted at him. "I know you. You attacked us behind the pub. Where're me mates?" He strode forward and pointed the knife at Nikolai with trembling hands.

"You attacked *me*, actually, and they're still in the drawers in the dungeon."

Medea swatted his arm. "Don't tell him *that*."

"Why the hell not? You said you could wipe his memory."

"I can only do it so many times. Eventually his subconscious will learn the pattern and he'll become harder to control. And telling him about the dungeon *doesn't help*." She swatted him on the last two words for emphasis.

"Let them out," the man cried. "You let them out right now!"

"No," said Medea.

"Who are you? What did we ever do to you?"

Medea regarded him coldly.

"You wouldn't leave Kate alone," Nikolai offered.

"Who's Kate?"

"The girl behind the pub."

The prisoner frowned, then comprehension dawned on his face. "Her? But we were just having a bit of fun, that's all. You know how it is."

"No, I don't. I'm not in the habit of propositioning fourteen-year-old girls."

The man laughed. "Fourteen? You're wrong about that, mate. She was a little well-developed for fourteen."

Medea stormed toward him. Her hand slashed in front of her, and his chest blossomed scarlet.

"What the . . ?"

Slash.

"What are you—? Stop!" He held up the knife.

This time a grabbing motion followed the slash. His severed fingers flew into her hand, where she clutched them like some grotesque bouquet.

He stared stupidly at the stumps and backpedaled. "Stop, no, *please*!" He halted at the edge of the cliff. "Please," he whimpered. "We didn't mean anything by it."

"You never do." She launched him over the edge, face a mask of quiet fury. The man's eyes barely registered his fate before he plummeted from sight. The symphony of his scream ended splendidly, but all too soon. Medea held out her hand and relinquished the fingers, five pink sausages toppling down. As much as Nikolai wanted to see what a fall like that did to a body, he couldn't take his eyes off of Medea. She glared imperiously over the edge, beautiful in her battle stance, wind tugging at her dress and hair as though emphasizing her power. *This* was where you fucked a woman like Medea, not in the library surrounded by books.

"I'll get the next one," he said.

She winced, going from statuesque to self-conscious and ruining the moment. "Sorry about that. This is why I avoid talking to them. You won't get as much practice now."

"It's alright."

"No, it's not. But we can always get more." Her voice hardened. "Men like that are disturbingly easy to find."

It would be a pleasure to hunt alongside her.

They returned to the hovel. As they passed the library, she said, "There's a book I read ages ago, I think it was by an Indian telepath—I'm afraid I don't have a copy of it. But he said it's better to show your target something they want rather than trying to block what is there."

"How is it that you can recall something that obscure, yet you can't remember names and need a spell to remind you to eat?"

She shrugged. "If I find something interesting, I remember it. Don't you?"

"Not like that. You recite things almost verbatim. Why even have a library?"

"I remember the *overview*. The library exists so I can cross-reference what I remember with the truth. The devil is in the details."

They returned to the dungeon and he started anew with the next prisoner, this time focusing on what would drive the man forward—a door, a promise of freedom and safety. As long as the prisoner received the message that neither Nikolai nor Medea would help, he took no notice of them. When they reached the cliffs, the prisoner's body collapsed. His vacant eyes stared skyward as Medea levitated the body and floated it back toward the hovel.

"It's not a clean memory wipe," she said, "not like you'll eventually be able to do. It just erases a recent block of time. If you get advanced enough in your telepathy, you should be able to cherry-pick which memories go, or even parts of memories."

She reset the prisoner a number of times. All went well until the eighth trip when, as she'd predicted, the prisoner's subconscious began to interfere. He'd walk up to the target door and freeze, hand poised over the knob, then back up and eye it with suspicion. Only after trying every other door did he reluctantly exit the laboratory. The same thing repeated in the common room. He stopped to examine the hearth, the chairs, the library door. Medea had warded the door shut, but that didn't stop the prisoner from slamming his shoulder into it repeatedly.

She scowled and declared him spent. "This time when you get him to the cliffs, make him jump."

"That won't be easy. I could barely get him out of the lab this time."

"It would be difficult regardless—the body fights its own extinction. I'm sure you'll think of something."

You hear Patrick's voice calling from outside the door. Better hurry.

The prisoner paused, listening, then made for the hovel door. He followed the suggestion across the meadow, though he glanced over his shoulder at them several times, expression dark.

Patrick's calls are getting urgent.

The prisoner faced forward and jogged to the cliffs.

Patrick's drowning. You have to help him! The jump is short. You can make it.

He ignored the suggestion and ran along the cliff face, searching for a way down.

Too late. He's going under!

"I'm coming, Patrick!" The prisoner dove head first off the cliff onto the rocks below.

Nikolai peered over the edge. The view was disappointing—both bodies remained intact. Weren't they supposed to splatter?

Medea joined him. "You're getting good at this," she said with a smile. Rare enough to get a compliment, but this one didn't seem to fit. Good work was the expectation and therefore unworthy of acknowledgment. Faults, on the other hand, had to be pointed out immediately so they could be fixed. Her expression was that of someone admiring a fine work of art.

Her words came back to him. *Is that all you're going to do? Surely they deserve more.* Maybe he should stop trying to impress her with his body and just gift wrap a bunch of catcallers. They were certainly more fitting than orange blossoms. At least *he* knew better than to dirty her lab. Medea might be a slob, but she couldn't stand other people's messes. Honestly, it was like Thomas hadn't known her at all.

"Let's get the last one," she said brightly. Autumn had put a chill in the air, but as they returned to the hovel Medea walked like a woman enjoying a fine summer stroll.

The final prisoner leapt just as willingly when his turn came. Nikolai made sure to stand at the edge and watch the fall. The man jumped feet first. His legs cracked with the impact, but his torso and head managed to land in a gap between the rocks. He screamed in pain.

Medea groaned. "I hate when they carry on like that. Go ahead. Do away with him."

As much as he wanted to, he might earn more points for making the man suffer. "We could just leave him. Not like he's going anywhere."

She shook her head. "We can't leave any of them. Do you have any idea how bad they'll smell after baking in the sun?"

"Very well." He used telekinesis to pick up a small boulder and positioned it over the man's head—*now* he'd see some carnage. His aim was slightly off. The boulder glanced off the man's head, leaving only a shallow gash in his scalp. Damn. He'd been hoping to crack it like a nut.

"Remember, the skull is designed to protect. You have to go in—"

"Through the eyes or the nose, yes I know." He tried again, this time using hand movements to aid his precision, and got a satisfying crunch.

Medea gave him a look. "*You* get to clean that one up."

She levitated them down to the beach and began slicing the bodies into bits. Whatever spell she used also cauterized the ends, filling the air with the scent of cooking meat. His stomach grumbled.

"Eat if you like," she said, perching upon a rock and summoning an apple, "but I want you tossing the pieces out to sea. No hand gestures this time. Here." She conjured an illusion of a golden hoop offshore.

He summoned a sandwich, holding it with both hands to help resist the urge to make a grasping motion. He willed a severed foot into the air and launched it at the target. Miss. Next came a portion of leg. The shattered bones made it flop around like a limp noodle. He dropped it several times before getting a firm hold with his mind and winging it out to sea. "Why is it so much easier when I use my hands?"

"Your brain is used to taking spatial cues from your body. Rather like losing an eye and adjusting to a world without depth perception. I suspect it's why so many people who can levitate fail to master flight. The latter has added dimensions."

"But it *will* get better in time?" Flight would be amazing.

"With practice. Hopefully."

After a time the water began to ripple with every toss. Medea dispelled the hoop and flew them offshore. As they hovered above the water, she willed a hunk of shoulder to them and plopped it into the sea. The surface became a writhing mass of fish. They jostled one another for a taste of meat as Medea watched, taking slow bites of apple. When the flesh had been picked clean and the crowd began to disperse, she willed another hunk over. A shark appeared in the fray, its sleek body darting in to snatch the prize.

He called another piece over—easier to bring it toward them than propel it away—and dropped it. The fish moved in, dispersing suddenly as more sharks arrived to claim the food. It was fascinating to watch. They'd dash together, forming a wriggling ball of sharks that lasted a mere instant before the meat was gone. He worked together with Medea, ferrying over body parts while she cut them into smaller portions to prolong the show.

They'd eaten dozens of meals together in diners with a multitude of conversations, but none compared to this mutual observation in silence. It almost felt like he could be himself around her, though he knew that wasn't the case. He couldn't be himself around anyone. Still, it was nice to imagine such a thing was possible.

STRANGE ENCOUNTERS

Nikolai held the funnel steady and poured. There, that was the last of it. He screwed the cap on tight and set the metal flask on the counter with the rest of his Frog's Fancy. He seemed to be going through it a lot faster, not because of more episodes but because he had to take more to have any lasting effect. A sip used to last all day; now he was lucky to get several hours.

Medea poked her head into the lab. "Oh good, I caught you in time. Can you come to the gateway room?"

"A moment." He scooped the flasks into his belt pouch.

Yesterday she informed him that she'd finally managed to secure a test site for their experiments. "I'm anxious to get started. As you've hit a certain . . . block in telepathy, I thought a change of scenery would do us good."

She said it like they didn't change scenery every time they stepped through a gateway, but he knew what she meant. A change *would* be nice. She asked if he had any unenchanted bags —apparently she would allow no enchantments on this trip—and when he said no, she gave him today off to gather whatever he needed.

Despite her directive, he planned to use the day to practice telepathy. She'd been right about taking a break to work on something else—yesterday's success had reinvigorated his drive to continue training.

Medea awaited him in the gateway room with a notebook. The control peg was already inserted into the map—some sleepy town in North Carolina. Definitely not his first choice for finding luggage *or* magically sensitive Mundanes.

"I thought I had today off."

"You do, but seeing as you're going into town anyway—" She pulled a sheet of paper from her notebook and handed it to him. "I need you to check on this stone. It stopped transmitting data."

The request was odd, given how controlling she usually was with this kind of thing. "Wouldn't you rather do it yourself?"

"Yes, but I have preparations to make for our trip and can't spare the time." In other words, she'd already made plans and didn't feel like changing them. "If you find the stone, bring it back here. And don't dally tonight. You still have packing to do before we leave tomorrow."

He stepped through the gateway, trading warmth and wall-to-wall maps for crisp autumn air and endless trees in varying shades of yellow, orange, and red. There was no path, only leaves blanketing the forest floor. "Medea!" he called behind him. "Which way is town?"

"Head straight out of the gateway. The land should slope downward. Just keep heading down and you'll find it."

The gateway closed and he took a few steps back to memorize the location—between two nondescript tree trunks. He'd have to use Magic Sight to pick them out from the rest when he returned. He followed Medea's instructions and eventually the land sloped down. Thirty minutes later he arrived at the outskirts of a town. Her paper said the stone was on Main, between Fourth and Fifth Street, behind the cobbler. The town was too small for cabs, which meant more walking, and it was another thirty minutes before he reached what passed for downtown. No wonder she hadn't wanted to come. He scanned minds as he walked but found no magically sensitive Mundanes.

He found the cobbler easily enough. It actually *was* a cobbler —he'd expected a modern shoe store—but there was no stone to be found behind it, enchanted or otherwise. Probably picked up by a kid or something. After a sweep of the entire block with Magic Sight, he counted it lost and moved on to finding himself new luggage. In the past he would've used his wide-mouthed drawstring bag to shoplift, but his telepathy had gotten good enough that there was no need. He simply grabbed the suitcase he wanted and headed for the door, tossing a quick *I paid for this* at the clerk in passing.

"Where do you think you're going with that, fella?"

Nikolai turned to find an older gentleman customer regarding him with distaste. "Don't worry about it, I've already paid. Isn't that right?" He smiled at the clerk, who nodded.

"That's right."

"No you didn't," the old man insisted. "I watched you."

"Look, I don't know what you think you saw, but *I paid for this*." He laced the final statement with telepathic power.

There was no change in the old man's demeanor. He simply motioned to another customer browsing the back of the store. "Bill, get over here. This guy is trying to pull a fast one."

Enough of this bullshit. He went to invade the man's mind and found nothing. Occasionally he'd glimpsed inside damaged minds, finding anything from a mess of confused thoughts and sensations to a still pond, but this was nothing like that. He couldn't even find the man's mind, though he clearly had one, given that he was moving and talking.

He flicked back to the clerk—still there, so there was nothing wrong with his ability—and then to the second customer—nothing. Not a damned thing. If Mundanes could be magic-sensitive, perhaps they could also be dead to magic. But to have two in the same place?

"Are you two related by chance?"

The men exchanged a look. "No. Why do you ask?"

"No reason. Anyhow, I'd appreciate you butting out. This is between me and the good man here." He gestured to the clerk and took a step toward the door.

"Check the till," said the old man.

The clerk opened the till and frowned. "You're right. I don't see enough cash in here to cover that suitcase." He smiled at Nikolai, trying not to offend. "I'm sure it's just an honest mistake."

"Fine. I'll pay again if that'll make you happy." He pulled Medea's paper out of his breast pocket and thrust it toward the clerk. *This is enough to cover the suitcase twice over.* "Here you go, my good man. Try not to lose it this time." *It's money. It's money.* He repeated the phrase like a mantra. He couldn't fool the customers, but he could sure as hell fool the clerk.

"That's just a sheet of paper!" said the older customer.

It's money. I paid. Those guys are lying. It's money.

"You think I can't tell money when I see it!" The clerk wagged the paper at his customers before thrusting it in the till and slamming it for good measure.

Tell those guys to leave.

"I think you two had better leave."

They did, shooting Nikolai dirty looks as they passed. He grinned and tipped his hat.

He spent the next hour or so wandering downtown, visiting the shops and scouring the local populace for magically sensitive Mundanes. Even though they were comparatively rare, he would have expected a town of this size to have at least a few. Maybe the place was like a magical black hole—he'd found two magically dead minds, after all. He made a mental note to tell Medea. It was definitely the kind of thing she'd want to study further.

But not today. His arm ached from carrying around the suitcase, empty though it was, and he struck back toward the gateway. The shadows had already begun to lengthen in the afternoon sun. After he dropped off the suitcase, he'd pop over to Los Angeles for some real hunting. Medea might retire early, but he'd never needed more than a few hours of sleep.

The land sloped up, sidewalk transitioning to gravel. Soon it would be hard-packed earth and forest. A shadow approached from behind, accompanied by the hum of an engine. It wasn't until the car began to keep pace that he glanced over. By then the blackjack, wielded by a man who had jumped out of the car, was in full swing.

He twisted sideways and instinctively threw out a telekinetic pulse. The force should have been enough to send the man flying, but his clothes only fluttered a little. What the—?

He barely registered that the man was the same irritable customer from the store before the blackjack cracked against his jaw. Someone—probably the second customer—made to grab his arms. He aimed a hand and cast Pummel, but there was no telltale crack or thump of impact. Had he missed?

Nikolai threw his head back into the man's nose. The man screamed and his grip weakened. Nikolai wrenched himself free.

Pain exploded in his arm, his hand, his other hand. Who aimed for the hands and not the head? He didn't recognize the third man, the one wielding the baseball bat, but his mind was invisible to telepathy too. Two blank minds might've been a coincidence; three was not.

He cast Lance between blows. Each spell had enough power to break clean through a rib cage, but the man didn't even flinch. Lance was hard to see, usually just a faint rippling in the air, but he swore he saw the spells connect.

He curled his broken fingers as best he could and took a swing. The man dodged easily and brought the bat across Nikolai's knee. The traitorous limb buckled, dropping him to the ground.

The older man with the blackjack approached. Nikolai tried to aim a spell but someone grabbed his arms and pinned them behind his back.

"Won't do you any good, sonny. You're only making this harder on yourself."

He had to cast something visual. He had to be sure. Medea once scoffed at how he thought spells had to originate from his body. He'd never managed to learn her technique of casting projectiles from any point in space, but his hands weren't the only part of his body. Perhaps it would be enough.

"Flamma!" He opened his mouth wide with the incantation, willing heat to coalesce. Fire erupted between his lips.

A hand clamped over his mouth, but it was too late—a fireball already winged toward the man. It got within an inch of impact before disappearing *into* his body. Well, shit.

The man thumped his chest. "I told you it was no use. The *Lord* protects us."

Witch hunters. It had to be. He hadn't even thought witch hunting was a *thing* anymore, not since the Collective cracked down on magic in public. Certainly no one in Haven had ever encountered one. And he'd never heard of witch hunters like this. Did Medea know about them? Surely she would've warned him if she had. Unless . . .

Goddammit. Was *that* what her stupid lectures had been about? She'd specifically mentioned the lack of Collective oversight in America, as if that were the important part. Why couldn't she have led with "America has ridiculously elite witch hunters with anti-magic capabilities" or mentioned them at least *once*?

The man laughed. "Boy, does he look angry."

"I was just imagining strangling my mentor."

"Mentor, eh?" The older man grabbed a fistful of his hair and wrenched his head up. "I think you have to be one of the most powerful witches we've ever caught. Magic without a wand? Without your *hands*? You'll have to tell us about this mentor. But for now . . ." He looked to the man with the bat. "Disable him."

The man with the bat took careful aim at Nikolai's chest and swung. There was no crack, just a meaty thud and a couple soft pops, but it felt like he'd taken a knife to the chest. They gagged him and bound his wrists. He really wished they hadn't gagged him. Breathing was suddenly difficult.

They lifted him and it was like he was being stabbed all over again. He screamed involuntarily and choked it back—the scream hurt almost as bad as the lift. They must have broken a rib. He scanned himself, slowly, one rib at a time, like Medea had taught. Two broken, and one had punctured the pleura—the lining around the lungs. Fuck. He could heal bone, though it took forever, but the pleura wasn't something he could fix on his own. When it came to "fine work" healing, he was more liable to fuse tissues wrong.

"Car."

They laid him down beside a Buick as headlights passed.

"Frisk him there. I'll keep watch."

They emptied his pockets, removed his belt, checked inside his shoes. Probably taking him someplace secure for interrogation. Whatever magical protection they had seemed to extend only to their bodies, but who knew what they had back at their base. He had to escape now.

He expanded his senses, taking stock of his environment. No rocks bigger than pebbles. The bat was propped up against the car. Bound as he was, his telekinesis would be too sloppy to take down all three with it before they had a chance to knock him out. It could be used as a diversion, but what then? It's not like he could run off with a busted kneecap and two broken ribs. The knee he could fix if he had enough time, but they were almost done. What he needed was a car.

"He's clean."

"Alright, let's get him into the trunk."

"Hang on, there's another car coming."

He latched on to the driver's mind. *Slow down. Stop when you get to me.* The bat wouldn't be enough—he needed something bigger. As the oncoming vehicle slowed to a crawl, he slipped the witch hunter's Buick into neutral and gave the bumper a tele-kinetic shove. The incline wasn't much, but it was enough. The Buick rolled backward down the hill, and the oncoming car swerved to avoid it. *Ignore that. Come to me.*

"Look out!"

Both men started to stand.

"No!" said the leader. "Davis, you stay here." He took off running down the hill after the car with the other witch hunter. Two down, one to go.

Stop your car and open the door. The oncoming car halted in front of them and the door flew open. "Is everything alright?" asked the woman inside.

The witch hunter tensed. "Everything is fine, miss. Just dealing with a man who tried to break into my—"

CRACK. The witch hunter slumped over.

Nikolai released his tentative hold on the bat and tried to stand. His chest screamed and his vision swam.

Help me!

The woman was suddenly at his side, offering an arm, but she wasn't strong enough to lift him on her own. Through a combina-tion of sheer willpower and telekinesis, he managed to help her enough to get to his feet. She tugged him toward the car.

He glanced down the hill. The remaining witch hunters were running back up. He gripped the bat with his will and sent it flying toward them. It cracked one in the face, but the other kept coming.

Nikolai stumbled against the car door. It felt like his chest was on fire. He wrenched the door open and crumpled onto the back seat. The woman tried to help him get settled. He shooed her away with a thought. She needed to drive *now*.

The car had just started to move when the door wrenched open and the witch hunter leader grabbed Nikolai's ankle. Nikolai met him with a grin. Magic might protect the man from direct spells, but it couldn't help him now. He shifted the gravel underneath the man's feet and slammed the door on his arm as he fell, pinning it tight. The man screamed and pulled at the door with his other hand, but the physical force was no match for Nikolai's will.

Drive faster.

He let the man drag for a few miles, thumping against the side, before the pain in his chest forced him to relinquish the arm and tend to his own injuries. He could at least get started on one rib.

The woman's mind was full of fear. None of what she'd seen made sense and she'd been horrified at the man trapped in the door. She'd wanted to stop but couldn't override the compulsion to keep driving. When she begged Nikolai to open the door, he telepathically informed her it was only a coat, nothing to worry about. The lie silenced her, but her subconscious knew the truth. She feared him but didn't know why, so she just kept driving as though she could outrun him, tears flowing silently down her cheeks.

"Where are we going?" she asked.

Good question. Even a mended knee wouldn't be enough to get him back to Medea's gateway. He could barely breathe, let alone walk for miles uphill. He needed a gateway they could drive right up to.

"Wh—" Fuck, that hurt. No talking then. He spoke with

telepathy instead, giving her the impression that they actually conversed. *Which is closer—Charleston, South Carolina or Norfolk, Virginia?*

"Norfolk, I think."

Take me there.

"But that'll take hours!"

Take me there.

She didn't argue, but the tears started again.

I'm not going to hurt you. He sent wave after wave of gratitude at her—she was strong, caring, kind. A hero even. He had to keep her going. Eventually her fear changed to concern.

"You look sick." She paused. "And beat up. Are you sure you don't want me to take you to a hospital?"

Norfolk. Take me there. He projected the path she should take through the city. The pain in his chest was excruciating, but that was just pain. More alarming was how shallow his breaths were becoming. It wasn't just painful to take a breath; it was like he couldn't breathe. He scanned his chest again. Fuck. The pleural space had filled with air, causing the lung to collapse. If he went cyanotic, if he passed out . . .

If I lose consciousness, keep going. You have to get me to there. EXACTLY there. He burned the gateway location into her brain. *Pull me out of the car and drag me through. You can do it. You can do it . . .*

11

MISSING

Medea jolted awake, heart pounding. That wasn't her alarm—that was the intruder ward. She thrust her covers away and dressed quickly. Outside, she blinked in the dawning sunlight. Ugh, she hated flipping time zones like this. One of these days she needed to find a second island. She flew to the beach gateway, conjuring all the effects—voice magnification, whipping wind, electricity sparking off her body.

"WHO DARES INTRUDE ON MY—" Oh, it was just Nikolai and some hysterical woman. She winced at her own internal vernacular. The Greeks used to think women were upset because their uterus detached and floated around inside their body. The stupid word had been used for ages by male Mundane physicians to refer to any female behavior they couldn't explain, and from there had moved to more colloquial use. She *must* be tired to think of that damned word.

She landed in front of the *frantic* woman, who gaped and dropped Nikolai's lax arm.

"I don't care how drunk he is, he's not allowed to have trysts here—" Oh shit, his fingers were blue. "How long as he been like this?" She asked it automatically, not listening to the answer but scanning the body. How the hell did he have such blunt force trauma? Irrelevant. She laid him on his back, tore open his shirt, and placed her palms over his chest. First thing was to oxygenate the blood, evacuate the pleural space, reinflate the lung . . .

The woman paced beside Nikolai. "This can't be happening. This can NOT be happening! Where am I? Where is this? Is he okay? He's been turning blue and then I couldn't get him out of the car. I wanted to go for help but I couldn't. I don't know why but I *couldn't*. You have to believe me. God, I hope he's okay. Is he going to be okay?"

A quick Sleep and the woman crumpled onto the sand. Medea would have liked to send the woman back through the gateway, but Nikolai might need her for some reason. She finished with the lungs and his fingers returned to a healthy tan, though his chest was still mottled with bruises. Minor injuries could wait. Her fingers traced the line of a rib, drawing the two edges together.

Nikolai gasped and coughed, wincing at the pain.

"Try not to cough, I'm not finished yet."

He blinked, trying to focus his eyes, then looked from her face to his chest and back. "That all it takes?" he croaked.

"What? You really shouldn't be talking. Don't make me paralyze you."

He watched her in silence, a weird little smile on his face. How anyone could be happy to be wounded . . . She shook her head. Nikolai had always been a glutton for punishment. Most apprentices approached their practical lessons with a certain amount of trepidation; Nikolai seemed to enjoy them no matter how badly he got injured. Even with full access to her library and all its spells, he'd take a sparring match over reading a demonology book any day of the week.

It made his recent interest in books even odder in retrospect. Before she'd had a chance to mull that over, he spoke.

"You couldn't bother telling me there were witch hunters in America?"

"Witch hunters did this to you?" If he'd let them beat him this badly, maybe he wasn't as promising as she'd thought. "There are witch hunters everywhere, and I told you every time we took the gateway."

"You told me not to *cast spells* in public. You never said *why*."

"Nonsense. I'm certain I told you—"

"You didn't. Not one fucking word."

She started running through her spiel in her head. Collective, no oversight, don't draw attention . . . Had she left out a part? It had been a while since she'd updated the script. Everyone *used* to know what it meant. I mean, why else not cast spells in public? Besides, it was good practice anyway, even for someone like her. Who wanted attention from Mundanes? They'd either try to kill you, which was annoying, or they'd ask you to do things for them, which was even more annoying. "I told you the important part—don't draw attention to yourself."

"It's a little hard to take that seriously when you're constantly contradicting your own advice."

"Do as I say, not as I do."

He rolled his eyes.

"Anyhow, witch hunters should be no problem for someone of your skill."

"There were *three* of them and they jumped me!"

She stared at him in disbelief. Was he messing with her? "Three? You got beat up by . . . three? And you what, forgot you're a telepath?"

"I couldn't read them! You could've told me they had anti-magic capabilities. Every damn spell I cast was absorbed. By the time I figured out what was happening, they had me on the ground."

It figured he'd lie to make himself look less incompetent. Disappointing, really, though not unexpected coming from Nikolai. More likely he'd been drunk or high and working the girl when they'd set upon him.

"I had to use telekinesis to get out of it," he continued, "and you know my control isn't great."

"What do you mean 'get out of it'? Didn't you kill them?"

"Don't you think I would have if I could? I barely got out of there before they shoved me into a trunk." He sat up, wincing as he did so. "I managed to knock two down. The third . . . well, if he's not dead, he'll sure wish he was." Nikolai smiled.

He hadn't killed a one? Unacceptable. She stood. "Witch hunters are to be eliminated."

"I told you—"

"*Always*. They're a bane on our kind. America is crawling with them, thanks to its puritanical roots and lack of oversight. They work in packs, usually small family groups—fathers, brothers, cousins—all indoctrinated since birth. If they see magic, they'll give not a sign they've marked you. They'll follow at a distance, noting where you go and who you meet, then come back with partners. Be wary if you ever find yourself being followed. They know to look for wands and magical talismans, and they'll try to bind and gag you so you can't cast spells. If they see multiple suspected witches together, they will wait until each is alone. Their goal is to catch you unawares, giving them an advantage." She glanced at the sleeping woman. "Get used to warding your motel rooms."

He followed her gaze. "It's not what you think. She happened to drive by and I made her give me a lift. Can you reopen the gateway here or do I have to carry her up to the house to put her back?"

"Just kill her. I don't want anyone knowing the location of my gateways, least of all when there are witch hunters nearby."

"I'm not in the habit of killing people who've been useful to me."

"If she were male, you wouldn't give a damn." She nodded to the stone archway, mentally activating the previous portal. Between the columns, a darkened street appeared with a lone car parked cockeyed, its back door ajar.

"You're surprisingly unsympathetic toward your own sex, you know that?"

"And you're not?

"I don't like competitors. What's your excuse?"

"She annoyed me."

"Everyone annoys you." He moved to lift the woman.

"I'll do that. You're still injured."

"Then finish healing me."

"It's just a few bruises and the knee. You could use the practice." She levitated the woman through the portal and thrust her into the back seat. "How long was she with you?"

"Three or four hours."

"I can't wipe memories that far back, not with any kind of precision. It's a shame you can't modify them yet." She frowned. "I really don't like her knowing about the gateway."

"Then wipe what you can. I'll drive her a few blocks away and imprint that it was all a dream. Maybe she drove here in her sleep."

Nikolai limped to the car and slid into the front seat. He wrapped his hands around his injured knee and began to mend it. The healing was slow and clumsy and it was painful not to intervene.

"I can *feel* you judging me," he said. "You can fix it later if I fuck up."

"I'm sure you'll do fine." She wasn't entirely convinced she meant it. "I'm going back to bed. Don't dally. You still have packing to do. We leave tomorr—er, today."

"Blyad."

"What?"

"Those fuckers took my suitcase."

Nikolai awoke to rapping. It felt like only minutes since his head hit the pillow. What time was it?

"I have something for you," called Medea through the door.

"Coming." He groaned and sat up. Despite the healing, his body had been full of minor aches and pains last night. He'd tossed and turned, finally giving up and wandering into the laboratory to make a healing potion. The aches were gone, but he still felt fatigued. He shuffled to the door and opened it.

Three suitcases of different sizes stood in a neat line with Medea behind them. "For you," she said.

They were evenly spaced, ordered largest to smallest. A shame she couldn't keep the rest of her home so well organized. Over the past two years it had become apparent that she only cleaned when a new apprentice arrived. The common areas had gradually degraded in appearance. A notebook she momentarily set down became a dumping place for every homeless paper or note. The laboratory tables were cluttered with ingredients, the sinks with cauldrons to be washed. She set out herbs to dry and then forgot to put them away. Rather than clean them up the next time, she set them aside and hung more. Cobwebs adorned the far corners of the common room, then the less frequently used shelves. Only the library remained pristine.

When she spoke again, there was an air of barely contained excitement in her voice. "Today marks the start of our experiments. The test site is far from both Mundane technology and magic. Unfortunately, that means we won't be near a gateway, so pack a week's worth of clothes and anything else you feel you might need, but nothing magical. I can't stress that enough—no magic. Can you be ready in thirty minutes?"

"Uh, probably. I'd have to take a cold shower but—"

"Great. Be at the gateway in thirty." She spun and made a beeline for her room.

"Cold shower it is." He shook his head, grabbed the middle suitcase, and tossed it onto the bed, passing over the Frog's Fancy stain on the floor—there was his first packing priority. He hoped Medea didn't count a tincture as magical, not that it mattered if she did—he wasn't going anywhere without his antidote. The damned witch hunters had taken his pouch. He'd have to get a new one. He yanked open the top dresser drawer and shifted the contents around in search of a vial.

Where the hell were his— Oh, fuck.

Right before he'd left for North Carolina, he'd rebottled his entire stock in sturdier containers. Medea had called him, and he'd swiped the whole lot into his pouch—the pouch that was now lost.

Gone. ALL of it.

"Blyad, blyad, blyaaaaaad!"

He roared and punched the wall, heedless of how his fists came back bloodied. He toppled the dresser and kicked it furiously. He'd find the rest and kill them. *He'd fucking kill all of them!*

"Nikolai? Nikolai!"

He barely registered Medea's voice. A bubble formed around him, floating upward until it bumped against the ceiling.

"Let me down!"

"Not until you're calm."

"NO. ONE. EVER. CALMS. DOWN. WHEN. YOU. ASK. THEM. TO." He punctuated each word with a punch to the bubble. When that didn't work, he started kicking.

The skinny bitch stared at him with her sour fucking face,

then left the room. He fell over as the bubble zoomed down to follow her. She exited the hovel and walked to the meadow.

"LET ME OUT!"

She hurled the bubble to the ground. It burst, sending him careening across the grass. He was barely on his feet when a spell sent him sprawling. He rebounded, shield up, and launched his own attack, flinging spells with mindless ferocity. Medea blocked them and returned in kind, a swirling blossom of red.

Cast, parry, cast. He needed to kill, but she couldn't be killed, though she satisfied his desire to unleash the deadliest of his repertoire. Sweat drenched his body with the exertion of casting so many high-mana spells in the afternoon sun. After a time, his desire to impress superseded the urge to destroy. A creative turn of a spell won him a rare smile. They danced in perfect concert around the meadow, two beings joined in the ecstasy of combat.

Only when the tip of mana exhaustion made its presence known did he pause. His breath came hot and quick. Medea approached. Did she feel it too? Violence, with its rush of blood and adrenaline, was a natural precursor to sex. He wanted to grab her slender waist, pull her into the grass and show her where his true abilities lay.

She handed him a mana potion and took a step back, forever maintaining a distance between them.

"Better?" she asked.

He nodded. "Thank you."

"You're right. No one calms down when told to." Her frown turned introspective a moment, then, "If you ever need a fight, just ask. Don't break your things."

Two years together, and she understood him better than anyone ever had. She hadn't asked why he was upset. She'd simply given him an appropriate outlet for his anger. Even Harper didn't know him that well, but then he never let Harper see his dark side. He concealed his true self from others in a web of lies and masks, maintaining a false sense of closeness, and yet he found he relaxed his guard most around her. She didn't judge him for who he was—well, she *did*, just not in a way that others would. Rather than running away in fear or demanding he be someone he wasn't, she met him where he was and challenged him to do better.

Unfortunately, she insisted on maintaining a veneer of formality around him. He'd have to get through that.

"What do you need when you're upset?" he asked. "Just so I know."

Her eyes widened. Probably no one ever thought to ask. Her brow furrowed a moment before she answered. "When I'm upset, leave me alone."

"That's it?"

"Any attempts at comfort will only make it worse. I know that doesn't make any sense." She pointed an accusing finger at him. "*Don't* hug me. Or pat me, or whatever. I've had people try that. I know that seems counterintuitive, but if you touch me when I'm upset, I will lay you out."

He chuckled and arched an eyebrow. "Do I seem like the hugging type?"

"No. But you mimic social protocols. When I'm upset, I need space."

"Fair enough."

They walked back to the hovel. The late afternoon breeze teased Medea's blonde hair and set the meadow grass undulating. Earthy scents mixed with those of the ocean, recalling the time she'd been so close to him in the cab. He fantasized about what he'd do with her if given the chance.

As they entered the common room, she said, "Well, that was fun, but we're getting behind schedule and I need to finish preparing. I'll meet you in the—"

"I can't."

Her face crumpled. He hated being the one to kill her mood, but it had to be done.

"I'm sorry, but I can't. My entire supply of Frog's Fancy is gone. It was in my pouch—taken by the witch hunters. I need to get it back."

"Nonsense." She waved a hand and started toward the stair-case. "I won't allow it on this trip. Once the experiments are complete, you may return to the jungle to replenish your stock."

"I can't. A wildfire burned most of the trees." She'd kill him if she knew the truth—that in his ignorance he'd burned the grove.

Medea turned to him with a perplexed #3 frown. "That place is humid even in the dry season. It's not prone to natural fires. Humans sometimes burn the jungle to make room for other crops, but there are no settlements in the vicinity."

"Maybe it was a lightning strike. In any case, only a few plants survived, and they've been slow to regrow."

Her frown deepened, and she looked on the verge of saying something. He continued before she could interject.

"So you see, I need to get my pouch back now." If he was lucky, it would still be near the road where they'd frisked him.

"If they've taken your pouch, it's gone. If they haven't, then it will still be there next week. I'm sorry, but we don't have the time."

"What do you mean we don't have the time? You're immortal! You're telling me you can't push the trip out by a day or two?"

"I've already made all the arrangements."

"So start without me. I'll catch up in a few days."

He hadn't even finished when she began shaking her head. "I need you there. I can't do this experiment alone."

It wasn't the first time he'd encountered her stubbornness around schedules. Once Medea got an idea in her head that they were doing something on a certain day, she was about as reluctant to let it go as a dog worrying a bone. Still, it rankled that she didn't take his personal problems seriously. He tried to make it matter.

"And what if my curse kicks in during the experiments? Your data will be ruined."

"I doubt it will trouble us. The curse seems predisposed to strike when you're doing well or having fun. As the experiments involve dull, repetitive work with no opportunities for your usual, uh, extracurricular activities, the curse will probably stay dormant. If not, we can just stay longer."

That wasn't good. He already battled boredom on a daily basis. Something in his brain craved constant stimulation. Violence and danger scratched the itch—probably why he wasn't as bothered by Medea's harsh physical lessons as previous apprentices—and manipulation kept him entertained. Sex satisfied another craving entirely. Now he was facing a week or longer without *any* stimulation, physical or mental. "You're *really* selling this trip, aren't you?"

"I don't *have* to sell it. I'm the master, you're the apprentice. Now go pack. Remember—nothing magical. Be sure to bring a lamp and plenty of books, or whatever you use to keep yourself entertained when we're not working." Medea resumed ascending the iron staircase to her room.

"I'll just pack a bunch of pornography, shall I?"

"If that's what you need to get through the week," she called over her shoulder without halting her stride.

12

EXPOSED

Medea felt Nikolai's seething gaze on her back. He was going to be a sour little shit all week. Would he go against her orders? If he bolted, she could always give him a nasty curse of her own when he returned, but then she'd still be out an apprentice for however many days. She would *not* allow him to jeopardize this experiment, not after how long it had taken her to make the arrangements. Better not leave him the option. At the top of the stairs, she warded the gateway room door.

Tino leapt onto her shoulder by way of greeting. She gave the gecko a pat and set him on the bed. "I'm sorry, I can't take you with me. I don't trust Nikolai at the best of times, and now, well, this is no time for introductions."

She pulled out a crumpled list. She'd packed the night before and crossed everything off, but it didn't hurt to do a final scan— books, paper and pens, a lamp, oil, blanket, clothes, shoes. They could make or purchase food once they were through the gateway and haul it with them. The site had a well with a manual pump. She'd been so ecstatic to find a willing seller that she'd forgotten to check if it worked. No matter—there was a creek a few miles from the house. She scanned the list twice before conceding she was stalling the inevitable.

Experiments were all about controlling your variables. The fewer variables you had, the more accurate your data was likely to be. Magic, unfortunately, was one such variable. Outside the experiment itself, they would cast no spells, nor would they bring in anything that held enchantments, as magic might influence the results.

With a resigned sigh, Medea removed her hip pouch and placed it on her nightstand. She frowned at the floral dress lying on the bed. It had taken nearly a month to find something marginally more comfortable than a burlap bag, but she still had her misgivings. True, it had felt okay in the shop, but who knew how it would hold up once she had to wear it continuously? She probably should have taken a day or two to wear it about the island, just to make sure. Too late now.

Medea stripped her enchanted red dress and donned the Mundane replacement. The skirt and sleeves were too short for her taste—the former extending just below her knees and the latter leaving her arms bare below the shoulder. There had been "jackets" available to wear over the top of the dress, but these proved to be stiff and unyielding. Her red dress felt like a second skin. This dress, while not unbearable, was alien enough to continually tug at her attention. Given what she still had to do, perhaps the distraction would be welcome.

She rubbed her arms and sank onto the bed, pulling a notebook close. Her personal enchantments would have to be removed. Teleporting was the quickest way, but she told herself teleportation sickness wasn't worth the time she would have saved, and anyhow she was overdue to update her list of spells.

It was like staring at an ice-cold pond she couldn't bring herself to dive into. As though easing into frigid water and hoping to acclimate, she undid her enchantments a spell at a time.

Gone were the reminders to eat and links to her wards. This week she'd be sleeping away from home, away from the protective enchantments she'd placed on the island.

Gone were Magic Sight, Poison Protection, Mind Warding. She'd be completely unguarded, cooped up with a male who once wanted her dead, and still might.

Gone were the *Servitus aut Mors* compulsion and hostile intent proximity detection—that last had activated during her own recent encounter with witch hunters. Someone could slit her throat in her sleep now. She'd probably wake in time to heal herself, but that meant contaminating the test site.

Gone were the rest of her protection spells. She bled spells onto the page, diminishing more with each scribbled notation. It was less like stepping into water and more like drowning. There was no acclimating to this.

When she rose from the bed, she was more naked than when she'd bared her skin to don the new dress. She gathered her things and paused at the bedroom door, taking one last breath of sanctuary before descending.

Nikolai tested the gateway room door and found it locked. Seemed Medea didn't trust him not to go against her orders and retrieve the pouch. He'd considered it, but she probably would have cursed him with something even more annoying than what he had now. His best bet was to get her to make a new gateway at their destination or, if that proved impossible, expedite whatever she wanted him to do.

Several loud thumps reverberated on the floor behind him—duffel bags. She wasn't kidding about not using magic. From the sound of the thumps, they probably contained a good number of books. How much crap was she bringing? If she expected him to carry all that stuff for her—

A slender Mundane woman appeared at the top of the stairs. Who the—?

The woman turned and Medea's face appeared. She wore something else! And not just anything—something *modern*, something that showed *skin*.

He drank in her new look as she descended the spiral staircase. Always she'd worn the same medieval-style red dress, long sleeved with a skirt that covered all but her feet. This dress was yellow with white flowers. If she were trying to fit in, she hadn't quite succeeded. The cap sleeves were more suitable for summer than fall. Her hair was all wrong and she wore no makeup, hat, or shoes. In a way, her usual wear made her other differences stand out less. Once people heard her accent, they generally chalked up her oddness to being a foreigner. This felt like watching a penguin attempt flight. Something else was different too, but he couldn't put his finger on what.

At the bottom of the stairs Medea glanced up, saw his face, and blushed. One hand tugged downward on the skirt of her dress, as though willing it to lengthen, while the other vainly attempted to cover a bit of her arm.

"Stop gawking."

"Sorry, I've never seen you in anything else. You seem to have forgotten something."

She twisted in place, examining her dress. "What?"

"Shoes. If we're not using magic, you won't be able to use an illusion to conceal your feet."

"Illusion? Oh!" She stuck out a foot and pointed to a leather anklet. "This is enchanted. See?" The leather sprang to life, splitting in two and extending in opposing directions. Each piece wound around her foot, crisscrossing and finally flattening under her sole to create a makeshift sandal.

"Handy."

"Footy," she mumbled. "Unfortunately, I can't use them on our trip. I bought shoes. They're in here somewhere . . ."

She took off the anklets and tossed them haphazardly onto the closest armchair. One rebounded and fell to the ground. She took no note and proceeded to rummage through her bags. He sighed internally and levitated the anklets onto the nearest table. *Someone* had to keep this place in order.

"Here we go," she exclaimed, pulling out a pair of work boots.

"Medea, those aren't even regular shoes. And they're for men."

"Technically, they're for adolescents. I had difficulty finding adult shoes in my size." She sat on the floor and started pulling on socks, oblivious to how her shorter dress crept up, exposing more and more leg.

"You wouldn't have had any trouble if you'd looked for women's shoes."

"Have you *seen* what passes for women's shoes these days? So uncomfortable." She finished lacing the boots and bounded upright, turning to admire her feet. "These aren't so bad."

"Not bad at all." The dress-and-boots combination was oddly erotic, drawing attention to her legs. He imagined running a hand along the pale, cool skin. "Can I get your bags?" He started forward, but she shooed him away.

"I can get them myself!" She shouldered them one by one— four duffel bags and a smaller satchel. How she didn't crumple was beyond him, until he realized she was using Levitate to lift the bulk of the weight.

"It's not realistic for you to carry all that. People are going to stare—I mean, more than usual. Plus I'm going to look like an asshole walking next to you."

She frowned. "You're probably right. I'll give you some later. We won't be going too far yet."

She brushed past him and entered the gateway room. In the close proximity, he felt it—the thing that was different—or rather, the lack of it. He cast Magic Sight. Sure enough, the morass of spells normally adorning her body was absent. The instinct to kill a weakened Competitor bubbled to the surface. He brushed it aside. Medea was an Ally now, or would be by the time he was through with her. In either case, she was still Useful. And now, she was vulnerable.

"You've stripped off all your enchantments," he said with a grin.

Medea jerked as if poked and spun to face him. A bag slid off her shoulder. She maneuvered it irritably back into place and shot him death glare #3 mixed with something else. Fear?

"Don't think for a second I can't defend myself without my passive spells."

"I'm well aware of your capabilities." He tapped his scars and offered a smile.

The glare didn't falter. He reached past her to open the gateway door and her body tensed, though she remained stoically in place. Interesting. She could kill him instantly, yet she feared him. He didn't know whether to be impressed that he caused such an effect or annoyed at the display of weakness. She was better than that.

"You'll have to dispel that illusion on your face when we get to our destination."

She was punishing him for the momentary discomfort he'd made her feel. No—that was something he'd do. Medea didn't make power moves like that. The timing was coincidental, though it didn't make her demand any less annoying. He looked down, locking eyes with her.

"No magic," she continued, as if he needed the clarification.

"I don't like—"

"I don't care what you like. It will just be me and you out there. I'm not even sure why you bother to maintain it here on the island." She strode through the gateway.

He spared a glance at the map. Omaha, Nebraska. Great.

The gateway exited in a brick alleyway. She pointed at the ground. "Put the bags here. I'll conceal them. We have work to do and I don't want to be encumbered."

"Why don't we just leave them inside the gateway?"

"Because then we'd have to go back through to get them," she said in a patronizing tone.

"And?"

"And we might be tempted to linger." Her face said she was serious.

He bit back the impulse to argue. Medea never budged on her eccentricities. He did as instructed, then moved to the mouth of the alley to get his bearings while she enchanted the area *around* the bags. Such an odd woman.

"What are we doing?" he asked when she finally met him on the street.

"First, we have to visit a few shops. Then we need to secure transport to the countryside." She fiddled with a small stone in her hands—one of those she'd enchanted to measure ambient magic.

"Why not get a car first?"

"Because the drive is far enough without asking someone to chauffeur us around all day."

"Medea, I can 'ask' someone to give us their car."

She looked scandalized. "That's like stealing someone's horse!"

Good thing he'd never told her about the Jaguar. "It's not like we plan to keep the car. We'd only be borrowing—"

"Absolutely not."

No wonder she'd budgeted a week for the trip. This was going to take forever.

He changed his posture and tone to mimic her on the day they'd first met. "When you do things in the *most ethical manner possible*, anything that *increases* your morality *decreases* your performance."

"What are you doing there?" she asked, unknowingly crossing her arms in the same manner he affected. "I have a feeling you're quoting me at me, but I would never say something so absurd. What do you care if I'm behaving ethically or not?"

"Because you're keeping me hostage on this trip, and the longer you keep me here, the greater the chances my pouch will be gone."

"Hostage!" She flung her hands out. People on the sidewalk swiveled their heads at the commotion. "You *volunteered* for this!"

"I didn't realize signing up would keep me from getting back my antidote!"

"You mean treatment. Antidotes are for poison, not chronic curses. And you wouldn't need treatment if you hadn't been so rash!"

"*Thank you* for that clarification. I couldn't *possibly* go another day without knowing the proper definition of 'antidote.'"

Two men guffawed as they walked by. One spun and hollered, "Just kiss her!" Medea turned crimson and clenched her fist, magic brewing within.

Nikolai sidestepped to block her view of the man. "*Now* who's being rash? We have work to do. I don't want to be here any longer than I have to. So where are we going, Miss We Can't Use Magic on This Trip but I'm Going to Blast a Guy in the Street?"

"Find us a taxi," she said through clenched teeth. Medea crossed her arms and propped herself against the building. She waited in silence, periodically plucking at her dress until he flagged down a cab.

"Where to?" asked the cabbie.

"Downtown. Somewhere with a lot of shops," said Medea.

The cabbie looked at Nikolai, who offered an apologetic shrug.

A few blocks from the gateway, Medea discreetly dropped her enchanted stone out the window. They sat in silence, Medea staring out the window and Nikolai pretending to stare out the window while stealing periodic glances at her bare legs. She continued to pluck at the dress, forever tugging at the hem or sleeves.

"You're not going to make it any longer by doing that."

She pierced him with glare #1.

He smirked. "That doesn't work on me anymore. I know your looks."

She rolled her eyes and went back to staring out the window. Her hand crept to the hem of the dress, then halted and balled into a fist. She shifted in her seat, wincing like she'd sat on a tack.

He passed the time chatting with the driver, a chronically single man who had lived in Omaha his whole life and was curious to hear the stories of strangers.

"Stop here!" Medea called, pounding the seat to grab the driver's attention. The cab hadn't even come to a full stop before she bolted out the door, making a beeline for a clothes shop, from which a good number of women were coming and going.

"Must be a sale," chuckled the driver.

"You'll have to forgive my sister," said Nikolai. "She has no manners. Please wait for us."

"You're a brave man," said the cabbie, nodding at the store, "going in there with all those dollies."

"Nonsense." Nikolai leaned over the front seat. "Here's a tip:

if you want to meet women, go to where they congregate." He winked and exited the cab.

Medea was nowhere to be seen—probably in the dressing rooms. Nikolai perused the racks, pretending to shop for his mother while chatting up attractive patrons. Far quicker than he would have expected, Medea reappeared wearing a new dress. No, not new—it was the same dress, though now turned inside out.

"Let's go," she said.

He debated whether to tell her. So many people looked askance at Medea's typical dated dress that she probably wouldn't notice the stares. The satisfaction of pointing out her mistake proved too good to pass up.

"I know you're not used to Mundane clothes, but I'm pretty sure you put your dress on inside out."

"I'm aware." Medea indicated he should move, as he was blocking the aisle leading to the door. When he didn't budge, she said, "The seams were bothering me."

"Then get a new dress. Surely we have time for that."

"There's nothing here for me."

He gestured at the numerous clothing racks with exaggerated astonishment. "How can there be *nothing* here for you?"

Her mouth pinched shut, and he found himself sliding backward, nudged by the force of her will. He leaned into it.

"You look ridiculous, you know that?" The nudge became a shove, and Nikolai stumbled into the next aisle.

The cabbie raised his eyebrows at Medea's inverted dress but said nothing as they drove on. A few blocks away, Medea demanded they stop again and turned to Nikolai.

"Your job is to ensure the employees are compliant," she said.

In the rearview mirror, the driver frowned. Visions of bank robberies and mafia movies danced in his head.

We're two law-abiding citizens. Pay no mind to what we say.

The driver picked up a newspaper lying on the seat next to him. Nikolai turned his attention to the storefront. They sold appliances—refrigerators, washing machines, and the like. "How are we going to haul anything without enchanted bags?"

"I'm going to ask them to deliver. Can you convince them to do that, even if it's out of their way?"

"I think I'll manage," said Nikolai. Then, to the driver: "Please wait for us."

As soon as they'd reached the entrance to the store, the cab pulled away.

"What the hell? I told him to wait!"

"He didn't seem to be paying much attention. Maybe he didn't hear you."

"Of course he—" And then it dawned on him that he'd telepathically commanded the driver not to pay any mind to what they said. Shit. He'd have to be more careful about his wording. "Never mind. Let's go."

The shop door tinkled, and a clerk bustled to greet them. "What can I do for you today?" he said cheerfully, directing his question at Nikolai, who shook his head and pointed at Medea.

She walked past the clerk and gazed around the shop. "I'd like one of everything."

"One of *everything*?" The man's eyes darted questioningly between them, then traveled the length of Medea, taking in her odd attire.

Medea opened something with a pronged rack inside. "One of each type of . . . whatever you call them." She glanced at Nikolai, as if hoping he would supply the word.

"Appliances," he offered. Did she expect him to be familiar with all this stuff? He'd left Soviet Russia at the age of twelve, spent time at the Academy and Haven—both of which banned electricity—then moved to Medea's island where he was lucky to have a modern toilet. What little he knew of appliances was from

American films, and they didn't typically center around the inner workings of the Mundane kitchen. Would Medea expect him to know how to operate all these things?

"That's a dishwasher," said the clerk. "Is that what you're looking for?"

"Yes," said Medea. "One dishwasher, one of those, one of whatever that is . . ." She gestured to a refrigerator, a television, then vaguely to the rest of the shop.

The clerk, who had been eying Medea's dress with consternation, perked up when he realized the scope of the sale. Money was money. "Certainly! We can start with the refrigerators. This model has many features—"

Medea waved her hand dismissively. "I don't care about features. Actually . . ." She paused, considering. "More is probably better. Give me the newest . . ."

"Models?" said the clerk.

"Yes. Whatever models have the most features. Do you deliver?"

"Absolutely!" The man practically vibrated with joy. Christmas had come early this year.

Medea brought out a hand-drawn map and passed it to the clerk. "This is the place. Can you have them there by tomorrow afternoon?"

The man's face crumpled. "This is two hundred miles away . . ."

Nikolai peered into his mind. Despite the length of the drive, a sale of this size would be worth it. But the place was so remote it might not have electricity yet. Did they have a generator? The woman seemed screwy. What if they arrived, and she got angry when they couldn't hook anything up?

"We'll need a generator as well," said Nikolai, "and whatever is required to run it."

"I don't sell generators, but you can get one over at—"

"Deliver us what we require and you'll be well compensated." Nikolai layered the command with telepathic power.

The man blinked a few times, dazed, then said, "Sure thing, mister! I can have everything delivered tomorrow afternoon. And how will you be paying?"

Nikolai looked to Medea. She felt for her hip pouch and made a frustrated noise.

"I knew I forgot to pack something!"

"I've got a dollar if you want to use that," he said in Latin.

"This isn't a meal. I don't want to bankrupt the man," she said, following his lead before switching to English. "Stay here, I'll be right back." The door tinkled again. Outside, Medea appeared to scan shop signs, then took off, evidently finding whatever she was searching for.

Nikolai fingered the dollar in his pocket. First the car thing and now this. His Frog's Fancy looked further and further away.

Fuck it.

"I've got your payment right here, plus a nice bonus for yourself." Nikolai shook the clerk's hand, palming him the dollar while pushing the telepathic message deep into the man's mind. "Don't spend it all in one place." *After you make the delivery, you'll forget all about this purchase.*

The clerk beamed. "Thank you, sir!"

This was way more fun than stuffing mattresses into magically enlarged sacks. "You're very welcome," Nikolai said with a grin. "When my sister returns, please tell her I've gone to fetch the car."

13

WHEELS

Nikolai prowled the street for a mark. This was going to be fun. Aside from the Jaguar, he'd had few opportunities to try his hand at driving. He knew the basics, like where the pedals were, but could use far more practice.

Pedestrians wandered in and out of shops. The perfect American nuclear family piled into their car. Too many people to deal with. A harried man fumbled with his keys. Easy target, but there was no way he was going to drive that piece of junk. Ah, there it was—a middle-aged man in an expensive suit exited a jewelry store and headed for a blue '57 Chevy Bel Air. He carried a small parcel with him.

"Excuse me," Nikolai said. "I need to borrow your car." *Agree. Give me your keys.*

The man laughed. "Are you nuts? I'm not giving you my car!"

"Are you sure? My grandmother is sick, and I need to get to the hospital quickly." *You want to give me your fucking car.*

"Positive. Now get lost." The man opened his door.

It had been a while since he'd encountered a mind with sufficient willpower to override his telepathic commands. Looked like he'd have to do this the old-fashioned way. Nikolai pushed the door closed and leaned against the side. The man shoved his parcel under his arm and yanked on the door handle with both hands, gold band flashing on the left.

"Get out of my way or I'll call the police!"

"Buying trinkets for your wife?"

The man ignored him and continued to struggle, but the prompt was enough to get his mind going. He'd bought a necklace for his mistress.

"Does your wife know you're seeing someone else?"

"What? I—" The man paused and took in Nikolai's appearance for the first time. Had his wife hired a private eye? What did she suspect? "I don't know what you're talking about."

"Your wife hired me to keep an eye on you. It would be a shame if I had to show her those pictures."

The man eyed him skeptically. "Do you have proof?"

"You're not going to like them." Nikolai reached into his jacket. *I'm pulling out the pictures. They're the worst scenario you can imagine.* He held out his empty hand.

The man turned crimson. "Whatever she's paying you, I'll double it. Just don't show her those."

"I don't know, she's paying me a lot."

"You don't get it—my job, I work for her *father*. I'll be canned."

"Look, you seem like a nice fellow. I really need wheels more than money right now. Just for a week or so. You'll get it back."

The man stared at his keys and then handed them over.

Nikolai tipped his hat. "Much obliged."

He slid behind the wheel, started the engine, and put the car into gear, ignoring the man's horrified cry as the Chevy lurched drunkenly into traffic with a loud grinding noise. The drive back to the shop was jerky, but by the time he arrived, Nikolai felt he had the hang of things. So what if the front tire ended up on the curb? Not like he'd be staying long.

The clerk's head swiveled toward the tinkling door. "Hello again."

"Did my sister come by?"

"Yes. She said to tell you to put the car back and meet her at the bags."

To hell with that. "Thanks." He paused halfway out the door. "Did she give you anything?"

"Uh, yes. I tried to explain that you already paid, but she insisted."

"She's like that. What did she give you though?"

The clerk hesitated a little too long. "Oh, not much, really . . ."

"It's okay, you don't have to tell me." And he didn't. Diamonds. She'd given the lucky bastard diamonds. How'd she done it? Transmutation? Another spell he'd have to learn.

He pulled the Chevy out and scanned the street for Medea, hoping to catch her walking back. Ten minutes later he cursed, realizing he'd been watching for a red dress. As he drove, he noted the locations of bars and clubs. Jazz clubs seemed particularly popular. Now that he'd secured transportation, there was no reason he couldn't come back in the evenings for a little fun. He passed a bookstore and slowed to a crawl, even circling back for a better look in the windows—no Medea.

He made it all the way to the alley with no sign of her. He parked the car and waited.

And waited.

He got out, checked the bags (still there), and entered the gateway. Despite Medea's hesitation to return to the island before they were finished, she might have gone back for something. All the rooms he could access were empty. A knock on her door didn't yield a reply. He summoned lunch, ate in the kitchen, and returned to the alley.

Still no Medea.

He loaded the car, then killed a bit more time going through Medea's bags. A fur blanket and a bedroll—would they be sleeping on the ground? He'd rather sleep in the car. Two near-identical copies of the Mundane dress. Only the pattern and colors differed. Books, books, and more books. Mostly fiction, and all of them well worn, as if she'd read them many times. *Gulliver's Travels*, *Pride and Prejudice*, *Candide*, *The Blazing World*. She seemed to have a fondness for science fiction, and H. G. Wells in particular. He stuffed everything back into the bags, not caring that she'd notice he'd gone through them.

Where *was* she? Surely a cab would have brought her here by now. She couldn't have walked, or he would have seen her, unless she'd gotten lost. Goddamnit. She was probably doing it on purpose because he'd taken a car. Well, the joke was on her—coercion wasn't the same as outright theft.

He drummed his fingers on the steering wheel. He could be off getting his pouch. If Medea took much longer, he just might leave. It would be her own damned fault.

The bars called to him. He grabbed a sheet of paper from Medea's bag and wrote a quick note. He deposited it in the alley where the bags had been and pointed the Chevy toward the nearest bar. There was the bookstore again. On a whim, he pulled over.

If there was a key to Medea's heart, it would be through books, and he already had a decent idea of her taste. He bought every new release in science fiction, some Mundane science texts, and a few novels he thought she'd fancy. As a subtle dig, he threw in a copy of *How to Win Friends and Influence People*. Sure, he could pass his time in a bar and come back to the alley reeking of cigarettes and alcohol, *or* he could meet Medea with something she valued, simultaneously increasing his standing and making her feel guilty for her tardiness. He smiled at his own cleverness as he drove back to the alley.

Medea stormed down the street. She'd returned to the shop to find Nikolai gone—off to steal a car. He wasted so much time complaining about the length of their trip, and yet there he was, out finagling. Now she had to find her own way back. Her eyes roved the street in search of a cabbie.

A block away she found a line of taxis waiting outside a large office building. A steady stream of businessmen exited the building and made short work of the line. By the time she arrived, all but one of the taxis were gone, and someone was already headed for the last. She swore under her breath.

The businessman took one look inside the cab and seemed to have a change of heart. He backed away from the curb and took a place next to Medea.

"Is that one out of service?" she asked.

"Might as well be." He tapped his foot as he scanned for another ride.

She tentatively approached the vehicle and peered inside. The driver flipped down the corner of his newspaper and gazed at her. "Need a lift?"

"Yes."

He made to come out and open her door, but she assured him it was fine. No sooner had she seated herself than the businessman from the curb banged on the window.

"You can't take that cab!" He looked upset.

She rolled down the window with no intention of relinquishing her seat if he'd randomly changed his mind. "I thought you didn't want it."

"I don't. But you should really wait for something better." His eyes kept darting to the driver. Did they know each other?

She glanced around the interior, but nothing stood out as

wrong—not that she'd know what to look for. "Is your vehicle sound?" she asked the driver.

"Yes, ma'am."

She returned her gaze to the businessman. "If you can't be more explicit in your objection. I'm going to have to ask you to step away." She began to roll up the window.

Before she could protest, he jerked the door open, saying, "Here, let me share the cab with you," and slid in beside her. He smiled and stretched his arm over the back of the seat. "Pretty girl like you shouldn't be traveling alone. Where're you headed?"

"None of your business." She scooted away until her back was against the far door.

"You should really let him drop you off first," he said, nodding toward the driver. Inexplicably, he leaned closer and whispered, "It's not saf—"

She cried out at the warm puff of air on her skin and swatted him back. What the hell was this guy's problem?

"Ma'am," said the driver, "I can drop you off first. What's the address?"

She shook her head and pointed at her uninvited seatmate. "Him first." The businessman didn't look at all happy, but he gave the driver an address.

"So, what brings you to Omaha, little lady?"

"None of your damn business."

He laughed and shifted to face her. After several more failed attempts to engage her in conversation, the businessman gave up. His eyes took in her dress, then her shoes, then her dress again. She pretended not to notice how his gaze occasionally flicked to her breasts or legs. No help for that. At least he wasn't a groper. Yet. His destination couldn't come fast enough.

The cab halted in front of a restaurant.

As if they were continuing some conversation in the man's

head, he said, "I know! Why don't you have lunch with me? This place is outstanding."

"I'm fine." Get out get out get out.

The businessman glanced at the driver and didn't move. Did they have some sort of personal history?

"I *really* think you should have lunch with me."

"I *really* think you should get out." She magically opened the car door and gave the man a telekinetic shove before slamming it again.

"Go!" she urged the driver. The cab peeled away, and she spun to look out the rear window. The businessman was on his ass. He dazedly got up but made no move to follow. She let out a breath and turned to the cabbie.

"You alright, ma'am?" His concerned face watched in the rearview mirror.

"I'm fine, thank you." At least *he* was professional. Unfortunately, he'd want an address, and she didn't have one. She knew landmarks, but most of them probably predated his knowledge of the town. What had been across from the alley? A bar? Something named for a cat? "Can you park for a moment? I need to get my bearings."

"Sure thing." He pulled to the curb. "Take whatever time you need."

She closed her eyes and expanded her senses, trying to locate the gateway. Back home, Nikolai's innate power blended into the ambient magic of the island. Here, in a landscape barren of magic, she found him almost immediately. But he wasn't at the gateway. Should she pick him up? No. He'd gone against orders. If he wanted to meet up with her, it would be at the gateway or nothing.

She let her senses drift wider. Unfortunately, the gateway's magical signature would be far weaker than Nikolai's, and much farther away. Searching for it was rather like fumbling with her toes for a single marble hidden at the bottom of a dirty pond. It didn't help that the drive had her all turned around. Which way was north?

Something registered—not the gateway, but a cluster of magic so small she almost overlooked it. What could it be? To her knowledge, there were no magical communities in this region, not since the natives had been pushed out. Had they left something behind? A magical artifact perhaps? She strained toward the magical signature, trying to decipher what it was.

Sharp rapping jolted her out of her trance. She instinctively shielded herself and raised a fist, power pulsing within. A police officer stood outside, tapping his stick against the glass. Medea lowered her fist and rolled the window down.

"Yes?"

"Are you alright, miss?"

Why did everyone keep asking her that? "Perfectly splendid."

He didn't look convinced. His gaze flicked to the driver and then to her inside-out dress. Damn it, Nikolai had been right about standing out too much. She hated when he was right. It wouldn't be so bad if he wasn't so condescendingly smug about it.

"Would you mind stepping out of the car, miss?"

"I would mind, actually. State your business." Dress or no, she wasn't about to let some Mundane derail her plans.

The officer seemed surprised by her answer but recovered quickly. He leaned on the windowsill and gentled his voice. "If you need a ride, I'd be happy to take you wherever you need to go."

Dear god. What was it with the people in this town?

"I'm fine. *Really.*" Medea cranked at the window, struggling against the weight of the officer's arm. She lent magical strength to the handle and he finally moved, allowing the glass to slide into place. He looked angry and started heading toward the driver's window. Shit. She didn't need to lose her ride.

"Drive," she said.

"I don't think that's a good ide—"

"Drive!" She pushed the car with her will. The cabbie cried out, grabbing the wheel as the car moved forward jerkily, fighting against the brakes.

"I'm sorry, ma'am. I don't know what's—"

"That's quite alright. Please keep driving."

She gradually relinquished control of the vehicle and flung her senses outward, latching on to the odd magical signature she'd felt before—much easier to find now that she knew it was there. The gateway could wait. Whatever this was, it bore investigating. "Turn left here."

Movement out the rear window drew her eye and she twisted to get a better look. The patrol car had turned down the same street.

"He's following us!"

"He certainly is," said the driver. When she gave him a puzzled look, he continued, "You're not from around here, are you?"

"No."

He nodded to himself. "Thought not. Not with that accent. What country ya from?"

"Uh . . . various places. But why should that matter? Is it my dress?"

"No, but that's not helping any. They see a white woman alone in a cab with a Negro and they get worried. 'Round here, white folks don't take our taxis. Not if they can help it. Some of them carry NCD signs—No Colored Driver."

"Ooooh." That made some sense. Well, not really. Negroes had long held subservient positions in America. From what she recalled, the country had abandoned the practice of slavery, but if whites were satisfied to have Negroes drive them before then, why not now? Resentment at having to pay them, she guessed, but that didn't explain why they'd acted concerned for her rather than critical of her employing him.

"I understand I broke a social convention, but why were they trying to get me out of the car? And why were they so agitated? Seems a bit extreme."

The driver didn't answer immediately. "You could say this city goes to 'extreme' lengths to protect its white women from Negroes."

"Extreme how? Why would they need protecting?"

He didn't answer, and she could feel herself getting irritated. She was just asking for clarification. People complained she was out of touch, but when she did ask a question no one would give her a straight answer.

"Extreme how?"

"Forget I said anything." He kept checking the rearview mirror, eyes on the police vehicle that followed.

"If I get rid of the cop, will you tell me?"

He chuckled and shook his head.

"Why are you laughing?"

"Because even if we stop and you go with him, he's gonna radio his buddies to pull me over a mile down the road."

"Why would they pull you over?"

"To remind me not to take fares from people like you."

That sounded inconvenient, not cause for concern. For an instant, she envied Nikolai's shameless ability to delve in and out of minds, unperturbed by what he found. Perhaps she could use fleshweaving in a similar way. It wouldn't tell her specifics, but it might tell her something.

She scanned the driver's body. Late middle age, overweight, minor body ailments that would have developed from sitting in a car all day. Lungs ruined from habitual cigarette use. She disregarded the obvious and searched for anything more subtle. Muscle tension and high levels of what the Mundanes had recently coined cortisol, a chemical released in response to stress.

"Look in the mirror again," she said. "Watch the police car. Keep watching." She waited until his gaze shifted before exploding the engine of the police car.

"What the—? Lord!" His attention drifted—they were approaching the car in front of them too fast. He slammed on the brakes, but it wouldn't be enough. The driver's mouth fell open as she lifted the taxi into the air, over the car, and set it down on the other side.

"Don't brake, they'll hit us!" She accelerated the cab and yanked them down a side street.

He stared at the steering wheel, which appeared to move of its own accord. "How did you— How're you—?"

"It was quite simple, really. You shouldn't use such flammable compounds in your machines if you don't want them to explode. As for the method—magic. I would think that's obvious, but so few people believe in it anymore. Can you take over again? I'm not good at this."

He placed his hands back on the wheel and swallowed. "Did you kill him?"

People were odd about that these days. "No. I confined the explosion to the area near the hood. And I won't kill you."

"What else can you do?"

She sighed. "I thought we were past the small talk."

"Humor me. I've never had a magical person in my cab before. Not that I know of anyway."

"We're not as common as we used to be, and it would be easier for me to list the things I cannot do."

"Can you fly?"

"Yes."

"So why not just fly everywhere? Why take a cab?"

"Because I don't like drawing attention to myself."

He laughed. "But you'll cause an explosion and make a cab fly?"

"An explosion could be caused by anything. And I figured most people would be too busy watching it to see what I did with the cab."

"Oh, I'm pretty sure whoever was in the car behind us noticed."

She waved a hand. "One person doesn't matter. Tomorrow they'll question what they even saw. As will you, probably. I usually try to keep my magic more subtle."

"Like what?"

She reached into his body and began setting things to rights. Joints were restored, arteries cleaned, lungs cleared, heart fortified. He didn't feel it at first, then gasped as all the little aches and pains he'd felt so long disappeared. He looked at her with a smile —the kind she'd learned to dread. Not gratitude or joy in what she'd done, though that was there too, but the realization of what she could do. More than anything, it was that smile that kept her from casting spells among Mundanes.

She cleared her throat. "I'd appreciate it if you answered my question now. What did you mean by extreme lengths?"

The cortisol was back. "I, uh, don't normally talk about stuff like that. Not with people like you anyway."

She sat up straighter. "I know I look young, but I'm over a thousand years old and have seen quite a lot. So please, be frank with me. I'm not one to keep up on cultural trends—there are far too many to recall, especially at the rate they change—but it's possible I'll be coming through this area somewhat regularly and I can't very well adapt if I don't know."

He gazed at her for another minute, then ran his fingers over his short curly hair. "In 1919, a white woman accused a Black man of rape. There were a lot of accusations like that back then, people tryin' to get us in trouble—most of them amounted to nothin'—but this story got picked up by the *Omaha Bee*. The police barely had time to arrest Will Brown before a mob started forming. They went to the courthouse and started chanting for him to be handed over. When the police refused, they broke into shops, stole guns, shot up the station, and set it on fire.

"I was only eight. My parents told us to hide, to keep quiet. The crowd was beatin' up every Negro they could find, and any white person who got in their way. The mayor tried to talk them down. They lynched him—or tried to. Had him strung up three times before he was finally rescued. Will Brown wasn't so lucky. Mob lynched him, shot him hundreds of times, drug him through the streets, and burned him."

"You speak as though you feel sorry for the beast. If I'd caught him, I would have started with the burning, then healed him up and done it again. Rapists deserve nothing but pain."

He gaped at her a moment. "Will Brown was no rapist."

"You're certain of that, are you?" Men always wanted to believe the best in one another. They didn't have to deal with the lurid stares, the groping, the subtle blocking of physical space, the backhanded compliments and patronizing remarks. They didn't have to fear traveling alone or at night, nor did they have to ask themselves if someone's motivation was merely to bed you— because it nearly always was, and when it wasn't, they aimed to take advantage of you in some other way.

"Positive. And even if I wasn't, Will Brown deserved a fair trial."

"Trials are rarely fair."

He scoffed. "We can agree on that."

She leaned forward, mind galvanized with righteous fervor. "I understand you feel empathy toward this man, but consider the woman. Accusations like this often go unpunished. In many places, the woman would be put to death for such a transgression or forced to marry her attacker. No one gives women power in this world. We have to take it where we can. If she said he raped her, I'm inclined to believe it."

The driver shook his head and mumbled something under his breath.

"What was that?"

"I said this is why we don't talk to you. There's no point."

"Of course there's a point! You're trying to convince me of something. Debate is good for the mind. And I asked you. I wanted to know."

"It's pointless because you *don't* want to know and you're not open to being convinced. To you this is . . . a mental exercise or somethin', a fun way of passing the time. It doesn't affect you. When someone like Will Brown is murdered, it happens to all of us. You think, there but for the grace of God go I."

"If you're not a rapist, you have nothing to fear. That woman wouldn't have accused him without good reason. I'm merely asking you to consider the evidence and—"

"What evidence?" he snapped. "That after the war white men were mad about competing with us for jobs? That they looked for excuses to bring us down? Or how about the fact that Will Brown had rheumatism and was in no shape to overpower anyone? The woman who accused him was a prostitute and her boyfriend— who helped rile up the mob—"

"With good reason."

"—worked for Tom Dennison, a crime boss trying to smear the newly elected mayor. Dennison controlled the *Omaha Bee*. Told them to print stories of Black mobs roaming the streets, stealing guns, and raping white women." He shook his head. "You don't know how unlikely somethin' like that is. We *know* not to mess with white folks. And I'm not talkin' rape or murder or theft. You look at the wrong man sideways and you'll get beaten. You look at a white woman the wrong way and it'll get you killed. I took a risk just givin' you a ride! Will Brown was a scapegoat.

The mayor unseated Dennison's man. It wasn't about Will Brown, or us, or lost jobs—it was a way to make the new mayor and his police force look incompetent. We were just . . . disposable. Dennison knew people hated us, so he fanned the flames."

He'd spoken so fast and with such fervor that she had trouble absorbing it all. Clearly he knew much about the workings of the city, something she'd never bothered with no matter where she lived. Why go through the trouble to learn when it all changed so quickly? Everything always seemed to come back to politics, that invisible machine that moved the world. She'd known far too many men like this Dennison, men who sought to use her for her abilities while hiding their true goals. This would have been yet another instance where she might've unknowingly done enormous damage had she tried to help.

The cabbie shook his head. "Debate isn't good for the mind when it pokes at old wounds."

"No, it isn't." She didn't mention he'd poked at hers. As he'd said, sometimes there was no point. "I understand," she said tentatively. "Or rather, I understand enough to know that I don't really understand."

"Well, that's something." He glanced at a bus as it drove past. "It's been nearly forty years and the fear is still strong. They only just started hiring Colored bus drivers. Everyone assumed that if a white woman was alone on the bus with a Black driver, he'd rape her."

"That . . . doesn't even make any *business* sense. Why would anyone risk losing a job just for something like that? You'd never have any repeat clients."

He laughed. "If there's one thing I've learned, it's that people who have nothin' to fear manufacture their own. It's like people can't exist without it. Some fears are sensible. Some aren't. You know what scares me? *You.* When you got in my cab I was petrified. What if someone sees me with her? What if I get stopped?

But it's not like I could kick you out either. What if you got angry? That's the fear I live with, only mine is real."

It was hard to imagine a Mundane male fearing her tiny, thin frame. The only people who feared her were those who knew what she was capable of.

He let her chew on their conversation for a few minutes before asking where they were headed. They'd been driving on the same road for a while now. She scanned again for the source of magic and found they were getting closer. "Keep heading this way. I'll tell you if we need to turn."

They drove until the buildings thinned, the weak magical signature creeping ever closer. At last they got close enough for her to make out the signature's cause—not some magical hot spot as she'd hoped, but five Magi clustered in the same location. Probably just a family reunion. Medea swore under her breath.

"You alright, ma'am?"

"Fine."

Should she continue on, or go back to the gateway? If Nikolai had been with her, she would have considered approaching the Magi and asking for their help with the experiments. Six test subjects were better than one. But her people skills were less than optimal. Every time she'd sought participants in the past, she'd been unsuccessful. She could return with Nikolai, but that might encroach on their experiment time. The control run needed to be completed before the appliances arrived at the test site.

They were close enough to the destination that it seemed pointless to turn around now. Might as well grab an address.

"Pull over just up there."

They stopped in front of a large building surrounded by an expanse of lawn dotted with trees. A tall, wrought iron fence served to keep out prying eyes and casual trespassers. A Magi compound at the edge of a large Mundane city? Interesting. If they practiced magic here, that was another strike against the Mundane-technology-causes-magical-interference hypothesis.

The driver peered out the window. "You got family in there?" Something like pity tinged his voice.

"Not exactly. Listen, I was supposed to meet my apprentice in the northern part of the city—we're leaving to do experiments in the country for a week—but I need him to come here first. I think it's off 24th, but I can't remember the address. Do you happen to know that area?"

He snorted. "Yeah, I know it. Do you remember what was nearby?"

She pursed her lips. Most of the landmarks she recalled were likely long gone. She listed them anyway.

"You weren't kidding about the immortal thing. They tore that building down ages ago." He chuckled at her dubious expression. "You ever want to know about a place, ask a cab driver. We know our cities inside and out. So your man, uh, your apprentice—he's nearby?"

"He should be somewhere along that block, probably near the mouth of an alley. Would you mind retrieving him? Early twenties, dark hair, tan complexion, smarmy smile." She sighed. "He probably has a car with him. If he does, I doubt you'll be able to convince him to ride with you, so just tell him to meet me here."

She reached down the front of her dress and fished out a diamond, proffering it to the driver. "I trust this is enough to cover the ride and buy a few more hours of your time."

His eyes widened, but he made no move to take it. "I have a better idea."

Oh no.

"My mother hasn't been doing so well—"

"No."

"Why not? You healed me easy enough."

"As I said, I don't like drawing attention to myself. Besides, I don't have the time. I'm leaving the city tonight."

"What about when you come back?"

"I'll have other things on my mind. I don't have time to be coordinating rendezvouses with people."

He gave her a look. "You're immortal and you don't have the time?"—if she had a coin for every time she heard *that*—"Then I guess I don't have time to go get your apprentice."

"Hey!"

"Fair's fair. And you owe me a second one." He smiled. "Fare, that is."

"I am offering you a *diamond*. Surely you can pay for medical care several times over with that!"

"Doctors can only do so much. I haven't felt this good since I was a boy. I can *breathe* again." He pounded his chest and took a deep breath. "My mother's in real bad shape. They think it's cancer. No diamond or doctors can fix that. But *you* can."

Damn it. This wouldn't end well. He'd tell others and it would become a whole *thing*. But she really needed Nikolai here. "Fine. I'll be coming through again in about a week. I can't give you a precise time because I don't know it. If you meet me by the alley where you find my apprentice, I'll heal your mother."

He smiled broadly. "Great. I'll see you in a week."

She hurriedly opened the door and started up the path before he could entangle her in any more commitments.

"Wait!" His voice rang out behind her and she flinched. Should she pretend she hadn't heard? He'd probably thought of someone else for her to heal. She took a chance and turned back toward the cab.

He leaned out the window, hands cupped around his mouth. "What's your man's name?"

"Nikolai," she called back.

She unlocked the heavy wrought iron gates and walked up the long path toward Shady River Hospital.

14

HYSTERIA

Medea entered the building. The sign outside said it was a hospital, which was perfect. If the Magi were here for treatment, she could heal them in exchange for their services in her experiment. More likely they were on staff, putting their craft to work as healers. Her smile blossomed at the thought of meeting other Magi with an interest in healing—such a lost art these days. She could barter a few of her better spells in exchange for their time.

She passed the front desk, boots clomping against the tiles, and headed for the double doors.

"Ma'am?"

Locked.

"Can I help you? Ma'am?"

She focused on the locking mechanism and slid the tumblers into place.

"How did you—? Barney, come help me out here!"

The double doors opened to reveal a long hallway with more doors. Fluorescent lights flickered irritably overhead. Medea cast Light all the way down the hall and severed the connection to each Mundane fixture. Much better. Unfortunately, the Magi were spread out within the facility. She'd have to visit them one at a time.

"Ma'am!"

She started to open a door, but a meaty hand pushed it closed. A bulky nurse looked down at her with a smirk. He wore a crisp white uniform starched to absurd stiffness.

"Where do you think you're going, sweetie?"

"I'm here to see someone. Five someones," she clarified.

"Uh-huh." His eyes ran down her body and he snickered softly. "Then you need to come to the front desk and sign in." He gestured to the double doors.

She could plow right through him, but the Magi might not take kindly to her injuring a coworker. "Alright."

The man led her back to the front desk, where a dour woman asked her name and business.

"My name is Medea and I'm here to see some people."

"Medea what?" The receptionist's pen hovered over the sign-in sheet.

"Just Medea."

"What's your last name, dear?"

She was getting really tired of the pet names. "I don't have one, *dear*."

"Uh, okay . . ." The receptionist's face morphed into the grimace of someone forcing a smile. "Who are you here to visit?"

"I have no idea. I was just passing by and felt them. Do you have anyone here who claims to do magic? If so, I'd like to speak with them."

The receptionist and the nurse exchanged a look. God, she missed the days when she could ask to be taken to the local shaman or wizard or witch and have Mundanes say, "Sure thing! I know just the fellow, he cured my kid last week." But no, everyone was hiding these days.

The nurse, who had been looming nearby, casually positioned

himself behind her. Under different circumstances, the behavior would have been alarming, but he was obviously on edge due to her attempted trespass. Even if their goals were opposed, she could respect a man who took his job seriously; she gave him a smile to show she meant no harm. He returned it, though he still sized her up as though expecting he'd have to tackle her.

The receptionist's toothy grimace somehow solidified, making her look like a wax caricature. She pulled out a blank sheet of paper and set it over the sign-in sheet, then continued with her questions. None of Medea's answers seemed to satisfy her. No address, no phone number. Next of kin?

Medea paused. Nikolai might have an easier time following her in if they thought he was her brother. Women were given so little power in Mundane society that they probably wouldn't believe he was an apprentice or even a colleague. She gave them Nikolai's name and a physical description. No, she still didn't know the last name. Probably for the best, given how Americans felt about Russians. The receptionist seemed very interested to know where Nikolai was.

"Does he know you're here?"

Medea waved a hand. "He was supposed to meet me in an alleyway."

"An alleyway?"

"Yes." Did the woman have trouble hearing or did she just repeat everything for clarity's sake? She tried to recall the street the cabbie had identified. Already the conversation was fading. "Up north 24th Street." Yes, that sounded right.

"The hell were you doing up there?" interjected the nurse. "You got jungle fever or something?"

His hostile tone was perplexing. Had there been an outbreak in the northern part of the city that she was unaware of? If so, his concern that she might transmit the disease into the hospital was justified, even if it was incorrect.

"I can assure you," she said, trying to sound sympathetic, "I'm quite healthy. No fever." She chuckled. "Though as a nurse you ought to know malaria doesn't spread that way."

The man made to say something else, but the receptionist, who'd been gaping, waved at him with a shushing sound.

"Look, I understand you have certain procedures to follow, but it would really be more efficient if I could just walk back there and find who I'm looking for myself." One way or another, she was getting into this place.

"I have enough for now," said the receptionist. "You just need to have a little chat with Dr. Hayes."

The conversation with the doctor was equally pointless and annoying. He took copious notes while she answered his questions, most of them repetitive, and seemed to be under the impression that she needed treatment. What they wanted to treat her for she had no idea, but if it helped her get in, fine. Eventually he had the receptionist lead her to an empty room.

"An attendant will come get you in a few minutes," she said, before closing and locking the door.

As soon as she'd gone, Medea unlocked the room and tiptoed down the corridor to find the Magi. Four were deeper in the facility, but one was fairly close.

Footsteps echoed behind her. She quickened her pace, magicked the door open, and darted inside.

"My name is Medea. I'm here to ask you—" A wave of ammonia momentarily left her speechless. She took shallow breaths and blinked against the sting in her eyes.

The room looked more like a converted storage closet than a hospital room. There wasn't even a bed for the sole occupant. An obese man sat on the floor next to a bucket, his pants damp with urine. He stared into space while absentmindedly twirling a red checker between his fingers. His movements were clumsy—so much so that the checker should've dropped several times over, yet it spun with rhythmic precision. Consciously or unconsciously, he used magic to stabilize the rotations.

She didn't know what she'd expected—but not this.

"Hello?"

The man didn't look up, nor give any indication that he'd heard.

"I'm here to talk to you about, well, magic." She paused for a response. Was the man even cognizant? "What brings you here? What are you doing with that checker?"

"Hey! How'd you get out?"

She spun to find the nurse from the lobby staring her down.

"What do you think you're doing? It's not safe to be wandering about, especially not in here." His eyes darted to the man on the floor.

Shit. The Magi was dark skinned, and she'd been alone in the room with him. It was the cab ride all over again.

"I just needed to talk to him." She gave the nurse what she hoped was a demure smile.

The attendant laughed. "Talk? He's mute."

Well, that explained that. Maybe she could get around it. "Have you a pen and paper?"

His face darkened. "Why do you want to talk to him so bad? He remind you of that *brother* you were gonna meet?"

"Why would he remind me of my brother?"

"You think anyone buys that little story? That you had any business in an alley up on 24th? And now you've broken out of a secure area and *this* is where I find you? It's not right." He glanced down the hallway, then stepped into the room and closed the door. "There is something wrong with your taste, dolly."

"Don't call me—"

In two steps he had her back against the wall, eyes raking her chest. "You need a reminder of what a real man is like."

"I know *exactly* what real men are like."

"Feisty. I like that." He reached for her face.

Nikolai's words drifted back like a poison. *Pretend for a second that magic doesn't exist. What would you have done?*

There was no reason not to cave the man's skull in. None at all. And yet she found herself trying to dodge his lips and wriggle free. His arms had her sufficiently blocked. She tried to go under, but he seemed to anticipate her every move. Hot breath puffed against her cheek, followed by disgusting wetness.

She aimed a kick at his crotch. He blocked it and grabbed her wrists.

"Let go of me!" She made to bite him, expecting him to let go with at least one hand, maybe make a grab for her hair. Instead he spun her into the wall, so hard it knocked the wind from her lungs. He pinned her arms behind her back while she gasped to draw breath. A hand snaked up her skirt.

A reflexive telekinetic burst sent him flying into the opposite wall.

She flipped around and took a shuddering breath. This . . . this was untenable. She felt sick. If she hadn't used magic . . . What the hell was she trying to prove?

The nurse rubbed his head and moved to block the exit. "You're stronger than you look. I was trying to be gentle with you, treat you like a lady, but it seemed our friend here"—he nodded to the Magi on the floor, who was now rocking and crying —"got a little rough."

"You do realize I can just tell them it was you?"

He laughed. "No one takes you schizos seriously. Tell them whatever you want. It'll only make you look crazier."

Crazier? What kind of hospital was this? The gates outside had been tall and foreboding. She'd thought they were to keep people out, but . . . "Is this an *asylum*?" At least in the old days they had the courtesy to label it as such, not hide it under a pseudonym like "hospital."

He laughed again.

Shit. No wonder he was so cocky. She'd wandered into a restricted area. He could do whatever he wanted and claim he'd found her that way. It's not like the Magi could speak up for himself, not that anyone would believe him if he could. And if they thought she was delusional . . . She felt a pang of sympathy for anyone who set foot in this place. If she were Mundane, she'd be completely at his mercy.

Thankfully, she was Magi. She did, however, need to be reasonably discreet.

"You're right. I *am* stronger than I look." With a flick of her finger, she sent him careening into the wall. She pummeled his body with invisible blows while he looked around wildly for his attacker. She sighed internally and started making hand motions. It was just no *fun* if they didn't know it was you.

The urge to rip him apart from the inside was overwhelming. It would be so easy to perforate his intestines or sever major blood vessels, but she had to be careful not to hurt him too bad. She kept her magic external and away from the face. A kidney shot here, a broken rib there, a few jabs to the gut. He screamed and the lights flickered.

He lost his balance and braced a hand against the wall—the hand she could still feel creeping up her thigh. She wrenched his fingers back and he screamed. The noise was unbearable now.

"Shut up shut up shut up!" She struck his jaw, his temple, his other temple.

Still he screamed. Casting Silence would have been efficient, but it was far more satisfying to knock his head to and fro, painting the wall behind him with crimson flecks. He had no right to complain about what she did to him, not after what he'd tried to do to her, what he *would* have done if not for her magic.

It wasn't until he slackened and fell that she realized the screams weren't coming from the broken body in front of her, but the Magi on the floor. He'd backed himself into a corner and begun striking his own head. What the hell was wrong with him?

What was wrong with *her*? This wasn't why she was here.

Before she could fully process that thought, the door opened to reveal three men in starched white uniforms.

"Okay, big guy, time for your— Oh no! No no no. Barney? What the hell did you do to Barney?"

In an instant, two were dragging their unconscious fellow away from the distraught Magi while the third ushered her from the room.

"How'd she get in here?"

"Figure it out later. I'm getting backup." The man left her standing against the wall and ran down the corridor.

"Barney? Barney! Can you hear me? Oh my God, look at his *face*."

"You son of a bitch. You're going to pay!" A shout, directed not at her but at the Magi. They were crowding around him, shoving him with every accusation. The lights flickered.

"It wasn't him." Her voice came out a whisper. How had she managed to make a mess of things so fast? She cleared her throat and tried again. "It wasn't him. It was me."

They didn't seem to hear, and she couldn't find the wherewithal to speak louder. She needed to think, but she couldn't concentrate with all the crying and shouting and thudding. Soon more people arrived. A woman steered her away by the shoulders, offering quiet words of comfort. She wanted to tell the woman to stop but couldn't get the words out. As they reached the end of the hall, the lights sizzled and went out with a pop.

What was wrong with her? Calm, control, calculation—that was her mantra for combat—yet she'd let her emotions get the better of her in a way she hadn't done in ages. She never let men like that bother her anymore. She was cool and contemptuous, allowing the desire for justice to guide her actions. Here she'd been, what? Afraid? No. She hadn't been in any real danger. Angry? That wasn't quite it either.

"Here we go, dearie."

Medea blinked back to reality. The woman was maneuvering her into a large room sparsely furnished with chairs and tables.

"This is the dayroom. You'll be here most of the day, aside from meals and treatments."

Patients milled about in drab green uniforms. They looked far more comfortable than the dress she wore. She looked down and was surprised to find herself in the same garb. When had she changed? She vaguely remembered they'd stopped in another room . . .

Odd movement caught her eye, snapping her attention back to the patients. Many sat on the floor, as they were short on chairs by at least half. One woman shuffled by, pushing some sort of broom, her expression vacant. A girl with long black hair—one of the Magi—stood rigid, her arms frozen mid-gesture as though she'd started a conversation and abruptly turned to wax. She took no notice of her surroundings. Someone had draped a sweater over one of her lifeless appendages.

With so many people, one would expect to hear the steady murmur of conversation, but there was only a chaotic cacophony of mutters and sobs interspersed with the occasional shout. A woman engrossed in a one-sided diatribe with an imaginary person approached, hands gesticulating wildly. Medea flinched away from the potentially contaminating touch. Not possible, she knew, but that didn't lessen the urge.

Physical deformities were repulsive enough, with their overwhelming sense of wrongness, but at least she knew how to fix them. Diseases of the mind were another matter. She had yet to decipher the peculiar magic of neurons, which somehow encapsulated memories and experiences, merging them to form consciousness. She could repair physical injuries to the brain, but unless she'd memorized every neuron placement and fold of cortex, the injured person likely wouldn't be the same as before—memories would be lost or their personality might be irreparably altered. It was enough to make her avoid such things, though that wasn't the only reason.

Regular people were unpredictable at the best of times, but you couldn't anticipate the actions of the mad, nor reason with them. They were like facsimiles of real people—close, and yet so undeniably *wrong* that they set her teeth on edge. Their movements were wrong and they made weird noises that tugged at your awareness. Sometimes they got in your space and tried to *touch* you. They could turn violent at any moment.

Medea hugged herself and gazed at the wretched inhabitants, anxiety overriding her earlier curiosity. This was a mistake. What use were Magi such as these?

The woman gave her a nudge. "Don't be shy. Dinner is at six. If you have any questions, ask an attendant." With that, she exited and locked the door behind her.

Medea fumbled behind her for the doorknob, unwilling to turn her back on the room. She had to get out of here. One of them was coming right for her! A Magi no less. Who knew what the woman's addled mind was thinking? She pressed against the door and flung up her shields.

———

Gloria approached the new girl, a pretty, slender wisp of a thing with long blonde hair that could use a good brush. She looked to be in her late teens. Poor thing must be terrified. Her hands worried the doorknob while her gaze darted nervously about the room.

As she got closer, Gloria realized she'd been wrong about the age. The woman's short stature and frightened stance made her look younger.

She stuck out a hand. "Hi, you must be new here. My name is Gloria."

The woman shrank back and stared at her outstretched hand like it was gangrenous. "Why did you approach me?"

"I, uh, as I said, you looked new and a little unsure. I just wanted to make you feel welcome."

"And that's the only reason? You didn't sense . . . something about me?" The woman's gaze was intense, like the world hung on Gloria's answer.

Schizophrenia, it had to be. Gloria had met enough of them in her stint here. There were those who spoke with their hallucinations or went catatonic, like Evelyn; then there were those who thought everyone was out to get them. To the suspicious ones, everything had a hidden meaning or message.

"I *sensed* you were new and you might need some help. What's your name?"

"Medea."

Odd. That was Greek, wasn't it? She didn't look Greek.

"Did you want me to show you around?" Gloria took a step toward the center of the room, expecting Medea to follow— almost everyone wanted a rundown of how things worked here— but the woman only frowned and drew herself up, changing her entire carriage. She now had the imperious air of a debutante plucked straight from a socialite party. Maybe she was. Rich people could afford to give their kids weird names.

"Not yet. You seem normal enough. I can start with you. What're you in for?"

What the hell was this, an interrogation? "A family disagreement."

"About what?"

"Oh, you know, the usual things. What about you?"

"Me?" The woman looked confused and somewhat affronted, then waved away the question. "Oh, I don't belong here. I was *trying* to get in."

Uh-huh. This oughta be good. "Why?"

"I can't *tell* you." Medea's gaze jerked over her shoulder. The schizophrenics were always staring at random things. "What about that one? Why's she— I mean, what's wrong with her?"

Gloria turned and followed Medea's gaze. She was looking at Evelyn. The woman had some nerve referring to the poor girl as "that one." A sweater dangled from Evelyn's outstretched arm. Damnit, someone was using her as a coat rack again.

"Hey!" Gloria shouted, striding over to the catatonic girl and removing the sweater. "Whose is this?"

"Mine." A buxom brunette bounded over. Of course it would be Doris.

"I told you to stop doing that," said Gloria. "She's a person. Stop hanging stuff on her." She threw the sweater at Doris, who caught it with a huff.

"It's not like she *notices*. Where else am I supposed to put this thing? It's too stuffy in here to wear."

"Put it on the floor. Or tie it around your waist."

Doris looked scandalized. "Bad enough I have to wear *this*"— she gestured to the green uniform—"and you want me to tie a sweater around my waist?"

"Who on earth are you trying to impress?"

"*Some* of us just enjoy looking nice." Doris sashayed away, draping the sweater around her shoulders like it was a mink shawl.

Gloria gave Evelyn's shoulder a sympathetic pat. "Sorry about her."

"No touching!" barked Nurse Phillips.

Gloria scowled and made her way back to Medea. Rude socialite or not, she deserved to know how things worked here.

Staff never bothered to tell them. The woman was talking to Bethany; from the look of it, things weren't going well.

"Hey, Medea," she called with a wave. The woman looked eager for an excuse to bail on the conversation and hurried over.

"Thanks." Medea glanced furtively back at Bethany. "I don't think she likes me much."

That makes two of us, Gloria thought, then chastised herself. The woman looked genuinely troubled. Probably hadn't been raised with any manners. If anything, she deserved sympathy.

"Bethany doesn't like me either. And look, well, she's in here for killing her son. You should probably stay away from her." She paused for the inevitable questions, but Medea only gazed back with disinterest, as though she'd mentioned the weather and not *murder*. Well, schizophrenics were like that—their facial expressions didn't always line up with what was going on. Gloria took a breath and continued. "Have you ever been in a place like this before?"

Medea pursed her lips. "Not as a . . . as a patient."

"Does your family know you're here? Did they commit you?"

"No, I— Well, I guess I committed myself. But I told them to send word to my brother."

Good. She had that much sense at least. "Will he side with you in getting you out?"

"He'd *better*." The absolute conviction made Gloria want to laugh.

"They'll keep you here for fifteen days. Sometimes they just observe, sometimes they start treatment. After fifteen days, you'll go to court and try to argue your case for getting released. Whether or not your family agrees can be the deciding factor. If your brother argues for you to stay, you could be here another sixty days for treatment. Trust me, you do *not* want that."

Medea waved dismissively again. "I'll be out of here tonight. I have somewhere to be tomorrow." That, too, was normal. No one wanted to believe they could be stuck in a place like this or that their family had so much sway when it came to their freedom.

"Do you know what diagnosis they've given you?"

"No, but it doesn't really matter because I'm not staying. I appreciate what you're trying to do, but what I really need is information. About you, about that frozen girl, the one I just talked to, and the other with the sweater." There was that intense gaze again. "Have you ever done anything that you couldn't explain? Something that seemed impossible?"

"What do you mean?"

Medea glanced around and took a step closer. "You know, *impossible* things. *Magical* even."

"Can't say that I have."

"Oh." Her disappointment was clear. "What about the others?"

Gloria shook her head and gestured around. "Look where you are. Half the people in here have hallucinations of some sort. If you want to get out, it's best not to talk like that. Tell them what they want to hear."

"I *hate* doing that," she pouted.

"Well, it's that or be stuck for what passes for treatment around here."

"What treatment do they give you?"

Gloria swallowed. Just thinking about the shocks made her palms sweat. "It's called aversion therapy and it's—" Awful, she was going to say, but Medea fervently cut across her.

"Pairing pain with behaviors to make people stop doing them!" she said with unnatural glee. "I use it on my apprentices. Very effective." She frowned. "Well, not for this last one, but he's an anomaly. What about you? What behavior are you trying to avoid?" Medea gazed up at her expectantly.

For a moment, all Gloria could do was stare. Medea acted as

though they were discussing the latest fashions, not torture. The fact that the woman was delusional did nothing to soften the casual callousness of her remarks.

"Nothing. I'm not trying to avoid anything. Look, it was nice talking to youuuooh shit."

Nurse Phillips sidled up with two attendants and a saccharine smile. "Gloria, it's time for your treatment."

Was it time already? She looked to the clock hanging out of reach of meddling hands. No, they were early. Treatments had gotten more aggressive this second stint. She'd lied her way through psychotherapy well enough to get released the first time, but they knew that now and were always watching. Everything she did, no matter how innocuous, was suspect. She probably shouldn't have talked to Medea. Or helped Evelyn.

"I've got to go," she told Medea. "Remember what I said. You *need* your brother on your side."

Gloria followed Nurse Phillips out of the women's ward and into B wing. She hated this walk. It was bad enough when you knew where they were taking you. The route took them past the lobotomy room. Every time, she was afraid they'd make a hard right into that room.

Her heart hammered in her chest as they approached it. She shoved her hands in her pockets to hide the tremors. Would today be the day they turned? Had they given up trying to cure her and decided this was the only way? Some people came out nice and compliant. Others came out as drooling vegetables unable to attend to their own needs. She didn't want to think about whether or not her family would prefer that.

They inched closer and closer to the door, but the attendants didn't make her turn. Aversion therapy was beyond this. It contained a table with two chairs, where she sat and gripped a metal bar connected to electrodes. They'd hold up pictures and shock her according to content. Looking away didn't help. They'd just keep prompting until she gave in. But today they passed that room too.

"Where are we going?" Gloria tried to keep the panic from her voice.

"The doctor wants to try something new today," said Nurse Phillips.

Shit. Maybe it was hydrotherapy. It wasn't great but was probably the least painful aside from meds and psychotherapy. Not that meds would work for her. Nothing would work for her.

But it wasn't hydrotherapy. They led her into a long room, maybe fifty feet, empty except for the doctor, two attendants, and a padded table at the far end. She'd heard about this from Doris and a few of the others. Most of them had to piece it together after the fact—electroconvulsive therapy caused short-term amnesia, a side effect of the grand mal seizure it induced.

"They make you do that long walk on purpose," Doris had whispered, double-checking to make sure the attendants weren't listening. "And they won't answer any of your questions, just keep prodding you along. I heard them talking to a trainee—the walk is *supposed* to scare you. That's part of the treatment. To punish your subconscious or something. Make you *wake up*. The second time is worse though, because you know what's coming and there's nothing you can do to stop it." She shuddered.

The treatment was mostly used on psychotic patients or those with mood disorders like manic depression, as was the case for Doris. Gloria's diagnosis was "sociopathic personality disturbance," so it shouldn't have applied to her, but they also liked to use ECT as a last-ditch effort when everything else failed. Couldn't hurt, right? Right . . . Ten doses was the standard, and the ECT patients got to know their schedule. You could always tell when their time was arriving by how agitated they got. Staff probably saw this as a sign it was working. The patients were wheeled back hours later, half out of it. Even the normally gabby Doris would be subdued.

"Come on, then." Nurse Phillips motioned for her to start the walk.

Gloria took a step forward, the nurse and attendants shadowing her.

Another step. The shocks in aversion therapy were painful. That was the whole point. And those were just her hands. How much would it hurt going through her *head*?

Some patients came back bruised, or with a wrenched back from all the convulsions.

Doris said they didn't get the voltage right for her the first time. They started low and cranked it up with each attempt until they hit the right threshold to cause a seizure. It took something like four tries to get it right.

Nuts to this.

Gloria bolted. The attendants weren't ready. It was her first time, after all. She wasn't supposed to know any of this. The attendants weren't big but they were fast. They caught her in the hall, with grips designed to immobilize, and dragged her back. The attendants from the far end of the hall came to help. There were hands all over her, grabbing her and pulling her toward the padded table. No matter how hard she thrashed, she couldn't break from their iron grip.

"Settle down, dearie, settle down," Nurse Phillips said as they laid her on the table. "My my my. Whatever are you so frightened of? Really now, you're just going to wear yourself out. It's best if you cooperate. Here, open your mouth. *Open your mouth*. That's a good girl."

They'd pinched her nose shut to get her mouth open, then shoved the bite block in. Nurse Phillips clamped her jaw shut and nodded to the doctor. Something cool tickled her temples—conductive jelly. The doctor pressed electrodes against her skin.

"Hold still now. That's a good girl."

Pain lanced through her skull. She screamed and thrashed, but hands held her tight. The pain relented and she sagged against the table.

"Negative," said the doctor. "Increase the voltage."

Two clicks, then more pain. Her teeth clenched. How could they do this to her? How could her family do this to her?

"Try the amperage now, and increase the duration." Click click. Pain.

Gloria's breath came hot and fast. She was choking on the bite block.

"Breathe through your nose, dear."

It took a moment to remember how. Would she die here? Had they ever killed anyone with this machine? She tried to ignore the clicks as they adjusted the dials again. Beside her, Nurse Phillips repeated insincere platitudes.

"That's a good girl. That's a good—"

A black hole of fire and pain swallowed Gloria, and she didn't hear the rest.

15

THE MAN WITH THE CHECKER

Someone tapped on the Chevy window. Nikolai looked up, expecting Medea's chastising glare—#2 at the highest—but it was only a middle-aged man with the dark skin and hair typical of the neighborhood. Probably a resident wondering why he'd been parked here for so long. Nikolai rolled down the window and plastered a benign expression on his face.

"Sorry to trouble you, sir," said the man, "but you wouldn't happen to be Nikolai, would you?" The man's mind held an image of Medea in the back of a cab, giving instructions to find someone matching his description. What the hell? She thought his smile was *smarmy*?

"Yes, I'm Nikolai."

The man visibly relaxed. "The name's Arthur. Your, uh, mentor wanted me to come get you. She's down at the mental hospital."

Mental hospital? What the hell was Medea doing? The man's mind revealed nothing. Whatever made her take a detour, she hadn't shared it with her driver. He seemed preoccupied with the alley, wondering about its importance. Ah, she'd offered him healing in exchange for his services.

"When y'all come back through town, will you be meeting here?"

"Yes."

Arthur nodded to himself. "I can give you a lift to the hospital if you like. She seemed a little miffed about you having a car."

"She would be. Directions will be fine."

On the drive, Nikolai ruminated on Medea's *smarmy* remark. He had more work cut out for him than he'd thought. The sun hung low on the horizon when he arrived at the hospital—a tall brick building surrounded by an imposing fence. A chill breeze rushed to greet him as he exited the blue Chevy and walked up the path to the entrance.

"We weren't even sure you were real," said the receptionist after he'd introduced himself. "Thank you for coming straightaway. Your sister wandered in off the street. Seemed a bit funny, you know. Didn't know who she was or where she was from."

"Where is she now? Can I see her?"

"You'll have to talk to Dr. Hayes first, but I'm afraid he's doing rounds at the moment. If you'll have a seat, I can have someone tell him you're here."

"That won't be necessary. I'm a doctor too. Just point me in the right direction." He used telepathy to reinforce his words but could see her mind waver. It didn't exactly match protocol. *He'll be happy to see me. I'm an illustrious colleague.* That did it.

The double doors opened, and a man in a white uniform approached the receptionist. "Damn light in the storage room is busted."

"But they just fixed it!"

"Apparently they didn't do a very good job because it's out again, along with half the hallway. Harrison is breaking out the flashlights."

"I'll call maintenance. See if they can get someone out ASAP." The receptionist moved to the front desk and picked up the telephone. She paused, looked at the orderly, and gestured to Nikolai. "Would you mind taking this gentleman to see Dr. Hayes? He's the brother of the new patient."

Nikolai followed the orderly through the double doors down a long corridor. For a few minutes, all was quiet save for the clacking of their shoes against the linoleum floor. The orderly shot Nikolai an appraising look.

"Sister, huh? She don't look much like you."

"I get that a lot."

They rounded a corner into a dark hallway, and the orderly clicked on his flashlight. "Sorry about the lights."

Several beams cut through the darkness ahead. The first was aimed inside an open door, from which emanated sounds of scrubbing. Odd time to be cleaning, what with the lights out. Probably vomit or shit. Something you didn't want to leave lying around. Nikolai glanced inside as they passed and halted his stride. Two men with brushes were attempting to remove blood from the walls.

"What happened here?"

"A patient attacked an attendant."

"How bad?"

The orderly tensed. "Pretty bad. Like beaten into unconsciousness bad. They had to take him to the hospital."

"Which patient? Was it a blonde woman?"

The orderly holding the light for the scrubbers laughed. "*That* little thing? No, but she was there when it happened. Darn lucky she didn't get hurt too."

Nikolai's escort loudly cleared his throat. "Um, this is the woman's *brother*."

"Oh." The man's eyes widened. "*Ohhhh*. Sorry. Uh, look, no one knows how she got out, but whoever failed to lock the door is probably going to get canned."

Nikolai's guide scowled at his coworker and motioned farther down the hall. "Let's go talk to Dr. Hayes."

Several people milled about in the hallway. Two bulky orderlies had their flashlights trained on a man seated on the floor. Nearby, a man in a suit stood talking with more orderlies. "We'll do it just before dinner," he said. "Call the parents and tell them he can be picked up tonight. I don't want him around any longer than necessary."

"Dr. Hayes," said Nikolai's guide, "this is the new patient's brother."

The doctor's head swiveled and his eyes widened. "You brought him *here*?"

"Betty said to—"

Nikolai stepped forward. "The fault is mine. I may be her brother, but I'm also a psychologist and insisted on seeing you straightaway. Your orderly was kind enough to show me the way."

Distrust brewed in the doctor's mind at the word "orderly." These were attendants, not orderlies, though that one was a nurse —something to do with the pattern of stripes on their uniforms. Surely a psychologist would know that.

"Really? What hospital do you work for?" Dr. Hayes delivered the question masterfully. There was no inflection or shift in body language to give away his suspicions.

"Haven's Rest. We're a small facility, so don't feel bad if you haven't heard of it. I came here to visit my sister—she lives at our parents' house in Omaha. I fear her caretaker took it as an excuse to slack off because she let my sister get out."

"Awful. I'm glad she turned up. Tell me, what treatments have you tried on her so far, doctor . . . ?"

"Apologies. I'm Dr. Featherline." Nikolai threw out the old moniker and extended his hand for a shake while plucking the relevant information from the doctor's mind. "I was just about to try chlorpromazine. We've had great success with it at our facility. That's what brought me home, actually—I wanted to observe the effects on her myself. Has your facility tried it yet?"

Dr. Hayes relaxed. "We only just started. Seems promising."

Telepathic commands were fun, but there was something immensely satisfying about winning with skill alone, especially against an opponent trained to sniff out bullshit. And now to turn the tide.

"I'm afraid I have to ask—what happened here? One of your attendants said my sister was involved. Is Shady River in the habit of allowing young women to walk freely in the men's ward?"

Dr. Hayes flinched and shot a look at the accompanying attendant.

"It wasn't me," the man said. "James blabbed."

The doctor drew a breath. "No, we are *not*. Rest assured, I'll be looking into the matter. We take security very seriously."

"And the altercation?"

"One of our attendants discovered her in the room of a patient—"

"Are you telling me she got through *multiple* locked doors? My god, man, what kind of place are you running here?"

"As I said, I'll be looking into it. Anyhow, my best guess is that the patient was about to attack your sister—don't worry, she's fine—and Barney intervened. He took the full brunt of the attack."

"I see." Nikolai arranged his face to ensure the doctor knew he was on thin ice. "Where's the patient?"

Dr. Hayes said nothing, but both he and the attendant glanced at the man slumped on the floor. The patient's hair was shorn nearly to his scalp, exposing a variety of cuts and bruises in varying stages of healing. Several were fresh and oozing blood. No doubt retribution for the supposed attack. He wore a faded green uniform, frayed and stained with more than blood. The shirt stretched taut across his wide frame, slowly losing the battle to contain his girth, and the hem of the pants only came to his calves. Nikolai went to skim his mind and shrank back—he was Magi. Was that why Medea was here? Did the man know something special?

"I'd like to question him. Alone."

"I'm afraid that's not possible."

He shot Dr. Hayes his best impression of Medea's #4 glare and had the pleasure of seeing the man quail.

"It's not! He doesn't talk."

Of course! A mute in a mental hospital, what better practice could he have? Even if the Magi noticed his telepathic probes, it's not like the guy could complain. If he couldn't crack the man here, they could transport him back to the island for storage. A man like this wouldn't be missed. He'd done well to pick Medea as a mentor. She'd thought of everything.

"I'd still like to try. Can you give us some space?"

"I suppose. Though I don't know what you expect to achieve." Dr. Hayes instructed an attendant to hand over his flashlight to Nikolai, and the group filtered back toward the bloody room.

Nikolai sat down cross-legged in front of the Magi, ignoring the murmurs that erupted from the peanut gallery down the hall. The man didn't look up. His focus remained on something in his hand, a red checker, that he spun with childlike fascination.

He brushed the man's mind. Despite the focus on the checker and seeming mindlessness, the Magi scratched absently at the back of his head. Nikolai pressed again and again with varying degrees of pressure, but still the man sensed him. Worse, he began rocking back and forth. That, at least, was new. Curiosity got the better of him—he could always practice properly again later—and he threw open the curtain on the man's mind.

Raw. That's how he felt. Just . . . too much of everything—the fabric touching his skin, the dampness of it, the voices echoing like jackhammers down the hall, the *scratch scratch scratch* of the brushes, and the smell, oh how he hated the smell! He could barely think through the bombardment of his senses. So he didn't. He focused on the checker, on the pleasant sensation of the ridges on his fingertips, on the dancing rhythm of its twirl. Somehow this made the other things less . . . loud.

The man's discomfort was infectious. Nikolai pulled back a bit, trying to separate himself from the swarm of sensations.

"I'm Nikolai." It felt odd to speak in his own voice again. "What's your name?" Even if the man couldn't answer, the priming should prompt him to think of it.

It took a moment for the man to process what he'd heard. Actually, it took a moment for him to realize he'd even been spoken to. His brain then scrambled to replay the words so it could interpret them. Eventually he got an answer, though. *Josh.*

Nikolai smiled. "Nice to meet you, Josh. Do you remember the woman that was here earlier? The blonde?"

This was the wrong thing to say. The man tensed, his mind calling up images of Medea's face contorted with rage, her will punching the attendant before her in a display the Magi vaguely understood on an instinctual level. She terrified him, and the checker twirled faster.

"Yes, her. What did she want from you?"

She hadn't made any sense, talking about magic and asking what he was doing there.

"That's it? She asked you about magic?"

The checker froze. How did he know that?

Nikolai leaned forward and whispered, "I can read your thoughts."

No no no. That's impossible. You're lying! The checker started twirling again.

"I can prove it. Think of something."

The checker slowed to a methodical pace. What would be impossible to guess? Nothing about him. He could have asked the doctors. It had to be random, like a number. 75,357.

"I like the way you think, Josh. 75,357."

The checker paused. When the ramifications of what Josh heard sank in, the floodgates opened. Elation that someone could finally understand him. Terror at the prospect of someone reading his thoughts and having no privacy. The two emotions warred with one another, oscillating in his mind until he got stuck in a sort of loop. The checker resumed spinning, so fast it became a red blur. Nikolai half expected it to escape the man's hand and fly across the room, but it didn't, and he realized Josh held it in place with magic. The man's thoughts continued to spiral, so rapidly Nikolai had trouble keeping up.

Calm down. The telepathic command got sucked up by the tornado of thoughts and whisked away, but the checker slowed.

What did you do? You did something.

"I told you to calm down."

But you didn't say it. Did you? Self-doubt.

"No, I didn't say it. It's just something I can do. How did you end up in this place?"

Embarrassment. *I left home. There was a toy store—it had these spinning tops. They were painted bright colors that blended into a pattern when spun. I wanted another look, that's all, and Grandma didn't want to take me. "Next week, next week," that's all she kept saying, but next week came and we never went. So I went on my own. I stared into the window, wishing I had something like that, and suddenly there was a top in my hand. I didn't take anything, I swear! It was just there. I tried to take it back in, hand it to the shopkeeper, but he called me a thief and all sorts of nasty things. He called the police too. I tried to run but they stopped me. It was so loud, I was scared . . .* His thoughts trailed off, replaced with sensations of physical force, being restrained, and then relief when something flung them all away.

"You threw off *five* cops?"

I didn't do anything! They were just gone, but it only made them madder. And scared. They . . . they . . . His thoughts were dancing toward a dark terror. Nikolai could sense the static, the mental tornado or whatever it was, just below the surface and rising fast. He tried to send more calming thoughts.

"You did magic. Usually our powers first appear in childhood or early adolescence, typically under duress. Telekinetic bursts are the most common manifestation. They're wild, performed by instinct. Learning to control magic takes a lot of trial and error. Most people need formal training. What I don't understand is why it's only showing up for you now."

As he hoped, the talk of magic intrigued Josh enough to keep the swirling tornado at bay.

Yes. Other kids used to pick on me. Sometimes they got hurt. Fell back. Pushed into walls. You're saying that was me? I always thought it was God. I couldn't explain it to Mama. Everyone thought I must be pushing them. Eventually they just started keeping me at home. Grandma watches me. Reminds me to do things. I . . . I forget.

Embarrassment again. He either couldn't sense or couldn't remember when he had to use the restroom. Grandmother had to remind him. Nobody had done that for him here, just given him a bucket. When he failed to use it, they made degrading remarks about his lack of hygiene, as if he'd chosen to soak in his own waste. Shame and anxiety flooded his mind at the prospect of Nikolai reading the thoughts.

"What does your grandmother help you with?"

Josh perked up. Maybe the man couldn't read all his thoughts. *Getting dressed. I can't tie my shoes or do buttons. My hands— they fumble most of the time. I drop things. Except this.* He visualized the checker. *I don't know why. It makes people mad, though. They think I'm pretending I can't do the other things. Or that I'm lazy.*

"Well, they're mistaken. You're using magic to spin it."

I am? Josh looked at the checker in wonder.

Dr. Hayes was headed back. Nikolai quickly stood. "It was nice meeting you, Josh, but I have to find my sister."

Your sister? Confusion.

The blonde. She's not really my sister, but the doctor doesn't need to know that.

Can you tell them I didn't hurt the attendant? There was desperation in the plea.

They wouldn't believe me. Telepathy could only do so much, and it wasn't exactly in his best interest to pin it on Medea.

Josh's shoulders slumped. *I figured. I just hoped . . .* The thought trailed away. There was no hope, not for someone like him.

"Any luck?" asked Dr. Hayes, though he clearly expected nothing.

"It was as you said. Still, I like to get the measure of a man myself. I'd like to see my sister now."

"I can have someone bring her up front."

"I'd rather see her where she's at, find out what drew her to this place."

"She said she 'felt' several people she needed to talk to. You know how schizophrenics get. It's not wise to cater to their delusions."

"I find it can offer subtle clues about their state of mind. Medea rarely leaves the house these days. Her caretaker and I are the only two people she really sees. I'd like to observe her inter-actions with other patients, if that's alright."

"As you wish." Dr. Hayes motioned an attendant over. "Dennis, please take Dr. Featherline over to the women's ward."

INTRACTABLE

Nikolai followed the attendant through the corridors until he was passed along to a female attendant, who led him to the dayroom. He barely had a chance to scan it before Medea appeared at his side.

"*There* you are! What took you so long? Never mind. I need your help." She grabbed his arm and pulled him away from the door. "Can you feel them?"

"You realize that makes absolutely no sense without context, right?"

"There are Magi here. Five to be exact. Do you know how rare that is in a place like this? In a Mundane city? The ratio is absurdly off!"

"Okay, so what? I thought we were here to do experiments." He couldn't keep the edge from his voice. Her excitement meant she'd latched on to something new, potentially extending their trip. But god forbid he have a couple days to take care of his own shit. No one could fuck with her schedule but her.

"Think about it," she exclaimed, smile unwavering. "Every generation, fewer Magi are born. Don't you find it odd that there are five in the same location? There has to be a reason." Her tone and mannerisms were reminiscent of a woman sharing juicy gossip. He suddenly missed her frown.

"And this is worth sidetracking our trip?"

"For a day or so, yes. Whatever's causing this spike in Magi, it could be the antidote to whatever is causing magic to die out."

"Antidotes are for poison," he said in a mimicry of her lecture tone. "And what about the delivery we have scheduled for tomorrow?"

Her frown reappeared. "I forgot about that. Maybe you could drive out to meet them and come back here once everything is set up."

"Oh, *now* you're fine with me having a car?" And pushing the experiment back a day. His pouch looked further and further away. He withdrew his arm from her grasp.

"No, but seeing as you already *have* it . . ."

His fist clenched at his side. It was no use arguing with her when she was like this. The best he could do was speed things along. He took a breath. "What exactly do you want to accomplish here?"

"I don't know." She gave a wandering patient a funny look and pressed against him like she was trying to melt into his side. "I've been trying to figure out why they're here, but some of them seem sickly."

"*Really?* Sick people in a nuthouse. Imagine that!"

She swatted his arm, then caught the fabric and held on. "Yes, though not all of them. I tried talking to a few, but I couldn't get them to open up to me."

"Shocking. What'd you do, ask if they'd cast any good spells lately?"

"*No.* I simply asked why they were here and if they'd done anything that seemed impossible."

Of course she had. "Did it ever occur to you that they

wouldn't feel comfortable opening up to a stranger? Particularly one that looks at them like *that*?"

"Like what?"

"Like you're terrified of catching something."

"I am not!"

He glanced meaningfully at her hand, still clutching his sleeve. She hastily let go and took a step back.

"I *know* I can't catch anything," she said defensively. "They're just . . . not right. Well, one seemed okay, but then they took her to therapy and now I can't get her to say anything. She's been sitting for over an hour, just staring off into space. The man did that, too, and statue girl, so maybe the therapy causes it. If so, that doesn't bode well for us—they just took another of the women. That only leaves one unaffected. Can you talk to her, get her to open up? If not, well, maybe we should try telepathy. I know you haven't had a chance to test your new method on a full Magi, but—"

"Actually, I have. The mute you encountered—his name is Josh. I had a nice conversation with him. He's in for theft. Sounded like he managed to summon a toy into his hand. Is such a thing even possible? I thought you could only summon food."

"Oh no, you can summon anything, though it takes extraordinary focus to do so. That's one reason my healing abilities surpass so many others. I can summon the raw materials necessary to rebuild tissue without relying on the body's own stores."

Incredible. And he'd *seen* it, back when she'd regrown a prisoner's arm. He'd wondered why the man didn't become gaunt from such rapid healing. Every time he thought he had a handle on how powerful Medea was, she'd nonchalantly do something that demonstrated he'd only scratched the surface.

". . . almost like something was hunting them. That's why you don't see many grand master summoners, not even in the old days."

He blinked. Apparently he'd missed part of what she'd said. "Fascinating. You'll have to tell me more later, but for now let's focus on why we're here. Which ones are the Magi?"

Displaying a rare modicum of common sense he hadn't thought her capable of when it came to human interaction, she said, "It would be rude to point them out. Here, I'll mark them."

He cast Magic Sight, and spots of light blossomed on the chests of various patients. There were only three in the room—a woman in her thirties slumped over in a wheelchair, a brunette who was already checking him out, and a girl with long black hair striking an odd pose. He made a telepathic beeline for the latter. He *had* to see what was going on in there. Was she conscious, or was her mind somewhere else?

He dove into her head, yet she barely seemed to notice. Her mind had a muted, dreamlike quality, though she was fully conscious of her surroundings. She was irritated with Doris, who'd hung something on her. People did things like that whenever she went catatonic, thinking her unaware. She always meant to tell them off later, but it was hard to keep her thoughts straight long enough to follow through. When she did remember, they just laughed off her concerns. At least it was only a sweater. She'd had worse things done to her by men. She yanked her thoughts away from those memories, carefully avoiding the *thing* behind her.

An ominous presence pressed against the back of her mind. Paranoia brought on by his telepathic intrusion? Curious, he tried to steer her attention toward it. She mentally dug her heels in. Whatever was back there, it was bad, not worth looking at, must be avoided.

Stop putting thoughts in my head!

I'm not. I'm just reading what's already here. What are you so afraid of?

She tried to ignore him.

Just show me what it is. Maybe I can help.

He'd never seen anyone so adept at avoiding a thought. Usually when you told someone *not* to think about something, it became impossible for them to think of anything else. This woman deftly avoided giving shape to her fear.

Whatever it was, she should learn to face it. People were scared of the silliest things. It couldn't be *that* bad, and it's not like it was real.

Not so gently, he pushed her toward it.

Stop. I can't look. Don't make me look!

Suddenly Grandmother paced before her, heels clacking against the floor. She wore the pale blue dress and apron she'd died in, still dusted with flour. Curlers adorned her head, pulling the skin of her face into an unnaturally tight grimace that seemed to melt like wax and drip up toward the ceiling.

"Stupid bitch." *Clack.* "Worthless, no-good whore of Satan." *Clack clack.* "Do you hear me, Evelyn?"

The hallucination was so vivid he had to temporarily retreat from Evelyn's mind to double-check it wasn't real.

"You should die for what you did. Filthy slut." *Clack clack clack.* "The family doesn't want you back. Or the church. Jesus died for our sins, but he didn't die for you. Kill yourself. Find something sharp and cut your wrists. Smash your head in the door. Tear your clothes into strips and make a noose."

He yanked his mind away from the insidious tirade and hovered at the outskirts of Evelyn's consciousness, reluctant to dive back in. Her thoughts were annoyingly close to his own when he was in the grip of the malaise. It felt like tempting fate to be close to something so similar without his Frog's Fancy.

How the hell could she live like this? At least his curse was externally applied; her brain inflicted this misery on itself. He could think of no evolutionary advantage for such a thing. Is that why her body shut down? Was it an overcompensating freeze response? Evelyn wanted nothing more than to cover her face and shrink away from the tirade.

"Everyone hates you, you fucking *slut*. Your father is ashamed. Your mother too. Gave birth to a monster, she did. Just *die* so we can all move on."

Fuck this bitch.

As he'd done with the test subjects, he attempted to influence what Evelyn saw. *There's a swordsman clad all in black.* Her brain latched on to the suggestion, making it far more real. *Look, he's after your grandmother!* He nudged the swordsman toward the old woman. In one smooth motion, the figure bolted forward and sliced off her head. It hit the floor with a wet thud and rolled across the room, coming to rest against a chair leg. Let Grandmother complain now.

Evelyn stepped back from the headless body—comically still standing—and screamed. Excellent. He'd managed to break her out of the trance.

An inhuman wail sounded across the room. Dead white eyes stared at Evelyn from Grandmother's severed head. "Look at what you did to me, you ungrateful harlot! Drown in your sins. *Drooown!*"

Blood spurted from the neck stump, a gushing fountain of it, and more leaked from the walls. The windows opened and a red torrent flooded the room. Evelyn yanked her feet away, but there was no retreating from the rising tide.

He had to admire her imagination. *It's not there. None of this is real.*

The suggestion fell flat. It was real enough to Evelyn and she reacted as any sane person would—she tried to climb onto the nearest chair. The current occupant hollered and tried to push her away.

"Let me up. *Please.*"

"Get off of me!"

"Drooownnn."

A good shove sent Evelyn to the floor. She came up gasping and bolted for the door. Blood sloshed around her ankles as she fruitlessly tried to work the knob. Attendants rushed to pull her away.

Medea was suddenly at his side. "What the hell did you do?"

"What makes you think that's *my* fault?"

She gave him a look.

"It broke her out of the trance, didn't it?"

The look intensified.

He glanced at Evelyn. No one was going to talk to him with that show going on. He pretended to stretch and sent Sleep at her. She crumpled to the floor, brain still misfiring, though not as intently. He telepathically sent wave after wave of calm at her and she eventually stopped twitching.

"Try not to break the next one," said Medea.

He approached the attendants fixing to move Evelyn. "Need a hand?"

The women looked at him like he'd sprouted a second head. Apparently doctors didn't stoop to such menial tasks. "Uh, sure," one of them said.

He figured they'd take her to a bed to recover, but all they did was move her to the side of the room and lay her against the wall.

"How often does she have outbursts like that?"

"Not often," said the older of the two attendants. "Mostly she just mutters to herself or goes catatonic." Their word for Evelyn's frozen state. When she was like that she'd hold whatever position she was in, sometimes for hours. "The family reported that she throws things when upset, but we haven't had any of that here. Of course, we don't give them things to throw."

"They said she made objects *fly*," interjected the younger attendant. "Just goes to show you she's not the only nutter in that family."

The older woman silenced her with a look and continued, "You know how it is with schizophrenics. Most are harmless, but their behavior scares people. Her family is deeply religious, so when the episodes started they called a priest."

"How'd she end up here?"

"She ran off. The police found her living on the street a few months later."

What she didn't say was that Evelyn had been picked up for prostitution. While some women willingly turned to that profession, he doubted that was the case with Evelyn. Her disconnect with reality would have made her easy prey. He could think of a hundred ways someone could take advantage of her catatonic state. She would have been conscious the whole time, too, unable to complain or fight back. Probably made some jackass a lot of money.

Inexcusable. Women picked *you*, that was the whole point. Anyone could harass or force their way into sex. Seduction took *mastery*. And satisfaction led to repeat customers—he'd learned that the hard way. As Medea said, reputation mattered. What they'd done to Evelyn was abhorrent. He'd have to ask Medea for that spontaneous combustion curse.

The attendants stared at him with alarm. Shit, he'd let the mask slip. He plastered on a concerned expression. "Sorry, I just hate to think of what might have happened to her out there. Thank goodness she's safe now."

They relaxed a bit, but they were less forthcoming about the other Magi and he had to rely heavily on telepathy. When he felt he'd tapped them all he could, he excused himself to go talk to Doris.

As if on cue, the brunette Magi bounded over and peered past him at Evelyn. "Goodness. I hope she'll be okay. Do you think she'll be okay?"

He'd feigned concern often enough to recognize the insincerity of her words. The spell identifying her as Magi was placed dead center on her sternum, making it a fair bit harder to avoid glancing at her breasts. Thanks, Medea. He wrenched his eyes upward. She was pretty, putting him in mind of a brunette Grace Kelly. Her hair was pinned to one side with a white flower made of twisted paper, as though she couldn't bear to be unadorned even in a place such as this.

"She'll be alright. Friend of yours?"

Doris laughed. "Evelyn? Goodness, no! She's, well . . ." The woman shifted to stand in front of him, blocking his view of Evelyn, and spoke in a flurry of whispers. "I heard she used to be a *prostitute*. Can you believe that? What kind of girl has sex for money? Shameful, positively shameful! Now me, I only go out with nice, *respectable* men. I'm Doris, by the way. Are you a new doctor here?" She twirled a mousy brown lock around her finger and smiled coyly.

"Doctor, yes, but I'm just visiting my sister." He smiled, cranking up the charm. "But for *you*, I might consider staying."

She tittered. "I wish you would. The doctors here are so *frightfully dull*. Maybe you can buy me a drink when I get out. You just have to promise not to tell my folks. They're so *old-fashioned*. Don't like me having fun with handsome men"—she gave him a sly look—"and you'd have to pick me up. I had a car—well, it was my *parents'* car—but I was in one teensy tiny accident and they refused to let me borrow it again. Can you believe that? I know where they hide the keys, but of course I prefer a man who has his own car. Some of the boys I've dated didn't have one. That's why I prefer men."

"I've got a brand-new Chevy, pretty powder blue, just like your eyes."

"Oooh, I've never been in a Chevy before. I hear they're a good size. Why I bet you could fit a whole bunch of people in the back seat. You must be a hit at the drive-in."

A woman after his own heart. It was about as direct as she could be, given how sex was viewed in Mundane America. He had half a mind to break her out and take her to the nearest club—if they even made it that far. They could drink and dance until they collapsed into the back seat and got to know each other more intimately. He glanced at Medea and found her watching them jealously. Oh, that was even better.

Medea glanced at Nikolai, leaning nonchalantly against the wall as he spoke with the brunette Magi. The girl twirled her hair coyly and smiled a lot. Was that flirting? It looked like flirting. He'd better not be slacking off. They had things to do. God she hated relying on others like this. It would be so much simpler if she could get the information herself.

Waiting wouldn't be so bad if they had books, but there wasn't so much as a scrap of paper. How the hell did people keep themselves busy here? It was enough to make one mad if you weren't already. She entertained herself by scanning the staff and patients and healing minor ailments. She found a few things of note—brain tumor, cyst—and almost cheered when she found a case of neurosyphilis. Fixing it required a good deal of concentration, though it didn't keep her occupied nearly long enough. Nikolai was still with the brunette woman.

How long did it take to get information out of people? It felt like he was purposely taking forever just to annoy her. He definitely knew she was watching, for he occasionally glanced her direction with a smug look on his face.

After what seemed like ages, Nikolai attempted to disengage from his target. The girl tried to follow and was rebuffed. She reluctantly returned to her friends, though her eyes tracked Nikolai across the dayroom.

"Took you long enough," Medea said when he reached her. "Would you like me to make you a chair?" Frustrated with the lack of seating, she'd waited until the staff weren't looking, conjured an illusion, and sat levitating on top of it.

"No thanks, and I took as long as needed. Building rapport can't be rushed."

"Oh, is *that* what you were doing? Looked a bit more personal."

Again the smug grin. "I can't help it if women like me. Besides, Doris told me far more than the attendants." He paused as though waiting for something, though she couldn't imagine what.

"Don't just stand there. Tell me what you've learned!"

He glanced around the dayroom. "Do you find it odd that four of the five Magi are women?"

"Please tell me they're not in here for something like hysteria."

"Might as well be. It seems intractability is enough to get women thrown into this place." His eyes fell to her illusion when he said the word.

"What kind of intractability?"

"Not wanting to be a good little woman. Smoking, drinking, hanging out with boys—things all women do, but doing it overtly and without guilt, not on the sly. That's why Doris is in here. Or being defiant with male relatives, as Gloria was, or seeming uncaring when a child dies, like Bethany. Men can haul their wife or daughter down here and tell the doctors they're being belligerent and uncooperative. Throw uncontrolled magic into the mix, and they have even more damning evidence. Evelyn—statue girl—her family saw her make objects fly."

"And they didn't think that was magic?" She knew Mundanes could be dense, but this . . .

"Oh, they did. They called an exorcist."

She rolled her eyes. "Of course they did."

"Well, it wasn't just the flying objects. You've seen her, frozen in space like that. Her family thought she was possessed. After months of so-called treatments at home, she managed to escape, but she couldn't function on her own. I'm talking living on the streets, being taken advantage of by anyone who sought to make a buck." He paused. "For her at least, being brought here was probably a good thing. I don't know what you plan to do about these people, but at least a few of them *are* sick and just happen to have magic too."

She slumped back and rubbed her forehead. There didn't seem to be any connection between them. Maybe this was a dead end. After all, two had obvious things wrong with them—one was a mute prone to self-flagellation and the other froze for hours on end. She toyed with the idea of breaking them out and taking them to a Magi town. Weak or not, they deserved an opportunity to have proper training. But that would be a logistical nightmare. They'd have to go through her gateway, her *home*, to a Magi town. And then who would take them in? Even with Nikolai's skills of persuasion, she doubted they could find enough people willing to house complete strangers. She sure as hell wasn't going to.

"You can just leave them here, you know."

She winced, then did a double take. "Did you use telepathy on me?"

Nikolai smiled wryly. "As you once told me, it doesn't take

telepathy to know what you're thinking. Just leave them. It's the simplest, most practical option."

Everything he said was true, and yet . . .

"I don't know that I can. Not anymore. There are so few of us left. Can we really afford to lose anyone?" Did it really matter? If they couldn't figure out what was causing the decline in magic and reverse it, gathering and training more Magi was like inviting passengers onto a sinking ship. Would they really thank her for showing them what could have been? For forcing them to live through the slow destruction of their hopes and dreams? And there was something else, something she couldn't quite put her finger on. She shook her head to scatter the thoughts. "I don't even know if it'll help. I don't know what's causing this. I just . . . I don't *want* to leave them here." Gods, when had she become so sentimental?

Nikolai studied her impassively. He'd gotten better at disguising the few emotions he felt—mostly anger and irritation—but she had the distinct impression she was being judged and found wanting. Nikolai only took action when there was some benefit to himself, if only just amusement.

"Okay," he finally said. "But you don't have to do it right this second. Why not wait until we're done with our experiments? That way your schedule doesn't get screwed up."

She chuckled despite herself. Damnit, he knew her pretty well. Probably a bad thing, but it was nice to be understood. "I suppose there's no harm in leaving them here for a week."

A loud tinkle came from the door; a nurse stood with a little bell in her hand.

"Dinner time!" she called. Patients began shuffling toward the exit.

Medea's stomach growled. When had she last eaten? She'd have to remember to do that this week without a spell to remind her. "I'm going to go get a bite. Can you arrange for my release? I don't want to cause a fuss leaving this place, especially when we have to come back for the others. Maybe lay the groundwork for that as well."

Nikolai nodded, and she joined the line of patients heading for the cafeteria.

17

INFANTILIZED

Josh twirled his checker and tried to ignore the grumbling in his belly. Down the hall the attendants were arguing about how to move him. He wasn't sure what the big deal was—usually they just told him where to go and he went.

He stood and started to walk over.

"What the heck?" said one of the attendants, taking several steps back.

"Who told you that you could get up? Get down on the floor now!" The second attendant stalked toward him like a man ready to brawl.

Josh tried to step back but his body wouldn't respond fast enough. The attendant shoved him into the wall.

"NOW NOW NOW!"

The sound bludgeoned him like stones. Josh cowered against the onslaught. Something hit his leg and he buckled. He instinctively tried to stand, but someone pushed him back down. He gripped his checker tight to his chest as a rough hand shoved him to the floor.

"And STAY down!"

NOW NOW NOW! The words echoed in Josh's mind. He thumped his head against the linoleum, but the broken record of *NOWs* refused to be silenced. Sometime later—he had no idea how long—a foot prodded him.

"Up and at 'em, boy!"

He shrank away from the shoe and the booming voice that accompanied it.

"Let me try," said a woman.

He glanced up. More people had arrived. Nurse Vickie and, behind her, the burly Nurse Carter. For some reason, he always shadowed Nurse Vickie.

"Hi, Joshy. Would you like to go for a walk with me? You'd like that, wouldn't you?" She used the singsong tone one might use for a child.

He gripped his checker tight and shakily got to his feet. Everything hurt.

Nurse Vickie beamed. "Good boy!"

She led him down the hallway, followed by two attendants and Nurse Carter. They entered the main corridor between wings and for once the lights weren't buzzing and flickering at him. He paused and tried to get a better look.

"Keep moving!" barked Nurse Carter.

Josh braced himself for a jab in the back but none came. He relaxed a bit and kept walking until they turned toward the darkened B-wing corridor. An electrician stood on a ladder, fiddling with the lights.

"Not again," exclaimed one of the attendants.

"I got yah covered," said the other, pulling out a flashlight.

Josh had a stab of guilt. Now that he knew he could do magic, he was certain he'd been the one knocking out the lights. It's not like he'd done it on purpose. They were just so painfully loud and bright. They combined with all the other icky sensations in this place until he felt as though he'd explode. It was like building a fire. You lit the kindling, usually in several places, and at first you could just as easily see the fire going out. But as the flames spread, there was no stopping it. You had a raging fire in the fireplace. The fire burned until it ran out of fuel, but it died out gradually in its own time. You could put it out quicker by dumping water on the flames, but then you'd be left with billowing smoke and the fireplace would be a sopping, ashy mess.

It was the same with him. Small things added up over the course of the day—the lights, the smells, the food, the feel of the clothing against his skin, the too-tight shoes—all kindling until he burst into flame. When the fire raged, the staff yelled and grabbed him. They didn't realize that by doing so they were throwing logs onto the fire.

An attendant and a female patient approached from the opposite end of the hall. The patient had sharp features and wild, frizzy hair. There was something odd about her, though he couldn't put his finger on what. She caught sight of him and scowled, and he returned his gaze to the linoleum.

The odd sensation got closer with every step, and when she passed alongside him, he felt an unnatural warmth radiating from her chest. He stared at it in consternation. What *was* that?

The woman lurched toward him with a hiss and kicked at his shins. Josh howled as her foot connected.

"Take a good look!" she spat.

Her attendant jerked her back. "Settle down, Bethany."

"I will *not* settle down until you get that filthy spook away from me! You should've seen what he did. What on earth is he doing here anyway?"

"The treatment areas are used by both sexes—you know that."

"Come along now, Joshy," said Nurse Vickie. "Don't mind her. We're going to get you fixed up nice and good in this next room." She gestured toward a waiting door.

Down the hall, the frizzy-haired woman cackled. "Serves you

right!" She turned the corner, howls of laughter echoing behind her.

Josh entered the room, which held a gurney, several metal tray tables, and a black box with cords running out of it. The lights buzzed oppressively overhead.

Vickie turned to him with a smile and ran her hand over the padded gurney. "See this nice, soft bed, Joshy? Doesn't that look nice? Can you get up here for me, boy? Can you?"

He tried, but it creaked ominously.

Nurse Carter whistled. "You sure that thing'll hold him? Boy might need two beds!" He laughed.

"Just help him up, would you?"

Nurse Carter made a grab and Josh lurched away with a hiss.

"I'm just trying to help you. Stand still!" Nurse Carter motioned to the attendants, and they swarmed around Josh.

He hissed again. He *hated* being touched. Why couldn't they leave him alone?

"Come on, Joshy-boy. Let them help you. I promise you'll get to go home after this."

Home? Really? He'd worried his parents had forgotten about him in here. They hadn't come to visit him once. Or maybe they weren't allowed. He stared at the gurney. Home. If he did this, he got to go home.

Josh reached for the gurney and tried again, keening as the men laid hands on him but doing his best not to flinch away.

"Good boy! Goood boooy!" Nurse Vickie patted his arm.

Josh winced at the touch. He did his best to hold still as the attendants strapped him to the gurney. Too tight! His breath came in short little puffs. He spun his checker and tried to stay calm.

"Oh, what's this? You'd better give that to me for safekeeping." Nurse Vickie pried his fingers apart and stole the checker.

"Where's he keep getting those? I swear I've confiscated ten of them." Nurse Carter glared at the attendants. "None of you better be sneaking them in."

One, he wanted to tell them, and it was from home. It had come to him that first day in his jail cell when he'd wanted so badly to run his finger over the worn ridges. He'd know that sensation anywhere. The cops had taken it, but it had come to him again in the hospital and every other time he'd needed it. His hand felt naked.

"It's alright, Joshy-boy. It's alright." Nurse Vickie smeared something cold and slimy on his temples. "Open your mouth, now." She tapped his chin.

He'd barely gotten his mouth open when she jammed something inside. He gagged but Nurse Carter held his jaw shut tight. The strap wouldn't allow him to turn his head. He was going to choke to death!

Nurse Vickie laid a hand on his chest. "Be brave, Joshy. It'll all be over soon. Think of your mama and papa. Won't it be good to see them again?"

Grandma—that was who he missed most. Her morning flapjacks made the kitchen smell like heaven. When she saw him watching rainbows dancing on the wall, she polished bits of glass and hung them in his room so he'd have his own kaleidoscope of color.

Josh closed his eyes and whimpered. He had to hold on long enough for them to finish the procedure.

Home. He was going home.

Medea brought another spoonful of mashed potatoes to her mouth.

"How can you *like* this stuff?" said the girl beside her.

They sat at one of several long tables that traversed the cafeteria. Interestingly, the Magi had instinctively clustered together. Medea had chosen a seat across from the one person she'd had a decent interaction with—the woman who'd introduced herself when she first entered the dayroom. What was her name? Something with a G, she was sure of it. The woman was older than the rest, but not *old* old. Thirties maybe. Straight-backed and serious, with a pleasantly matter-of-fact way of talking. Medea mentally dubbed her The Reasonable One.

She had asked the rest for their names, though she promptly forgot them and resorted to monikers. Next to Reasonable sat Statue Girl, who was now conscious and seemed none the worse after her outburst in the dayroom. The girl to Medea's right was the one Nikolai had spent so much time with. She had a manic energy about her and barely stopped talking long enough to eat. She dubbed that one Chatterbox. Then there was the frizzy-haired woman with a dour face.

Medea paused, spoon poised in front of her open mouth. "Uh . . ."

"I mean there's no flavor. No texture. And you're shoveling it down like you haven't eaten in weeks." Chatterbox leaned back and eyed Medea's body. "Then again, maybe you haven't."

"I eat," said Medea, putting the spoon in her mouth. Did they really think this food was bad? She found it heavenly. Smooth texture, not a lump in sight, no pepper or other rogue spices to impale her tongue. Even the meat was good. She poked at the rectangular pink blob. "What do you call this?"

"Spam," said Reasonable. She was out of the wheelchair and seemed to be better, though she didn't want to talk about where she'd been.

"I love Spam," mumbled Statue Girl. "I thought everybody did." She had a faraway look in her eyes and always seemed to be distracted. As she leaned over her plate, her long black hair swept against her mashed potatoes. Medea shuddered and looked away.

"I got sick of it during the war," said Reasonable. "The GIs called it 'ham that didn't pass its physical.'"

A man farther down the table barked out a laugh. "In my unit, it was 'meatloaf without basic training.'" He looked at Reasonable amicably. "What were you to be that close to enemy lines? A nurse?"

"Mechanic in the Women's Army Corps." There was a subtle challenge in Reasonable's words that Medea didn't understand.

The man's expression soured. "Oh, one of *those*." His attention returned to his food. He stabbed a piece of Spam and held it up. "You know who really loves this stuff? That big colored feller. Would probably eat ten pounds a day if he could." He chuckled and shoved the pink blob into his mouth.

Medea glanced around but could see no sign of the male Magi with the checker. She hadn't thought to look for him at first—the sexes seemed to be segregated here—but male patients had filed in after the females had been seated. According to Chatterbox, the head doctor thought it would do the patients good to have supervised mingling, so long as they were on their best behavior. But the male Magi had never entered.

"Where *is* he?"

"Your brother?" asked Statue Girl. "Didn't he leave? I saw him leave. At least I think I did." She frowned and gazed around at the Magi. "Your shirts are being really loud today."

Medea nearly choked on her potatoes and hastily canceled the spell she'd cast earlier to identify the Magi to Nikolai.

"Oh darn, they've stopped! I could almost hear them singing." Statue Girl started humming, earning a sympathetic glance from Reasonable.

"I hope your brother comes back," said Chatterbox. "He's

dreamy. Is he single? I didn't see a ring. Think he'll visit you a lot while you're in here?"

Nikolai dreamy? *What?*

"I prefer a man with more muscle," said a Mundane woman farther down the table. She held out her hands as though encircling something the size of a dinner plate. "*Big* muscles . . . and other things." Several women giggled.

"I bet he's pretty fit," said Chatterbox. Then, to Medea, "What's he look like under that shirt?"

"He's her brother," said Reasonable. "Why would she pay attention to that kind of thing?"

"They grew up together. She must have seen him in swim trunks or something." She gave Medea a playful nudge that felt more like a stab and gazed at her with unnatural interest. "Well?"

"Uh . . . I mean, yeah, he always seems to be going about shirtless these days."

Reasonable frowned, but Chatterbox leaned close. "See! So, how is he? Got any muscle?"

"I guess. He exercises a lot." Heat rose in Medea's cheeks. How could Chatterbox talk about Nikolai that way? She didn't even *know* him. And why did she care how he looked under his shirt? It's like personality didn't even factor into the equation.

"She's blushing! Ooooh!"

Medea shook her head. What the hell had she even tried to ask? She could've sworn it was important. Food. The Spam. Ah, the missing Magi. "Not my brother. Where's the guy with the checker?"

They looked at her blankly. She turned to the man farther down the table.

"The big guy who loves Spam. I don't remember his name."

"Oh, the Negro," said Chatterbox.

"They prefer the term Colored," said Reasonable.

Chatterbox waved her hand as if to say it was irrelevant. "Why do you care where *he's* at?"

"Because it's *dinner time* and he's *not here*." Medea looked around the table. Several people averted their eyes and picked at their food. She had the impression she was being ignored. She turned to Chatterbox. "Don't you find that odd?"

"Not really. I mean he sits separate from us anyway." Chatterbox nodded across the cafeteria.

Medea followed her gaze to a stool and a milk crate in the corner of the room, as far away from the other tables as could be managed.

"People get discharged all the time," said Reasonable. "It's best not to get attached."

"I know where he's at," said a frizzy-haired woman, another of the Magi. The woman paused, smirking until nearly everyone at the table gazed in her direction. "They've taken him to the lobotomy room."

There were more than a few sharp intakes of breath and everyone suddenly showed a keen interest in what lay on their plate, all except Statue Girl, who stared vacantly into space, and Reasonable, who stared at the frizzy-haired woman.

"What the heck is wrong with you, smiling over something like that?" she said.

The frizzy-haired woman got all huffy. "I'll have you know that animal was staring at my chest earlier."

"So was Evelyn. Doesn't mean he deserves to be lobotomized. No one deserves that."

Chatterbox piped up. "I heard he put an attendant in the hospital today—"

"That was me," Medea interjected, but her words were swallowed up by the breathy girl at her side.

"—and when he was arrested, he beat up six policemen! His kind have inhuman strength—fine if you need a job done, but when they're violent like that . . ." Chatterbox shuddered. "He's dangerous. Honestly, I'm surprised they haven't done it before now."

Medea turned the word over. The roots were Greek. *Lobos* for lobe and *tomē* for cut. "What lobe? What are they cutting?"

Chatterbox stared at her blankly.

"His brain," said the frizzy-haired woman. "They're going to chop up the Negro's *brain*."

"*What?* But that will kill him!"

"He'll be fine," said Chatterbox cheerily. "They shove an ice pick up his nose and scramble his brains a bit is all. Makes people tame as kittens, I hear. Then they'll send him home."

Reasonable leveled a gaze at Chatterbox. "You don't know what you're talking about. You haven't been here long enough to see what that does to people."

Chatterbox shrugged. "Whatever it does, it has to be better than how he is now."

Medea slumped in her seat. Mundanes had always had ridiculous notions of healing, but the literature she'd read the last century had shown vast improvements. Clearly not enough. They couldn't wait a week to get the Magi out. They couldn't wait *five minutes*.

She sat up and addressed the frizzy-haired Schadenfreude. "How long ago did you see him? And where's the lobotomy room?"

Schadenfreude snorted. "What do you think *you're* gonna do?" She laughed and shook her head.

"It's at the edge of B-wing," said Reasonable. "Take a left when you exit the cafeteria, then head all the way down the hallway and make a right. It's hard to miss. The lights are nearly always out in the B-wing corridor these days."

"Don't *encourage* her!" hissed Chatterbox.

But Medea was already getting up.

"Not so fast, honey," said an attendant.

She nudged him aside with her will and exited the cafeteria.

"Hey! Stop!"

Multiple shouts echoed behind her. She threw up an invisible barrier and made her way down the hall toward B-wing. Hopefully she wasn't too late.

18

ORBITOCLAST

Josh blinked and immediately regretted it. The sting was worse than the times he'd opened his eyes just as Grandma sent a deluge of soapy water over his face. He reached up to wipe them clear but his arm wouldn't move. Something was holding it down. Where was he? All he remembered was pain.

"Orbitoclast." Dr. Hayes' voice.

Someone touched the corner of his eye and pried it open. Hazy shadows resolved into Dr. Hayes and Nurse Vickie.

"Mallet," said Dr. Hayes, and Nurse Vickie handed him a small metal hammer.

Josh hollered through the gag as Dr. Hayes aimed an ice pick at his eye. What were they doing?! This wasn't getting him home. They'd lied! He frantically squirmed against the restraints but they held him tight.

"Drat, he's awake," said Dr. Hayes. "Crank up the voltage and flip the switch again, Carter."

This could not be happening. This could *not* be happening. *This could not be happen—*

Pain lanced through Josh's skull.

He woke to something cold and sharp pricking the corner of his eye. He shrieked.

"Not again." Dr. Hayes shook his head. The others just stood there, seeing him but not really seeing him.

He couldn't breathe. He couldn't scream or cry or fling himself off the table. He was doomed.

"Again, Carter."

NO!

A loud pop sounded overhead and the lights went out.

"Blast it!" said Dr. Hayes. "Run and get the electrician. Tell him he needs to come here next."

The door opened, spilling a sliver of light into the room.

Dr. Hayes looked at it hopefully, then shook his head. "I can't work without enough light."

Nurse Carter pulled a flashlight from his pocket and waggled it. "I got a light. Let's get this done. I don't feel like hoisting this tub of lard onto the table a second time."

Dr. Hayes smiled. "Glad to see one of us is prepared. Flip it."

Josh tensed for the shock but none came.

Nurse Carter flicked a knob on the black box back and forth several times. "I think whatever got the lights fried the ECT machine too."

Dr. Hayes put a palm to his face. "It's no use. We'll have to reschedule."

"The parents will be so disappointed," said Nurse Vickie. "They've already been notified to come pick him up. The mother sounded so relieved."

"Couldn't we do it without the ECT?" Nurse Carter asked. "Not like we ever knocked them out for transorbital lobotomies."

Dr. Hayes frowned. "True, but we still used a local anesthetic on the scalp. Of course that's not a problem now that we go in through the eye socket, but we'd still need something to keep him still."

"I can get an IV going," Nurse Carter offered.

"But he'll still be awake and able to feel it," said Nurse Vickie.

"So? You know they have a high tolerance for pain, and anyhow it's no worse than a black eye."

"He's right," said Dr. Hayes. "There's no reason to wait, especially if we have to order a new ECT machine. Let's get this over with and send the boy home."

Nurse Carter grinned. "I'll run and get the IV right now."

Josh balled his hands into fists and started to cry.

Nikolai approached the receptionist. "Sorry to trouble you again, but I need to speak with Dr. Hayes about getting my sister released."

She smiled apologetically. "I'm sorry, but he's in the middle of a procedure."

Great. One more roadblock to getting out of this place. Medea's little side trip was taking forever.

"Do you know when he'll be done?"

"It's just a lobotomy. They don't take very long. He should be back shortly."

"Alright. I'll wait." Nikolai took a seat and reached for a newspaper. Might as well get caught up on Mundane news.

Medea rushed down the corridor and turned left, following the faint magical sensation of the Checker Man. The doors on either side were windowed, but she'd have to stand on her toes to see inside. Not that she wanted to. All that mattered was getting to Checker Man in time, and he was ahead—somewhere.

The corridor terminated in two more double doors. She passed through, wincing at the lights. No time to deal with that now. Checker Man was to the right. She tried the rightmost door and found it unlocked. Inside was a large communal bathroom. Showerheads lined the tiled wall with no privacy separators between. The tiled wall was in the middle of the room, hiding whatever lay behind—probably more shower heads. She swallowed her reservations at potentially encountering a naked man and entered, circling around the wall. The far side of the bathroom was just as empty.

She swore and backtracked to the corridor. What were Reasonable's directions? Something about a hall where the lights were out. Other than that, she couldn't recall. She'd trusted her own ability to sense Checker Man's magic, but this place was a maze. Breaking through the walls was an option, but that would definitely get Mundanes asking questions. The last thing she needed were Mundane police tracking them to the farmhouse and interrupting their experiments.

This whole trip was a mess. Why had she allowed herself to get sidetracked? Yes, the Magi cluster was a curious anomaly, but she could have left as soon as she realized there was no greater mystery to them being here—they were sick and that was that.

They thought she was sick too.

Medea pushed the thought aside. What she needed was a more precise idea of Checker Man's location. She halted and cast her senses wide, gut twisting at what she saw. The doors she'd so casually passed contained people—probably those less able to interact with their peers. Some wore straitjackets. Others were bound to beds with heavy metal cuffs. It wasn't that the treatment was barbaric. She'd seen far worse in her lifetime—most of her lifetime, really. By comparison, this was actually quite tame. So why did it bother her now?

She remembered Nikolai's assessment in the dayroom—that intractability was enough to get women thrown into this place.

Intractable—people had always called her that, though in less polite terms. How many women like her were thrown into places like this? The Magi here hadn't been privy to magic. They didn't grow up enslaved to a healer, watching him ply his craft. Nor did they have access to scrolls detailing the specifics of his profession. So many variables lay beyond her control. If she'd been born in another time or place, she'd likely be dead by now or incarcerated behind those locked doors.

In her youth she'd often turned a blind eye to injustice, convincing herself that if someone was determined enough, they could find a way out of anything. After all, she had. Admitting that people could be victims meant admitting her own status as one. It meant admitting that her survival was due not just to her determination but to her proficiency in magic, to luck and circumstance. Odd to think of herself as lucky after all she'd been through, and yet she was.

It made the slow demise of magic that much worse. One could be physically weak or crippled or mute and still excel at magic. Magic evened the odds, offered you a choice. It gave you a say in your own destiny. A young girl could duel a master several decades her senior and *win*. In a generation or two, even the weaker Magi would be extinct. Magic, that great evener of odds, would be no more than a distant memory, until people doubted it had ever existed at all.

Medea blinked back tears and halted her magical sensing. The incarcerated patients behind the doors faded from her awareness. She couldn't face that reality, not now. These people didn't have magic. The few that did couldn't wield it well enough to help themselves. Checker Man was facing a lobotomy with no way out. Worse, it was likely her fault. She'd accosted a man and they blamed him for it. She *had* to get him out of here.

She sprinted down the corridor, bare feet slapping against the floor. Evil lights hummed overhead, mocking her lack of progress. Every step seemed to take her farther from him. Had she come this way yet? Everything looked the same. She rounded a corner and skidded to a halt. Ahead of her was the cafeteria. She swore and spun back around.

Nikolai glanced up from his newspaper as an attendant burst into the lobby and ran up to the receptionist.

"We need every available staff member outside the cafeteria *now*."

"What's going on?" she asked.

"It's the new girl. She—" The attendant halted, catching sight of Nikolai. "Look, just get everyone you can to come help. We've got a situation."

Nikolai folded the newspaper and set it aside. "I'm happy to assist in any way I can. What's my sister done now?"

"She bolted out of the cafeteria. We tried to stop her but"—he shook his head—"I can't explain it. It sounds nuts if I try to explain it."

An image of five attendants banging on an invisible barrier featured prominently in the man's mind. So much for discretion. Nikolai sighed and got up. "Tell your men not to worry, I'll handle it."

"I can't just—"

"I said I'll handle it." He reinforced his words with telepathy. "Tell everyone to go back to their rounds."

"Yes, sir. Right away." The man pushed through the double doors and jogged down the hall.

Nikolai followed at a slower pace. What the hell was Medea up to? He caught up with the attendant at the barrier. Four more clustered in front of it. A workman with a ladder stood trapped on the opposite side.

"I'm telling you," the telepathed attendant said, "we can go back to our rounds. Her brother's going to take care of it."

"Have you lost your mind, Paul? Look at this!" The attendant slapped his palm against the invisible wall.

Go back to your duties. Nothing is amiss. My sister pushed chairs in the way. Nikolai reinforced the command with the visual image of Medea running and overturning chairs and tables. The attendants dispersed, some glancing back with looks of confusion. When they were gone, Nikolai punched through the barrier with his will.

The workman on the other side gaped. "How did you do that?"

"Magic." Nikolai winked. *You saw nothing. Now go about your business.* The workman wandered toward the lobby and Nikolai continued down the hall. Though he had trouble distinguishing the Magi in the facility, he had no trouble following Medea's magical signature. He found her a moment later screaming and kicking the walls.

"What the hell is your problem?" he asked.

Her face was crimson, her hair disheveled. "This—fucking maze." The words came out clipped. "Can't find guy."

"What guy?"

"The guy!" She sputtered a moment. "*You* know!" She angrily mimed spinning something in her hand.

"You mean Josh? I thought we were leaving the Magi here for a week. What changed?"

"Giving him, uh, uh . . . *Stabbing his brain!*"

Never had he seen her so flustered. She forgot words from time to time, but this was ridiculous. A fine time to demonstrate how cool and collected he could be.

"Where was the last place you sensed him?"

She glared accusingly at the wall in front of her, and put a hand to it. "Magic burst. That way. No time!" She raised a fist pulsing with magic, as though she intended to blast through the wall.

"That won't be necessary." Nikolai closed his eyes and searched for the familiar mind of Dr. Hayes.

Attendant. Nurse. Nurse. Attendant. Ah, there he was. *You have an urgent matter at the front desk. Stop what you're doing and go right now.*

"There," he said. "I sent Dr. Hayes back to the front desk, though I don't know if he's completed the procedure yet. I take it you can't heal brain stabbing?"

Medea slumped against the wall, body shaking, and rubbed her face. It was several minutes before she spoke. "I can reform the structure, but I don't know if he'd be the same. Brains are uniquely wired; I would have had to do multiple detailed scans first. I can repair myself, possibly even you, but I don't know Checker Man's brain well enough to replicate it with any reasonable accuracy."

"You've scanned my brain in detail?" he asked with a smile. "Why?"

She gave him an exasperated look. "Morbid curiosity. Can't we talk about this later? We still need to find Checker Man."

"His name is Josh."

"Yes, yes, Josh. Don't start lecturing me on names again. This day is miserable enough already."

An attendant appeared at the far end of the hall.

Medea frowned. "That's not the doctor. You sure you got the right person?"

As if he couldn't tell the difference. He bit back several sarcastic replies. "Positive." He strode toward the attendant. "Excuse me, the receptionist said I could observe Dr. Hayes perform a lobotomy, but I seem to have gotten turned around. Could you point me in the right direction?"

The attendant paused. "You're that visiting doc—Featherline, right? Down that way, to your left. Don't know how much you'll get to see. The lights went out. The electrician didn't happen to pass through here, did he?"

"I saw a workman headed to the lobby with a ladder."

"That's him. Thanks!" The attendant took off at a jog.

Nikolai waited for Medea to catch up and gave her the news as they walked. "See? Nothing to worry about."

"Unless they move him to another room. I'll feel better once he's found." Medea wrung her hands and kept a brisk pace. Every so often, her gaze flicked to the doors on either side. Why did this matter so much to her? Her eccentricities had been more obvious since they arrived in Omaha, but this place had her particularly out of sorts.

"You worry too much," he observed.

"That's about as helpful as when I told you to calm down."

He smiled. "At least anger is productive. It spurs action. Fear makes people panic, freeze up, or make irrational decisions."

"And destroying your room is rational, is it?" She spun to face him. "Name *one* rational decision you've made in the heat of anger." When he didn't reply, she arched an eyebrow and faced forward again. "You assume anger is better because you don't experience fear. Neither is useful in large quantities."

He liked that she, too, categorized things according to usefulness. Pragmatism wasn't celebrated nearly enough in women. If Mother hadn't suffered from a lack of it, perhaps they'd still be on speaking terms. Medea was right—anger tipped him too far in one direction. That she could impartially and logically point out his failings was one of the things he liked most about her. They might not agree on many things, but she always pushed him to improve.

Dr. Hayes appeared and passed them without a word on his way to the lobby. When he'd vanished, Medea said, "After we get Checker Man—uh, Josh, I want you to arrange for the release of all the Magi. Tonight."

He smiled. "And yourself. Don't forget, you're a patient here too." She could blast this place wide open, remove the patients, and nuke the staff into oblivion, but for subtlety, she needed him. It was a power imbalance of her own making, one he was enjoying immensely.

"I'm quite aware of that, thank you."

Voices emanated from down the hall.

"Why would he just leave?"

"We could finish without him."

"I'm not going to risk screwing that up."

"Not like it matters. Especially with him. Here, I'll do it. I've seen Dr. Hayes perform lots of lobotomies."

Medea sprinted down the hallway, blonde hair whipping behind her. Talk about fear making one irrational . . .

Nikolai hastened after her, grabbed her uniform, and hauled her back. She spun and launched a spell at him. He'd half expected this. Scared animals reacted on instinct, not higher-level thought. In one swift motion, he dropped her shirt and blocked the spell. Her face went from fury to recognition to something like surprise.

"Discreet. Remember?" He had the pleasure of seeing her flush. He walked around her and entered the room. "Not to worry," he announced in a booming voice, "Dr. Hayes sent me to wrap things up here and—"

He stopped at the sight of Josh's face. A thick metal knob protruded from the corner of one eye.

19

ROCKET SURGERY

Medea felt a jolt of pride at how Nikolai blocked her spell. At such close range too. He was coming along nicely, and his telepathy had been a boon on this trip. She waited outside while he used his power on the remaining staff. The nurse didn't sound convinced.

"It's alright," he told the woman. "I have my own assistant to help. Nurse Rhodes, would you come in here please?"

Was he referring to her? He had to be. Medea took a breath and stepped inside.

The nurse frowned at her. "But that's—"

"My assistant," Nikolai said more forcefully. "You may have seen her around, that's why she looks familiar."

"Come *on*," said one of the attendants. "He's got this covered." The man held a metal cylinder with a light on one end. He passed it to Medea on his way out the door. "Just leave that at the front desk when you're done."

The staff filed out, the nurse still shooting suspicious glances at the pair of them. When they were gone, Medea shut the door, set down the metal cylinder, and cast Light.

"Don't scream." Nikolai stepped away from the gurney, revealing Josh, and her stomach turned to ice.

Embedded in his skull was a long metal pick. They'd entered through the orbital cavity to avoid cutting through bone and jammed it into the forebrain. The tissue surrounding the pick had been mangled.

Brutal. Pointless. What was the purpose of this? The prefrontal cortex controlled a variety of functions, including planning, memory, attention, reasoning. Personality was located there. Destroy it, and what did you have left? An automaton. Throughout history, Mundanes had tried all kinds of quack methods of healing, but at least their intentions were good. She couldn't fathom how anyone could look at this procedure and fool themselves into thinking it was healing. It wasn't even *helping*. How dare they call themselves a hospital!

She clenched her fists. All who were complicit would pay with their lives. No—she'd perform the same procedure on them, see how they liked it.

"Medea," Nikolai said calmly. "You need to focus on the problem at hand. Josh is still in there. He's conscious."

"And his thoughts feel the same? The pick hasn't affected him?" she asked hopefully.

"Of course it's affected him. His thoughts are more rudimentary. Like he's hungry, but he can't even put one and two together enough to imagine going to the cafeteria."

Her stomach dropped.

"But that's beside the point." A subtle smile played across Nikolai's lips at the word "point." Of course he'd find this funny. But his next words proved he still contemplated the problem, even if he didn't care one way or another about Josh. "He needs healing. And you're the best healer alive."

She shook her head. "If he feels different, there's no guarantee I'll repair him to exactly how he was before."

"So? No one goes through life unchanged. You of all people should know that. And you'll have me to guide you."

Was he daft? "You're terrible at healing!"

"One of these days I'm going to die under all the unsolicited praise you heap upon me, but that's not what I'm talking about. I'm in his *head*. I can tell if your healing is making his mind closer to what it was."

So great was her distaste for telepathy that she'd never considered using it in conjunction with healing. In retrospect, it was a glaring oversight.

She approached the table. Josh stared at the ceiling with one open eye, his expression vacant. She had to trust Nikolai that Josh was still in there. A quick scan of his body revealed him to be far younger than she'd previously supposed—late teens at most, for the growth plates on his long bones had not yet fully fused. A heavyset boy, but a boy nonetheless. His brain had several anomalies in tissue density. Some areas were ludicrously overdeveloped while others lagged far behind. No wonder he struggled with speech and fine motor control.

She held his head steady and slowly extracted the pick from his orbital cavity. Her heart dropped a little further with each exposed inch of steel. When the tip came free, she exhaled and flipped the cruel instrument onto the metal tray beside the gurney.

Bit by bit, she reconstructed the brain tissue along the path of injury, trying her best to mimic the density of neurons in the surrounding frontal lobe.

"He says that feels weird," said Nikolai.

She looked up in alarm. "There are no pain receptors in the brain. He shouldn't be able to feel anything."

"I don't think it's physical. He's conscious of what you're doing. To some degree anyway. Keep going. He's getting more lucid. Unfortunately, that also means he's panicking."

"Talk to him. Tell him about magic, about what we are and what he is."

"I've done that. It's not helping." Nikolai cocked his head. "No, that's not right. Whatever you did, strip it out and start again."

Medea swallowed and regretfully destroyed the cells she'd created. She tried again.

"That's even worse."

Again and again she tried, her guilt increasing with each attempt. They'd blamed Josh for what she'd done to the nurse, all because of a momentary lapse in judgment. This is what happened when she intervened with mortals. People got hurt, and it was never her.

"Not even close," Nikolai said after the eighth attempt.

She spun away from the gurney, cursing.

"I can't do this! I can't get him exactly the way he was. The best I can hope for is"—she shrugged—"whatever I've been doing until now. But it won't be Josh. That Josh is dead."

"I have an idea. Check his hand."

She turned his palm over. "What am I looking for?"

"His checker. It's not here. Do you see it?"

She spotted it on a metal tray. "Here!" She handed it to Nikolai.

"Can you give him use of his left hand?"

She cast Paralyze, excluding the left forearm and hand, and removed the IV from his arm. Another spell temporarily sped up Josh's ability to metabolize the drug they'd given him. She poked his hand every few seconds until he pulled it away. "There."

Nikolai pressed the checker into Josh's palm. His fingers closed around it and began twirling the game piece. Nikolai looked to her. "Try again."

She stripped away the regenerated tissue once more and studied Josh's brain. Different places were active now, including the prefrontal cortex. It was almost as though the checker were helping to ground him. For what she hoped would be the last time, she set to work regrowing neurons. The checker rotated rhythmically beside her, a steady tug at her awareness. She shifted to block her view of the distraction. With the prefrontal cortex active, she could better sense minute differences in tissue density along the path of destruction. Any moment she expected to be interrupted by Nikolai, but he said nothing.

"Done," she announced and watched him with trepidation.

Nikolai remained focused on Josh. After what seemed like an eternity, he canceled Paralysis.

Josh's other eye flung open, and he took several quick, shallow breaths. Then he curled onto his side, threatening to over-turn the gurney, and bawled like a babe.

2 0

———

MAGUSMANIA

Nikolai left Medea to tend to Josh while he sorted out their release. She'd looked positively stricken as he walked away. Good—she was coming to rely on him.

He mulled over the best way to deal with Dr. Hayes. Getting Medea released would be easy, but five other patients? Telepathy could only do so much. It worked best when the target stood to benefit from his command—a man was more inclined to believe in a sudden windfall than he was to give up something. It wasn't all that different from motivating people without telepathy. Figure out what the target needed—or better yet, manufacture a problem —then convince them you were the only person who could solve it. What problem could he solve for Dr. Hayes?

Voices drifted from around the corner. He paused and used telepathy to eavesdrop.

"You just left him alone with the patient?" asked Dr. Hayes. First an attendant hospitalized, then the thing with Josh's parents, and now a rogue doctor on the loose. This day just kept getting worse.

"Nah, he had an assistant," said an attendant.

"Are you blind?" said the nurse. "That was his sister."

"Sure, honey."

"How could you *not* see that was his sister? She was wearing a patient uniform!"

"Hey, doc, I think Vickie needs an exam too. Seein' things now." The attendant laughed.

"That's not funny. I know what I saw. You two are the ones acting strange. How could you leave in the middle of a procedure?"

"I had an urgent matter at the front desk." Dr. Hayes spoke with conviction, though his thoughts were troubled. Why *hadn't* he finished up? It was reckless and irresponsible.

"What urgent matter?" Vickie pressed. "And how could you even *know* that? No one came in and told you."

Smart woman. As quick as he could, Nikolai envisioned an attendant bursting into the lobotomy room to notify the doctor and shoved the image into the men's minds. It wasn't the same as altering a memory, but he had no doubt it would take. People were always looking for ways to rationalize their behavior.

The attendant laughed. "See? I told you she needed an examination. Doesn't even remember Jacobson coming to get you."

"But he *didn't* come to get you."

"Enough, Vickie," snapped Dr. Hayes. "Maybe you need to go home and rest." The silence that followed was deafening, then sharp footsteps retreated down the hall.

Nikolai waited a moment longer before he rounded the corner. "Ah, hello, Dr. Hayes. Just the man I wanted to see. I've finished the procedure."

Dr. Hayes and the attendant exchanged a glance. That couldn't be good. He flitted between their minds, trying to piece together what he found.

His command to send Dr. Hayes to the lobby had been perfectly timed. The man had arrived to find a middle-aged Black couple arguing with the receptionist. The woman had dressed in her Sunday best, and her eyes held the wrath of God. "We did NOT give you permission to do that! Why weren't we notified? Why weren't we *asked*? You tell us to come down here and pick up our son, then tell us you've SCRAMBLED HIS BRAIN?"

"Your son put a man in the hospital," said the receptionist. "He's dangerous. Now sit down before I'm forced to call the police."

"Is everything alright here?" Hayes had asked.

"Doctor!" Relief blossomed on the receptionist's face. "This woman—"

"Mrs. Jones," said the woman.

"Mrs. Jones. She wants the procedure on Joshua halted."

That explained their discomfort—Dr. Hayes and the attendant were on their way to stop the procedure, or what was left of it.

Dr. Hayes turned to the attendant and said, "Well, that settles it. Collect Josh and bring him up front."

The attendant nodded and took off around the corner. Nikolai followed his mind and sent a command after him. *Take a break for fifteen minutes, then go about your normal duties. Do not bring Josh to the front.*

"Thank you for covering for me, Dr. Featherline. How did the operation go?" Dr. Hayes struck a snail's pace toward the lobby. The doctor didn't look forward to notifying Josh's parents that the lobotomy had gone through as planned. Perhaps that was a weight he could take off the man's shoulders.

"It went fine. Is something the matter?"

Dr. Hayes rubbed his brow. "The parents are in a tizzy about the procedure. I told them it was too late, and anyhow, something had to be done. The boy was violent. At least this way they can take him home. The state hospitals—well, you know how they are. Underfunded and overcrowded. I try not to send people there if I don't have to."

And there it was—Dr. Hayes' need.

"Ours is a difficult profession and we all do what we can, but I may be able to help you. I've recently opened my own facility—state-of-the-art—for a condition I've been studying. I've already transferred a few patients from my old facility, but I'm in need of more."

Dr. Hayes perked up. "Really? What's the condition called? How does it present?"

Good question. Several of the Magi patients had been diagnosed with schizophrenia, including Medea, so he'd start there.

"I first noticed it in my sister. It presents similarly to schizophrenia—both conditions can have hallucinations—but there are subtle differences. The symptoms begin earlier in life, for one. My patients often have violent outbursts, extraordinary strength, delusions of magic, a strong dislike of fluorescent lights—"

"Delusions of magic?"

"Oh yes. That's how I came up with the name for the condition—magusmania." He couldn't wait to see how Medea would react to *that*. "Ever since she was a little girl, my sister fancied she was a powerful mage who could cast all manner of spells. Overactive imagination, right? But it persisted well into her teens and on into adulthood. If we contradicted her, she'd rage and smash things about the house. One time, she pushed me off a balcony, claiming she could make me fly. First time I'd ever broken a bone." He rubbed his left arm for effect. "So we walked on eggshells and tried to keep her away from others. I swore one day I'd find a cure for her."

Dr. Hayes clapped a hand on his back. "You're doing all you can. Though many won't admit it, a lot of us got into this profession because we've known someone who needed help. For me it was my mother, but she's long past being helped these days."

"I'm very sorry to hear that. I pray I can find a cure for my sister. The standard treatments don't work—that's why I need to specialize. I've obtained a generous grant, now all I need are patients."

They arrived at the double doors leading to the lobby.

Dr. Hayes paused. "And you think we have some here?"

"I'm sure of it." Nikolai gave the names of the patients. "I think they'd fit in wonderfully at my facility, and it would free up some of your beds."

"Yes," mused Dr. Hayes, "it would. I don't suppose you could take more? I mean, if we get more of them in."

"Certainly. Especially if you can help me with transport tonight. I wasn't expecting to come out here, so I only have my personal car. If you have a vehicle I could borrow, perhaps something older that you rarely use, I could shuttle patients to the new facility and return for another load." *You want to loan me one of your vehicles.*

"I really don't have anything to spare. Unfortunately, we don't have any, uh, generous grants at the moment. But I'll draw up the paperwork so the patients can be transferred at your leisure. Except for Josh. He'll be going home with his family tonight." Dr. Hayes drew a steading breath. "Speaking of which, it's time I faced the music."

"Wait." He halted Dr. Hayes with a hand to his shoulder. Medea wouldn't let Josh go back to the Mundane world, especially not after everything she'd done to heal him. It was all or nothing with that woman. "Let me inform the parents. I'm the one that completed the procedure, after all."

The doctor smiled wanly. "Thank you for the offer, but it's my patient and my responsibility." He pushed through the double doors and approached the couple waiting at the counter.

Josh's mother was shorter than the memory had led Nikolai to believe. Perhaps her demeanor cemented her in the doctor's brain as larger than life. She certainly stood tall and proud, but there was an unmistakable tension in the set of her jaw and the way she clasped her handbag. Her mind was a coiled spring, twisting tighter at the doctor's approach.

"Mr. and Mrs. Jones, Josh is perfectly healthy and ready to come home. An attendant should be bringing him up at any moment."

Mr. Jones relaxed, but Mrs. Jones wasn't fooled. "Perfectly healthy—then the procedure wasn't performed?"

Dr. Hayes pretended not to hear and asked the receptionist to bring him the paperwork for Joshua Jones. He flipped through the stack, scanning the page with a pen and feigning notations. Just a little longer and he could avoid a confrontation entirely. The attendant would arrive with Josh and they would be on their way. No sense worrying the family. Josh would be more tractable, they'd see.

"Doctor," said Mrs. Jones, "what about the procedure? Were you able to stop it?"

Dr. Hayes returned the paperwork to the receptionist, taking the opportunity to step behind her desk and place a physical barrier between himself and the Joneses. "As I said before, it's a routine procedure, quick and painless. Dr. Featherline"—he gestured to Nikolai—"was kind enough to step in and finish when I was called away. But don't worry, it was a complete success."

The words drove into Mrs. Jones like knives. Her poor boy— would he ever be the same? Her voice shook. "It's not right, what you've done. Josh is our boy. We should've been the ones to decide what happened to him."

Mr. Jones placed a hand on her arm and spoke softly. "Now, honey, there's nothing we can do. It's done." His eyes met the doctor. "This'll make Josh better, right?"

Dr. Hayes relaxed at the possibility of an ally. "The procedure removes excess emotions and should reduce the frequency of his outbursts."

Relief flooded Mr. Jones' mind. He wasn't sure what that all meant, but it sounded better than what they had now. What had he done to deserve a son like Josh? All his friends and family had normal kids. The reverend said God wouldn't give them anything they couldn't handle. That Josh was a test of his faith and his ability as a father. Well, he didn't want a test. He wanted a son that would become a proper man, not stay a perpetual child. When Josh was taken into custody, he'd hoped they'd send him away forever. This wasn't as good, but it was the next best thing. A fantasy blossomed in Mr. Jones' mind. Josh sat at the kitchen table with his parents, laughing and conversing like a normal person. He'd give anything to have that.

"See, honey?" He squeezed his wife's shoulder. "Josh will be better off."

"Better off? *Better off?* They scrambled our son's *brain*, and you think he's better off?" Mrs. Jones yanked away from her husband and glared at the doctor. "What are the side effects?"

"In rare instances, patients can lose speech or intelligence." Dr. Hayes chuckled nervously. "I think we can all agree that's not a risk in this case."

"But will it make him normal?" Mr. Jones pressed. "Could he learn to talk?"

"I'm sorry, but if he didn't have the aptitude before, it's unlikely he'll develop it now."

Mr. Jones' face fell. "Then what's the point in taking him home? If he can't hold a job, if he can't make something of himself—why can't you put him somewhere else? Aren't there asylums for this kind of thing?"

"Dear! You can't be serious."

"What else are we gonna do? Your mother's getting too old to look after him. He'll just get out again. He can't take care of himself. What happens when we get old? Where's he gonna go? Who's gonna take care of him? If we can get him into a place, we should do it."

Mrs. Jones stared at him, aghast. "You want him to go live with strangers? We don't know what'll happen to him or how he'll be treated."

"But, honey—"

"Absolutely not!"

Nikolai took a step forward. "If I may interject. Mr. Jones, your wife's fears are not unfounded. The state facilities already have too many people and not enough beds. You don't want your son going someplace like that. Fortunately, I have another solution." He expanded on the story he'd given to Dr. Hayes, adding detail about the facility grounds and other things he thought might appeal to them.

Mr. Jones looked interested, but Mrs. Jones eyed him with skepticism. "A research facility? You really want us to hand over our son so you can do experiments on him? *Never.*" She turned away and directed her attention to Dr. Hayes. "Bring us Josh now and we'll be on our way."

He liked this woman, the way she carried herself and how she'd so casually dismissed him without a word. Like himself and Medea, she was a survivor, someone who would never give up. Such a woman demanded to be treated as an equal. Since arriving at the hospital, he'd adopted the mannerisms of a competent but deferential guest. Now he threw the mask aside and replaced it with something closer to the truth—that he owned this hospital and everyone in it.

"I'd like a private word with Mrs. Jones." He spoke to the room but kept his unwavering gaze on Josh's mother. "Dr. Hayes, kindly show us to your office." His tone was polite but brooked no argument.

There was a pause as the receptionist and doctor came to grips with the new world order. The receptionist sent a questioning glance to Dr. Hayes, but he didn't contradict the order, which meant he had to follow it.

"Uh, right this way," said Dr. Hayes. He led them to an office off the far side of the lobby. Nikolai sank into the doctor's chair while Dr. Hayes stood awkwardly by the door. Mrs. Jones squared her shoulders and entered as though she were stepping onto a battlefield.

"Please be seated, Mrs. Jones," said Nikolai. Then, to Dr. Hayes, "Would you ask the receptionist to bring us two coffees?"

"I— Sure." Dr. Hayes left, closing the door behind him.

Nikolai sat back and smiled.

"I don't care what you have to say," said Mrs. Jones. "Josh isn't going to your facility." She paused, waiting for him to state his case. When he didn't, she felt pressured to fill the void. "Lobotomy or no, he's my son. You think I don't know how we're treated in places like that? I may not be a doctor, but I'm not stupid."

"That makes two of us." Nikolai grinned. "I'm not a doctor either." He rose and opened the file cabinet, flipping through names and pulling out the file folders for each Magi. Each folder hit the desk with an audible slap.

"What're you playing at?"

"Many things." *Slap.* "I've played the responsible older brother." *Slap.* "The best friend." *Slap.* "The doting lover—my favorite, I might add." He shot her a smile. "Most recently, I played at being a doctor to get a colleague out of this place. Funny how much control people give you when you act like you belong."

Slap. The final folder landed—Joshua Jones. Nikolai resumed his seat.

A horrified expression crossed her face. "Are you serious? And you operated on *my son*?"

"Not at all." With satisfaction, he saw her relax slightly. "My colleague did that." The horror returned. God, he loved playing with emotions. Fear, relief, anger, gratitude—he could flick them on and off with the same ease as a light switch.

The door opened and the receptionist entered with two cups.

Mrs. Jones shot out of her seat and pointed an accusing finger at him. "He's not a doctor!"

"Thank you, Betty. Just put them on the desk."

The receptionist moved warily past Mrs. Jones and set down the cups.

"Did you hear what I said?" asked Mrs. Jones.

"Oh, and would you give these to Dr. Hayes?" Nikolai held out the files to the receptionist. "They're the patients I need released into my care. I'd appreciate it if he could have them all brought up front." She took the files and turned to leave.

"Not that one!" The receptionist recoiled as Mrs. Jones snatched Josh's file from the top of the stack. Mrs. Jones brandished the file at him. "Josh will not be going with you!"

The receptionist eyed the folder as though unclear whether she was supposed to grab it back from the deranged woman. "Do you want me to send a couple attendants in here?"

"It's alright, Betty. Just see that Dr. Hayes gets the rest sorted. And would you mind having someone pull a hospital car around front? Thank you."

The receptionist left and shut the door. Mrs. Jones clutched Josh's folder to her chest as though daring him to pry it away.

Nikolai laced his fingers together on the desk. "Let's talk about Josh. Specifically, what's best for him."

"What's best for him is to *come home*."

"You really think that's what's best for him? To go back to a home where he's hidden away, where his father can't look at him without feeling disgusted, where he has no chance at a real life? Is that what you want?"

"Why do you care? You said you're not a real doctor, which means you don't have a hospital."

"I don't."

She took a breath and steeled herself. "I don't know what kind of game you're running here or why you're trying to get so many patients when you said you were only here for one, but leave my son out of it."

"I can't. You see, Josh is special. Every one of those files I handed to the receptionist belongs to a Magi—someone born with magic. Without training, their powers come out in violent or unpredictable ways. And it doesn't help for them to be in a city like this. Electricity, lights, appliances—they all mess with Magi abilities. Most Magi live far from technological advancements. That's where we're taking them—away from all this, so they can learn to control their powers."

He knew she wouldn't believe him, but he'd expected an interruption far sooner. Instead, she stood in silence. She thought he was crazy, but she kept those thoughts to herself. Whatever this was, she didn't want to get any more entangled in it.

"I know that you require proof. And you shall have it."

He rolled up his sleeve and picked a letter opener off the desk. Mrs. Jones' eyes widened. She bolted for the door, hands fumbling for the doorknob, twisting it in vain.

"It won't do you any good—I've locked it with magic—and in any case, it's not you who's going to be hurt."

When she turned toward him, he slashed the blade across his forearm, flexing it to increase circulation. Blood ran in rivulets down his skin and pattered the floor.

"This is nothing compared to what they did to your son. When we found him, they'd already started the lobotomy. There was an ice pick"—he tapped his eye socket with the letter opener—"buried here up to the hilt."

Mrs. Jones sucked in a breath.

"Thankfully, my colleague is a master healer. She removed the blade, and with my help she patched up Josh's mind. It took her many tries, but I doubt anyone else would have done it in a million. I'm nowhere near as good, but I can still heal this."

He tossed the letter opener onto the desk, splattering blood across the wood, and held out his arm for her to see. Mrs. Jones stood transfixed as he drew his finger across the cut and willed the wound to close.

Mrs. Jones bolted to the desk and grabbed the letter opener. "Open the door and let me go."

"You mean this door?" Without touching the door, he magically opened it, just long enough for the people in the lobby to catch a glimpse of Nikolai's blood-splattered arm and Mrs. Jones holding a blade, and closed it again. It wouldn't hurt to have some leverage. "Magic is real, Mrs. Jones, and your son has it. He's intelligent. Did you know that? He may not talk, but he understands everything you say." Nikolai held out his hand for the letter opener. "Let us take him to where people understand him. Where he can be with his own kind and hone his craft."

Someone pounded on the door and a voice called out, "Dr. Featherline! Dr. Featherline, are you okay?"

Mrs. Jones' mind raced. For a moment he thought she'd back down, but then she straightened her stance.

"You've got everyone in this place fooled. That makes you a damn good con artist, and a damn good con artist can fake magic." She drew the blade across her palm and threw out her hand. "If you are what you say you are, heal *this*."

What a woman! How the hell had she married that lump outside? She might be worth a trip back to Omaha someday. Such a treasure deserved better than whatever her husband was giving her.

He reached forward and lifted her arm. "Not the best move. If I *were* a con artist, I could just claim you attacked me, or that you'd tried to kill yourself." He focused on the slender line weeping blood and willed it to heal. "Lucky for you, I was telling the truth." The flesh knit itself closed.

She stared at her arm and the letter opener clattered to the floor.

He took a handkerchief from his pocket, dipped it in the untouched coffee, and began wiping away the blood. A long thin scar now marred her beautiful brown skin. "Apologies. I'm no good with fixing scars."

"You did it. You really did it. And you think . . . you think Josh could learn this too? He can't talk, can't remember to use the restroom, he can't even tie his *shoes*"—she closed her eyes and shook her head—"and you're telling me he has magic and that he's . . . there? How can he be? He just sits there, spinning his toys, staring off into space. He's never given any indication that he understands us."

Funny how the existence of magic was easier for her to buy than the idea her son wasn't an imbecile.

She took a deep breath and continued, "How do you *know*? How can you be so certain?" Her hands flew to her mouth and she gave him the look he'd seen a thousand times before. "Dear Lord, you can read *minds*."

He let a smile tease the corner of his mouth. Smart woman. He liked that. "Josh seems particularly sensitive to modern technology. That could be why he struggles so much. He should be given the opportunity to learn and thrive in a more conducive environment."

The pounding on the door was getting louder. Frantic voices called out from the other side.

"Let me take Josh. Let me give him a chance to succeed."

"He's just a boy. My only boy."

"A boy who's already using magic haphazardly. He told me what happened with the police, how they suddenly flew off of him—that's what we call a telekinetic burst. It's a self-defense mechanism. Magic often reveals itself first under duress. I don't have to tell you that it can get practitioners into trouble. But with proper training Josh can certainly learn to tie his shoes and care for himself. If he stays here he'll be stifled at best and incarcerated or lobotomized at worst."

A tremor ran through Mrs. Jones and she nodded. "If you really think you can help Josh, then . . . then, yes, you can take him."

He tied the handkerchief around his bloody arm and opened the door. Dr. Hayes and an attendant burst into the room. Behind them, the receptionist and Mr. Jones looked on anxiously.

"Everything's fine," said Nikolai. "Just a little accident. I slipped and nicked myself, that's all."

Dr. Hayes breathed a sigh of relief and dismissed the attendant. "I, uh, presume everything is settled then?" He looked to Mrs. Jones. When she nodded, he continued as though she weren't there. "Betty tells me you asked her to have one of the cars brought up. I told you—I can't spare any right now." As he spoke, he rounded the desk and sat down. Sneaky little bastard, trying to reclaim his space.

"You're going to give me a vehicle, Dr. Hayes."

"What on earth makes you say that?"

"Because if you don't, I'll tell the papers how you can barely keep the lights on in this place, how you perform surgeries in the dark and can't even be counted on to finish them properly, and"—he paused for dramatic effect—"how you let my beautiful sister get through *multiple* locked doors into the men's ward, where she encountered a dangerous criminal who bludgeoned an attendant nearly to death."

Dr. Hayes gaped, mind whirling at the sudden change in his supposed colleague.

"You think your hospital can survive a scandal like that? Whose head do you think will be on the chopping block when the time comes to assign blame?" He took a step forward. "Look, I'll make it easy for you. I'll buy the car. As soon as I get back to my facility, I'll draw up the paperwork to send payment. But I'm taking those patients tonight."

Dr. Hayes sat in stunned silence for several moments. "I . . ." He shakily cleared his throat. "I'll have someone bring the car around."

Mrs. Jones nodded to Nikolai and exited the office. He was about to follow when Dr. Hayes spoke again.

"You *will* be back to pick up more patients, won't you?"

Nikolai shrugged. "We'll see."

LEADERSHIP

The crying set Medea's teeth on edge. She wanted desperately to conjure her sound shield but worried she'd forget to dispel it before they got to the farmhouse.

"Josh?" she said tentatively. "We're going to get you out of here, but I need you to walk with me to the lobby."

The keening continued as though he hadn't heard. Maybe she could lift him onto his feet. She wrapped the sobbing boy in her will and started to raise him off the gurney. Josh screamed and thrashed wildly. She hastily set him back down.

At this rate, she wasn't even sure she could wheel him out on the gurney without causing a ruckus. Sleep would knock him out, but what then? He'd probably still be in this state when she released it. It felt wrong to cast Calm. That was for people with bloodlust in their hearts, not this. One didn't solve grief by ignoring it. He needed time.

"I'm going to wait outside." In the corridor she settled on the ground and hugged her knees.

This was a mistake.

She should've known better. Anytime she gave free rein to her feelings, anytime she interfered with the lives of mortals, it all went to shit. What was she going to do with Josh? What was she going to do with *any* of them? They couldn't come to her island. Bad enough sharing her home with one person. She wouldn't do it with six. They had to go someplace else.

But where? Reasonable seemed okay and Chatterbox, though annoying, appeared sane enough, but Statue Girl heard voices, Josh couldn't talk and acted strangely, and Schadenfreude was an accused murderer who reveled in a teenage boy being lobotomized. A Magi town wouldn't want that burden. Nikolai might be able to find a home for a couple of them, but not all five, and it didn't solve the problem of their training. There was no telling what kind of damage they could cause in their ignorance. As much as she loathed the Academy, they did provide training to adults. But would it take students like these? And if they couldn't learn magic, what then? Would the Collective quietly put them down, as it did so many others who could not or would not toe the line? She chased the thoughts round and round but could think of no decent solution.

Eventually the crying stopped and the gurney creaked. Josh joined her in the hall, eyes on the floor, checker twirling between his fingers.

She got to her feet. "We need to meet my apprentice in the lobby. Do you know how to get there? Because I don't."

Josh struck off down the hall, which she took to be an affirmative. She winced as they entered a hall with the lights still buzzing overhead. She severed the connections and cast Light. Josh looked up a moment as though puzzled.

"Magic is nice," she said, "when you can control it."

They reached the lobby door without incident. The second they stepped through, a woman hurled herself at Josh.

"Joshua! My sweet boy! Are you alright? Is everything

okay?" The woman put her hands on his cheeks, forcing him to face her.

"He's fine," Medea mumbled, stepping away from the pair. Josh's distress was palpable, but it wasn't her place to intervene. She glanced around, searching for refuge, and spotted Nikolai leaning nonchalantly against the reception desk. She fled the commotion and made a beeline toward him.

Nikolai straightened. "Everything's settled." He held out a bundle and nodded toward a door. "Your clothes. Bathroom is that way if you want to change."

She hesitated. Even when she wore the Mundane dress inside out, the fabric wasn't that comfortable, not like the hospital uniform, which was soft and loose. If she wore it on the street it was apt to draw attention, but they'd be going to the farmhouse soon, or so she hoped, and then it wouldn't matter how she dressed.

Nikolai smirked. "Are you *really* considering wearing that thing?"

"No." Even to her, it sounded lame.

He laughed. "So she *does* lie!"

Heat crept into her cheeks and Nikolai laughed harder. She snatched the bundle of clothes and swept toward the restroom, his cackles hounding her every step of the way. He'd never let her live that down. It was a stupid thing to lie about. They both knew it, yet she hadn't wanted to give him the satisfaction of being right. He was already too smug by half.

She dressed quickly and tugged on her boots, startling momentarily when she rose and caught sight of herself in the mirror. She gazed at her reflection, more to give herself a reprieve before returning to the lobby than out of any desire to gauge her appearance. What was the point? She already knew what she looked like. The island had no mirrors—well, aside from the one Nikolai had installed in his bathroom—he was both smug *and* vain—and she couldn't recall the last time she'd seen herself in something other than water or a window.

Her flaxen hair was as straight as ever, though she could see little snarls beginning to form. It hadn't even been a full twenty-four hours since she'd canceled her detangling spell. She combed her fingers through her hair, wincing every time they snagged, until at last they flowed smoothly. Satisfied that her hair was in proper order and, more importantly, that Nikolai was no longer waiting to mock her, she exited the restroom.

The tension in her chest eased at the sight of him preoccupied with signing documents. When he finished and turned his attention to her, the mocking expression was blessedly absent.

"Come on." He nodded toward the front door, then projected his voice toward Josh and his family. "We'll be out front whenever you're ready."

They stepped into the chill night air. Goose bumps formed on Medea's exposed arms and calves, and she had to mentally slap herself to keep from using magic. Temperature control—yet another thing she'd be forgoing this week. She shivered and rubbed her arms.

"Would you care for my jacket?"

"No," she said reflexively. A negative was usually the safer option, but the chill *was* horribly distracting . . . "I mean yes."

He handed over his too-big coat and she tugged it over her shoulders. Her calves were unprotected but it was better than nothing. At least it didn't smell bad. Nikolai watched her with a self-satisfied smile.

"What?" she asked.

"Nothing. Just glad I could help."

He led her toward a blue car parked inside the gated courtyard. The car seated five—six at most if they packed in tightly—but Josh would take up half the back seat by himself. If she cast Volume Increase on it, they couldn't drive it to the farmhouse without possible contamination, not that they could take the Magi to the farmhouse anyway. Any errant spell could ruin the experimental data. What had she started? What the hell were they going to do?

"Relax." Nikolai gave her a knowing smile. "I took care of everything. The hospital is giving us one of their cars."

He hadn't used telepathy on her. She knew he hadn't—she would have felt it, wouldn't she? His coat was suddenly heavy and uncomfortable on her shoulders. She wanted to hand it back but feared the move would betray her unease. Maybe she could take it off once in the car, if it was warmer inside.

As if in answer, Nikolai opened the door. She tensed, but he only reached inside and withdrew a folded sheet of paper, which he spread on the hood of the car to reveal a map of Nebraska.

"What other gateways do you have in this state? Any located farther from big cities? Out in the wilderness?"

"I have a garden gateway near the northern border. The closest town was maybe a day's ride." She approached and scanned the modern map for landmarks she recognized. Ah, there was Valentine. She traced a line about forty miles west. A few small towns dotted the highway in between. "Here."

Nikolai circled the gateway. "Not too far by car if they need supplies."

He couldn't be serious. He wanted them to stay there? "I don't want people tromping through my plants."

"I'll ask them to tread carefully. Don't give me that look. They need a place to practice magic away from the Mundane. But they need shelter. Are there any buildings nearby?"

She considered whether to answer. The garden contained a variety of plants introduced to her by the Pawnee. A nomadic people who only used the land seasonally, they'd given her permission to take what she needed. At first she continued to encounter them on her brief forays to the garden, but their numbers dwindled and they eventually vanished. When she heard of the Homestead Act, she'd staked a claim on the spot to prevent others from doing so, though she considered herself merely a caretaker. She didn't mind sharing the location with apprentices, which were few and far between, but five people she barely knew? What if they drew attention to the place or ruined the land?

"They don't have to be right on top of the gateway," said Nikolai. "Just close enough that we can check on them."

The words were comforting, though the fact that he seemed to read her thoughts sent another chill up her spine.

"There's a sod house about a mile to the west," she offered. "But that doesn't solve the problem of who's going to look after them, who's going to train them. We have work to do. *I* don't have time. *You* don't have time."

"I have someone to train them," he said with a hint of a smile.

She waited for him to say who, but he stared at the map as though engrossed in thought. Finally, she blurted out, *"Well?"*

"You'll find out soon enough. The others will be here at any moment. You'll see as soon as—"

"No. You will tell me now. I don't like surprises, least of all when they involve my own . . ." She struggled to find a word for what the Magi were to her. "Project," she finished lamely.

"Project, eh? I thought you wanted to cut ties as soon as possible."

She opened her mouth and closed it again. What *did* she want? Not to train them. One apprentice was more than enough. They were an anomaly worth further study, but she had no interest in them outside of professional curiosity, though she still felt some guilt over what had happened to Josh. That didn't mean she wanted to form any lasting relationships with them. Already she could imagine them crowding around, asking how she was, expecting her to do the same, to care about their brief lives. What a personal hell that would be. She couldn't fake concern or rapport like Nikolai. She suspected he fed on that kind of attention, but for her, they would be leeches draining her dry.

"I want to study them further. Perhaps enlist them in our experiments later. Aside from that"—she took a deep breath—"I want nothing to do with them. But that doesn't mean I wish them *ill*." Lord knew they'd been through enough, especially Josh.

Nikolai waved a hand. "You have nothing to worry about. My instructor is perfect."

"Then who is it?"

He smiled. "Yoxtl."

Nikolai watched Medea closely. Fear, anger, revulsion—all flitted across her face at the mention of Yoxtl. The fear was of particular note. What did Medea have to fear from a spirit?

"Yoxtl?" she repeated, as though hoping he would correct her.

"You know it's been after me for a year to build it a following."

"So you're going to offer up the Magi? They know nothing of what a bargain with a spirit entails! And they don't need one. They have their own powers."

"Precisely. Even if I convince Mundanes to worship Yoxtl, their souls won't be forfeit until they die. That could take years—possibly decades—unless I speed up the process." He shot her a devilish grin. She didn't reciprocate, so he adopted a more contemplative expression and continued. "But I don't think Yoxtl's that bloodthirsty. The spirit will wait until its followers die naturally, and I'll be forced to perform parlor tricks to keep them loyal. If Yoxtl had a stable of Magi, they could cast spells without its help. They wouldn't *need* to give it their souls, just access to their abilities."

"Thereby relinquishing you from the burden."

"Just because I stand to benefit doesn't mean they won't either. Yoxtl gets five Magi for the price of one, they get training, and you get Yoxtl off the island. Everybody wins!"

She frowned. Doubtless she saw the sense of it, though it made her uncomfortable. "Is there no one else you can think of? Anyone at all?"

"Can *you*?"

"What about your friend, Harold?"

"*Harper* has his own life and quite enough secrets already. He also lives in a large Mundane city, or did you forget?"

"Right, right . . ." She was wavering. He had to tip the scale.

"You've been antagonistic toward Yoxtl ever since it saved my life. Is that why you hate it? Because it interfered where you wouldn't? Perhaps you'd prefer I died."

"Don't be ridiculous."

"You were perfectly fine with Yoxtl before then, and it's not like you don't have other spirits on your island. So if it's not that, what is it?"

"That is between me and Yoxtl." She closed her eyes and took a deep breath. "Maybe it would be for the best. We have no other options, and as you said, everyone wins."

A large white car pulled around the side of the building and parked behind the Chevy. Nikolai walked closer to look it over. It was perfect—two seats up front, a half bench in the middle wide enough to comfortably accommodate Josh, and a bench in the back that could sit two or three people.

An attendant emerged and handed him the keys. "She's all gassed up for yah."

"How do people get in back?" The car only had three doors—two in front and one in the rear, but the rear door was blocked by the back seat.

"Here." The attendant opened the front passenger door and folded the seat forward.

The hospital doors opened and the Magi filed out, led by an attendant. Gloria came first, eyes alert with suspicion. Doris chatted amicably with a frizzy-haired woman he didn't recognize. She had to be Bethany, the accused murderer who'd been absent from the dayroom during his interviews. Evelyn trailed behind with another attendant. She paused, a faraway expression on her face, and the attendant nudged her forward. They marched single file toward the white car.

Last came Josh and his parents. They shadowed him as though afraid he might bolt. Mrs. Jones made to take Josh's hand, but he ignored her and shambled toward Medea, who'd sagged against the Chevy like a wilted flower. Surprising she'd lasted this long, given they'd spent all day in a Mundane city.

"Okay," Mrs. Jones said to herself, her voice choked. "Okay."

"He'll be fine," said Nikolai. "I'll take good care of him."

She nodded and reached into her purse, extracting a slip of paper. "Here's our number. Please give us a call as soon as he's settled."

"There's no phone," Medea said flatly. Great, she was entering her snippy, don't-give-a-fuck part of the day.

Mrs. Jones stared in alarm. He quickly took the paper and steered her away from Medea.

"We try to live simply. As I told you, modern technology interferes with magic. We make a supply run into town every few weeks and I can call from a pay phone then."

She set her jaw. "Saturday, two o'clock, two weeks from now. If I don't hear from you—"

"Then I'm dead in a ditch somewhere, or will be when you find me." He winked and she gave a laugh.

"Darn straight."

"We best get going," said Mr. Jones.

Mrs. Jones threaded her arm through her husband's and strode toward the gates with the regality of a queen. Splendid woman.

Lovely curves, strong will, and a quick mind. Definitely worth getting to know better.

A woman's sharp cry tugged his attention back to the white car. Gloria stood with her arms out, barring entry to the vehicle.

"This is ridiculous! You can't transfer us without consulting our families. Something's not right."

"What's not right is you making a fuss," said an older attendant. "Now move!"

Nikolai strode over. "Thanks, I'll take it from here." *Go back inside.*

The attendants made for the hospital entrance without a backward glance. He waited until they were inside before addressing the Magi.

"I'll get straight to it. Magic exists and you all have it. We're not taking you to another hospital. We're breaking you out and taking you somewhere you can learn magic in peace."

Gloria met him with stony eyes. "You're insane. I don't know what kind of con you're pulling, but we're not going with you."

Before he could reply, Medea stepped forward. "We don't have time for this." She raised a hand, palm up, and the women shot into the air with startled gasps and cries. "What he says is true, so shut up and listen. Don't make me seal your mouths."

It was blunt even for her. When she lowered the women, they gawked at her in horror. All but Evelyn, who seemed more focused than usual.

"There's no need for threats." He directed the comment at Medea, who crossed her arms and leaned sourly against the Chevy. "We're all Magi here." He focused again on the patients. "You have magic, but it's untrained, which means you can't control when and how it manifests. It can show up in a number of ways." He pointed to Josh. "Knocking out lights or throwing back aggressors with telekinetic bursts." He looked to Doris and Evelyn. "Causing things to fly or break when upset."

"What about seeing ghosts?" Evelyn asked hopefully. "Demons? Can they be made to go away?"

Medea shook her head. "Spirits sometimes mess with mortals that way, but I have not sensed any pestering you."

"But you're not sure. There *could* be some."

Medea's face darkened at the perceived questioning of her abilities. Before she could respond, Nikolai interjected.

"Your instructor will help you sort out your magic from your schizophrenia."

Gloria looked from him to Medea. "You mean neither of you are training us?"

"I'm busy," Medea said flatly, ever the charmer. He should've asked her to wait in the car.

"I have someone different in mind. Someone even more powerful than us." He ignored Medea's are-you-fucking-kidding-me glare and stepped back from the cars until there was a sizable gap between himself and the Magi. With a flourish of his hand, he summoned wind into the space. Leaves and scattered litter danced within the cyclone as he chanted nonsense in Turkish, hoping it would sound sufficiently exotic to American ears. He ended with booming English: "I summon thee, oh great god Yoxtl!"

The fox-like spirit appeared at his side, black fur unaffected by the wind. The Magi took no notice, focusing on the cyclone before them, except for Josh, who stared directly at the spirit with a puzzled frown.

"What are you doing?" Yoxtl asked.

You're invisible, I presume? Nikolai projected the thought while doing his best to maintain the cyclone and chant more gibberish.

"They can't see or hear me." Yoxtl nodded to Josh. "That one can sense me though. Who are these people?"

Your new followers. He explained the situation, emphasizing that there were probably more Magi stashed in asylums around the country, ripe for the picking. Yoxtl's tail twitched as it stared at the patients, and Nikolai could see the spirit adding things up. This was an untapped source of potential followers, people who'd been rejected by society and thus were more open to influence.

"What have you told them about me?" it asked.

Only that you're more powerful than me or Medea, and that you're going to train them. I didn't know how you wanted to play this.

Yoxtl frowned. "That's a lot to live up to. The soul magic Medea gave me is almost gone, and I can't have them knowing I'm this weak. Think I'll just be a 'servant of the god Yoxtl' for now." The spirit stepped into the center of the cyclone. "Can you do a lightning strike in the middle here?"

Sure. Nikolai changed the air current, blowing it outward toward himself and the Magi, whipping their hair and clothes. *"Fulmen!"* He didn't need the incantation any longer, but as Medea had once told him, it added to the show. Lightning struck the ground and the spirit made itself visible.

"The great god Yoxtl has sent me to aid thee!" The booming voice was horribly mismatched with the tiny body. Why hadn't it chosen a more impressive form?

"Is it just me," said Bethany, "or does it look like a fox?"

Gloria cocked her head at Yoxtl's tail. "That or a weird cat crossed with a raccoon."

"Awww," cooed Doris. "It's so cute! Come here, little fella." She knelt and patted her legs.

Yoxtl flew at her—tail bristling, amber eyes blazing with golden light. Doris fell backward.

"Listen, you! I am the servant of the GREAT GOD YOXTL. I only took this form to avoid frightening you. Disrespect me again and you will find my next form far less pleasing!"

"Oh!" Doris got to her feet and nervously brushed off her uniform. "I'm so sorry."

"That's better," said Yoxtl, relaxing its fur. "Now pick me up and scratch my ears."

Doris gently lifted the spirit, cradling it against her, and gave its head a scratch.

"Definitely a cat mix," Gloria muttered. She looked at Nikolai. "And this thing will be teaching us?"

"The spirit speaks for the god Yoxtl and can be referred to by that name."

"Yoxtl." She turned the word over in her mouth.

"It's a god of southern Mexico, often overshadowed by the Aztecs. I know the servant doesn't look like much, but it knows magic and can guide you in learning to control your powers."

She didn't look convinced.

"I know it's a lot to take in, especially on such short notice, and I hate to throw even more at you, but I was wondering if you'd mind driving?"

"Driving?"

"To the countryside. Medea has a place where you can safely train. I'd like someone who's responsible and good behind the wheel. If you're not comfortable, I completely understand. Doris mentioned she can drive—"

"No!" Gloria shot a nervous glance over her shoulder, but Doris and the others were chatting with Yoxtl. "I mean, no, I don't mind. Where are we headed?"

"Medea can show you on the map." He directed her toward the Chevy, then projected his voice to the clustered Magi. "Everyone, please find a seat. You too, Josh."

Gloria joined Medea at the Chevy while Josh ambled over to the white car.

"Now just hold on a minute," said Bethany. "You expect us to ride alone with *him*?"

He waited half a beat for Yoxtl to take charge, but it only

peered at Bethany curiously from Doris' arms. Apparently he had to do everything himself.

"There's five of you. Six if you count Yoxtl. That's hardly alone. And yes."

Evelyn and Doris shrugged and climbed into the vehicle, settling onto the back bench. Yoxtl perched between them and tried to strike up a conversation. Josh studied the car, red checker spinning frantically between his fingers. His gaze alternated between the middle seat, which would sandwich him between two groups of white women, and the ostensibly forbidden front.

"It's alright, Josh. Either seat is fine, though I think the middle would give you more room."

Josh offered no acknowledgment but squeezed inside with a look of relief. Doris wrinkled her nose and scooted closer to Evelyn.

Nikolai moved the front seat back into position and smiled at Bethany. "All yours."

She glared back defiantly. "I *said*, I'm not riding with a—"

"Shut up and listen." He glowered at her, then transferred his gaze to Evelyn and Doris. "You too. All of you. I don't care how you lived before. I don't care how you got here. This is all you need to know—you're Magi, and Magi take care of one another. It doesn't matter what they look like or where they're from or what language they speak. Because when it comes down to it, it's us against *them*." He pointed to the psychiatric hospital.

"*They* locked you up and put you in straitjackets. *They* drugged and electrocuted you. *They* threatened to stab your brain." He looked at each of them in turn. Bethany tried to interject, but he cut across her. "*They* blamed you for the death of your son. And when you couldn't handle the grief, when you were no longer a 'good little wife,' *they* threw you in here."

The color drained from Bethany's face and she took a step back.

"Mundanes did this to you. Non-magic folk. They don't understand you. They've *never* understood you. And they *will never* understand you."

He gave them a moment to let that sink in, then pointed to Josh. "You think they wouldn't do to you what they tried to do to him? Think again. Mundanes like their women complacent. Your job is to stand there, look pretty, and make babies. The gifts you've been born with are a threat to that. You push back against the prison they've built for you, and they will cut out whatever pieces they can to get you back in line."

Bethany wept softly, eyes downcast. The other women watched him as though entranced—even Gloria and, to his surprise, Medea. Doris had swapped places with Evelyn and rolled down the window to hear better. Josh didn't look up, but the checker made slow, steady revolutions. Yoxtl stared from the back seat, face unreadable. A tendril of thought reached him, and it was as though the spirit whispered from his shoulder. *What are you doing?*

He ignored the question. This was right, he could feel it. He'd always had a way with people, but these Magi were different— clean slates with no preconceptions of how magical society ought to be. They'd be completely isolated where they were going. Why not take the opportunity to shape them as he saw fit? A world of possibilities unfurled. To hell with Yoxtl, he could build an empire from this.

He pointed again to Josh, more forcefully this time. "*He* is not the enemy. Mundanes are. And when they come for you again— which they *will*—with fetters disguised as lace and gold, you have the choice to submit and be used again, or stand tall and fight with other Magi at your side. With the power you wield *together*, you'll be unstoppable."

Gloria took a step forward, determination and longing in the set of her jaw.

He leaned into it. "Whatever happens next, remember that you're *family* now. You might have your differences, even disagreements, but at the end of the day, you have to rely on one another, for no one else will come to your rescue. This world, the Mundane world, is dangerous. There are people who would kill you simply for being what you are, but to deny your abilities is a fate worse than death, for it makes you a danger to yourself and others. You must protect one another."

He wielded his gaze like a sword, aiming it at Bethany and stretching the silence until the others were forced to look too. She glanced up and withered to find herself impaled by so many eyes. He'd have no more resistance from her. He softened his voice.

"I don't mean to frighten you. Tonight should be a happy occasion. This is a start of a new life for you—all of you." He extended a hand to Bethany. She took it and allowed him to lead her into the car.

Yoxtl shot him a sour expression from the back seat, then turned its charm on the ladies. Bethany smiled wanly at some question, then stared vaguely ahead.

Gloria was suddenly at his side. "Are you sure you can't train us?" There was a yearning in her voice that had nothing to do with why women usually approached him.

He offered an apologetic smile. "I wish I could, but duty calls, unfortunately. Did Medea show you where you're headed?"

"Yes. This place you have us going to is in the middle of nowhere and doesn't have any amenities. How are we supposed to survive? It's almost November. We need proper shelter. We need access to food and medical care and—"

"Magic will take care of several of those things." He paused. How long would it take them to learn how to summon food? Cast spells for warmth? Well, he knew how much mana was required for that. And healing definitely took time to learn. He put a hand to his chin as though considering. "It wouldn't hurt for you to have a buffer to alleviate the pressure of learning spells quickly. Is there a department store nearby where we could pick up supplies? Something with camping gear and winter clothing?"

"Yes. But this late they're closed."

He smiled. "That won't be a problem."

They each went to their vehicles, Gloria leading the way in the white car and Nikolai following in the Chevy. Medea rode beside him in silence for a time. When they pulled onto the main road, she spoke.

"Your speech. That was—"

"Amazing?"

"Frightening. I've seen men like you lead others to their deaths too many times to count. Did you use telepathy?"

He smirked. "No need. I'm just that good."

She rolled her eyes.

He turned the Chevy onto a wider street. "Remember, most people are just sheep waiting for someone to come along and tell them what's what and that everything's going to be okay. They don't want to think about, well, *anything* really. They'd much rather hand the reins to someone else."

"By that definition I'm a sheep. I foisted their care onto you, after all."

"Only because you couldn't be bothered."

"Isn't that the same thing?"

"No." Her comparison was irksome. Yes, she'd been completely out of her element here, but she wasn't a sheep. She just had a different skill set—magic, not people. "You discarded a Useful tool because it didn't fit your hand. You passed it to someone you knew could wield it properly."

She laughed ruefully. "And then you passed it over to Yoxtl." She pressed her forehead firmly against the window and gazed at the darkened buildings. "How well do you think *that* will go?"

"They'll be fine," he lied. "Are you okay? You seem exhausted."

She took a deep breath and exhaled, fogging the glass. "Today was hard. Being away from home, the sights and sounds, all the people, all the *interactions*, and then the thing with Josh—it's taken a lot out of me. I'm tired. And hungry. I hardly ever notice when I need to eat, but the past few hours I've been famished."

"You can summon something now."

She waved a limp hand. "Dinner was satisfactory. I just want to get to the test site and get settled. I need to know what's going to happen next. Right now . . . too many variables."

"We'll be on our way soon enough. Look, here we are."

The white car pulled to the curb and he parked behind it. A department store with dark windows towered to their right.

"Why don't you stay here? I'll get done as quickly as I can."

She didn't respond but drew her legs up onto the seat and then under the coat. He left her in the Chevy and went to meet the women at the store entrance.

"Josh not coming?" he asked.

"We tried to get him out of the car," Gloria said, "but he got agitated, so I told the girls to leave him. What about Medea?"

"She's out of sorts. All this"—he gestured to the streetlights and buildings—"can impact magic-users. That's why we have to get you settled out in the middle of nowhere."

He approached the door and waved his hand theatrically. *"Recludo."* He pulled the door open and cast a globe of light in his palm. The women gasped.

"Oh, this is exciting!" Doris squealed as they entered the store. Yoxtl perched upon her back and shot him a look of reproach as it passed.

He positioned himself at the counter. "Everyone pick a wide-mouthed purse and bring it to me."

"Wouldn't duffel bags be better?" asked Gloria.

"If you like. Just make sure the opening is big on whatever you grab. Take this." He passed the globe of light to Gloria and conjured another.

The women dispersed and he gave the register a curious peek. Empty. Honestly, people had no trust. He closed the till and a black shadow leapt onto the counter.

"What do you want?"

Yoxtl's tail bristled. "You stole them from me. Every last one."

Don't you need to have something before it can be stolen? He gazed levelly at the spirit. "I had to get Bethany in the car somehow. All I did was convince her that it was in her best interest to join us."

"By propping yourself up as leader!"

"Not at all. If you remember, I told them they'd need to rely on one another." They both knew it was a play. On a subconscious level, the Magi internalized another message—that if he were the one offering them power, then he alone had the ability to grant it.

"But not me. Nothing about how I'd protect them."

"Because you can't. What happens if they do magic in public and attract the attention of witch hunters? What if they expect you to protect them? I won't set them up to fail."

"No, you'll only set *me* up to fail." The spirit's amber eyes burned.

"They might love me now, but soon I'll be out of sight and mind. You'll be the one teaching them to feed themselves. If there's one thing I've learned, it's that children cling to the parent they're with, not the one who's always away."

"Or maybe they'll take the commonplace for granted and idealize that which they never see."

"What do you expect me to do? *Someone* has to set them up, and you lack the magic to do it yourself."

"I *expect* you to defer to me as leader."

He would've laughed if it hadn't been so irritating. "That's not how leadership works. Leaders *lead*. They—"

Didn't ask for things. They made things happen. Yoxtl was cunning, but it had always been small-time. No wonder the conglomerate of Aztec spirits refused to let it join. When they killed its followers, Yoxtl didn't establish a new religion elsewhere. Instead it hid in the jungle for centuries and latched on to the first Magi to pass by. The spirit had contrived to weasel a following out of him but made no other moves to better its situation.

He was the one who'd freed the Magi, gotten them a car, convinced them to work together. And the speech! How he'd missed swaying a crowd. At the Academy, he'd clawed his way up the social ladder from nothing. He'd had half a dozen dueling partners, twice as many lovers, and a network of people feeding him information on staff and students. In Haven, his gravitational pull had ensnared the younger generation. He'd been the one teaching them, spicing up their otherwise dreary lives. For years he'd feasted on a buffet of devotion and influence. This trip was a stark reminder of how much he'd given up to train with Medea.

"Leaders what?" prompted Yoxtl.

Even now, the creature looked to him for guidance, rather than simply taking what it wanted. Propping the spirit up was blasphemy.

But it wasn't the time to cultivate his political power. He only had one day off a week—hardly time to train Magi, let alone build an empire. In eight years or so—ugh, that was so *long*—when training was over, he'd be free to do as he pleased. For now, he had priorities: seduce Medea and learn immortality. And it all started with getting Yoxtl off his back, even if the spirit wasn't fit to lead a tea party. He swallowed the wrongness of passing the reins to such an unworthy creature and put on an accommodating face.

"Nothing. You're right. I've been sloppy. I'll start invoking your name when I perform magic, or make it look like you're casting the spells."

"That's more like it!" Yoxtl said cheerily.

Nikolai wanted nothing more than to bash in its skull, or whatever was the spirit equivalent.

Bethany and Doris returned with purses. Gloria arrived a moment later, coaxing Evelyn along.

"Found her wandering around, mumbling to herself." She tossed several duffel bags on the counter. "She can use one of these. Stay with us, okay, hun?"

Evelyn nodded vaguely, eyes wandering about the store, then squeezed between Gloria and Doris, sending nervous glances over her shoulder.

Nikolai pulled a bag over and demonstrated the volume-expanding spell, this time invoking Yoxtl, who attempted to appear Useful by making the bag glow temporarily.

"I'm creating about a car trunk's worth of space in here. You can pack anything that fits through the mouth of the bag. You won't be able to do this on your own yet, but it shows you what's possible. Fill these with necessities only. Camping gear, warm clothes. No food. No first aid stuff."

Gloria raised an eyebrow.

"Magic," he said. "I'll fill this one with enough food to get you started." He handed all but one of the bags back. "And, Gloria, pack some things for Josh." He eyed Evelyn, who'd begun to wander again. "Evelyn too."

"I got her," said Yoxtl. Gloria looked at the spirit with some surprise, then nodded and made her way to the men's section. Yoxtl trotted to Evelyn's side.

Bags stocked, they returned to the cars. Gloria asked Josh to step out and held up a jacket to his chest. Josh shook his head and backed away.

"At least try it on. I need to know if it fits."

"Oh, don't worry," said Doris. "He'll wear it if he gets cold enough."

Josh shook his head more vigorously and slapped the coat out of Gloria's hand. She turned a worried expression to Nikolai. "He's going to freeze come winter if we can't get him in some decent clothes."

"What's the problem, Josh?" asked Nikolai.

It's stealing. You guys stole those clothes!

I left money in the till.

No, you didn't! I watched you open the register and you didn't put anything inside.

"He's upset because we didn't pay."

Gloria frowned. "How do you know that?"

"We have a unique way of communicating. Give me a minute." Nikolai returned to the Chevy and tapped on Medea's window. She raised her head and stared at him bleary-eyed. "Whatever spell you used to pay for the appliances, I need you to do it again."

She blinked a few times, then rolled down the window. "Bring me something that has either a lot of mercury or a lot of carbon." Her head slumped back down.

"Gloria," he called. "Bring me a bag of charcoal!"

Gloria arrived with the bag. He took it and sent her back to the white car so she wouldn't see whatever Medea was about to do.

She stripped the bag off and tossed it aside. The charcoal briquettes hung suspended in the air. She cupped her hands around the black mass, her brow furrowing in concentration. He sensed mana flowing into the space between her hands, though nothing appeared to be happening. Eventually he noticed bits of the charcoal dissipating near the bottom. They flowed downward like sand through the pinch point of an hourglass and reformed into something clear and solid. It took a good ten minutes to get through all the charcoal, but when she was done, Medea had several small diamonds in her hand. She thrust them at him as if they were of no consequence.

"When we get back," he said, "you're teaching me that spell."

"It takes more focus than what you have."

"And the mercury? What would you have made with that?"

"Gold. But that takes more mana *and* focus than what you have."

He returned to the white car and held up the diamonds to Josh. "See these? I'm going to leave them inside in one of the cash registers. That way we're paying for what we take."

Josh shook his head vigorously. *You stole the charcoal from the store. You can't pay for things you stole with other things you stole.*

"But we increased their value. Diamonds are worth exponentially more than charcoal."

Bethany laughed. "If he doesn't want them, I'll take them."

You didn't have permission. What if they don't want diamonds? What if they don't understand why they were left there? You can't just walk in and take things without asking. It's wrong.

He squelched the desire to embed the diamonds into Josh's face.

"You had no say in what we did. There's no sense in freezing to death over it. If you want to pay the store back, do it. *Survive, learn magic, and pay them back as soon as you're able.*"

Josh twitched at the telepathic command. *What was that?*

He opened his mouth to evade the question with one of his own, but Doris leaned over the front seat to chime in.

"Think of it as a loan, big guy. Banks loan money, don't they? And people pay them back all the time!" Her tone was singsong and light.

Josh crossed his arms and turned away from Doris. *I'm not*

stupid. Tell her. If you take bank money without asking, it's still stealing.

"Stop talking down to Josh. He understands everything you say." This was getting too complicated. Leaving Josh behind might be the only option. That or simply letting him freeze. It would be his own damned fault. The bastard was as stubborn as Medea.

Medea . . .

He strode back to the Chevy and banged on the window, startling her awake. The look she gave him was murderous.

"I need your help. We have a situation with Josh."

She clutched the coat he'd given her tight about her and pushed open the car door, nearly catching her arm when it swung back. She rubbed her eyes with one hand, yawned, and stumbled toward the white car.

"What problem?" she asked.

"Josh refuses to wear any of the clothes we bought to keep him warm, because they're stolen, and he doesn't want to use the diamonds either."

Medea said nothing, simply shook off the coat and held it out in front of her. The women gasped as the fabric grew, enlarging the coat. Every so often, Medea glanced at Josh as though sizing him up. When the coat was several sizes larger, she rubbed a hand over it and muttered something, then tossed it to Josh.

"That's his coat." She jerked her head toward Nikolai. "Though for all I know, it's stolen as well. It won't fit perfectly, but I've added a temperature regulating enchantment. Speaking of which . . ." She took a step back and held her hands out in front of her, palms out.

"Oh!" Doris startled. "Do you feel that? It suddenly got all warm."

"You're right!" said Bethany.

Nikolai extended his senses to the car. It felt like Medea was dumping mana into the frame.

She dropped her hands. "The enchantment should be good for a year. If you get *frigus*, retreat to the *currus*." She'd yawned, slurring her words so badly that he almost missed the Latin, and wobbled back to the Chevy.

"Can *she* train us?" Gloria asked.

He forced a smile. "I'm afraid you're not ready for those lessons yet. Yoxtl will take excellent care of you."

Gloria glanced at the spirit enshrined on Doris' lap enjoying an ear scratch, unable to hide her skepticism. Better add something to cheer her up.

"But that doesn't mean you should travel empty-handed." He passed her the diamonds. "For any incidentals. I'll check in on you when I can," he lied. Best to cut ties with all of them. So much for getting to know Mrs. Jones better, but then he had another woman to focus on at the moment.

He returned to the Chevy to find Medea snoring. She roused long enough to give him directions and promptly fell back asleep.

2 2

HOME ON THE RANGE

Nikolai studied his sleeping mentor in the rearview mirror. Medea had curled into a fetal position on the back seat, one hand dangling over the side. He memorized the line of her collarbone and the curve of her hip. Easy enough to imagine her head in his lap or his hand sliding up her bare leg, disappearing under the folds of her dress. One day she'd welcome his touch. He shifted his gaze to the inky terrain passing by.

Despite his annoyance at coming on this trip, there was no reason he couldn't use it to his advantage. In the Magi world, Medea was a paragon. Out here, with her ridiculous self-imposed restrictions, she'd been forced to rely on him a number of times. Once they got to the farmhouse, she wouldn't be able to use magic at all. He knew more of Mundane things and had physical strength to compensate for not using magic. If there were any time to prove himself Useful and win her affection, it was now.

Delicate fingers of light had just begun to appear on the horizon when Medea woke. She stretched and yawned, then climbed into the front seat, nearly kicking him in the head with her thick boots.

"Pull over," she said, rubbing her eyes.

He maneuvered the Chevy onto the dirt shoulder. A dilapidated fence of sagging barbed wire bordered a vast field of grass. This stretch of road looked the same as any other. Here on the American plains, there were no hills or mountains to differentiate the landscape.

Medea turned to him with a preemptively accusing expression. "We're nearly there. From here on, no magic without my say-so. *None.* Dispel that." A nod indicated the illusion masking the scars on his face.

For the first several months he'd worn it, the illusion had to be recast every morning, having fallen off during his sleep. Maintaining it took no effort now, and when he attempted to release the spell, it was like prying open fingers cramped stiff with cold.

"Just let go!" Medea burst out after a minute.

"I'm *trying.*"

She made an exasperated noise and grabbed his chin, jerking it forward. Her grip was too hard, almost painful, but his body warmed at the contact. Deft fingers picked apart the spell disguising his mouth and nose.

"Honestly, no one cares how you look," she muttered.

Medea wasn't one for false platitudes. If she said something, she meant it. When she said no one cared about his looks, it meant *she* didn't care about his looks, either because she didn't care about him or because she didn't see him in that way. He had his work cut out for him, though it was a small comfort that she didn't find him hideous.

She gave his face one last critical glance, turning his chin before finally letting it go. "Do you have anything enchanted on your person? Pouch? Jewelry? Tattoos?"

"Tattoos?"

"Yes, tattoos. I took mine off the night before we left. But from your expression, I gather you don't have any."

"No, I don't." He'd often wondered what was under that red dress she usually wore, but he never imagined there'd be tattoos. Is that why she preferred long sleeves? And how the hell had she taken them *off*?

"We'll have to get you some when you're older. They work like any other enchanted item, holding spells it might otherwise be difficult for you to cast. Unfortunately, few masters of the craft remain, and they lack for apprentices. When they die, their knowledge will go with them." She chuckled bitterly. "Maybe we *shouldn't* wait until you're older."

"But the knowledge is still there. You have a whole section on tattoos." Back when he'd first toured the library, he'd scoffed at her eccentric interests, not understanding how they were connected to magic, nor how Useful many of them were. "We could take the designs to a shop—"

She hissed and gave him a look like he'd just shat in her lap. "You can't just take them to a Mundane shop and expect them to *work*."

"I wasn't suggesting a *Mundane* enchant them, only that they complete the artwork. *You* could enchant them after the fact."

Her mouth fell open and she stared at him in abject horror. "That's not how it's done! And I am not a master."

He was careful to keep a neutral expression even though he wanted to roll his eyes. "You're the most powerful mage in the world. And you have notes to draw from."

"That doesn't make me a—" She rubbed her face and shifted in her seat. "Look, I may have an unsurpassed breadth of knowledge, but I'm not a master at everything. Take telepathy—I'm a journeyman at best."

"Only because you dislike the magic. If you applied yourself, I'm sure you could do far better."

"It's more than that. Whenever I meet a fellow master, I feel like an impostor, for they have a level of skill I can't hope to obtain in the few scant years I train with them." Her lips pinched together a moment, then she said, "Look out the window and tell me what you see."

He complied, though he already knew what was out there—a whole lot of nothing. Occasionally they'd passed trees, usually alongside a river, but it was all grass, grass, and more grass, whether natural pastureland or fields of wheat. "I see grass."

"I see a land barren of magic, in more ways than one." Medea spread her hands wide and gestured toward the field beyond the barbed wire.

The horizon became dotted with dome-shaped earthen homes. Smoke puffed from the center of each dwelling as people clad in leather and deerskin went about their business. The figures were faceless and oddly blurred, as though Medea had forgotten what they looked like, and he found himself extrapolating detail from body movements. Some of them unloaded bundles of corn. Others sat in groups, chatting as they husked. A man leading a horse stopped momentarily to check its hoof. Three women worked to skin a buffalo and cut its flesh into strips, while young children chased one another, full of life and laughter.

"After Thomas left, I traveled west. I had wanted to do so earlier, but he was always distrustful of the natives. I tried to learn their languages and their magic. To learn a magic, *really* learn it, requires an apprenticeship and years of study. I could have stayed in one place, focused on a single tribe, become a master, but in the end I cast my net wide. My goal then was to get as much information down as I could before it was gone, and I still didn't make it to half the tribes I intended."

Medea stared into the distance, idly pinching the tips of her fingers. "It hasn't even been that long, and now look at this place." She waved her hand and the illusion vanished. "Civilizations die. I'm used to it. But there is knowledge stored in people, not all of which can be easily transferred with a few words and a pen. That is what we stand to lose. Even if ambient magic recovers, who will be around to take it up?"

He didn't understand her concern. Who cared if others took part in magic, so long as there was enough for the two of them? All that mattered was being on top. Then again . . .

He looked out over the plain, to where the illusion had stood. The people had been wiped out, along with their magic, and replaced with a people who knew nothing of such things. "Those spells Yoxtl gave you from the Aztecs—how many were dead?"

"More than half. I would have thought the spirit made them up to give the appearance of helping if I'd not encountered the pattern before. There's a definite correlation between dead spells and dead peoples."

"Do you think there has to be a minimum number of casters with knowledge of a spell for it to work?"

"I've considered that. Sometimes I feel I should run into the middle of a city and start casting. No one believes in magic anymore, not really. But even if such a show garnered interest, what would I tell them? Sorry, you lack the innate ability for magic? The scale has tipped too far in the wrong direction, and now you must bow down before a spirit to cast anything?" She shook her head.

"It wouldn't work. Casting magic in public, I mean. They'd be awed for a day and then forget about it. Or they'd start to doubt they'd seen it at all, rationalizing it to be something else. People are perfectly willing to believe in luck and god subtly influencing their lives, but the big, flashy magic you can do—they wouldn't be able to wrap their heads around it, not unless they saw it every day." He didn't add that any government would probably take a keen interest and seek to subdue her.

"You're right. In that respect, it's good we found the Magi. Perhaps if more could be located and trained, we might stem the tide, if that is indeed what's causing the downfall. Though I suspect it is more of a by-product. Oh, how I wish I had started tracking this all sooner!"

"No use fretting about it now. We'll find out the cause soon enough." He reached over and patted her hand, not out of any particular desire for physical contact but because it might mean something to her. Women liked that kind of thing and she seemed to be having a moment.

Medea jerked her hand away and rubbed the spot he'd touched as though it were tainted. "Don't touch me."

"Sorry, you looked as though you needed comforting."

She crossed her arms and leaned back. "The only kind of *comfort* I need is for you to perform your duties. I cannot do this experiment by myself. Follow my instructions explicitly, for if you do not, the whole experiment may be compromised. A sample size of one is poor enough, but it should give us a place to start, and depending on what we discover, we can come back here with more Magi later."

He cleared his throat. "Shall we get going then?"

"Not yet. I still have work to do."

"Work" entailed triple-checking the car and its contents for enchantments. Satisfied there were none, she summoned a host of food—butter, cheese, eggs, dried meat, and fruit—things that would survive without refrigeration. He expressed concern when she didn't summon any bread, but she declared it wouldn't be needed. When everything was wrapped in cloth and stowed in the bags, she bid him drive a mile before turning down a bumpy dirt road.

They arrived at a small two-story farmhouse. Faded yellow paint peeled away from the siding, exposing the wood to the elements and inviting plants to take up residence between the boards, which they had done in numerous places. Many of the windows had long ago lost their glass, and the front porch sagged, threatening to fall. No doubt it would be worse on the inside. He glimpsed an outhouse around back and sighed internally. It was almost like Medea had a vendetta against proper housing.

They unloaded the trunk of the car, or rather he unloaded while Medea went inside to check the rooms. He half expected the structure to collapse when she opened the front door. The ancient floorboards groaned in protest as he followed with a load of bags. He paused to let his eyes adjust to the dim interior. The first floor consisted of a living area adjoined by a kitchen. Spiders had taken up residence in every corner of the ceiling. Dark brown pellets and the faint scent of ammonia hinted at rodents. A dusty rocking chair sat before a fireplace. He made a mental note to check the flue.

A startled cry erupted from the kitchen and he arrived to find Medea glaring at the cabinets.

"Rats," she said. "We'll have to use the cabinet on that side. This one has a hole in the back."

"Do you want me to kill them for you?"

She gave him a funny look. "I can kill a *rat*."

"I didn't mean to insult you," he said, setting the bag of food on the rickety kitchen table. "Only I'm younger and probably have more recent hunting experience."

Anyone could kill a cat or a dog. They weren't wary enough of humans, though they learned to be once the food ran low. Rats were intelligent and cautious. They took note of how their fellows died and avoided making the same mistake. Hunting rats took *skill*, and he'd been quite good at it back in his youth. He pushed the unpleasant memory aside and went to get the rest of the bags.

When he was done unloading the car, Medea handed him a few rags and bid him dust off the scattered furniture. "Then take care of the cobwebs. No magic," she reminded him, before exiting the building.

He'd wanted her to rely on him, and yet he couldn't help but be irritated that he was the only one working, especially when she was making him perform such homey tasks. Couldn't she at least have asked him to do something strenuous, like chop firewood? He stewed until she returned carrying a makeshift broom. She'd bound stiff grass to a stick with twine, and it occurred to him that she was probably more used to roughing it than he was. He'd been poor, yes, and without food, but never without shelter, and he'd grown up in a large city. But Medea was over a thousand years old. Despite having magic, she'd lived the majority of her life without access to modern conveniences or factory-produced products. Perhaps she wasn't as out of her element as he'd supposed. He liked the way she'd seen a problem and solved it.

"Why are you looking at me like that?" She paused her sweeping to frown at him accusingly. Damn, that one didn't fit on his carefully calibrated scale. He'd have to reorder everything if he were to add it—call it a #3.5 for now.

"I just never see you clean."

"That's because I hate it. Seems pointless when everything just gets dirty again." She blew a strand of hair out of her face, then irritably flung the rest over her shoulder. "At least at home I have spells to manage the worst of it."

Which wasn't saying much, given the state of her kitchen when he first arrived on the island.

They worked in companionable silence and within an hour they had the house as hospitable as they could make it. Upstairs were two bedrooms, one with an old dresser and the other with a rotted mattress. Medea took her time deciding between them and eventually chose the one with a dresser.

"Meet me in the kitchen," she said, digging around one of her bags. "We have to complete the control experiment before the delivery arrives." She frowned into her bag, then shot him an accusing glare. "Did you go through my things?"

"I needed to write you a note and I knew you'd have a paper and pen. By the way, there's a surprise for you in the other bag."

He smiled and left before she could ask what, savoring the thought of her upending everything, searching in vain for some trickery only to find a stash of new books. However, when she joined him in the kitchen she said nothing, merely deposited an armload of items on the counter and grabbed a pot from the cupboards. She left again just as suddenly, front door creaking behind her. Had she resisted the temptation to search her bags? Or did she wish to avoid thanking him?

He rose to examine the items she'd dumped on the counter—pen and paper, notebook, stopwatch, Bible. The notebook contained hand-drawn grids. Most of the squares were blank, aside from the row at the top, which contained letters that were probably some sort of abbreviation. It offered no clues as to what data she intended to collect. The stopwatch was more modern than what he would have suspected, as was the Bible—a recent edition, thick, with a hard cover.

The front door creaked and Medea came into the kitchen with a pot full of water. She'd covered it with twigs for some reason, and the act of balancing them on top caused her to slosh water over the sides.

"Let me help you with that."

"I've got it. I've got it."

Despite her protests, he snatched the twigs and put them on the table. She set the pot on the counter with a huff and blew a stray lock of hair out of her face.

"Beaker, beaker . . . Where are my beakers?" she muttered. In a whirl she was out of the kitchen and headed back upstairs. She returned with several beakers and began filling them with water.

"The goal of today," she said, sticking a thermometer inside one beaker and jotting down the temperature, "is to get a baseline of how well your magic performs under normal circumstances. I'm going to have you cast a variety of spells. They will be rudimentary, they will be boring, and you'll be casting them repeatedly. Please do not cast anything outside of what I tell you to, and only *when* I tell you. Do you understand?"

"Yes." He thought she would explain further, but she launched immediately into the exercises. Each had to be completed ten times before they moved on to the next. All the while, Medea stood with the stopwatch and notebook, jotting things down. First he had to summon bread—not just any bread, but a particular type of rye. She inspected every loaf before setting it on the counter. After that he had to set the tip of a twig on fire. Whenever he succeeded, she blew it out and snapped off the burnt tip. She placed the Bible on the edge of the table closest to him and told him to push it across with telekinesis.

His precision wasn't the best, but he got it reasonably straight with the opposite edge. "Why a Bible?"

"I needed a heavy book that's both readily accessible and that I don't mind getting damaged."

"Damaged from what? Falling off the table?"

"I don't *know*. But it's important we keep things consistent. I bought multiple copies, just in case something happens to this one." She slid the Bible back to its starting position. "Again. By the way, if at any point you feel mana exhaustion approaching, tell me immediately."

The monotony of the tasks began to chafe. "Can you tell me anything more about what we're doing?"

"I told you, it's to get a baseline for how well your magic performs."

"Yes, but why?"

Medea stopped scribbling and peered at him curiously. "I really shouldn't tell you. It could influence the results of the experiment. Now, please, continue."

He bit back his frustration and finished the task. Medea exchanged the Bible for a white sheet of paper.

"I want you to create an illusion of a black line. Bisect the page directly in half the long way."

As it wasn't a school of magic he'd studied, his first few attempts were barely visible. Medea had him keep trying through faded, wobbly, and broken lines.

On the twentieth try he asked, "Isn't this contaminating your test site?" Hopefully she'd disregard this particular spell.

"None of these spells are very powerful. Are you saying you can't cast magic meant for a novice?"

Cute how she thought to use his competitiveness against him, but one didn't con a con man. "Maybe I just have the same distaste for it as you do for telepathy."

He expected to see her flush with embarrassment, but she only stared at him, puzzled. "I never would've thought you'd admit to something like that," she said, and he realized his error. His words had betrayed an old hurt. As if scenting weakness, she sat down across from him with a grave expression. He leaned back and feigned disinterest. She seemed unsure, sitting quietly for a time, pinching the tips of her fingers before finally speaking.

"That which wounds us also has the capacity to wound others. A master disregards no tools."

Did she know it was the perfect thing to say? If anyone else heard the first line they would have taken it as a sort of golden rule, do-unto-others nonsense, but not him. He'd cast aside a potential weapon in a fit of anger. His disdain for illusions suddenly seemed childish and stupid—not surprising, given he was a teenager when Mr. Couture tricked him, but he'd never taken the time to reevaluate his views as an adult. Once again, Medea had seen into his soul and asked him to examine it for himself.

She opened her mouth as if to say more, then abruptly stood. He pulled the paper close and tried again. It took several more attempts before a solid black line appeared. Medea had him repeat it well over ten times to ensure it remained consistent, then removed the paper and replaced it with a beaker filled exactly to the top line.

"I think you know what to do here," she said with a half smile.

Indeed he did and set the water to boil. The seventh time, mana exhaustion hit.

"I hoped I'd get more out of you, given it's been a year."

He slumped in his chair with a grin. "Seven times and she complains I lack stamina. Now what?"

"Now we wait until your mana replenishes naturally. Shall we break our fast?"

"Since when do you remember to eat?"

"I didn't. It's nearly noon."

She grabbed one of the summoned rye loaves and cut it into slices, examining each before placing them on the table, while he set out a small spread. He seated himself, wrinkling his nose as he smeared butter on the rye, and tore off a small corner to be discarded. Even with the added lubrication, the bread was dry and scratchy going down. Still, food was food. He'd survived on worse. He cut himself a slice of cheese and popped a couple grapes in his mouth, savoring the combination of flavors, simple as they were.

Medea shoved a huge hunk of cheese into her mouth so as to have her hands free to cut the next loaf. Now he understood why she hadn't summoned any bread back at the car. They had a week's worth already, though her incessant cutting was going to make the already-dry bread stale. She continued to examine each slice as though expecting to find mold.

"What *are* you doing?"

"Hmm? Oh. Checking for consistency."

"Careful now—you're going to make me insecure about my work."

"I doubt that's even possible. Here"—she tossed him two slices—"make me a sandwich while I do this."

He caught the bread and reached for the dried meat. "I'm surprised you trust me with this, given how particular you are about food."

"It's three ingredients. I doubt even you could mess it up."

"Ha-ha," he said, slapping cheese on top of the meat.

When she finished slicing the bread, she plopped down across from him and reached for the sandwich. She took a bite and froze, staring in consternation at her food. "I was wrong."

Her face was dead serious, and for a moment he wondered how the hell she could be *that* picky, when she burst out laughing.

"I'm *joking*," she said between giggles. "It's fine. Though the bread *is* rather dry."

"I can do a nice sourdough next time."

She shook her head. "I doubt we'll have time before the delivery arrives. You still have to finish three more water boils, and we can't change the type of bread mid-experiment."

An hour later, his mana had replenished enough to continue. He'd scarcely finished the last boil when a rumbling announced the arrival of their appliances. Medea scribbled a final note and dashed outside to greet the truck.

The foreman eyed the house with healthy skepticism. "Well, I can see why you wanted a generator. Are you sure you have the proper hookups inside?"

"I doubt it," Medea said. "But bring them in anyway. Put everything in the first room up against the walls. Just don't block the stairs," she added needlessly.

The foreman glanced to him as if to confirm this idiocy, then quickly looked away. "Pardon me, sir, but is that right?" The tone was too formal, a shield to hide the man's discomfort. But why?

He itched to use telepathy but wasn't sure if Medea would snap at him for contaminating the test site. On the one hand, he wasn't sure she'd be able to sense it. On the other, he didn't want to give her an excuse to start over elsewhere. "Follow the lady's instructions."

Two other men were already unloading a refrigerator. One of them glanced at him in passing, did a double take, then looked away as though embarrassed. What the hell was going on?

"Do you gentlemen need any assistance?" he asked by way of testing their discomfort.

Sure enough, the workers deliberately avoided looking at him. One answered, "It's alright, sir, we've got it." Was it his imagination, or did they move faster to get inside the house? He stowed his curiosity and followed them inside.

"No, no, no, not the kitchen. *Here*." Medea pointed to an empty spot next to the fireplace. "Put it all in here."

"Ma'am, the dishwasher won't work without a water hookup," said the foreman.

The workers paused to see where this was headed. They gazed appreciatively at Medea, though she was too busy to notice.

"The house has no running water," Nikolai interjected. "As I understand it—and she'll correct me if I'm wrong—we only need to be able to turn the machines on and off."

"Are you sure about this, ma'am?" Once again, he avoided looking at Nikolai. Given the Mundane proclivity for putting a man's word above a woman's, it was odd to see the foreman deferring to her so automatically.

A whisper and a giggle came from the corner of the room where the other two workers stood. Though they could be making fun of Medea's ridiculous demands or inside-out dress, he suspected he was the butt of their joke.

He stalked over. "That's my sister you're looking at."

The declaration seemed to throw them, though something like comprehension passed over their faces, and one said, "Ahh . . ."

This time they did look at him, but their gazes lingered on his mouth and nose.

His scars. It was the goddamn scars! That's why they wouldn't look at his face. They had thought them a married couple and couldn't understand why a woman like Medea was with someone disfigured. His announcement that she was his sister made her tolerance of him understandable.

He strode upstairs to his room. It took every ounce of willpower not to slam the door. Medea made him cast an illusion dozens of times for her experiment, yet she wouldn't allow him to wear the illusion that concealed his ravaged face. It didn't matter what the Mundanes thought—they'd be gone soon enough—yet he hated to be seen like this. He tamped down the fury building within. Someone once said that success was the best revenge. Well, he'd have his revenge on Medea by succeeding where others failed. She *would* care about him, and then he'd own her, heart and soul.

He returned downstairs to find the disgruntled workers setting up the appliances. The generator was placed in the living room and everything plugged in around it, like some weird technological cult. He had to hand it to the foreman—despite the baffling setup, he patiently explained to Medea how to work the appliances. When everything was to her liking, she curtly dismissed the workers. They piled back into the truck with many backward glances and left in a cloud of dust.

"Now the real work begins," she said.

She made him wait in the kitchen while she went into the living room and shut the door. Though she refused to say what she was doing, it was obvious she'd gone to turn on one or more of the appliances. When she returned, he had to run through the cycle of exercises again—summon bread, ignite a twig, push the Bible, create an illusion, and boil water—ten sets of each. It was tedious work, especially since Medea insisted on no chatter during the experiments, claiming the distraction might somehow influence his magical abilities. He found himself looking forward to running out of mana so they could take a break.

"Tomorrow why don't we trade off?" he asked after the setting sun forced them to quit for the day. "After all, you never run out of mana."

"I'm not a good control. With my power, it's possible I wouldn't be affected by—" Medea cut herself short, perhaps realizing she was about to discuss the experiment, which she seemed determined not to do.

"I already know what we're doing, you know. You want to see which machines change the way my spells work."

A troubled expression crossed her face. "You're assuming they *will* cause a change. That alone could impact the results of the experiment."

"You know what I meant."

"But that's not what you *said*. Words matter, and yours reveal an inherent bias. The less you know of what we do, the better. It's bad enough that I can't conduct a double-blind study, but I don't have anyone else to help with this."

Odd she hadn't asked him to recruit others, as if it hadn't even occurred to her. Yoxtl had seen that potential in him right away. It was as if she existed in her own little bubble and was afraid to step outside of it, or perhaps she feared relinquishing control.

The autumn air rapidly grew chilly. He checked the fireplace flue and found it blocked with some sort of animal's nest, though thankfully he was able to make short work of it with Medea's broom. She lit a fire, but there were too many gaps in the house for the room to retain much heat. The appliances squatted around them like metal sentinels, reflecting the cold. He wasn't bothered, having grown up in Russia's bitter winters, but Medea soon began shivering.

"Let me get another coat for you."

She pursed her lips but said nothing. He hurried upstairs to grab a coat before she changed her mind, though the hesitation seemed to have gone out of her since last time. Seeing her in his coat outside the hospital had been incredibly erotic. She swam in it, her bare legs poking out underneath, but it was the fact that she wore something of his that made it so tantalizing. She'd hesitated to accept it, yet she did in the end because she knew she wanted it desperately. One day she'd feel the same about him.

He returned with the coat and draped it over her thin shoulders. "We can sleep down here in front of the fire." Perhaps she'd huddle against him for warmth.

"I think not." She stood abruptly and walked toward the stairs.

"My apologies, I forgot you have to undo your weaving before bed."

She paused with a smile. "Nice reference. But no, I must unpack and settle in before we lose all light. I shall see you on the morrow when the sun rises." She walked upstairs and closed her door.

So much for getting close. Well, he still had a car and the night was young. Time to find the nearest town to see about getting a real meal, among other things. His days here might be dull, but there was no reason his nights had to be.

Medea rushed to the window at the sound of a car. Who was it, coming all the way out here? But it wasn't a visitor. The blue vehicle Nikolai had stolen retreated into the distance. Had he given up on the experiments already? Was he abandoning her here? No, of course not. He was probably just going into town to do his whoring. A relief, actually. It would get it out of his system.

But what if he didn't succeed? What if he came back drunk and empty-handed and— She shook her head to scatter the thoughts. No use focusing on variables beyond her control. Time to fix those she could.

Neither bedroom had a working lock, so she'd chosen the one that could be made the most inaccessible. Nikolai's room had a window overlooking the tapered edge of the chimney—an easy climb for someone as determined as he was. Her own window had a sheer drop. He'd have to levitate to gain access that way. Even without her wards, she was sensitive enough to changes in magic that such a thing ought to wake her.

She put her hands to the only furniture in the room—a battered old dresser—and pushed, straining against the weight as it scraped slowly across the wooden floor. The boards were pitted and none too sound, and the dresser kept snagging. She often had to lift the corner while pushing to get it uncaught. Dust particles wafted around her, stirred up by her exerted breaths. Attempts to blow them aside failed. With a cough, she spun and braced her back against the dresser, pushing until it was in position in front of the door.

It wouldn't stop Nikolai—not really—but it was enough of a barrier to give her some warning if he tried to enter without magic. If worst came to worst, she could always use magic to defend herself, though she'd have to restart the experiments elsewhere with a new apprentice.

She stared at her bags, debating whether to unpack. Unpacking meant repacking, and the inability to leave quickly should anything go wrong. Leaving everything in the bags meant she'd have to fumble through them every time she wanted to extract something. She compromised by unpacking her books, stacking them neatly in the dresser drawers to add weight to her blockade. Several books were unfamiliar, and it took her a moment to remember Nikolai's offhand comment about a surprise. She fanned them out inside the drawer and read the blurbs—all science fiction, and recently published. Well, except for the one on making friends and influencing people, but that was obviously a jest.

What had he meant by gifting these? The last book he'd given her had sent a clear message—almost a challenge—calling out her teaching methods, but here she could decipher no pattern. Was it a ploy to win favor? It had to be. Men like Nikolai were never nice without purpose. He'd be after something.

When the books were unpacked, she chose one at random and lay down to read. It had been ages since she'd used a bedroll, and the once-fine traveling companion offered no reprieve from the hard surface upon which it rested. Soon her hip was screaming in protest. The pain, combined with the cold, made it impossible to focus.

She snapped the book shut and rose, teeth chattering, to dig through her bags. Her single blanket seemed woefully inadequate now. What had she been thinking? Why hadn't she brought anything warmer to wear? She tried pulling a second dress over the first, but the modern outfits weren't designed to be layered in such a way, so she added them to the bedroll to serve as extra padding. Normally she hated to wear coats—they restricted movement far too much—but Nikolai's was large enough that it didn't matter. She pulled it back on and snuggled under the blanket, carefully tucking the edges in around her. At least the long sleeves allowed her arms to remain relatively warm outside the blanket as she clutched her book.

Cold seeped into her bones and her fingers turned to ice. Every exhaled breath puffed a small cloud in front of her face, temporarily blurring the words. What she wouldn't give for a heating spell. After what seemed like ages, her body warmth filled the cocoon she'd built, and she was able to read in earnest.

A resounding crack shook the floor. She bolted to her feet, heart hammering in her chest as the chill of the room rushed to snatch away what little warmth she'd gained. Someone was trying to break in. Nikolai? No, she would have sensed him. The effort required not to cast spells as she approached the door was almost physically painful.

The dresser still stood vigil in front of the door—no one was there. Had she imagined the noise? It was an old house, and cold —the place was probably just settling for the night. Perhaps it was a raccoon or a rat. Despite her brain's attempts to be reassuring, she remained poised for combat, ears straining. It was only when the chattering of her own teeth became loud enough to obscure any other noise that she returned to her bedroll.

Concentration eluded her, words sliding by without meaning. At last she gave up on reading and resolved to sleep. The dresses padded the bedroll well enough, though they didn't make it comfortable. She slept fretfully, as one does in a new place, tormented by unknown sounds and a dull ache in her abdomen.

ACCOMMODATIONS

The headlights scarcely cut through the darkness, but a faint glow appeared on the horizon. Gloria squinted at the map beside her. Nikolai had given them a magical ball of light, but Evelyn had dropped it on the floor. Now she stared out the window, absently tugging her long black hair. The others snoozed behind them.

"Evelyn, can you lift up the magic ball? I need to check the map."

Evelyn glanced down and wrinkled her nose. "I don't want to touch it."

"I'll get it." Yoxtl bounded onto the front seat and ducked under Evelyn's legs. The spirit reemerged with the ball floating impossibly on its back.

"Thanks. I think this town coming up is the last one for a while. We better stop for the night."

"I don't think that's wise. Why don't we keep going?"

"We have a ways to go yet, and I can barely keep my eyes open."

"Can't you just pull over?" the spirit pressed.

Bethany leaned over the seat, making sure to avoid touching Josh. "I want a real bed."

"I thought you were asleep," said Gloria.

"I was only pretending so Miss Chatterbox would shut up. If I had to hear one more thing about the handsome magical doctor—it's no wonder her family locked her up. There, I think that's a motel."

Gloria eased the Suburban off the highway and parked. Doris and Josh stirred.

"Wait here," said Gloria. "I don't even know if they have a vacancy yet."

Doris yawned and stretched, nearly punching Bethany in the face. "My butt is numb. I need to get out and walk around." There was a murmuring of agreement.

"How are we going to pay?" asked Bethany.

"Nikolai left me some diamonds."

Bethany's eyes narrowed. "Why did he leave them to you? Why didn't he give some to each of us?"

"I don't know. Does it matter right now?"

"Not as long as I get my share when you get back to the car."

Gloria shook her head and went to the front desk. She could hear the others filing out behind her. Great, she'd have to herd everyone back into the car if they didn't have room. Yoxtl trotted up beside her.

"Won't you be seen?" she asked.

"I can choose who sees and hears me." It offered a toothy grin.

Given the late hour, the front desk was empty. She dinged the bell on the counter and waited until a disheveled man in a nightcap and overcoat shuffled in.

"What can I do for you, miss?"

"I need three rooms."

"How many are you?"

"Five."

He gave her an appraising look. "Just so long as there're no unmarried couples staying together. We don't go in for that kinda thing 'round here."

"No, sir. Nothing like that. Only one man, and he'll be in his own room."

"See that he stays there. You'll have to sign in. Let's see, three rooms . . ." He muttered to himself as he fingered the keys hanging from hooks on the wall.

Gloria took the registration book and signed her name. Hopefully he'd be satisfied with first names for the rest.

"What in the gosh darn—" The man slammed the keys on the counter and hustled out the door. "Hey you! You can't be here. Go on now!" He waved his arms at Josh.

Gloria sprinted to catch up. "That's our, uh, driver."

"I don't care what he is. He ain't staying here!"

"Can you recommend a place in town that will take him?"

"Ain't no other place in town. No place 'round here that I know of. Maybe you drive another few hours, you'll find someone to take him, but I doubt it."

"Thank you for your time." Gloria turned to the others. "Looks like we're moving on. Can one of you take over driving for a bit?"

Bethany opened the rear door and grabbed her purse. "You can do whatever you want. I'm staying here."

"Me too," said Doris. "It's late. Just let Josh sleep in the car."

The owner shook his head. "Uh-uh, nope. Not in the car. Not on my property. When you ladies figure it out, you let me know. But he's not staying here." The man trudged back to the front desk.

Gloria gave the women a beseeching look. "We need to keep moving. You heard what Nikolai said—we have to stick together."

Bethany strode up to her. "But he's not here, is he? He left us alone with that rat." She jerked her head toward Yoxtl.

The spirit trotted to stand beside Gloria, providing a unified, albeit short, front. "Gloria's right. We need to keep moving."

"No one asked you." Bethany thrust her hand out. "I want my share now."

Doris bounded forward. "Me too."

Evelyn, who'd only just seemed to notice what was going on, mimicked the other two.

Gloria eyed them coolly. "What about Josh? He needs a place to stay. We can't just ditch him."

Bethany shrugged. "Not my problem. He should never have been with us in the first place. It's not proper." She flexed her fingers.

"Why don't you drive him to the edge of town and let him sleep in the car?" Doris offered.

"Because then I'd have to walk all the way back in the dark by myself."

Bethany smirked. "Not by yourself—you have the rat."

Yoxtl's tail bristled. "The *rat* has a name."

"Why can't Josh drive to the edge of town by himself? Then you wouldn't need to walk back." Evelyn was so soft-spoken that it took a moment for her words to sink in, then Bethany and Doris talked over one another in their rush to discredit the idea.

"Give him our *car*—"

"Are you nuts?!"

"You can't trust him!"

"—trying to leave us *stranded*?"

"Probably can't even drive."

Yoxtl floated upward until it was at eye level. "I am the servant of the GREAT GOD YOXTL and you are my charges! The safest thing is to move on to the site indicated on the map. I will guide you in the dark, I will—"

Bethany scoffed and started for the front desk.

"I'd like to see you get a room without paying!" Gloria called to her back.

Bethany spun and dug her hand into her purse. She withdrew a golden watch and waggled it. "*Some* of us planned ahead. Come on, girls!"

Doris shot Gloria a sympathetic look and hurried to catch up with Bethany. Evelyn trailed behind. Gloria returned to the car and wrenched the door open. She stared at the interior as though hoping it would give her answers. Several slow, methodical steps crunched the gravel behind her.

"I don't know what to do, Josh. None of this is okay. We should be working together, we should be . . ." She shook her head. Life was so much simpler in the Corps. Everyone had their job, their orders, and they did it. They might not agree on everything, but they were unified in purpose—support the troops, win the war. She turned to face him. "Nikolai said you can understand everything we say. What do you think? What should I do?"

Josh simply stared at his feet.

Gloria gave a rueful laugh and looked to Yoxtl. "You're supposed to be leading us. I need a solution here. 'Cause right now it's looking like I need to drive the three of us out to the middle of nowhere and sleep in the car." At least with the others gone they'd be able to stretch out on the seats, though she doubted that'd be comfortable for Josh. And what if someone found them? A lone woman sleeping in a car with a man like Josh —yeah, that would go over well. "If you really work for a god, you should be able to help us. Isn't there some sort of spell you can use?"

The creature's amber eyes were unreadable. "Tell the clerk you want the third room for yourself, then get the car out of sight. I'll distract him long enough for you to get Josh inside."

Josh shook his head and backed away.

Gloria grabbed his shoulders and he cried out. She let go. "Shhh! Josh. Josh! Look, we're gonna take care of you, okay? But I can't do that if you're sitting in the car somewhere by yourself. You don't want to be alone, do you? This will work. No one will see—right, Yoxtl?"

The spirit grinned. "Trust me. I'll keep the manager plenty busy."

Gloria started back toward the front desk. The girls exited, Bethany and Doris headed one way, Evelyn standing idly by with a key in her limp hand, looking confused. Gloria gave Evelyn's arm a squeeze and said, "Wait there, hun." She jogged up to Bethany and Doris. "Where are you two going?"

Bethany unlocked a room and tossed her purse inside. "To bed. Do I need permission from you to do that?"

"One of you has to stay with Evelyn. She can't be left alone."

"We thought you were," said Doris.

"I thought so too, but now I have to look after Josh."

Bethany's eyes narrowed and Doris slunk into the room before shots were fired. She busied herself with unpacking, though she surreptitiously watched them.

"What do you mean by that?" asked Bethany.

"I mean I'm going to sneak Josh into a room."

"How dare you! This isn't your establishment. They have a right to decide who stays here. Have you *smelled* him? Filthy. Probably have to burn the sheets afterward. Most of them are no better than trained mongrels, and *that* one's not even housebroken. There's no telling what he'll do to that room. I'm going to tell the owner right now."

Bethany started to walk away and Gloria grabbed her by the arm. The look she received was murderous, and she hastily dropped it.

"*Please*, Beth, I just need a good night's sleep. I'm exhausted. It's only one night."

Bethany's expression softened a fraction, then a stern resolution took hold. "He never should have come along in the first place, and the owner of this place made his feelings clear. Better to be rid of the boy now before he causes any more trouble. Now, will you take him somewhere else or do I have to report you?"

The night seemed even colder. Gloria thrust her hands into her pockets and tried to think. Her fingers brushed against something.

"What if I give you half the diamonds? One night, Bethany. That's all I ask."

The woman seemed to reconsider. Gloria fingered the stones nervously as she waited for a reply.

"I'll do it," said Bethany. "For all of them. I don't see why a morally compromised woman like yourself should be in charge of our finances." At Gloria's sour expression she added, "Oh, don't worry, honey, I'll leave you enough for a room."

Gloria gritted her teeth and handed the diamonds to Bethany, who passed back two.

"Thank you," Bethany said in a singsong voice. She flounced into the room and began pulling things out of her purse—expensive dresses and shoes, hats, jewelry. She giggled with Doris over their haul, laying everything out on the bed to compare. The most practical thing either of them had taken was a mink coat.

Gloria cleared her throat. "What about Evelyn?"

"Forget it," said Bethany. "Have you heard her in the ward at night? She's a screamer."

Gloria gave Doris an imploring look.

"I'm sure she'll be fine alone."

"No, she won't. You *know* she won't. Please, Doris."

"Give it a rest," said Bethany. "Just leave Josh alone and go sleep with Evelyn. Honestly, I don't know *why* you're fighting it so hard." She turned with a wicked smile. "Or are you finally listening to the doctor's orders? Is that why you're so desperate to bunk with the Negro?"

Doris shot Bethany a quizzical look and Gloria flushed. "If someone sees me coming out of Evelyn's room in the morning, they're gonna know I didn't sleep in my own."

"And we can't have *that*, can we?" Bethany laughed. "Relax, Gloria. If someone sees, tell them you were getting everyone up early."

Gloria backed away and closed the door. She held the handle for a moment, taking measured breaths and consciously relaxing her muscles. When she felt reasonably composed, she returned to the front desk. "I need a room."

The clerk eyed her suspiciously. "I thought you were staying with those other girls."

"That was before the other girls decided to leave me high and dry." She slapped a diamond on the counter. "Can I get a room or not?"

"No need to get *testy*, miss." He grabbed a key off the hook and held it out, yanking it back at the last second. "This room is for you and you *only*. I don't even want to see your driver so much as bring the bags inside. Got it?"

"I got it."

"Good, 'cause I got my eye on you."

Gloria took the key and stepped back with a squish. She frowned and glanced at her feet. The carpet was soaking wet. "I think you have a leak somewhere."

"What?" He leaned over the counter to see where she was pointing. "Oh no. No no no!" He bolted into an adjoining room.

Gloria followed him and poked her head inside. It was like a janitor's closet, boiler room, and bathroom all rolled into one. There was a mishmash of cleaning supplies, a water heater, and a toilet. Brown water leaked over the edge of the bowl and dripped onto the floor.

"You'd best get to your room now, miss. No reason for you to get filth all over your shoes." The clerk grabbed a plunger and set to work on the toilet, sloshing water all over his slippered feet.

That didn't make sense—the water at her own feet was warm, and there was a lot more of it than she'd expect from just the toilet. She craned her neck to look at the water heater—the drain valve was leaking. "The toilet isn't the problem. You have to—"

"No offense, missy, but the day I take plumbing advice from a woman is the day I die."

Her jaw clenched and she took a step toward the boiler. She'd show him what a woman could do.

Yoxtl materialized inches from her face. "What are you *doing*? Go move Josh!"

Gloria blinked, momentarily stunned by her own stupidity. "I'll, uh, leave you to it then." She backed out of the room and exited the lobby, Yoxtl floating alongside her. "I'm sorry. I was expecting your diversion to be more magical I guess." She gave the spirit a sheepish smile.

"Sometimes the simplest solutions are the best. And don't worry about him fixing the leak too soon." The spirit cackled. "I've got plans to keep him busy all night."

BARRIERS

edea woke to sunlight tickling her face. The room was still frigid, but she smiled at the day and its promise of renewed warmth. Stretching on all fours and arching her back like a cat, she rolled out of bed to ready herself for the day. Her brush was missing and it was only after sifting through her bags twice that she realized she'd forgotten it. She combed her fingers through her hair, battling the desire to chop it all off and be done. It wasn't until she turned back to the bed that she saw the blood—a few flecks at first, then a pool of deep crimson smeared across the dresses that had been her pallet.

What the hell? She glanced down at the dress she wore, but the front was clean. Where had it come from? Was she wounded? Had whatever caused the crashing sound last night hurt her, and why hadn't she felt it? She stripped and began searching her body. The source of the blood soon became apparent, and she cursed.

Why hadn't she anticipated this? Annoying enough having her hair in her face all the time, but now she had to deal with menstruation as well. She knelt to examine the dresses, swearing at the damage she'd inadvertently caused. How the hell had it soaked through *both*, plus the one she had on? She never remembered there being that much blood before. It was as though her body was getting revenge for the millennial pause in her cycle.

She rolled up a cloth and shoved it between her legs, then donned the dress with the least amount of spotting. Perhaps she could wash the others at the well before Nikolai woke. Males were odd about such things. They could be drowning in the blood of their enemies, smiling all the while, but the sight of a woman's blood made them shrink away in horror. *Uncleeeeean*. She shook her head at the follies of men.

The dresser in front of the door refused to budge. Right, the books. She opened each drawer and pulled them out, stacking them neatly beside the door, and tried again. Still it would not move.

She took a step back.

The dresser sat at a list. She examined the back and found one of the legs had broken through the floor—that had been the crash—and was stuck. She tried to maneuver it out, throwing her full weight against the dresser, but the leg remained stubbornly in place. Great, just great. A warm trickle down her inner thigh alerted her that her bundle had shifted. She swore and reposi-tioned it.

Second story, completely isolated, no chance of intruders sneaking in the window—all the qualities she looked for in a room yesterday now prevented her from getting out. She moved to the window, knowing damn well it was fruitless but praying she'd been mistaken, that a shed or trellis had magically appeared during the night. Nothing but a sheer drop.

The floorboards beyond her door creaked—Nikolai must be up. She was never going to live this down, but what other choice did she have?

"Nikolai! Nikolai!" She banged on the wall by the door.

The creaking stopped in front of her door. "Yes?"

"I'm trapped inside my room. I need you to go below my window and catch me."

Like an idiot, he tried the door and it smacked into the dresser. "Trapped how? What's blocking your door?"

"The dresser. Look, I need you to go outside and wait below my window."

"Why the hell is the dresser in front of your door? And why don't you just move it?"

"Don't you think I've tried that?" she snapped. He was so dense sometimes. "It's stuck. Go outside my window and prepare to catch me. Please," she added as an afterthought.

"Alright, alright. I'm going." Nikolai's mumbling faded away with the creaking floorboards.

She moved to the window and looked down. It took him forever to appear. This was going to be painful, not just because of the distance of the drop but because she'd have to allow him to hold her. No doubt he'd take the chance to grab something he shouldn't.

When he was in position, she put one leg out the window and then the other, balancing precariously on the creaky windowsill.

"I'm ready," he said, arms outstretched.

She took a breath and readied herself to jump, shifting her weight slightly. The wood beneath her snapped, and she plummeted with a yelp. A moment later, she was in Nikolai's arms. She tensed, expecting an "accidental" grope, but his grip didn't wander as he set her on her feet.

"You're even lighter than you look," he remarked. Abruptly, he cocked his head to look at her backside. She nearly pummeled him but halted at his words. "You're bleeding. Did you cut yourself on the ledge?"

Goddamnit. She twisted around to confirm what he'd seen. "No, I didn't cut myself. I just . . . I haven't been without spells for a long time. I'd forgotten that one of the benefits of magic was not having to deal with, well . . ."

Much to her surprise, he laughed.

"It's not funny, you know."

He grinned. "Yes, it is. Though maybe not to you. Can I get you anything for that?"

Her mouth pinched shut. Was he serious, or was he having a go at her? She hedged her bet on the truth. "Yes, actually. Dry leaves. A handful of them. And go on the other side of the house, I need to wash up a bit."

"Dry leaves, sure thing." He walked around the side of the house, chuckling as he went.

She waited until he was out of sight, then extracted the rag from between her legs, rinsed it at the water pump, wrung it out, repositioned it. The damned thing wouldn't do. It kept slipping.

"Are you decent?" Nikolai called out from the other side of the house. Nice of him to ask, although knowing most men, he'd probably peeked first.

"Yes."

"Here you go." He swaggered forward and held out a fistful of red-orange leaves.

Reflexively she reached out, then jerked her hand back when she realized what they were. "I can't use those!"

He'd broken them off at the stem, retaining the unmistakable three-leaf arrangement. Leave it to Nikolai to find the only unsuitable plant in the area. Had he done it on purpose, hoping she wouldn't notice? Was this petty revenge for some perceived slight? Most people wouldn't sacrifice their own comfort for the sake of a prank, but Nikolai had a high tolerance for pain. She searched his face for answers but found none.

"What's wrong with them?" He sounded indignant.

"They're poison ivy. Your hands are going to have a rash tomorrow."

He dropped the leaves as if bitten. *"Blyad!"*

"No, don't rub them on your pants!" She ran forward and grabbed his wrist. "The poison is an oil. You'll spread it around if you do that. Come here."

She led him to the water pump and pulled the handle while he scrubbed his hands with dirt and water.

"Could have been worse, I suppose," he said. "Imagine if you didn't recognize them and offered me some of your tea."

"Tea? What do you me— Oh!" She supposed that made sense. There were certain teas that helped with cramping. "I didn't want them for that, and if I was going to make tea I would've asked for specific plants."

"I'd wondered, but why else would you need leaves?"

Did he really want specifics? "You know, to catch the blood. You get a stick about the size of your finger and wrap the leaves around it. Then, you know . . ." She made a circle with one hand and pushed a finger up through it. His expression grew increasingly horrified. She should have known better than to discuss such things with a man. If he couldn't handle this sort of talk then he shouldn't have asked.

"You were going to shove them *inside* you? It's 1957! They must have invented something better than *leaves*." He covered his face with his hand. "Bloody leaves," he mumbled, shaking his head.

"Well, that's what we used back then!" She felt her cheeks burn. Never in a million years did she think a man could make her feel insecure about something like this. What *did* women use these days? "I suppose you're right. But I can't risk going anywhere right now and even if I could, I wouldn't have the slightest idea where to—"

"I'll go."

She stared at him in disbelief. Why was he being so nice? And why would he risk his reputation as a male to get her something like that? She didn't know much about the culture these days, but from what little she'd seen, menstruation probably carried the same stigma.

"Why?"

"Are you kidding? I'll take any excuse to get away from this dump." His blatant self-centeredness was oddly reassuring. For once he wasn't lying, and his interests really did align with hers.

She took a breath. "Alright. But don't dally. We still have work to do."

He flashed a grin and was gone.

Nikolai returned to the farmhouse in high spirits. Apparently a man willing to buy sanitary products for his "little sister" was catnip for women. The young lady behind the counter was more than happy to assist him. Ignoring her father's horrified expression at the open discussion of such items, she led Nikolai to the aisle and proceeded to show him what they had in stock. When he told her he'd be purchasing one of each box just to be on the safe side, she was about ready to tear his clothes off right there. As she rang him up, she asked how long he was in town and where he was staying, while her father glowered from a stool behind the counter.

"An old farmhouse off Havershine Road. My sister's of a mind to fix up the place. Sadly, it's in no state to entertain visitors yet."

"Too bad. I'd love to come 'round and meet her."

"She's not too fond of people, but I'll be here all week. Tell me, what do folk around here do for fun?"

"The bar in town has a dance floo—" Her father loudly cleared his throat, and she mouthed *sorry*. "That'll be three ninety-two, sir."

Nikolai locked eyes with the old bastard and withdrew a blank slip of paper from his pocket. He passed it to the young woman, telepathically informing her it was a five-dollar bill. "Here you go, darling. Keep the change."

The spat that ensued was highly amusing. Father demanded he pay. Daughter insisted he already had. Neither could figure out what the other's problem was, nor were they willing to back down. Eventually he tired of the exchange and made to leave, at which point the old man pulled a gun. Nikolai met his gaze coolly. The man jabbered on for a time, making demands, though his voice began to waver under the unflinching stare, until at last he simply ordered Nikolai to leave.

Maintaining eye contact with the father, Nikolai held his hand out for the bag. "And will you be at the bar tonight?" he asked the woman.

She chanced a look at her father, then straightened her shoulders and slid the bag across the counter. "Yes. Yes, I will."

Nikolai drove back to the farmhouse and swaggered into the house, bag of products slung over his shoulder.

Medea materialized at the kitchen door to accost him. "Were you successful?"

"In more ways than one." He smiled and upended the bag on the table, spilling out an assortment of boxes. Medea picked up a box of Tampax and mumbled to herself as she read. He liked that she was coming to rely on him despite herself. The bloodstain on the back of her dress had faded to brown, though the front was now covered with dust. What had she been doing while he was gone?

"So these are the same thing, just cotton. I don't know why you made such a fuss about my method." Her gaze snapped up. "Stay here!" She left the kitchen and creaked upstairs.

He bagged the remaining boxes and set them on the counter next to a book—one of the novels he'd purchased for her at the shop in Omaha. A sheet of paper had been stuffed halfway through. Had she read that much already? When she returned, he held up the novel.

"Were you able to get back inside your room?" he asked, hoping she'd remark on the gift.

"What? No. No, I left some books by the door and was just able to reach one through the crack." She glanced down at her filthy dress. "Though I had to lie on the floor to do it."

Not even an acknowledgment! She couldn't be disappointed in it, not when she'd read halfway through already. Did she have so many books that she couldn't keep track of those she'd bought for herself? Not one to back down from a challenge, he seized on another opportunity.

"I can give you some of my clothes. I packed extra, and I can always get more when I go into town. You look like you could use a change."

She turned a #3 frown toward him. It took a good thirty seconds for her to answer, as though she sought a reason to say no. Sure enough, she replied, "They'll be too big."

"We'll make do." He sprinted up the stairs before she could argue. Seeing her in his clothing suddenly became a desperate need. He returned with pants, a shirt, and a belt.

"Hold these up to your waist," he said, handing her the pants. It was a power play, though he doubted she'd recognize it as such. She did as she was told, involuntarily making herself complicit, and he cut the excess fabric off at her ankles. His next move carried more risk, but she'd already allowed him to get this familiar. He looped the belt around her waist and cinched it tight. For a wonder, she didn't complain, and allowed him to mark where to drill a new hole in the belt.

When she returned after changing, he basked in the glory of his creation. He'd intentionally chosen yesterday's clothes, hoping his scent still clung to them. She wouldn't notice until they were on, at which point it would be impolite for her to ask for something else, especially after his alterations. The shirt was too loose by far, but did little to hide the fact that she wore no bra. The fabric that had covered him, absorbed his sweat, and rubbed against his skin now cascaded over her bare breasts, almost like he was caressing them by proxy. A devilish thrill of pleasure shot through him, especially when she took a step closer with a pleading, self-conscious expression.

"Can you trim these?" she said, unrolling her sleeves. "They keep falling down."

"Of course." He neatly severed each sleeve.

Medea rubbed her arms and smiled, admiring herself. "This is surprisingly comfortable."

Given she was effectively wearing his second skin, there was little she could've said that would have been more arousing. There was no way he could work around her in his current state. It was distracting as hell and she was bound to notice. "I need to run to my room for a few minutes. I'll be right back."

"Whatever it is, it can wait. We're already behind schedule."

And so he sat, grateful for the table between them.

The morning's experiments passed in sensual torture. Every move Medea made was a subtle taunt, from the casual flick of her hair to the way she sucked on the tip of her pen. The machines had to be turned on or off between rounds, and whenever she passed by he caught a subtle whiff of her fragrance mingled with his. He soon realized there was more to it than scent alone. She'd told him that magic could be sensed without Magic Sight, and the more time they spent in this environment barren of magic, the more keenly he was aware of her presence. Even stripped of her spells, there was no mistaking the magic burning within her. It sang to him in a way he couldn't explain.

She refused to allow conversation during the experiments. The boredom, normally held at bay by their sparring matches, both verbal and practical, threatened to smother him. Even their Latin lessons had never been this dull. At least with those, he could entertain himself by getting a reaction from her, either by intentionally mispronouncing a word or asking her with a straight face to translate something he knew to be risqué.

Barred from his normal outlets of violence, sex, and mischief, he turned to mentally undressing her and imagined fucking her in all manner of positions around the kitchen. When he accidentally set fire to her shirt instead of the twig, it was all he could do to keep from encouraging the flames to spread. He longed for her to tear the shirt off and cast it aside, for the flames to lick up the cabinets and set the room ablaze. She'd come to him with a coy smile, pale breasts glistening in the heat, skin tasting of sweat. He'd take her on the table, house burning around them. They'd climax together, and as he shot himself into her, so too would her magic shoot into him—a perfect joining.

"I think I'd best stand behind you next time you cast that spell." Medea finished slapping the last of the flames from her shirt. The chill air made her nipples erect.

He averted his gaze before she noticed. "I'm out of mana."

"Already?"

"Yes," he lied. At least now she'd allow conversation.

"It's just as well," she said with a sigh. "I could use a break myself." She scribbled a final notation, then slumped into the chair across from him and rubbed her face.

"Everything alright?"

"Fine. Fine," she muttered, idly pinching the tips of her fingers.

"Medea, you're not fooling anyone. What's troubling you?"

For a moment it looked as though she might answer, but then her face changed and she said simply, "Nothing."

Abruptly she stood and went to slice the bread he'd summoned. In an effort to appear helpful, he began laying out their lunch. The loaves were less uniform than yesterday. One had oats baked onto the surface and a few were lighter in color. Two weren't even loaves but custard-filled pastries. He nearly laughed at the sight of them, recalling his daydreams.

"What's that one?" he asked as she cut into a golden-brown loaf.

She held it to her nose. "Sourdough. Were you aiming for that despite my orders?"

"Of course not. But seeing as we have it . . ." He leaned over and stole two slices from her cutting board.

Medea took her time with the bread, frowning and making detailed notes in her book. Once again, his attempts at conversation were rebuffed. By the time she sat down with a plate of fruit and cheese, he'd long since finished eating. He leaned forward, eager to start a conversation, but she whipped out the book he'd given her and began to read.

"How is it?" he asked.

She offered only a monosyllabic grunt in reply.

He wasn't sure if he should be offended that she ignored him for a book or pleased that one he'd chosen could hold her attention so well. It was risky to interrupt her reading, but she'd only just started and it's not like she'd given him any other opportunities. He cleared his throat loudly. "I said, are you enjoying that?"

"Huh?" She looked up as though surprised to still see him there. "Oh. I don't know—I haven't finished it yet. Have you read it?"

"No. I just asked the clerk for the best new science fiction. I usually read nonfiction, instructional texts—things like that."

"Fiction *is* instructional. About everything—human relationships, governments, philosophy." She let the book rest on the table. He should've known the only thing that would get her to stop reading would be an opportunity to correct him. "Science fiction in particular is interesting. It postulates new technologies and poses questions about where humans are headed." She smirked. "And I get to see how accurate their guesses are. Sometimes they even give me ideas for new spells."

It was the perfect opening—Medea could talk for hours about magic. "What kind of new spells?"

But she was already staring at the page again. "I'm trying to *read*." She lapsed into silence, devouring more words than food.

Their second break passed in much the same way. How could he gain ground if he couldn't even talk to her? Given her propensity for retiring early, it was unlikely he'd have any opportunities once they were done for the day. The week unfolded before him —Medea in attractive but unyielding silence, himself mired in drudgery, unable to make any progress. He couldn't let that happen.

Thankfully, her bedroom door was blocked. No doubt she'd ask him to clear it. He'd head her off, giving no inclination that he planned to fail, and declare the door a lost cause. Deprived of her room and most of her books, she'd be forced to spend time with him.

When the last water boil was done for the day, he rose from the table and stretched. "Now let's see about that door of yours." She followed him upstairs and watched as he opened the door a crack. It only went a couple inches before slamming into wood. He reached through the crack, intending to jiggle the dresser before giving up, but the top wasn't where he expected it to be. Why was it so tall? It shouldn't be that high if it had fallen over. He groped his way up the dresser—there was the smooth lip and then the flat surface of the top.

"Why is the dresser upright?" he asked. Come to think of it, he was pretty sure it had been on the far wall yesterday. Had she barricaded the door? He knew she was paranoid, but they were out in the middle of nowhere. He withdrew his hand.

"Can you move it?" she asked.

"It's stuck really good. Look, you can have my bed tonight."

"No no no, that's not going to work. My things are in that room. And yours is . . . insufficient." She rubbed her arm, looking small and helpless inside his oversized clothes.

Her power lay in magic. It must be terrifying for her, giving that up for a week. And he'd gone into town last night, leaving her all alone to jump at shadows. He should have thought to stay and act as her protector. No wonder she was upset.

He took a step closer. "I know it must be frightening to give up your magic, but I'm here to protect you."

The frown she gave him was one he didn't recognize. Disbelief?

"We're out in the middle of nowhere," he continued, keeping his tone calm and reassuring. "The odds of someone attacking you are nil. I promise I won't go out tonight. I'll stay here and watch over you, if that makes you feel better."

Her voice was flat. "It doesn't." She turned heel and walked downstairs. He caught up with her in the kitchen, where she was shoving the book and some cheese into a sack. When he approached, she extended her hand. "The keys. To the car."

Now she wanted to stay at a hotel? "Medea, you don't even know how to drive."

"The keys. Now."

He fished them out of his pocket and handed them to her. "This is silly. At least let me drive you."

"I'm not driving anywhere. I'm going to sleep in the car." She walked outside and threw her bag into the Chevy.

"The sun hasn't even set yet and you're already shivering. No one's going to attack you out here. Just come inside. You don't need to sleep in my bed—and I didn't mean with me," he added, in case that was the problem. "You can sleep by the fireplace. Or I can, and you can take my room."

Medea slid into the back seat and shut the door. The lock

clicked. She'd asked him for the keys—yet she had no intention of driving.

Realization stabbed him, and he glared at her through the window. "You're not afraid of strangers, are you? You barricaded your door against *me*."

She didn't answer, just stared at the seat in front of her, jaw clenched.

"You're still afraid I'll try to kill you? I told you—I don't want to do that anymore." The past year—he'd been so fucking *good* the past year, doing everything she asked, training in a magical school he didn't enjoy, bending over backward to gain the slightest bit of praise, and she thought he was still out to kill her?

"I'm just being cautious."

"Cautious? What the hell do you take me for? Do you really think that I'd be that sloppy if I *was* trying to kill you? Why would I throw my apprenticeship away? I have more to learn, don't I? We haven't even *touched* necromancy yet."

She refused to meet his gaze.

"And why haven't you been leery of me all day? Do you think I randomly turn into a werewolf at night?" He brought his fist down on the roof of the car. "*Say* something, damnit!"

She jerked and turned glare #3 toward him. "You forget your place, *discipulus*."

"Is that all I am to you?"

Her puzzled expression slapped him. "What else would you be?"

This whole trip he'd been at her beck and call, sorting out her problems no matter what trouble she'd gotten into. He'd bought her gifts, offered her his clothes—hell, even brought her tampons —none of which she'd even *acknowledged*, let alone thanked him for. He thought he'd been making progress. Slow, yes, but progress nonetheless. Now he found he was still on square one.

He was suddenly back at Petrov's shop, being called "the boy." She didn't care about him at all.

His roiling anger coalesced into a solid mass. He tapped on her window—one, two, three—slow and methodical. "I'm going to open your fucking room, since that's all I'm good for."

He turned and made a running leap, catching the listing corner of the patio cover and hauling himself up despite the precarious swaying. Behind him, the car door creaked.

"What are you doing?" she shouted. "Get down here!"

He ignored her and continued his ascent of the roof. Ancient shingles tore loose under his feet and he heard her cry out. He smiled at the challenge—not as good as an adrenaline rush, but it was the best he'd felt all day.

Medea's room was on the far side of the house. He crested the peak of the roof and edged down. Several shingles gave way at once. He scrabbled to regain his footing as he slid downward. Finally, some fucking *excitement*. One meter. Two.

He grabbed at the shingles, splinters be damned. His hands were already beginning to sting from the poison ivy—what was one more injury? Pain layered on top of pain, but his descent slowed. How close was the edge? He felt around with one foot until he discovered it. Making sure of his grip, he called out, "Am I above your window?"

"Don't be a fool! You'll get yourself killed."

"It's not like you've never lost an apprentice before."

"My apprentices die of their own follies. If you fall, I can't help you." She meant it too.

He glared down at her. "You *won't*. Words matter, remember? You've made it abundantly clear how expendable I am."

Her reply was slow. "You're not . . . you're not expendable." The lack of conviction said it all. Well, fuck her.

"But I'm not worth as much as a clean test site. Hard to find those. Turn over a rock, though, and you'll find a new apprentice." Let her feel guilty if he died. It would serve her right. "Now am I above your window or not?"

Medea's hands cupped her mouth. She said nothing.

"Fine." There was no gutter, only shingles and bare, rotting wood. Without hesitation, he eased his legs over the edge and dangled by his hands. Below him, Medea unleashed a string of Latin curses.

"Shut up!" he barked. "Left or right?"

"R-r-right."

Inch by inch, he worked his way along the eave, wood groaning under his weight.

"There."

He swung his legs forward and back, trying to get momentum enough to hook his foot on the edge of her window.

"It won't work," she cried suddenly. "The sill broke off when I climbed out, remember?"

He did remember, a second too late. He'd already released his grip on the eaves. His feet reached into the unknown. They scraped against wood but caught nothing. He pitched backward and plummeted headfirst toward the ground.

RISE AND SHINE

Josh lay in the hotel bed and stared at the ceiling. He wished Grandma was here. She knew when he needed help. It was harder to make Gloria understand.

She'd tried to get him to shower, but the water bit into his skin and a moment later she was pulling him back out with many a "shush!" Instead, she brought him fresh clothes she insisted were *not* stolen. He tugged the shirt up his arms but fumbled with the buttons. Gloria helped him with those, but she didn't help him with the pants, not even when he nudged them with his foot. She simply looked away while he stood awkwardly in his drawers waiting for help. Eventually his stomach growled.

"I forgot you missed dinner. You must be famished! I'll fetch you something."

When she returned, she looked askance at the pants on the floor and handed him jerky. It was tough and chewy and made him thirsty. He guzzled cup after cup of water until she shooed him out of the bathroom.

"That's enough for now," she said, approaching the bed and pulling back the covers.

He lay down, tugging the blankets under his chin.

Gloria sat on the edge of the bed with a sigh. "Josh, I need you to listen to me. It's really important. No one can know you're here. You can't yell and carry on like that again, and no one can see you. Do you understand? We'll get in so much trouble. They'll call the cops and you'll be thrown in jail or worse. Stay here. Be quiet and *don't move*. Do you understand? Do you?" She stared at him, repeating the same thing over and over. Mama got like that sometimes. He got it. What else did she want?

"I'm going to sleep in Evelyn's room but I'll be back to check on you first thing in the morning. Please stay here until then. Please please *please. Don't move*."

She got up and cracked the door. After one final glance in his direction, she left.

The bed was soft, with nice thick blankets. Much better than the hospital floor. Better than his bed at home even. He closed his eyes and tried to fall asleep, absently reaching up to scratch his nose. He jerked his hand back, heart pounding.

Had anyone seen? Did they have peepholes? He strained to hear anything—sirens and barking dogs and police bursting through the door to drag him off to jail. Nobody came. He'd gotten lucky this time, but what if he did it again? What if he rolled over in his sleep? Better to stay awake, but that was easier said than done. Even after napping in the car he was so very, very tired. He stared at the ceiling. It had a white, puffy texture of bumps that formed shapes if you looked long enough. There was a flower. There a car. A whale. His eyes drifted shut. He snapped them open again. A leaf, dog, tree . . .

A dog stood next to a great oak tree. He backed away—dogs were loud and jumpy and slobbery. The dog sniffed the trunk and lifted its leg. A yellow stream hit the bark and trickled to the dry earth. The dog moved to another tree—there was a forest of them now—and lifted its leg again. Again and again it urinated, until sunlight pierced the faded curtains and he groggily opened his eyes.

He'd fallen asleep! The thought was like a vise on his chest and his breath quickened, but there was no shouting of police and no barking of dogs. He was still flat on his back with the covers up to his chin. If he'd done anything in his sleep, it hadn't been enough for them to see.

When you wake up, fit as a fiddle,

Go to the bathroom and have a nice piddle.

Grandma's morning rhyme echoed in his head. He'd always had trouble knowing when it was time to go. Others just seemed to remember.

"Can't you feel it?" she used to ask.

"Feel what?" he'd wanted to say. All he'd ever felt was damp pants and the warm pooling of liquid in his shoes. So she'd come up with the rhyme and sung it to him every morning. After meals he was supposed to go too, and before bed.

Before bed!

He hadn't remembered to go. Everything was so different here. He'd slept and changed and eaten and bathed all in the wrong order. How was he supposed to remember after all that? He should go now, while he was thinking about it, but Gloria's warning echoed too.

Please please please. Don't move.

Going to the bathroom definitely counted as moving, so he waited. And waited. It was difficult to tell how long, but the beam of sunlight had definitely moved along the bed.

Gloria said she'd be back first thing in the morning. Where was she? Why was she taking so long? Maybe she'd left and driven off with the others. That had to be it. That or she'd forgotten all about him.

He could dash to the bathroom but that would mean police breaking down the door. After his last encounter with them, the bed seemed safer. Gloria would come back. She said she would and she seemed pretty nice. He could hold it.

He had to.

———

"Evelyn. Evelyn! Open the door!"

Gloria startled awake. She blinked toward the door with blurry eyes. Someone was hammering against it. Bethany, by the sound of it.

"OPEN. THE. DOOR."

Evelyn sat in a chair with her hands folded neatly in her lap. She stared straight ahead as though she couldn't hear the commotion.

"Just a minute!" Gloria threw back the covers and stumbled to the door. She opened it a crack and Bethany burst in.

The woman wore a pale blue polka-dot dress and nylons with perfectly straight seams. Her nails and makeup were immaculate, and her unruly curls had been pulled back and adorned with a pale blue hat that matched her dress.

"Planning on sleeping all day, dear? I had you pegged as the early-to-bed-early-to-rise type. It's eleven thirty."

"Eleven thirty!"

"We thought maybe Evelyn stabbed you in your sleep. Or did she just keep you up all night?" Bethany asked with a smirk.

That's exactly what had happened. Every time she started drifting off, Evelyn would abruptly cry out, lurching her back into consciousness. But there was no way she was giving Bethany the satisfaction. *"No."*

"Mmm-hmm. Anyhow, Doris and I already had breakfast at a little place down the street. When we came back the manager wanted to know where you were. Apparently he heard a man blubbering and crying inside your room." Bethany's smile couldn't be more pleased.

She couldn't have led with that?! Gloria ran to her bag and started yanking out clothes. She donned a pair of denim pants. "Where is the manager now?"

"Still trying to get into your room. For some reason, the lock seems jammed. But the Negro keeps howling to raise the dead."

"Drat drat drat." She thrust her feet into shoes. "Can you get Evelyn and our bags and put them in the car? I have to get Josh out of there."

Bethany's expression grew severe. "I *told* you that boy was trouble. We should leave him."

"I'm not having this discussion right now. We need to get out of here, with or without Josh. Now can you please help with Evelyn and the bags?"

"Fine. Since you asked so *nicely*."

Gloria dashed to Josh's room. Sure enough, the manager was trying fruitlessly to unlock the door. What Bethany hadn't mentioned was that Yoxtl was the one preventing him from opening it. The spirit hovered above the lock, its paw stuck *through* the wood toward the locking mechanism.

"I can't keep this up forever," the spirit said. "I told Josh you were on the way and he calmed down a bit, though you can still hear him whimpering."

The manager yanked out his key and whirled at Gloria. "You! I told you I wouldn't stand for this. You get that boy out of here right now! I'm holding you personally responsible for any damages he's caused. And you owe me extra. I can't have people knowing I let a Negro stay here. No one will ever want to sleep in that room again!"

Fat lotta nerve this guy had, considering they'd paid in diamonds. "I'm sure everything's fine. We'll be out of your hair soon enough. Mind if I try my key?" She shot a glance at Yoxtl, who extracted its paw.

She unlocked the door and tried to open it slowly, but the manager pushed past her and waved his hands.

"Out! Get out! What in tarnation did you do to my place?"

"He didn't do anyth—" The reek of piss slammed into her. Oh no. "Josh, are you okay?" He lay on the bed whimpering.

"He's made a mess is what he's done. Look at this filth!" The manager yanked off the covers. Underneath, Josh's pants were soaked. "That's it. I'm calling the police. You're in serious trouble, missy." He stormed off.

Gloria shot a desperate look at Yoxtl.

"I'll take care of it," the spirit said. "In the meantime, you've got to get him out of here. Give me your finger."

She held out her hand. Yoxtl flew over and bit down hard. She jerked back with a cry.

"Blood pact so I can find you later. Leave without me. I'll give you a long head start." Yoxtl vanished, presumably to the office.

Gloria returned her attention to Josh, who hadn't moved. "Josh? You need to get up. We have to leave right now!"

He just lay there whimpering. Had he even heard her?

"The police are coming soon. We need to go *now*. Please get up." She reached for his wrist and tugged on it.

Josh gave a bloodcurdling scream and rolled off the bed with a heavy thud.

"Are you okay?" She crept around the bed to where he lay sobbing on the floor.

Doris' silhouette appeared in the doorway. "What's going on? The manager is pitching a fit."

"I'm trying to get Josh but he won't get up."

"Where's that cat spirit? Can't it help?"

"Yoxtl is keeping the manager from calling the police. Is Evelyn in the car? Did Bethany get all our stuff?"

"I think so."

"Good. Grab Josh's bag and put it in the car. I'll be there as soon as I can."

Doris eyed the sizable wet indentation on the mattress without moving. "Why don't we just leave him?" she said quietly.

"He's one of us."

"But he isn't, is he?"

"He can do magic."

"Even if he has magic, he's more trouble than he's worth."

Gloria shot her a stony gaze. "Would you say that about Evelyn?"

Doris glanced over her shoulder and took a step into the room. "Maybe. But Evelyn is different. She's—"

"White?"

"A woman."

Gloria scoffed and returned her attention to Josh. He no longer cried, but his body shuddered with each ragged breath. He looked exhausted. Had he even slept last night, or was it from the crying? Why wouldn't he move?

"I wish I could understand what he needs."

"That's another thing," Doris said. "Evelyn can talk."

"Nikolai could talk to Josh."

"Yeah, but he's not here. Come on, just leave him. It's clear he's not right in the head."

"Are any of us?" Gloria muttered to herself. Then, louder, "We're not leaving him. If it takes magic to talk to Josh, maybe Yoxtl can convince him to get in the car."

"Then the police will come. Small town like this, they'll be here fast."

"We have to try." She wouldn't leave him to be arrested and sent to an asylum.

"Bethany's not going to like this. He smelled bad enough yesterday, but now—"

"I don't give a *damn* what Bethany likes! Get his bag and go back to the car. Not a word about how he smells. Not *one* word." She stormed from the room and headed for the front office.

Yoxtl was in a standoff with the manager over the phone. Whenever the man picked up the handset, Yoxtl stuck a paw through the cradle, somehow depressing the little prongs that were supposed to pop up. The manager huffed, slammed the handset down, then picked it up again. Gloria cleared her throat and he looked up in annoyance.

"Yoxtl, I need you to convince Josh to get in the car. *Now*."

The manager's face changed to confusion. "Yox— What?"

For a miracle, the spirit didn't question her and vanished. She grabbed the phone off the desk, yanking the cord out of the wall.

"Just what in the Sam Hill do you think you're doing, missy?"

"Call me 'missy' one more time and I'm going to strangle you with this cord." She brandished it at him and he shrank back, gaping.

"Now really, there's no need for . . . for that."

"I paid you with a *diamond*—more than enough to cover the room *and* the cleaning. We're leaving. And if you call the police on us, I swear to God I will come back here and piss on every single bed myself."

"Missy!"

She cracked the handset over his knuckles. He yowled and jerked his hand away, staring at her in horror.

"Do *not* test me!" She held his gaze until his eyes darted to the window. Outside, Yoxtl ushered Josh into the Suburban. She snapped her fingers in front of the clerk.

"Remember what I said. Forget we were here."

"Wh-what about my phone?" he stuttered.

"It's my phone now."

TAPPED OUT

The car arrived at the end of the dirt road. A sea of grass lay before them. Gloria opened the door and stood on the car's running board to give her some added height. There were a few darker spots on the horizon, but from this distance she couldn't tell if they were trees or a house.

"I think we're going the wrong way," said Bethany.

"Medea said it was out in the middle of nowhere. I just hoped the road went all the way to the cottage or wherever we're staying." Gloria turned to Yoxtl. "Do you know the way from here?"

"I can sense Medea's gateway and her protective wards that way." The spirit nodded to the northeast.

Gloria stepped down. "The building is supposed to be a ways west of that. Suburbans aren't designed to go off-road though. We'll have to leave it here and bring our stuff." She leaned into the car. "Everybody out."

For once, Bethany didn't contradict her. She stepped out and folded the front seat forward so the others could exit. Evelyn emerged, holding a hand across her face and blinking against the sun. Gloria noted with concern that the girl hadn't changed since yesterday. Josh still wore his soaked pants. Doris wore a bright red dress with matching lipstick, sunglasses, and heels—an outfit better suited for a date than traipsing across the countryside. Only Gloria and Josh wore pants.

Everyone shouldered their bags—thankfully light, given all they were carrying—and trudged west through the grass. They'd barely gone five minutes before the complaining began.

"Ugh, this grass is so annoying," said Doris. "My stockings are covered in stickers!"

"Are you certain this is the right way?"

"This place we're going had better be nice."

"How much farther is it?"

Yoxtl led the way, body passing through the plants as though they weren't there.

Gloria eyed the ground as they walked. There weren't many rocks or prairie dog holes. The Suburban might make it through next time if she took it slow. If there *was* a next time. Bethany had continued her cattiness through the whole drive, with Doris following her lead. Evelyn and Josh were off in their own little worlds. Even she was finding it hard to stay enthused.

If only Nikolai had come with them. She'd been suspicious of him at first, but he had the intangible qualities of a good officer, unifying the group with ease, and he'd shown them real, practical uses for magic. Even his grouchy sister Medea would have been better than Yoxtl. The woman's casual displays of power were enough to intrigue anyone. Yoxtl had helped out here and there, but never with magic and only in emergencies. It was eroding the creature's authority and making them forget why they were here.

"Hey, Yoxtl," she said, "why don't you tell us what our training's going to be like?"

There was a murmur of interest behind her, but the spirit simply said, "You'll find out soon enough."

So much for that. Bethany and Doris stopped complaining, but the walk seemed drearier.

Doris was the first to spot the roof above the grass and ran toward it with glee. Gloria called out in alarm—the careless girl was going to break an ankle running in those heels—but Doris' mood was infectious and the others followed her at a jog. Even Bethany perked up a little, though her frown returned as soon as they saw the place.

"I think we found Laura Ingalls Wilder's house."

"You can't expect us to stay in *that*!"

Gloria stared at the settler homestead in dismay. It was half sod and half wood, and it looked as though it hadn't been maintained in at least fifty years. Detached boards clung to the side by solitary nails that stubbornly refused to relinquish their burden. Prairie grass had rushed through the missing front door to reclaim the interior.

Gloria straightened herself and tried to sound chipper. "It's functional—that's all we need. Sod is a good insulator and we can shore up the rest with magic, right?" She looked to Yoxtl, but the expression the spirit gave her was anything but reassuring.

"I'm from the jungle. No use for warming spells."

Great, just great. At least the Suburban was heated. If she could get it out here, they could park it alongside the open door, maybe tent it to trap heat. Maybe. It would work in the short term, but they'd need real shelter once the snow started. She approached the building and examined the wood. The boards were badly weathered, but the frame seemed solid enough. It wouldn't take long to patch up the holes and add insulation in any gaps. They could make this work.

"This isn't going to work." Bethany stood inside the house with her hands on her hips. "It's filthy. There's no heat, no lighting, no running water. And just look at how tiny it is! It's meant for a single family all living in the same room, not four people and a"—she halted at Gloria's glare—"a *man*. We should go back to the nearest town and see if they have a motel."

"That's not a long-term solution."

Bethany gestured around the room. "Neither is this."

As much as she hated to side with Bethany, Gloria agreed. How long would the training take? How long would they have to stay hidden? And where would they go once their abilities were under control? Nikolai had made it sound as though there was a whole community of Magi. Would he check in on them as promised and take them somewhere else when they were ready? And why wasn't Yoxtl being more helpful? Her first instinct was to set up camp, but the others would never agree, not in this mind-set.

She turned to Yoxtl. "Why don't you give us our first magic lesson?"

"Shouldn't you settle in first? It gets dark pretty early here." A lame excuse, considering it couldn't be far past noon.

"Come on, just one quick lesson? Then we can have a late lunch and unpack."

"That's the thing—magic takes time. Meditation, fasting, spiritual cleansing, uh . . ." Yoxtl paused at her not-so-subtle expression signaling the urgency of the request. "Okay. I guess I can give you a quick demonstration. Sit in a circle over there. I'll be right back." The spirit disappeared into the sod house.

Doris and Bethany sat on the grass, murmuring with excitement. Josh plopped down opposite them with a bored expression. Evelyn didn't move from where she stood against the house, picking at strands of her long dark hair. Gloria approached her.

"Come sit with us, Evelyn."

The girl shook her head. "Grandmother said magic is evil."

"I'm sure we won't be doing anything bad. Magic has helped us so far, hasn't it?"

Evelyn frowned. "Back at the store . . . we stole stuff, didn't we? Josh was upset about it. And he should be. Stealing is a sin."

"I didn't think you'd remember that."

Evelyn's face darkened. "I'm not stupid. Just because I get confused sometimes doesn't mean I don't know what's going on."

"I . . . I know, hun. I'm sorry. I didn't mean to make you feel—"

"You drag me all the way out here, away from my family, and demand I fornicate with the devil. Well, I won't! I'm a good girl, and I won't do that. You can't make me!"

Gloria shrank back from the sudden vehemence. "No one's going to make you do anything."

"But you did! Again and again after I told you no!" Evelyn looked to Gloria's right, and it occurred to her that the girl's remarks might not have anything to do with magic. "It's not my fault! I *told* you it's not my fault."

"Evelyn. *Evelyn.*"

The girl's eyes snapped back.

"Nobody here is going to make you do anything, okay? We're here to learn magic, but you can just watch if you want."

Evelyn's eyes flicked to the side, as though checking an invisible specter for permission, then back to Gloria. "I'm a good girl. Leave me out of your devil worship."

"I found what I needed." Yoxtl reemerged from the house with a chipper expression and trotted over to the others.

Gloria reluctantly joined them, keeping a watchful eye on Evelyn.

The spirit spat out a small pile of corn kernels. "Okay, first lesson—growing your own food."

Bethany eyed the pile suspiciously. "Why do we have to grow our food?"

"Huh?"

"At the store, Nikolai magicked a whole bunch of food out of nothing."

"You must be mistaken." Yoxtl shot Gloria a questioning glance.

"He said he was gonna fill a bag with food for us, but I didn't see what he put in there. I was busy getting clothes for Evelyn and Josh."

"I saw it," said Doris. "He held out his hand and food appeared on the counter. Are you saying you can't do that?"

Yoxtl looked aghast. "I . . . That magic is forbidden."

"By who?" Bethany asked. "Nikolai didn't seem to have a problem with it."

"Yeah, well there are a lot of things Nikolai doesn't have a problem with. I don't know where he learned that spell, but forget you've ever seen it."

Bethany's mouth pinched shut. She leaned over and whispered something to Doris.

Yoxtl ignored them and continued. "Now, *growing* food is perfectly acceptable. You need the same things seeds normally require to germinate—sunlight, nutrients, moisture—you're just encouraging them to grow much faster. Allow me to demonstrate."

The spirit batted one of the corn kernels aside and crouched before it, staring intently. Gloria had to squint, but she could swear she saw it move. A white tendril snaked from the kernel and burrowed into the ground. Green blossomed from the kernel and shot skyward, impossibly fast. The shoot extended and thickened until it towered nearly ten feet. Yoxtl grinned at them.

"Wow," Bethany said flatly, her tone anything but amazed. "That's a really big cornstalk you got there."

Yoxtl's smile became a toothy grimace. It batted a kernel toward Bethany. "I'd like to see you do it. Concentrate on the seed and tell it to grow."

Bethany huffed and turned her attention to the seed. Doris leaned over expectantly. After a minute, Bethany shoved her aside with a snarl. "Stop breathing on me! You're breaking my concentration."

"It's not as easy as it looks," said Yoxtl. "Keep trying. The rest of you, come get a seed." It looked expectantly at Evelyn, who still leaned against the rustic house.

"She's not coming," said Gloria. "Thinks we're doing devil magic."

"Are we?" giggled Doris. "My parents would be so upset."

"We are *not*," Yoxtl said emphatically. "Put aside what you think you know about religion and magic. Focus on your seeds."

Gloria poked an indentation in the ground with her finger and set the kernel inside. She stared at it as hard as she could, willing a little white tendril to pop out, but nothing happened. A glance around the circle showed the others were having the same difficulty.

"This is ludicrous," Bethany burst out after a few minutes. "You're not even telling us what to do."

"I told you, magic is best mastered after a cleansing period to free the mind. If it were easy, everybody would do it."

"Oh!" Doris exclaimed and pointed to the ground in front of Josh, where a cornstalk was rapidly erupting. It surpassed the height of Yoxtl's stalk and kept growing. Josh didn't seem to notice. He stared intently at the base, as though all his thoughts were on the corn.

"Josh?" said Gloria. "You can probably stop now."

Still it grew, towering above them, twenty feet high. The soil surrounding the stalk cracked and paled. A root emerged and made its way toward Josh's exposed ankle. Josh didn't even flinch when it pierced his skin.

"Josh!" Gloria bolted forward and grabbed the roots, yanking them back, but they bit into her hands. "Help me! Josh. *Josh!* You have to stop!"

Josh blinked at her, confused, then looked down and began to wail. He tugged his foot away, inadvertently jerking her along with the roots.

"Hold on! Hold on! Doris—get the knife from my bag. I left it propped against the house."

Josh continued to struggle, but the roots refused to release his ankle. Gloria stared in horror at her own hands. She'd seen combat wounds—not often, but enough that injuries no longer made her squeamish. There was something entirely different about the roots though, the way they raised trails under the skin like parasitic worms.

"Got it!" Doris arrived with the knife.

"Cut Josh loose first. He's pitching a fit."

Doris hesitated, then moved to Josh. She hacked the roots and he scrambled back, sobbing. The roots in Gloria's hands slowed and stilled. Gritting her teeth, she began tugging them free. Her gorge rose. She took a breath and willed it back down. They were *not* worms, no matter how much they looked like them.

A loud snap resounded behind her.

"Look out!" Doris cried.

Gloria had barely turned when something cracked against her head. Spots of light flooded her vision. Evelyn's voice came as though from a great distance: "I told you magic was evil."

<hr>

Yoxtl turned in time to see Josh's cornstalk—now a good thirty feet tall—snap under its own weight and crack over Gloria's head. She rolled over and kicked the air as though expecting an assailant. Finding none, she slumped back and closed her eyes.

Humans were fascinating creatures. You could almost feel their souls swell with every little burst of emotion. Doris' pulsed as she ran over and yanked Gloria upright, while Bethany observed the scene with indifference.

"Up. Sit up! She has a concussion. We have to keep her awake. Bethany, *help* me."

"She made it perfectly clear she doesn't want my help."

Yoxtl studied Gloria. There didn't seem to be much blood, but head injuries were bad. Cut off a limb and humans would keep going. Cut off all four and they were slow, but their mind—the part that mattered, the part that fed their *souls*—well, that was still intact. Medea had once given yit power enough to heal Nikolai, and there was still a bit left over. Yoxtl had been saving it up for a big, showy miracle or an emergency. This might count as the latter.

"I'll heal her," yit announced. The mortals had been itching for any sort of magical display since leaving Omaha. Hopefully this would satisfy their curiosity. Of course, yit'd have to make a show. Yoxtl illuminated Gloria's head as yit worked—such trickery cost no power to a spirit—and the mortals watched in fascination.

Gloria's unfocused eyes snapped back to attention, then drifted toward the sobbing Josh. Her soul rippled. "We have to help him."

Doris tried to restrain her. "You need to take it easy."

"He's hurt." Gloria pulled herself away and crawled to where Josh lay taking ragged breaths. She tried to lift the cuff of his pants but he yelped and shrank back.

No no no it hurts! The thought was flung wide, but humans were notoriously terrible at picking up that sort of communication and probably hadn't heard.

"I can't see how bad it is with your pants on. Can you take them off?" Gloria tried to slowly scoot closer.

Josh lurched away. *No. It will snag and hurt more.*

Yoxtl inserted yitself between them. "Can she cut the pant leg open?"

Josh thought for a long moment. *Yes.*

"Doris, give her the knife."

Gloria approached cautiously. "I'll try not to touch you. *Hold still*." She pulled the pant leg taut and began sawing through the cuff. Once through the thicker material, the blade parted the fabric easily and she opened it with a grim expression. Roots ran under the surface of his entire leg like bumpy veins.

Josh heaved, and his soul quavered. *Oh God oh God oh God.*

"How could this have happened?" Gloria whispered.

"I told you magic was evil," said Evelyn.

"Magic is *not* evil," said Yoxtl. "Plants need nutrients to grow. When the soil was depleted, the roots sought whatever was available."

"Why didn't you stop Josh?"

"I tried, but his focus was unbreakable. He couldn't feel what was happening to his leg, let alone hear my pleas. I've never seen anything like it." Yoxtl glanced at Josh. Even now, the man seemed oblivious to their conversation, chanting *oh God oh God* ad nauseam. As if YHWH would ever be bothered to help mortals. Yit would have to break them of such habits if they were to truly convert. Nikolai should have been here helping, but the mortal had grabbed for power regardless of their bargain. Better to go at it alone than deal with such a fickle partner.

Yoxtl returned yits attention to the task at hand. The roots needed to be removed, but Josh was unlikely to sit still for that. If they had been in the jungle, yit could have directed them to a number of medicinal plants. But the land here was cold and dry, with few life-forms beyond the unfamiliar prairie grass. How could humans stand living here? Yit should've asked to take the Magi back to the temple. They would have been warm and well fed.

Yoxtl tried to make yits tone reassuring. "Josh, you're going to have to sit still so Gloria can remove the roots. They have to come out if you're to get better."

Josh's soul reverberated with the thought of such pain. *Nooooooo!*

Gloria frowned. "You make it sound as if you're not going to heal him."

"I'm not."

Gloria's soul flickered with indignation. "You healed me!"

"Only your head, not your hands. This isn't life-threatening."

"Like hell it's not. We have no antiseptic. No bandages. Nikolai told me not to pack first aid supplies because *you* could heal us."

Damnit. Why did Nikolai have to overstate yits abilities? First the food summoning—yit really had to ask about that—and now this. It's not like spirits had an unlimited supply of magic at their beck and call. They required a certain threshold to maintain consciousness. Dip too low and yit would return to a feral, mindless state. Josh's injury wasn't so grievous as to risk that, but healing it *would* consume what little remained of Medea's magic, draining Yoxtl back to yits limited inherent abilities. No power for miracles, let alone another healing if one of them managed to get *really* hurt.

Yoxtl tried to sound firm but reassuring. "You can get supplies in town. As long as the roots are removed, he'll heal fine."

Gloria stood with a glare. "If I have to go to town for first aid supplies, I'm not coming back."

"What?"

"You heard me. Heal Josh or I walk."

"You leave here without learning to control your magic and you'll end up right back in the mental hospital."

Gloria looked at yit coolly. "I wasn't thrown in there because of that. It won't happen again."

"Where would you go? I've seen how other humans treat Josh. He needs a place where he can be treated with respect."

"It's like that everywhere." She stole a glance at Bethany. "What matters is who he's with. And right now he needs people who *look out for him*. Can you do that? Will you heal him?"

She had no idea what she was asking. Healing Josh would put the whole group at risk. Yit had to regain control, and fast. Yoxtl drew yitself up and made yits voice a commanding boom.

"The Great God Yoxtl helps those who help themselves. Greatness awaits those who—"

Gloria scoffed and shook her head in disgust. "Doris, stay with Josh. Bethany, keep an eye on Evelyn until I get back." She stalked off through the grass, taking Yoxtl's every hope with her.

Why did mortals have to be so obstinate?

Help me.

"I can't." Yoxtl targeted the words for Josh alone. The man couldn't share the truth anyway. "I'd like to, really I would, but healing takes power and I don't have much left."

Please. Hurts so much. The words came out jagged and clipped, as though it took all his effort to form a coherent thought.

Yoxtl studied Josh's leg. While not deep, the damage was extensive. Did yit have enough power? Perhaps, if yit opted for surface healing more than internal. At least sealing the wounds would prevent infection. Yoxtl sighed and teleported to Gloria— at least *that* didn't consume power—appearing right in front of her torso. She jerked back in surprise.

"I'll heal him, but you still have to take the roots out."

She stared at yit a moment, then nodded curtly and returned to Josh.

"I need you to hold still," she said, crouching beside him. "This is going to hurt." Her fingers had only brushed the first root when Josh wailed and wriggled away.

Stop stop stop!

"I can't do this if he won't hold still."

"I'm not sure he *can*." Could yit afford a sleep spell? If Josh thrashed the whole time, yit probably couldn't afford *not* to. Yoxtl put a steadying paw on Josh's chest. "I'm going to put you to sleep."

Not bedtime.

"Not that kind of sleep. Just so that you don't feel what Gloria's doing. Okay?"

Feel better when wake?

"Yes."

Gloria watched the exchange with a furrowed brow. "You can talk to him?"

"When he thinks *at* me, yes. Lie back, Josh." Yoxtl waited until the man was prone before casting Sleep. "Go ahead, Gloria."

She grasped the end of a root and gently tugged, using far more care than she'd shown her own wounds. The root gave ground reluctantly and with a great deal of blood.

"Will all training be this dangerous?" she asked.

"I didn't intend for it to be. Growing corn usually isn't this exciting."

Gloria eased the last of the root free and tossed it aside with a grimace. Several of the tips had broken off under the skin. Great, something else to drain yits power. Yoxtl broke down the roots, cleansed the wounds, and started healing the worst places. When yits power dwindled, yit sealed up the entry points and made them look pretty. The rest would have to heal on its own.

Gloria nodded in satisfaction at yits work and held out her hands. "Can you do me now?"

"I can't. I'm . . . tapped out for today." Better to let her think yits magic needed time to replenish.

She frowned but didn't complain. Hopefully she'd forget tomorrow. The magic gifted by Medea was gone—no more healing, no more miracles. The mortals better not get themselves into trouble.

BEIGE

edea stared in consternation as Nikolai scaled the roof. The idiot was going to get himself killed. How could he be so careless, so stupid? What the hell was he trying to prove?

The day had gone from bad to worse. Turning on the refrigerator had resulted in an incessant low-pitched hum. She'd hastily returned to the kitchen, but its subtle vibrations followed her through the closed door. Nikolai hadn't seemed bothered, but if it was enough to grate on her nerves, who knew what kind of effect it was having on him? Sure enough, his first bread summoning had been wildly erratic. It took more willpower for him to push the bible across the table, his water boiling time increased by a full minute, and he'd even set her shirt on fire. If she didn't know any better, she'd say he was distracted, but she'd done all she could to ensure a sterile work environment. He performed every task diligently and without complaint.

The second machine wasn't quite as bad—for her or for him. His bread was still off, as was his water boil. Ironically, both times his illusion work was fine—though that aligned with the conventional wisdom that illusion spells weren't affected by

Mundane machines. She was curious to see if the trend held the entire week.

As the day progressed, the dull ache in her abdomen became a roaring beast clamoring for attention. She wanted nothing more than to curl up around a hot water bottle and read, but retreating to her room wasn't an option, nor was even sitting, for it would change an experimental variable. Thankfully, Nikolai had run through mana like a novice, giving her more breaks in which to rest her body if not her mind. He peppered her with questions, seemingly craving human interaction as much as she craved silence.

The day couldn't end fast enough.

She'd anticipated the possibility of being permanently locked out of her room. What she hadn't anticipated was Nikolai's reaction to the barricade. What the hell did he expect? He'd wanted to kill her! Not that death frightened her as much as it did in the old days. Even if he succeeded, her soul was powerful enough to cling to consciousness, body be damned. What she feared was far more personal, and stayed with a person forever—not that she was about to dispel Nikolai of his ignorance. She sat in silence, mentally and physically exhausted from the day, hoping he'd get over it and move on. He hadn't let up though, ceaselessly haranguing her through the car window. Why couldn't he just leave her alone? His words pecked holes in her mind until she felt she would crumble, and she'd sternly reminded him of his place. Now the fool was on the roof. Why did he put himself in such ridiculous situations? Every time she started to see him as a man grown, he proved he had the sense of a teenaged boy.

A patch of shingles detached and sent Nikolai sliding toward the edge. She gasped and rushed forward, the instinct to catch him overwhelming, even though logically she knew it would only hurt them both. But he didn't topple down. Heart pounding, she took a step back and found him clinging to the shingles. He repositioned himself, then asked, "Am I above your window?"

He couldn't be serious. The eaves were too far out and the window too far below. He'd never reach. "Don't be a fool! You'll get yourself killed."

He seemed intent on doing so anyway. The question was whether to intervene if he fell. She had a general rule against helping idiots out of self-manufactured problems. On the other hand, she needed him for the experiments.

Magically arresting his descent would contaminate the test site. Their work, barely begun, would be put on hold while she found an acceptable replacement. Just thinking about all she'd have to do to secure and set up a new location made her head ache.

She could allow him to fall. Actions had consequences. Why not let Nikolai feel the brunt of his? As long as he fell legs first, he'd sustain no more than a few fractures. It would mean dragging him to the car and taking him at least a mile away to do any healing, but the test site would remain clean, and perhaps he'd learn not to be so reckless. Of course, if he landed on his back or head, that was a different matter. She might not be able to move him without aggravating his injuries, which meant contaminating the site by healing.

Or he could die.

The risk was low, but it was there. She had to keep him from following through on his ridiculous plan. "If you fall, I can't help you." There. He wouldn't risk his own neck if he knew she had no intention to help.

The look he gave her was murderous. He accused her of thinking him expendable. It made no sense. Unless he found immortality for himself, she'd outlive him, just as she'd outlived everyone else, and her memories of him would fade into oblivion

—the very definition of *expend*. Most people were expendable, or at least interchangeable. Surely he knew this?

She tried to speak the lie that would make him happy. "You're not . . . you're not expendable."

"But I'm not worth as much as a clean test site. Hard to find those. Turn over a rock, though, and you'll find a new apprentice."

Well, yes, she wanted to say, then thought better of it. It was true that apprentices could be found everywhere, but that didn't mean she didn't enjoy his company or need his help. One could be expendable and still hold value, and Nikolai had proved invaluable on this trip. It was almost like he was resentful, or hurt. Ridiculous thought. Nikolai didn't get hurt. Angry, yes, but never upset, not like most people.

Once again, Nikolai asked if he was above her window. He could make no move without direction. She had half a mind to go back to the car. Let him spend the night up there!

"Fine," he said, and began lowering himself over the eaves.

What the hell was he *doing*? Was he *mad*? There was nothing to cling to besides the shingles, and he'd be putting his full weight on—

"Shut up! Left or right?"

Pointless not to direct him now. There's no way he could pull himself back up. The only safe way down was through the window.

"Right." She hated the quaver in her voice. Goddamnit, why did he have to be like this? Always pushing himself too far, taking too many risks. It's like he had a death wish. Each small movement coiled her tighter than a spring—would this be the time he lost his grip? Nikolai's muscles strained as he inched along the roof, but his face remained impassive. He might as well be going to tea.

He wasn't afraid.

It shouldn't have been surprising—his amygdala was smaller than average—and yet she'd rarely had the opportunity to witness such a striking example. She'd always hoped that as his forebrain finished developing, it would counteract the imbalance in his amygdala. Now she wasn't so sure. Could one make rational decisions without being tempered by fear?

Her heart sank. Talented as he was, he'd never make it to immortality. The cards were stacked against him. It wasn't until that moment she realized she'd been rooting for him to make it that far. Despite his many faults, he'd proven to be a capable mage, and someone she could count on.

He reached the window and she called out to him. Like a pendulum, he began to swing his legs toward the window—what was left of it. Rotted wood had broken away, leaving a gap. She cried out, trying to warn him, but he was already flying. The momentum flipped him on end. In terrifying slow motion, he fell head first.

Actions had consequences, and his would be death.

She was willing him upward before she was even fully conscious of it. Damnit, she couldn't let him die, not yet. He had so much *potential*. Did parents not protect their children? Well, hers hadn't, but that was beside the point. Some did. Was he not her responsibility while he was her apprentice? Wasn't it her job to train him to the best of her abilities—to the best of *his*—taking his faulty brain into account?

Up, up he went, then through the window in one fluid motion.

She stood a moment longer, heart pounding like she'd been running. What had she done? She'd contaminated the site. Worse—she'd intervened to save his life. Immortality had to be earned. It *had* to be. Her knees buckled and she sank to the ground. All her work to secure this place, half a year of searching for sites that met the qualifications, of swallowing her discomfort and talking to people, of trying to convince them she didn't need a husband to make decisions—gone in a flash, thanks to the whims of one idiot apprentice.

If she went upstairs to her room, she'd see him, and that was more than she could handle right now. She tried to will herself to stand and walk back to the car, but her body had never obeyed her as well as the magic had. He could have the house to himself. It was worthless now. When she had the strength, she'd teleport back home.

Nikolai strolled around the house, grinning like he'd won a damned prize. "Hey, what are you still doing out here? I got your room unblocked."

She launched herself at him, intent on slapping the grin off his stupid face.

Nikolai grinned at Medea. She'd used magic to save him—she *did* care! A slap rang across his cheek.

"YOU. MADE. ME. CONTAMINATE. MY. TEST. SITE." Medea punctuated each word with a slap, her face contorted with rage.

Though not the reaction he'd hoped for, it still proved she cared enough about him to act against her own self-interest, and that was a win. He just had to make her see it that way, or at least calm her down. He grabbed her wrists. "The site isn't contaminated. And you know it, otherwise you'd be attacking me with magic."

"Don't tempt me!" She kicked his shins.

"You used telekinesis to move me. Just like I've been using telekinesis to move the Bible—it's the same thing."

"IT'S NOT THE SAME THING!" She made to jerk her hands out of his grasp and he released them. She took a step back, chest heaving pleasantly as she caught her breath. "I used significantly more mana lifting you!"

"Yeah, but what are the odds that it stuck around and is affecting the environment? I mean, really, the whole *point* of this experiment is to see if the hypothesis bears further testing. It doesn't *have* to be perfect because you're going to do the experiment again with other people, *right*?"

She stared off to the side, wearing her contemplative #3 frown.

"Based on the last two days alone, would you say the hypothesis is worth pursuing?"

She said nothing, though it looked like she wanted to say many things. Finally, "Yes," through gritted teeth. She charged toward him again, not with her fists, but with an accusing finger. "But I'll have to get a whole new test site. You had no right to jeopardize my experiments. None!"

He ignored the second part. It would only lead to more arguments. "I'm sure the test site is fine. I'm even willing to stay here longer and replicate the work we did today, just so you can see if there's a difference. If the test site *has* been compromised, I'll take full responsibility for securing a new one." He suspected that was the real sticking point. Medea didn't do well in the Mundane world, or with people in general.

"I . . . okay." She rubbed her eyes with shaky hands, as though trying to conceal tears.

He wasn't sure why the test site thing affected her that deeply, but he'd long since given up trying to understand the intricacies of emotions. All that mattered was cause and effect. If you knew people's buttons, you could push them to get a desired result. He'd already discovered that one of Medea's buttons was being accused of lying, but this was something else. Compromised objective? He'd have to think on it. In the meantime, he'd give her an out. "Will you come inside? If you're cold—"

"I'm not cold. I mean I *am*, but . . . god, I need a drink." She hid her face and wiped her eyes again.

"We should've thought to summon alcohol."

She chuckled softly. "I didn't think we'd be needing it. I should've known better, being around you." She gave him a shove.

"Come on, let's go to town. I know where there's a bar." Shit, no, he'd told the cashier he'd be there. He'd have to reschedule. "Or how about a restaurant? We can get some real food."

Medea pondered it for some time, and he was certain she'd say no, but then, "Yeah, fine. I'm not going to get anything done now anyway."

He wondered what work she had left to do and how she'd expected to get it done while locked inside a car.

They got into the Chevy. No sooner had he started the engine than Medea exclaimed, "Your hands!"

He glanced down. Angry black splinters decorated his palms. Dulled by adrenaline, the burning pain came rushing back at her words. "It's nothing. I'll pick them out later."

"Don't be ridiculous. I'd hate to see what your shoddy healing would do to such nice hands. Drive a mile away and park so I can heal you."

Nice hands, eh? Just where exactly had she imagined his hands? What did she like about them? He joined the main road and began scanning the highway for a side street he'd seen on his last trip to town. To hell with the restaurant—he needed more time alone with her. There it was. He pulled down a dirt road and drove until they could no longer see the highway.

"You could've just parked on the shoulder," she said.

"I thought you might appreciate a quieter atmosphere." He smiled and got out of the car. The sun sank low over a field of grass and wildflowers. He couldn't have picked a more romantic spot. They'd watch the sunset and he'd pretend to be interested in the beauty of nature. Away from the test site and work, he might finally get Medea to relax. There was no wood for a fire. If she got cold enough, she might let him put his arm around her. He flattened a swath of grass and sat, beckoning her over.

Medea knelt beside him with a frown. "We can't get drinks this way."

Drunk Medea—even better. He couldn't summon liquid without a container but doubted she had any such constraint. "You're already going to use magic to heal me—why stop there?"

Her frown deepened, as though she searched for a rebuttal, then magic rippled over her body. "Remind me to cancel my temperature control spell before we leave."

Well, there went his excuse to hold her.

"Give me your hand," she said.

Her magic, a continual pressure against his consciousness at the farmhouse, was like a roaring fire this close. He'd gladly throw himself upon that pyre. He extended his hand. A jolt shot through him at her touch, but her fingers were cool against his burning palms.

Distress flashed across her face as she examined his hand. Did he feel like a void by comparison? A black hole next to her blazing sun? She cupped his hand and looked up at him with concern. "How on earth did you manage to hold on to the roof like this?"

Ah, so that was the source of her discomfort. He shrugged. "It's not like I had a choice." Abruptly, he lost the feel of her against his skin. "Please don't turn off my nerves."

She gave him a puzzled look. "It's going to be painful when I take these out."

"I don't mind. Really." He fished around for a lie. "If I can feel it, maybe I'll get a better idea of your healing process."

She said nothing, but his hand tingled back to life, bringing with it the caress of her fingers. Her head bent over him, golden locks shielding her face. He breathed deeply and caught the scent of meadow flowers in her hair. One by one, she coaxed each splinter out with her will. He allowed himself to wince at the pain, knowing she would expect it. The concern and meticulousness she showed wasn't something he'd witnessed in previous healings. Was it because she longed to see his "nice hands" returned to normal? Or because she was beginning to care for him? When both hands were healed, she massaged them as though testing their feel against her skin. He resisted the urge to embrace her and topple them both into the grass.

"There," she said. "I think I managed to stave off the poison ivy reaction as well. We'll find out in a day or two." She gave him a conspiratorial look. "And now, the alcohol. Hold one of your hands as if clutching an invisible ball, then conjure a shield in your palm, extending between your fingers."

He did so, but intentionally made an amorphous blob around his entire hand.

Medea laughed. "Not like that." She took his hand again, sending the same jolt through him, and pulled the shield into the shape of a cup. Satisfied he could hold it, she conjured her own and filled her hand with amber liquid. A hint of vanilla reached him. Bourbon.

"That's not what you usually drink," he said.

"I usually only drink when I'm upset, and I'd rather not be reminded of that. Would you like to try some?"

"Please."

She tipped her hand over his, then leaned back and took a swig of her own, closing her eyes with pleasure. He took a sip—a bit smooth for his taste—then downed the rest.

"Would you care for more?" she asked.

"No, thank you. I prefer vodka." He summoned water into his palm, sipping it to maintain the pretense. Too much alcohol and the mask slipped. His jokes became too dark, his tone too acerbic.

Men called him an asshole, while women shrank away, eyes wide and fearful. But Medea would only continue drinking if she thought he joined her. She sipped slowly, gazing at the setting sun with a wistful expression.

"It's beautiful, isn't it?" he asked.

"It looks much the same as it always has."

Damn, he'd defaulted to an inane topic. Maybe something philosophical would grab her. "I suppose there's a comfort in that —that some things never change."

For a time she said nothing. Had he hit a dead end? Then, "It's nice when things like *that* never change. Sunsets are innocuous. Human nature though . . ." She gazed out over the plain before taking a long swig of her drink, coughing.

Shit. Had he reminded her of the missing natives? The magical knowledge lost with their passing?

Medea emptied her hand in one final gulp. She did not refill it but shifted as though to rise.

"We should play a game," he said before she could suggest leaving.

Medea's neutral frown automatically deepened. "What game?"

He cast about for something that might get her to open up. "Truth or Dare."

"I already don't like it."

"But half of it revolves around truth, and that's your favorite thing!" he said with mock enthusiasm.

She rolled her eyes and settled back on the grass. The dipping sun behind her set her hair ablaze. "How is it played?"

"Players ask each other 'truth or dare?' If a player chooses truth, the other person poses a question that must be answered honestly. If a player chooses dare, they're assigned a daring task to perform."

"That sounds like a terrible game. Why would anyone want to

play?"

"To pass the time. It's quite popular among teenagers."

"I can see why. Teenagers only have half a brain anyway."

He laughed. "Come on, it's all in good fun. Play with me."

"Why? You do realize what will happen, don't you? I'll always pick truth and you'll always pick dare. You'll choose a question I don't want to answer, I'll choose a dare that's not thrilling enough for you, and we'll both be left unsatisfied."

He grinned. "I *always* try to make sure my partner's satisfied."

"I doubt that."

Had she intended to insult him, or had the innuendo gone over her head, as they so often did? "Look, you can switch to dare if you don't like the question I ask."

"That's even worse. Then I'd be stuck committing to a dare that I definitely don't want to do."

"I'll go easy on you, I promise. And you can quit anytime you're uncomfortable."

"It sounds like the whole point of the game is to make someone uncomfortable," she said sourly. "Why do you want me to play?"

"You have to ask 'truth or dare' first." He met her scowl with a playful smirk. If he could get her asking and answering, she'd play despite her protests. He just had to get past that first barrier. "I won't make you say it. I choose truth. Why do I want you to play? Because I'm bored and I'd like to know more about you. My turn. How old were you when you won your first duel?" She had to answer that—she loved dueling.

"I didn't agree to play. And you didn't ask 'truth or dare' either!"

"You're just going to pick truth anyway. We both know it. Well, how old were you? I know you don't remember your exact age, so give me a rough estimate."

"Ten or so."

"Did you kill them?"

She straightened, indignant. "You already asked your question."

He smiled inwardly—he had her now. "My apologies. I pick dare."

"We're in an open field in the middle of nowhere. I can't think of a single dare for you. No, if we play this, we play for truth and truth alone."

"That's not how the game is played, and I'm not sure you want honest me. No one does."

"I'm sure I don't. But I'll take honesty over fiction in any case. Truth or nothing, but if you fail to answer or if I think you're lying, the game is finished. You can't expect me to open up if you don't do the same."

Why did she have to be so damned serious? "Fine. Ask."

"Why do you take such stupid risks?"

"Pardon?"

She shifted closer, piercing him with her gaze. "Like the roof. You could have gone inside and tried the door again, but you chose the stupidest, riskiest way to get inside. And it wouldn't be the first time you've done something like that. I understand that you don't get scared, but you don't act like someone who wishes to be immortal. On the contrary—it's as though you have a death wish."

He feigned a nervous laugh. "I think I grossly underestimated your skill at this game. Then again, we are playing to *your* rules."

"Are you saying that to avoid the question, or to give yourself time to think of a lie?"

Jesus Christ. For someone who couldn't read people for shit, she could see through him with startling precision. "I did it to give myself time to think. I'm not sure I can explain it properly." Or that he'd want to.

"Try."

As always, his first instinct was to lie, but she'd see through that and the game would be over. Better to earn credibility for now. Medea knew enough of him not to be thrown by the information, and there was a chance it would make her more understanding.

"Imagine walking down a beige hallway, deafening in its silence. It's perfectly uniform and it stretches as far as you can see. That's life. You walk, you run, hoping to see something, *anything* unique, but it's just the same flat, dull walls. So you make changes. You run down the hallway screaming, hoping for an echo. You mess with the lights—maybe they'll flicker or break or electrocute you. You don't care, so long as it does *something*. Get desperate enough and maybe you'll punch a hole in the wall. Or scratch open your wrists and paint the walls with blood. It doesn't matter what the consequences are—you're not even thinking about that—all you're thinking about is how sick you are of the endless fucking beige.

"Life is boring—tell people that and they'll commiserate, but they don't really *understand*. I've been inside people's heads when they're bored, and their experience isn't even close to mine. They always feel *something*. They call up memories to entertain themselves, and somehow that works for them. I can't do that. I can't replicate the experience in my head. Memories are just a record of events, flat as photographs. The endorphins, the adrenaline—they're gone. The only way to get those is to *do* something, even if it means punching a wall and hurting my hand. I prefer pleasure, but pain works just as well."

Medea studied him intently. "So you're saying that because you lack internal emotional highs and lows, you seek external stimulation to artificially generate a temporary change in your brain chemistry?"

"I . . . Yeah."

"And you feel this way all the time?"

"For the most part. It's not that bad on the island now that I have days off. Practical lessons are challenging and sparring gives me a nice boost, but here"—he gestured to the wide-open plain—"nothing but beige. Not that I don't enjoy talking to you," he added hastily. "That helps—a lot, actually—but during the experiments, it's just sitting and quiet and repetition. There's nothing to keep my mind engaged, not even conversation. It's better when there's people around, because then I have something to play with. I can have a lot of fun in a crowded room."

He paused as Medea's face tensed. She probably saw herself lumped in with everyone else he manipulated. She was, of course, but most people fooled themselves into thinking they were the lone exception. Seeing it was different than hearing him talk so candidly. What the hell did she expect, asking him to open up like this?

"I'm not telling you anything new," he said, an edge creeping into his voice. "Everyone tries to influence the people around them—to get favors, sympathy, praise, whatever. What I do is no different. It's subconscious for most people. When a baby cries, does it know how each wail stabs its mother? No. It just knows that crying brings food or comfort. I'm just more intentional." And better at it.

Medea said nothing, but her frown deepened. She likely wouldn't recall any of this during their future conversations. Few people did. As long as you made them feel good in the moment, they'd forget your past transgressions. But right now, he was losing her. He had to make her see she was in a category of her own, above the rest. "Medea, I—"

"Stop. Just stop." She took a deep breath, opening and closing her mouth several times before speaking again. "I should never have brought you here. I see that now."

He had to head her off before this got any worse. "You're impor—"

"Would you *shut up.*" She pierced him with a glare. "I'm trying to tell you I'm sorry."

He froze. Clearly her mind had gone off in another direction.

"I didn't realize the experiment would be so hard for you. That by making you sit in silence all day I'd be encouraging you to act out in ways that put yourself at risk." She shook her head. "Between this and the site contamination, maybe I ought to scrap the whole experiment."

It never ceased to amaze him how people could twist things around in order to blame themselves. Guilt was painful, wasn't it? And yet some people willfully bathed in it. Medea's guilt gave him leverage, but if she canceled the experiment now, she'd end up resenting him.

He softened his voice. "You didn't know. How could you? I'll admit it hasn't been easy, but I'm willing to finish the experiment if you are. Maybe if we took more breaks, if you allowed me to talk . . ."

She nodded. "I'm sure I can think of some way to entertain your brain. Now, what's your question?"

"What? Oh." Right, the game. The sun had dipped below the horizon; stars appeared in its place. So many potential questions. She'd changed the rules of the game, making it Truth or Truth. He could use that. "Why did you and Thomas have a falling-out?"

It was a personal question, one he was certain she'd never answer. She'd ask to pass and he'd counter with a softer alternative, one she'd then feel obligated to answer, having locked herself into a game of Truth or Truth.

Medea summoned more bourbon into her hand and raised it to her lips. She took a measured sip, savoring the taste, then rested her hand in her lap. "Dare."

COMPLICATIONS

Mama and Papa were arguing again. No, two women. Josh opened his eyes a crack. It was Bethany and Gloria.

"I'm not sharing a room with him. Especially not one this small. It's indecent!"

"Fine. Throw your back out sleeping in the car."

Bethany laughed. "I'm not sleeping in that thing. Doris and I are driving to town to find a motel."

"Like hell you are."

Josh rolled over and tugged the blanket over his head. What had he been dreaming about? It had been something nice. He reached for the dream, but like most dreams, it faded away the harder he tried. The loud voices were difficult to ignore, as was the dull pain in his leg. He sat up and threw back the covers. Goose bumps erupted over his bare skin. The injury was gone, so why did it still hurt?

Yoxtl sat atop an old metal stove, watching Bethany and Gloria. Its tail twitched.

You said I'd feel better when I woke up.

The spirit shot him a glance. "I healed you as much as I could."

What's that mean? Were you interrupted?

"It takes power and I don't have any left."

What kind of power did magic use? Electricity? Sunlight? It couldn't be anything like that, or he wouldn't have been able to use it in the hospital. Or was he somehow sucking electricity from the lights? Was that why they flickered so bad and no one else seemed to notice?

What kind of power? Maybe I can help.

Yoxtl crept along the stove, eyes on the arguing women. It paused to look at him, though it didn't speak right away. Josh could empathize with that. Sometimes the right words were hard to find.

"You can," said Yoxtl. "Spirits get their power from souls. If you pledge your soul to me when you die, I can use its power to help others."

My soul is going to heaven.

"There is no heaven or hell. That's a lie told by another spirit."

Heaven is real. Mama and Grandma and Pastor John said so, and they'd never lie.

Yoxtl's ears twitched. "Look, can we talk about this later?" Its gaze fixed on the women.

"Give it to me!" Bethany lunged at Gloria, who held something out of reach.

"You are *not* taking the car," said Gloria.

"Ugh, you guys are giving me a headache!" Doris walked up to the pair, hands on her hips. "Maybe we should just stay here. Gloria said she could fix this place up right quick, didn't you?" She looked to Gloria, who nodded. "There. It's just for a few nights. We can sleep in the house and Josh can sleep in the car."

I don't mind sleeping in the car. It's warmer.

"Doris, I don't think you should sleep here," said Bethany. "In fact, I don't think any of us should. It's not right to leave Evelyn alone with someone like Gloria."

"What do you mean?" asked Doris.

"Bethany." Gloria's voice was a growl.

Yoxtl stood up. "Ladies, I think this has gone far enough. Josh is willing to sleep in the car so the rest of you can have the house."

"I still want to know what you meant," said Doris.

Bethany smiled. "Gloria wasn't in Shady River because she had a magical outburst or anything like that."

"Stop."

Bethany walked over to Doris, still smiling, and put an arm around her. "Have you ever been down to C-wing?"

Doris shook her head.

"They have this room with two metal rods. You put your hands on them and they show you pictures." She looked at Gloria. "If you look too long at the wrong picture, they give you a little shock. Gloria's pictures were of men and women."

Doris frowned. "So she's not allowed to look at people?"

Gloria took a step forward. "Please, Bethany. I'm begging you."

"This isn't helpful," said Yoxtl.

"Gloria got the shock for looking too long at pretty girls. She has a thing for pretty girls, don't you, Gloria?"

Doris' mouth fell open. She looked at Gloria and took a step back.

"So you see," said Bethany, "we can't leave Evelyn alone with her. Lord knows what might happen to that poor girl, left alone with a sexual *deviant*."

"That's enough!" Yoxtl's tail bristled. "You're way out of line, Bethany."

Gloria opened her hand and the key fell to the earthen floor with a dull thud. She walked past Bethany and out of the house.

Bethany snorted. "How rude." But she retrieved the key and, a minute later, she was driving away with Doris and Evelyn. Josh shivered and wrapped himself tighter in the blanket.

They were long gone before Gloria came back inside. She rummaged around her bag and took out a Coleman portable stove, setting it on top of the dated wood-burning one. She'd brought lots of things—folding chairs, tents, blankets, pots and pans for cooking. There had been an old wooden table and two chairs inside the house when they arrived. Josh had tried one of the chairs and it had promptly broken. Gloria had thrown them outside and checked the table, which seemed sturdy enough for her liking. She laid food on it now, silently taking inventory, then filled a pot with water and began cutting potatoes.

Grandma always narrated while she cooked—"you gotta pop the yolks before you beat the eggs" or "you can never have too much butter." When he was little she tried to enlist his help, but he always seemed to drop things and had trouble remembering all the steps. Papa came in once right as Josh dropped a plate. It smashed to pieces and Papa ranted about what a clumsy oaf he was, how he was a burden on the whole family. Grandma struck the back of Papa's head with a wooden spoon.

"Don't you talk like that! Everyone's good at somethin', you just gotta figure out what. And even if he weren't, he's still a gift from God, and you don't look a gift horse in the mouth. Now get outta my kitchen."

It took some time, but she was right—there were things he could do. He could help carry the groceries. He couldn't set the table, but he could wipe it down after meals and take out the trash. His favorite was kneading dough. He liked the way it smelled and how the dough squished between his fingers. Best of all, he liked how it allowed him to be helpful.

Gloria was laying out ears of corn. Shucking he could do—

kind of. He had trouble with the little stringy bits, but he could tear off most of the bigger leaves. He walked over and grabbed an ear.

"I still have to cook those." Gloria promptly took the ear from his hand and set it back down. "I'm going as fast as I can, Josh. I'll let you know when it's time to eat. Why don't you go answer nature's call?"

Josh draped the blanket over his shoulders and exited the house. Aside from the breeze rustling over the grass, it was quiet. No bird calls, not even the chirp of a cricket—not that he'd be able to answer them if there were. It was just him and the wide-open plain. The back of his throat tightened. Why did he have to come out here with these strangers? Grandma never would have shooed him away. He missed her food and her company and his bed. He missed how she reminded him to do the things he forgot, and how she still read to him every night, even though Papa said he was too old for that and he wouldn't understand it anyhow. He missed Mama. Would he be allowed to see them once he learned magic, or would he be stuck here forever, with a woman who hated him and others who just didn't care?

Josh sank to the cold hard ground and rocked gently until Gloria called him for dinner.

"Gloria! Gloria, wake up!"

She opened her eyes to find Yoxtl floating above.

"Get up quickly, mortal! Josh is missing."

"What?" She jerked upright and looked to where Josh should have been sleeping. In the dim dawn light she could make out an empty pallet. His grey pants lay crumpled on top. She crawled over to the pallet and picked them up. They were damp, as was the bedding underneath.

A knot formed in her chest. Doris was right. Not that they should have left Josh back at the hotel—that was unthinkable—but he clearly required more care than what they could provide. They weren't equipped to deal with someone like this. He needed a full-time nurse. He needed to be institutionalized.

Shame fell over her like a cloud at the thought, but what could she do? It was hard enough trying to keep the group together with Bethany making trouble. She hated to think of how Evelyn must be faring. What if they let her out of their sight? What if she had a psychotic episode? Yoxtl should have been leading them, but the spirit had been no help at all.

She whirled on Yoxtl. "Why weren't you watching him? It's not like you have to sleep!"

"I went to check on the others, and when I came back he was gone."

"Can't you find him with magic?"

"I don't have a blood link on any of the others, just you."

Gloria swore and reached for her shoes. "We have to find him before someone else does." She didn't want to think of what would happen if someone found Josh wandering around half-naked on their homestead.

She fished a clean pair of pants from her duffel bag and stepped into the grey morning. Fog blanketed the plains as far as the eye could see. Yoxtl came to hover beside her.

"Do you see him?" she asked.

"If I could, I wouldn't have woken you up."

"I'm going to follow the car tracks back to the road. Can you head in the other direction?"

Yoxtl nodded and vanished. She'd have to trust that the spirit could find her if it located Josh.

Gloria jogged along the car tracks. By the time she got to the road she had a stitch in her side. No sooner had she paused to catch her breath then she spotted Josh's round silhouette.

"Josh! Hey, Josh, wait!"

His slow walk became a hurried shuffle.

"WAIT!" She took off after him. He was limping and it didn't take long to catch up. She frowned. Had he twisted his ankle or had Yoxtl done a poor job healing his leg?

Josh saw her. He made a noise like a cornered animal and hobbled faster.

"Josh, it's me. Please stop. You're only making that leg worse." She tried to block his path but he pushed past her. To her chagrin, she saw he was crying. "I brought you clean pants."

He paused, giving her hope, but as soon as she held them out he wailed and limped away.

"Josh. Josh, stop! You need to— Oh, no." Headlights sliced through the fog. They were coming fast. "We need to get off the road."

Josh didn't seem to hear. He doggedly ambled along, oblivious to the oncoming car.

"Josh, move!"

She ran up beside him and shoved hard toward the side of the road. Josh cried out as they toppled together into the grass. A heartbeat later the Suburban roared by.

Gloria shoved the pants into Josh's hands with a harsh, "Put those on!" and went to see about the car. It had skidded to a halt and was slowly backing up. Doris pulled alongside them and rolled down the window.

"What are you doing driving like that?" said Gloria. "You could've killed us!"

"Oh, please. I wasn't going that fast. And what are you two doing out here anyway?"

Bethany leaned into view. "By the look of it, I'd say she's trying to cure herself. Really, Gloria, you can do better."

Heat crept into Gloria's cheeks. She glanced behind her at Josh. He stood in full view and made no attempt to cover himself.

"He had an accident and ran off. I was bringing him a change of clothes."

Bethany smirked. "Looks like he needs some help getting into them. How does it feel to play servant to an imbecile?"

Gloria ignored the jab and returned to Josh. When she asked him to put the pants on, he stared at them as if he didn't know what to do. Then he sat on the ground and tried to push one leg in at a time. The pants kept shifting away. She had to tug each pant leg onto him, but he refused to stand and pull the waist up. Finally she got him to raise his butt off the ground enough for her to slide everything under. The whole thing was highly improper. She could sense the judgmental stares. It wasn't fine. None of this was fine.

Even dressed, Josh refused to get up. He rocked and shook his head and whined. All the while, Doris and Bethany loudly complained from the car. Gloria tried to talk sense into him, but she was starting to doubt Nikolai's assertion that Josh understood everything they said. She begged and pleaded for ages until the others became restless and began talking about driving ahead without them.

"Get up!" Gloria snapped. She reached for Josh's arm and tried to pull him up. He screeched like she was killing him.

At his size there was no way to get him up without his help. Or magic. Medea had levitated them all easily. Where the hell was Yoxtl?

As if it heard, the spirit appeared. "You found him!"

"No thanks to you! And now I can't get him up. Can you please float him to the car?"

Yoxtl looked taken aback, then said cheerily, "I'll talk to him. Can you give us a few minutes?"

Gloria nodded and stalked back to the car. So much for the all-powerful god Yoxtl.

HUNGER

Medea stared at her bourbon. She should've summoned a stronger proof. Why had she let Nikolai talk her into this? His expression was unreadable.

"You said we weren't doing dares. That it was truth or nothing."

Shit. She *had* said that. Wait, did this mean he was disappointed she'd chosen dare? He had to know she'd never answer a question that personal, so what was his goal in asking? It had to be a play, but *what*?

She sized him up as she would any opponent. They'd been drinking. But that was her idea. Wasn't it? He was larger than her. That would forestall the effects of alcohol. The game blurred the lines of master and apprentice, which put her at a disadvantage— informal communication had never been her forte, and he knew that. It was very much a strength of his, however. Nikolai never acted without a thought for himself. Something was going on here, some manipulation, but she couldn't for the life of her figure out what, and that made it dangerous. She never should've let him goad her into this.

"You're right. I forfeit." Careful not to spill the bourbon, she stood and took a step toward the car.

Nikolai threw out an arm, pleading more than blocking. "Hold on now. Don't go. Just give me a moment to think of a dare. I wasn't prepared for you to change your mind. If you like, you can take an extra turn while I think of something. Please. You haven't let me speak to you all day."

Guilt crashed against her, halting her stride. Maybe he *was* just bored. No, it was another manipulation. Wasn't it? "Why don't we just talk? Why does it have to be a game?"

"It doesn't, and without the option of a dare, it really isn't. Though might I remind you that *you're* the one who pried into my personal life first."

She sat down with a sigh. "I'd hardly call it prying to ask the motivation behind a particular behavior. Very well, what's the dare?"

"A moment, please." Nikolai watched her with unnerving intensity, chin resting atop his hands.

Careful, careful. She had to be careful. This one, if he made a move against her, would come at her with a smile and a benign gesture.

"I have it," he said, and her stomach dropped. "Close your eyes and open your mouth."

Instantly she envisioned a penis heading straight for her face. She jerked back, physically and mentally. Nikolai would never be that stupid. She'd kill him. Worse than kill him. She shook her head and clenched her jaw. Improbable. More likely something equally disgusting. Feces? Poison? An eternity passed before she was able to croak out, "Why?"

"I want you to try a new food. Your taste is depressingly narrow."

Not reassuring. *"No."*

"We eat together all the time. I know what you like. Hell—I

know your orders by heart. Give me a chance to pick something different you'll enjoy."

"If it's just food, why do I have to close my eyes?"

He scoffed. "I've seen how you scan dishes for any pepper or stray speck of green. I don't want you getting turned off by appearance. If you close your eyes, focus on smell—"

She shot to her feet, magic burning in her fists. "I'm not closing my eyes!"

He should have been cowed or upset, but he merely looked at her with impassive calm. Fuck him. She *wasn't* overreacting. It was her body, her say what went inside it.

"Alright." There was no condemnation in his tone, only infinite patience, which somehow made it more reproachful. "You can keep your eyes open."

"*And* I'm warding my mouth against any nonfood item."

"Anything is food if you're hungry enough," he muttered. Then, louder, "Do as you please." He motioned for her to sit. She lowered herself cautiously onto the grass and he scooted until their knees were nearly touching. He summoned a brown fritter into his palm and held it up. "This is called *tulumba*."

Tension eased from her chest. It *was* food. Not only that, but something she recognized—a sort of sweet pastry, similar to a churro. She'd had them ages ago on one of her trips through the Middle East. "What's the green dusting? Pistachio?"

He nodded. "It's good, I swear."

She curled his fingers over the fritter. "I know. I've had it. So that's not a real dare."

He frowned at the *tulumba*. "You've had it? *Blyad.*"

She held out her hand. "Give it to me and summon something else. I can save it as a palate cleanser if I don't like the next one. Summon . . ." God, could she really be that daring? "Summon something *you* like, but you know I'd never try on my own."

"You sure about that?" He said it cautiously, as though worried she'd bolt.

"No." She laughed weakly. "No, but that's the point of this game isn't it? To make each other uncomfortable?"

"We can stop if you want."

The fact that he'd given her an out—*multiple* outs—said a lot about his character. Had she misjudged him that badly? His talk of the beige hallway, though it didn't excuse everything he'd done, explained much. With enough experience, people could stretch, but ultimately they were confined by their own neurological limits. Herself included.

Immortality had allowed her to fall into comfortable routines, especially in the centuries since Thomas left. Not much had changed. Same apprentices. Same foods. Same spells. Only the books differed, and the outside world—that changed exponentially these days. Nikolai was an odd bridge, equally comfortable in both Magi and Mundane worlds, yet he held himself apart from each. Always she felt him edging her toward the modern. Perhaps because he lacked fear, he found it difficult to fathom hesitation in others. Where she asked, "Why should I?" he asked, "Why not?"

What's the worst that could happen if she ate his food? If she didn't like it, she could spit it out. Though the taste would remain. Or the ungodly sensation of a terrible texture. Her brain tacked on a number of other worst-case scenarios—she didn't have her anti-poison spells active, he could feed her something that wasn't food, he could slit her throat, he could— She shook her head to dispel the nagging doubts.

"Do it." She tried to add certainty to her voice. "Summon the damned food."

She closed her eyes.

He would *not* poison her. And if he did, she'd feel it in time, even without the spell. Everything would be fine. It was only food. She'd warded against nonfood items. She might not like it, that was all. That was all . . .

His summoning spell tickled her awareness, then something pattered to the ground behind him. Again, the summoning and the sound. And again.

"What are you doing?" she asked.

"Sorry, I'm trying to get one with a smoother texture."

He *did* know what she liked. Still, it was hard to keep the tension from creeping back into her chest. What if he was only summoning to trick her? What if he summoned something awful? What if he—

"Okay, got it. I'm going to touch your face."

Even with the warning, it was hard not to jerk back as something brushed her lips.

"Smell that?" he said.

"Onions? You know I hate onions."

"You hate the *texture* of onions. You won't notice these."

"I don't know . . . and parsley?"

"Yes." His response came out husky, breath warm on her face. When had he gotten so close? Had she imagined it, or did he just touch her thigh? His finger caressed her chin. "You still need to open your mouth."

Her jaw clenched. His earlier comment about the ward indicated he might be able to get around it. What was she doing? God only knew what he'd—

"Here. You do it." The thing he'd pressed to her mouth withdrew. He tucked it into her palm, relinquishing control.

Relief flooded through her. She wanted to thank him but couldn't think of a way to explain the depth of her gratitude. Ridiculous, getting worked up over something so simple. The lump in her hand was oval-shaped, its rough surface grainy against her thumb. A pellet of some kind. Eyes still closed, she raised it to her face, refusing to pause or reconsider, and took a small bite.

A mishmash of unfamiliar flavors greeted her tongue—too many to pick apart individually, though it tasted overwhelmingly of tomato paste. The coarse texture was only just bearable. Seemed impolite to spit it out now.

"Well?" asked Nikolai. He wasn't sitting anywhere near as close as she'd imagined.

"It's not terrible, but I can't say I care for it." She swallowed as fast as she could, then summoned water into her hand and drank.

"Sorry. I tried to summon as bland a version as I could. It wasn't spicy though, was it? Hard to get *mercimek köftesi* without chili *and* pepper *and* have it be a smoother texture. Too many variables."

She smiled at his word choice. "It was fine." She took a bite of the *tulumba* in her other hand. It was sticky sweet and smelled of orange blossoms.

"Uh, heh, I'd advise you not to make any sudden movements just now."

She lowered her hand into her lap. *"Why?"*

"Because there's a snake on your left."

Her gaze jerked down. What was he going on ab—

"Your other left."

She made an irritated face and checked the other side. Sure enough, a rattlesnake nestled against her thigh. Well, at least Nikolai hadn't been trying to feel her up. "What the hell is it doing right next to me?"

"I think it's attracted by your warming spell. It's almost like it sought you out." He was damnably calm, almost cheerful.

"You watched it slither over and you're *just now telling me*?"

Amusement danced in his eyes. "You were pretty wound up and I wasn't sure how you'd react. What if I startled you into getting bit? Besides"—he smirked—"I wanted you to try my food first."

Fucking Nikolai. "Well, I best move it."

"Not yet." He leaned forward, a smile playing across his scarred lips. "It's your turn to challenge me, and I choose dare."

She threw back her head. This boy. "You're ridiculous."

"Come on, I'll answer however many truths you want, but you owe me *one dare*, and that right there"—he pointed to the snake—"is *perfect*."

"Perfectly stupid." Of course neither of them were in any real danger, not with shields and her healing abilities, but his brain probably needed this spike. "Fine. I dare you to get rid of the snake."

"You sure?" he asked coyly. "You can always dare me to strip naked and run through poison ivy."

"Why in god's name would I dare you to do that? *I'd* be the one who'd have to heal you."

His grin widened. "I know."

She stared at him, mouth agape. "You—"

He laughed with no regard for his well-being. Completely inappropriate. She ought to—

In a blink he was upon her, hand flashing silver. Thank god her shielding was reflexive by now. He nearly straddled her lap, and she had to lean back to avoid contact. She ought to react, fling him back and put an end to the clumsy assassination attempt, but his gaze held her. His hand came down like lightning, dagger crunching through the serpent's skull. Her heart hammered in her chest. Not once had he broken eye contact, not even to ensure his aim. His expression was gleefully confident.

The rattlesnake's body thrashed against her leg, its head pinned by the dagger. Death was never truly instantaneous. Organisms were nothing more than interconnected systems, and sometimes it took a while for one part to register the status of another.

Still Nikolai held her with his gaze. She longed to look away but felt as pinned as the snake. When had it gotten so hot? She wiped her palms against her pants. At last his eyes released her, dropping to her mouth—a much more reasonable place to look during a conversation. He leaned forward, lips parting as though about to whisper something, but a quick glance back at her eyes seemed to change his mind. He jerked his dagger free and rocked backward.

She took a deep breath and slumped. Why did it feel as though she'd run a marathon? Had Nikolai worked some subtle magic on her? She'd detected nothing.

He pulled the snake from his blade and sliced it down the middle. "Have you ever eaten rattlesnake?"

"Yes, actually. Do you always carry a dagger?"

"I try to. Especially when my master tells me magic won't be allowed." He severed the neck and began tugging the skin off the body.

"Are we still playing?"

He paused. "Do you want to?"

Did she? There was something oddly freeing about conversing within a specific set of rules, even if it was uncomfortable at times. And what conversation wasn't uncomfortable? Oh, she could talk of magic for hours, but this, whatever this was, had always lain beyond her abilities. Yet she felt she'd learned more of Nikolai in one evening than she had in a year and a half. "Yes. I believe it was your turn."

"A moment." He levitated the snake, now bare, and cast a flame in his hand, running it underneath.

"It's going to take forever that way, and you're going to get hot grease dripping on your hand. Just hold it steady and I'll cook." She focused on the carcass, willing it to heat.

Nikolai leaned back. "Is that like water boiling?"

She smiled. "Is that your question?"

"Hell no." He leaned forward, hands together. "Why did you break your own rule and teach immortality to Thomas?"

Fuck. Of all the things he could've asked. It was better than his last question, though it danced incredibly close to the same topic. At least this one gave her a bit of leeway. But how had he even known?

"I don't recall ever mentioning that to you."

Nikolai ran a hand through his hair and looked abashed. "I, uh, found out the time I was in your head. Sorry." He took a breath, then the words spilled out. "And I'm sorry I brought it up, but it's been bothering me ever since. You have a rule, and I've respected that, but I can't help thinking—what else could I be doing? Is it something that's secretly only offered to grand masters? I know I take risks, but I don't want to *die*, not after all I've been through. If there's something more I could be—"

"Hush." She moved to his side. Should she pat his back? No, that seemed inappropriate for student and master. "The fault is mine, not yours." He couldn't be allowed to think he was to blame. As painful as it was to admit to breaking a rule, he deserved an explanation. She took a breath. "Have you ever been in love?"

"No."

"I thought not. For every human affliction, there is a percentage of the population that is immune. I suspect you fall into that category, but then I used to think that of myself. I watched in alarm as friends became infected, and I resolved to find a cure for the disease. Stupidity, loss of will and identity, heightened emotions, increased bravado, mania—for years I catalogued the symptoms, yet I did not immediately recognize them in myself. Sometimes I wonder how my life would be different if I'd caught it early. But then, it's strongest in its early stages." Too late. She'd noticed too late. That had been a melancholic day—realizing what was happening and being unable to stop it.

Nikolai watched with the youthful indifference of one who thought it could never happen to him. If he was lucky, it never would.

"Imagine, if you will, giving up everything for another person, being willing to do things you'd swore you'd never do, just to make them happy. Except it's never enough. They always want more." She hugged herself. "The symptoms lessen over time. Problem is, by the time the sufferer begins to recover, they've often made life-altering decisions, irrevocably intertwining their fate with another—women especially. They get married, have children. I didn't go that far, but I gave up my method of immortality, hoping to satisfy Thomas, and even that wasn't sufficient."

"How did you rid yourself of the affliction?"

She laughed sadly. If only she'd had that much strength. Thomas had been the one to leave. Her only strength had lain in taking steps to ensure she couldn't acquiesce to him should he return, but he never did, and when his grimoire appeared in the library one day, she knew he never would. That particular gift only returned upon death.

"I didn't. I know that must seem alarming, but I'm aware of no cure. All I can advise is that you look for the symptoms in yourself, or better yet, have a confidant look for you, and distance yourself from the object of your affection before things get out of control. Remember, love is strongest in the beginning."

He smiled faintly and leaned over. "Will you be my confidant, at least while I'm your apprentice?"

"Of course. After all, it would likely affect your work, making me the first to notice."

Nikolai turned his head aside and coughed. "Ahem. Excuse me. I think the meat is done."

The meat had gone from pink to white. Nikolai pulled off a chunk, blowing to cool it. He'd never heard someone speak of love with such sound reasoning. It was refreshing. Unfortunately, Thomas had left scorched earth behind. Medea would be much warier in the future, though from what she said, she'd be unable to resist her emotions if he'd thoroughly secured her attachment ahead of her awareness. In that respect, her obliviousness thus far was a good thing.

He'd avoided being too overt to keep from scaring her off, but after months with nothing to show for his efforts, he'd begun to think he was too circumspect. When she'd dared him to kill the rattlesnake, he dared himself to get a reaction from her. And it worked—sort of. Her body had given every sign of interest, but when he'd leaned in for a kiss, her eyes offered him nothing. He'd withdrawn. Too soon. She had to be in wholeheartedly. Perhaps slow was the best course after all—small acts, gifts that would ingratiate himself on the sly, and his hands—he had to think of a way to showcase them.

"Here," he said, seating himself beside her and proffering a bit of rattlesnake.

She took it, reminding him to watch for bones. He retrieved another section for himself, pinched off a bit and flicked it into the grass, then proceeded to eat. It tasted like bland, rubbery chicken, but the juice ran down his fingers, giving him an excuse to lick them, making it as sensual as possible.

"That's disgusting."

He froze. "What do you expect me to do, wipe my hands on my pants?"

"Don't you have a kerchief or something?"

"No," he lied. "And your hands are just as greasy."

Medea raised her index finger, then clenched the rattlesnake in her teeth, freeing both hands. She held them up, showing the grease, then tilted them downward. The grease slid off, but in an odd way, as if she'd discarded a glove. "Eelds," she said through clenched teeth.

"What?"

She took the rattlesnake from her mouth. "Shields. Just conjure them over your hands and dispel when you're done."

"I have a better idea." He opened his palm and conjured a shield, like a rimmed plate. Into it he summoned *İzmir köfte*, trying his best to minimize the spices. The dish was basically meat and potatoes—aligning perfectly with her tastes—though the meatballs were spiced, and the whole thing was accompanied with tomatoes and peppers, swimming in a tomato sauce.

"That smells good." Medea inched closer and took one of the torpedo-shaped meatballs. She bit into it with the same expression she wore during a lesson she expected him to fail. Her face mellowed a moment later. "Not bad. Another Turkish dish, right? Why no Russian foods?"

"I can't think of anything you'd like," he lied. Aside from a few comfort foods he'd had before the war, his culinary experiences in the Soviet Union weren't something he wished to relive, let alone replicate. Istanbul was where he'd truly learned to eat.

She didn't pry further. They discarded the rattlesnake, which was plain even by Medea's standards, and finished off the köfte, though Medea carefully avoided the peppers. For dessert he summoned *tavuk göğsü*, a thick pudding made with chicken and flavored with vanilla and cinnamon. Medea ate most of it and leaned back, belly protruding nicely. The Milky Way stretched out overhead, a band of stars bordered by pink and purple clouds of dust. On either side, the black veil of night was dotted with a million specks of light.

She pursed her lips and glanced at him. "Truth or dare?"

"I thought we'd finished with that."

"So did I, but I've just now thought of something I've been meaning to ask you."

"You're assuming I'll pick truth."

"It would be nice."

He scoffed. "Fine. Truth." She was in a good mood and he intended to keep it that way. One more question couldn't hurt.

"It's about what happened in Safe Harbor," she began, "during the first year of your training."

Shit. That was when he'd tried to poison her. Ridiculous for her to still be upset about it after all this time. Their relationship was entirely different now.

"A man challenged me to a *Servitus aut Mors* duel," she continued. "I gave him a chance to forfeit and turned to you for confirmation of his intent."

He recalled the incident vividly. The man had seemed ill prepared and immediately regretful of his decision. At the time he'd found the man's behavior odd. It wasn't until later, when Medea drank herself into a stupor, that she confessed to having a spell compelling would-be attackers to issue a verbal challenge.

"You told me he was lying. That he still intended to kill me. Was that true?"

He still couldn't fathom why she'd asked him to confirm. Sure, he'd since learned that her telepathic capabilities were limited, but the man had obviously given up. Anyone could have seen it—anyone, perhaps, but Medea. How she could misread most people so easily and yet read him so well was a mystery.

Telling the truth now wouldn't earn him enough goodwill to make up for the previous lie. Medea would rightly blame herself for putting her actions in his hands.

"Yes," he said. "The man was set on killing you."

"I see." The words were as flat as her expression. She turned away, making his miscalculation plain.

Worse, he *felt* her withdraw. He hadn't noticed it before, but her magical presence had seeped into the area around them. Perhaps it leaked out of her when she was happy, or perhaps she'd cast spells and now dispelled them—whatever the cause, the magic retracted, leaving the ground hard and the air thin.

Of *course* she didn't believe him. She knew him too well—that's why she suspected the lie in the first place. She'd once lectured him on the importance of reputation. He'd built a reputation as a liar, and as long as he maintained that, she would keep him at a distance. Medea's core value was truth. Her lust for knowledge was merely an extension of it. The odds of her sleeping with someone she even *suspected* of lying were nil.

To stand a chance, he'd have to change her perception of him. He could appear to consistently tell the truth to everyone, but then she'd wonder what he was playing at, and anyhow he wasn't about to give up his greatest asset. There had to be another way.

And then he realized there was.

He didn't have to tell the truth to *everyone*—just her. Even if he lied to others, as long as he seemed to tell Medea the truth, she would eventually begin to trust him. Then when he *did* lie to her, she would believe him without question. Being truthful to her alone also sent the unspoken message that he cared about her enough to try, and that while he didn't agree with her values, he respected her enough to make the sacrifice. And, a small part of him argued, it would be nice to take the mask off once in a while. Not fully—never that—but there was a certain allure in being seen without being cast aside. No one could give him that completely, but with Medea he might get close.

"I lied," he said, allowing discomfort to show on his face. "Just now, and back then. I won't say I'm sorry because I'm not, but you wanted the truth, so there it is."

Medea turned back, expression neutral. "Why?"

"I wanted to see what you'd do. I'd heard all these stories about how you dueled twenty men at once, fired spells from every angle without a wand, littered the street outside the Hanged Man with bodies. And you didn't disappoint. You exploded the man's head." It had been spectacular to behold. A blossom of red to match her dress, a falling body, and Medea standing nonchalantly in the street, radiating power.

She closed her eyes and took a measured breath. "I suspected. As soon as I'd done it, I suspected. Your reaction was . . . hungry."

"What I don't understand is why you asked for my confirmation at all. You knew me for a liar since the day we met."

"Because you're a telepath, and I couldn't tell if he truly meant to give up. He'd already failed to poison me, and—"

"I poisoned you." Why was he telling her this? He was supposed to get her to open up, not the other way around. Yet he craved to see how far he could peel off the mask before she turned aside in horror. She'd wanted truth. Let her see what that truly meant.

"You?"

"Yes, me."

She frowned, but it was only a mildly confused #3, not the expected glare. "Your dosage was completely inadequate."

He laughed. It was such a Medea thing to say, complaining about the poor job he'd done poisoning her. "I wasn't trying to kill you, only see if you *could* be poisoned."

"Ah. That makes sense." She frowned again. "I never figured you for a poisoner."

"Why not? It's a perfectly acceptable way to kill someone." This was fun. The exchange wasn't going at all how he'd anticipated. Usually when he peeled back the mask even slightly, people turned aside in horror.

"You always seemed a bit . . . stabby."

"You're not wrong. That's how I killed Petrov."

She groaned and covered her face. "Don't tell me that! I don't need to hear that . . . I liked the man."

He grinned. "Fine. I won't tell you that. I baked Petrov a cake, and it was so delicious that he ate himself to death. But seriously, I love poisoning. It deflects blame. I dosed half of Haven with laxatives just to get Petrov out of the way so I could meet you alone. At the Academy, I poisoned one professor over a period of years. Harper was apprenticed to him at the time, so I couldn't have him dying too quickly—I *do* take care of my friends."

Medea gaped at him for several moments. "Why are you telling me these things?"

He stretched out languidly on the grass. "Call it a dare to myself. I've decided to tell you the truth from now on."

"Why?"

"Because you see through most of my bullshit anyway, and I'm curious what it's like to be mostly myself around someone. And because you value truth and I want you to take me seriously." Partials counted as truth, didn't they?

She was silent for a moment. Then, "Leave it to you to turn a truth into a dare."

"Speaking of which, it's my turn." He sat up, steepling his hands before his mouth. "Why are you so terrible at reading people, to the point where you can't even tell when a man has *obviously* given up, yet you can see through me better than anyone else? You do it so well that for a year I thought you were using telepathy against me. I *still* get that feeling, even though I know you're not."

Medea tensed and studied her lap before replying. "I— With challengers, I've learned not to trust myself. Too many times I've had people feign giving up—very convincingly, to my mind— only to launch their attack anew. So I err on the side of caution. If you hadn't been there, I don't know what I would have done. I'm trying not to kill people as much as the old days, not Magi anyway. As to the rest of your question—" She shrugged. "People are a mystery to me. They always have been, and it seems as though every time I make headway, the customs change and I have to start all over again. But one thing always stays the same —people like you." Her voice hardened. "The power-hungry, manipulative liars who will do anything to get what they want. Your kind are easy to predict simply because I've met so many of you. I may not pick up on every pattern of human behavior, but once something is pointed out, once it has cost me dearly—well, that's difficult to forget."

"Do you truly think that ill of me?"

"I think you are who you are and nothing is going to change that. I think the only reason you're acting different than your first year is because you realized you couldn't defeat me and decided to take the smarter path—learning what you can while you can. To your credit, most apprentices don't. But I will be very disappointed if you turn around a few years hence and try to kill me. *Very* disappointed."

"Duly noted." The night's progress had evaporated, leaving bitterness behind. He set it aside and tried to salvage what he could. "I meant what I said, though, about being honest with you."

"No doubt another calculated move."

He bristled. "So what if it is? The result is the same."

"And what exactly is the *result* you wish to achieve with me?"

This was why the truth sucked. It painted you into a corner. Then again, it would be an interesting challenge to give Medea enough truth that she'd believe him. "Because I respect you and I want you to respect me. Not as an apprentice, but as a man." An unpleasant thought occurred to him. "You *do* see me as a man, don't you? I'm not still a 'boy,' am I?"

She opened her mouth but didn't respond immediately, which told him all he needed to know. He started toward the Chevy.

"Give me a damned minute!"

He paused to look back at her.

"I don't *see* people the way you do. Or how anyone does, I expect. It takes time for me to parse out these things." Medea shook her head at his impatience. "You *are* much younger than I and always will be, but no, you're no longer 'the boy.' I just see you as Nikolai." She gave an apologetic shrug. "Whatever that means. It's not like the Botanist where I can distill all that you are into a single word—-uh, well I guess I *have*, except that it's your name and not some other identifier. I don't know where I was going with this . . ."

She categorized everyone by their specialty—even the Botanist, with whom she was on good terms. Thomas was the only apprentice she'd ever referred to by name. And now him. This was real progress.

He came back and sat beside her. "I understand what you're saying, and I'm sorry about—no, that's not true—I *apologize* for walking away. I get irritable when I feel disrespected."

"I don't mind it. We all have our moments."

He blinked. Did she prefer when he was an asshole? Some women liked that sort of thing. He just never thought Medea would be one of them. But then she clarified.

"Your irritability is, well, I wouldn't say *refreshing*, but it's always felt the most honest. Like you've stopped telling me what I want to hear and are finally being yourself. I swear, sometimes it's like we're back in the Hanged Man and you're trying too hard. I prefer when you're *authentic*, even if that shows your rough edges. Why hide who you are? I already know what you're like. I knew before we even met"—she scoffed and rolled her eyes—"opening Petrov's letter despite all my warnings. Was it beige that day in the store?"

He laughed. "Every day in Haven was beige before I met you."

What the hell did he mean by that? Compliments were annoying enough when they weren't indecipherably vague. Did he mean that Haven was an especially boring place? It probably was, relatively speaking, but what did that have to do with her? He'd said that every day in Haven was beige before he *met* her, indicating the meeting itself had some sort of lasting effect, but of course that wasn't true, not if the beige worked as he described. It would have returned the moment she left Petrov's shop. And it's not like they'd spent that much time together in Haven—an hour a day for a week. Certainly that wasn't enough to be remarkable? Regardless of what he meant, how did one even *respond* to such a remark?

"Yes, well . . . not much going on in Haven I suppose." Fucking brilliant. Well, that's what he got for saying something so inane.

Nikolai's hand covered his mouth, stifling a noise. Was he sniggering at her? It wouldn't be the first time someone had made a joke at her expense. She just hadn't expected it from him.

"I don't see what's so funny. If you wanted a different response, you should have been more clear!"

He rolled away from her, body shaking with restrained chuckles.

"Well, if you're going to act like that, we might as well get back to the farmhouse." And to think, only a moment ago she'd felt a kinship with him. She should've known his ego would force him to act like a jackass. She rose and brushed off her pants. "On your feet, *discipulus*."

Aside from his shaking, Nikolai didn't move. Was he having a fit or something? She scanned his body for injuries but found none. Nothing but—oh.

Bravo. Here he was trying to conceal the curse he knew she

despised, and she had accused him of laughing. Some master she was.

A hoarse cry erupted from Nikolai, and her chest filled with lead. She'd witnessed the curse take hold of him countless times, but never had she felt anything besides revulsion, disappointment, exasperation. Nikolai, being Nikolai, had impulsively killed his previous mentor to get out of a contract. Actions had consequences, and his would haunt him for the rest of his life. Was it fair, given what she'd learned of him tonight? How much could be chalked up to his need for stimulation, combined with a youthful lack of reserve and judgment? It's not like she'd never killed anyone. Granted, not for anything so stupid, and not for such a nefarious reason, but if she'd received a death curse for every man she'd killed, well, she'd have a lot of curses.

But it wasn't her call. Only Petrov could absolve Nikolai of his crime. She wouldn't interfere by lifting the curse.

Another sob tore through Nikolai. She knelt and tentatively placed a hand on his shoulder. Comfort wasn't interference, not really. His breath changed to rapid gasps and he groped for her hand. For a moment he held on as though she were a lifeline, and then he relinquished his grasp and sobbed anew, curling into a fetal position.

She considered levitating him into the car, but she wouldn't be able to levitate him back out, nor would she be able to move the vehicle all the way back to the farm with magic. They'd have to remain here until the curse subsided.

It had been a while since she'd last used her camping spells. Vermin repelling—would that work on rattlesnakes? Probably not. It was designed for small mammals and bugs. She grabbed the remnants of the rattlesnake and wove its essence into the spell. Might not work for *every* species, but good enough for tonight. Wards for humans were a standard she never forgot. Since it was only for the night, she set them to ensnare anyone who got too close. A temperature control spell seemed too personal. She drew a circle on the ground and conjured a fire, adjusting the intensity to ensure Nikolai wouldn't overheat, then knocked him out with Sleep. She warded herself to ensure she'd wake when Nikolai did. Cursed or not, he wouldn't catch her unawares.

Satisfied she'd seen to his physical comforts, she returned to the car. She retrieved her book and curled up in the back seat to read. Half a page later, Nikolai cried out and thrashed in his sleep. She tried to ignore the ruckus and focus on her book, eventually casting a sound shield. The number of spells she'd have to remember to cancel before returning to the farmhouse . . .

Where was she? She found her place again and began to read, but Nikolai was still visible through the window. He jerked around a bit before rolling over and sobbing into his hands. She slid down the seat until he was out of view, but it was like trying deliberately not to think of something. She found herself expanding her awareness to his body to see if he'd settled. No.

It was going to be a long night.

She canceled her sound shield and got out of the car. Nikolai had seemed to take comfort from her hand. Perhaps if she sat with him a while, he'd calm down.

"*Please* look at me," he whimpered in the old Turkish. "I'm not dead. Don't treat me like I am."

She froze. This was personal, not something he'd willingly share. It wasn't fair to listen. Then again, it was his own fault for getting cursed. He should have to bear the consequences. She settled with her back against his.

"I did it for you. Don't you see that? I did it for you."

The pain in his voice was palpable. Nikolai naturally had muted emotions. Even when entering someone's mind, he probably didn't feel what they felt, only observed it with dispassionate indifference. He had a conceptual understanding of emotion, that much was clear, but concepts paled in comparison to lived experience. She'd learned early on that study only got you so far. You had to see how things worked in practice because the world was filled with variables unaccounted for in books. Experience was everything. Guilt, sadness, self-doubt, fear—prior to the curse, Nikolai had probably never felt them. What must it be like for him, being magically forced to experience something so foreign? Were emotions blinding in their brightness?

Nikolai's back tensed and he roared, "I should've just let you die!" Then, softer: "I didn't mean that. You're everything to me. Please. Can't we go back to how we were?" The agony in his voice twisted something inside of her.

"You're dreaming. It's not real." She immediately regretted saying it. The feelings caused by the curse were no less real to him. She searched around for something better and came up empty. Words wouldn't solve this, only a cure, and she wouldn't give him that. She draped her arm over his shoulder and rested her chin upon it. "I wish I could take away your pain, but I can't. All I can say is that this too shall pass, and I'll stay with you until it does."

SHADOWS

Yoxtl watched Gloria stalk toward the car, disappointment wafting off her soul, then bounded into the bushes and landed beside Josh.

"What's the matter?" yit asked.

Josh didn't answer. His soul roiled with discomfort and confusion.

"What can I help you with?"

Home. The message was brief, as though it was all Josh could consciously manage, but the weight of it was immense.

"I can get you back to the house, but first you have to stand up and get in the car."

No, MY home.

This didn't bode well. If Josh left the group, it was only a matter of time before others did as well.

"Are you unhappy here?"

Yes.

"Why?"

I want to go home. A tidal wave of information accompanied the word *home*: the scent of cooking food, the sound of a woman humming softly as she helped him get dressed, the sensation of cool linens against his skin on a hot summer night, and a host of other things—family and routine and food and comfort.

Yit tried another tactic. "We were worried about you when we saw you were missing. Why did you run off?"

Embarrassed.

"It's not your fault. Is there something I can do to help you with that? Is there something you need?"

For the first time, Josh looked thoughtful. *Remind me.*

"Remind you of what?"

Remind me to use the bathroom. I forget. And I don't feel it until after. Morning, meals, and before bed. Gloria didn't remind me. When I woke up it was too late. He buried his face in his hands, soul like a thundercloud before a storm.

"It's okay. I'll remind you."

And I need help with clothes. I can't work the buttons and there are so many steps it's hard to remember them all in the right order. And tell Gloria I'm not stupid! I can do things like shuck corn. I just have trouble with smaller things—buttons and pouring water and stuff.

"I'll tell her. Let's go back to the house and get you some food. Then we can practice magic again."

His soul flinched. *No magic!*

"Okay, no magic. Breakfast? Are you hungry?"

Josh stood up. *I don't know. Maybe. It's hard to tell when I feel like this. There's just . . . too many thoughts and they all fight with one another. They make my body feel icky.*

They settled into a routine over the next few days. Yoxtl did yits best to remind Josh to relieve himself, and though the man didn't attempt to run away again, it was clear the group resented his presence—even Gloria, who did her best not to show how uncomfortable she was with helping him in and out of his clothes. It seemed that in this culture, males and females weren't permitted to be naked around one another outside of sexual relationships. Yit didn't understand what difference it made—a body was a body—but yit had long since given up trying to make sense of human customs.

At sunset every day, Doris, Bethany, and Evelyn piled into the car and drove to town. Bethany had pawned her diamonds for paper money and booked them two rooms at a hotel—one for Bethany and Doris, the other for Evelyn. The trio ate dinner at the only restaurant in town. Bethany and Doris chatted and laughed and made no effort to include Evelyn in their conversations. One time, the girl began talking to herself, drawing stares. From then on they left Evelyn in the room and brought her food. Yoxtl reported this to Gloria, who chewed them out and insisted someone stay with Evelyn at all times. Bethany made Doris switch rooms, but this helped little as Doris took to sneaking out to meet boys at the local bar. Bethany acted pleased to have the room to herself, but Yoxtl often found her drinking alone at night, a vacant expression on her face.

Magic lessons progressed slowly. Josh hung back, listening but refusing to participate. Evelyn had the most power out of any of them but seemed distrustful thanks to her Christian upbringing. By the end of the second day, both Bethany and Doris had managed to sprout their seeds. Rather than celebrating the small victory, they immediately asked when they could move on to fancier spells.

Gloria watched them with envy day after day. She tried the hardest, but she had the least amount of power and failed to show any improvement. After five days she still hadn't been able to sprout her seed and went to bed dejected. When she woke the next morning she declared she was going into town for supplies.

"It's getting colder. Someone needs to shore up this house before we freeze."

She returned with a car full of lumber and spent the day

making repairs while the others practiced. Yoxtl hoped she'd stop being so hard on herself.

When lessons had finished and the others were gone, yit went to observe her handiwork. Not bad. Yit was glad to see Gloria turning her mind to other things. Some humans weren't cut out for magic, and it was good to have followers with a mix of skills. True, her soul would never be as powerful as one that had practiced magic, but there was something to be said about a life well lived. It added a nice bouquet.

Gloria stood at the well, drawing up a bucket. She pulled out a cloth and tipped water onto it, then began wiping the dust and sweat from her face.

"Nice work today," yit remarked.

She only grunted in reply. Another tip of the bucket and she was scrubbing her arms. "What I wouldn't give for a shower."

"I can keep an eye on Josh tomorrow if you'd like to join the others for a night."

"Maybe," she said halfheartedly. "How soon until they can start learning the good stuff?"

"The good stuff?"

"Yeah, warming spells, enlarging bags, making diamonds, levitation, healing—stuff like that."

Aside from healing and levitation, yit had no clue how to do those things. Watching Nikolai and Medea had given the woman an inflated perception of what was possible. This wasn't at all how it was supposed to work. Mortals were supposed to be grateful for whatever magic they got.

"We'll get to that when they're ready. In the meantime, it's good that you're repairing the place."

"That's another thing—we're getting low on funds. What happens when the others can no longer afford a hotel? I doubt they'll want to stay here. Unless I can make this place really comfortable, add another room or two, I don't see them sticking around."

That was definitely a problem. Yit had hoped they'd stay for the sake of magic alone. If Doris and Bethany left, all yits functional casters would be gone. Josh and Evelyn might be coaxed into participating someday, but who knew how long that would be? Yit needed to teach them something that looked fancier than it was and would unify the group.

The next day, Yoxtl declared they'd be fixing the house. Gloria arched an eyebrow. Josh and Evelyn gave no acknowledgment that they'd heard. But Doris and Bethany erupted into a chorus of complaints.

"Now, now—I didn't say you'd have no magic lessons today. What I have in mind works better at night. We'll use the daylight to fix the house, and this evening I'll show you something new."

That mollified them. Bethany and Doris chatted excitedly about the prospect of learning something besides growing corn. But the chipper mood turned to resentment when Gloria started instructing them on how to pull off rotting wood and replace it with new boards.

"But that will ruin my new dress!" Doris examined the bright yellow fabric as though checking for smudges.

"Then you should have picked some sensible clothes," said Gloria. "Haven't you ever been camping before? You don't wear *heels*."

"I agree with Doris," said Bethany. "This is man's work. Why not make the Negro do it?"

"Josh isn't good with his fingers. He can help haul the wood. Besides, this house is for all of us."

Her last remark did little to mollify them. Bethany and Doris reluctantly began prying off old boards, but as soon as Gloria left to pick up more supplies they decided to take an extended break.

Yoxtl hesitated to intervene. If yit told them to get back to work and they refused, that would only further diminish yits authority. Instead, yit shadowed Evelyn, trying to engage her in conversation, but she acted like yit wasn't even there.

Gloria said nothing of their lack of progress when she returned, merely glanced at Yoxtl and pursed her lips before calling Josh over to help unload.

"I picked up a few more hammers," she said to the others, passing them out.

Doris and Bethany reluctantly returned to prying but, like errant children, wandered off at every conceivable opportunity. Doris needed a drink. Bethany caught her dress on a nail. Doris had to pee. The sun was in their eyes. Doris moved to the other side of the house and promptly snuck inside. Bethany soon joined her. The two conversed in whispers while Gloria pretended not to notice. She'd already prompted them back to work a dozen times. Josh carried boards until he got a splinter in his palm, collapsed into tears, and refused to go anywhere near the wood again. He spent the afternoon under the lone tree, twirling his checker.

Eventually the light began to fade and the group retired to the house to cook their dinner, though this resulted in more complaints. Yoxtl left the petty squabbling and scanned for a suitable backdrop outside. The bonfire should have been cultivated in front of a stone wall, but they had none and the rough siding of the house was unsuitable. The smooth white surface of the vehicle would have to do. When the humans finished eating, Yoxtl bid them build a fire.

"With what?" Gloria asked.

Yoxtl silently cursed the wood-scarce plain. Then, "You cooked food, didn't you? I just need something that will cast shadows."

Gloria nodded and entered the house, reemerging a moment later carrying something by a thin metal handle. The bottom was metal and green and stamped with the word "Coleman." Light shone from the clear upper half. Gloria set the device down. Yoxtl stepped between the light and the car, throwing a swath of darkness up against the white.

"Tonight I will teach you to manipulate shadows."

There was a murmur of interest, and Yoxtl resisted the urge to smile. Shadow magic was pure trickery—illusion, as Medea called it. Back in Yoxtl's heyday, the spell was reserved only for the most loyal of priests. With it, they could warp shadows into various shapes to recount stories, give omens, or strike fear into the hearts of dissenters. Humans loathed the dark, and a man cursed with shadows doubly so, for he'd find himself pursued by them wherever he went. Some would kill themselves rather than live in fear. Odd, considering the illusions were incapable of causing harm, but then humans weren't the most rational creatures. Yit once saw a man set fire to his own house in a vain attempt to banish the darkness. He'd died laughing.

But they'd be learning no curses tonight.

Yoxtl twitched yits ears and the corresponding points of the shadow began to elongate. They bifurcated once, twice, thrice and spread out like the limbs of a tree. Yoxtl frowned. The car was too short for decent shadow trees—more like shadow bushes. Yit made them rustle as though caught in the wind, and the humans *ooh*ed and *aaah*ed. Well, Gloria and Doris did. Josh was silent as always. Evelyn watched with disinterest. Bethany didn't seem impressed.

The shadows swirled and reformed into a large panther. Yoxtl peeled the creature off the car and sent it pouncing toward Bethany, who shrieked and ducked. It passed harmlessly over her and plopped down next to Doris, where it sat licking its paw.

Gloria laughed. Doris stifled a giggle as Bethany sat up with a scowl.

"Shadows can't hurt you. To make them move, you have only

to concentrate on what shape you wish them to take. It's easiest to stick with the wall. I don't expect any of you to make fully formed shadows like that tonight."

One by one, they took turns trying to manipulate the shadows. Josh, still in a mood, refused to participate. Doris tried, but nothing came of it. Gloria went next and unsurprisingly didn't succeed, though she seemed to take it better after Doris' failure.

"You're next, Bethany."

"I don't know what to make."

"It's easiest if you pick an object that looks somewhat like the shadow already."

"Nothing looks like your head," she complained.

Doris thrust her hands over Yoxtl. "Look, a bird!" she exclaimed, moving her fingers to make the shadow flap.

Bethany said nothing, merely stared at the shadow with a frown. The shadow bird detached itself from the wrist and Doris put her hands down with a gasp. The bird hung above the shadow of Yoxtl's head, wings still, bobbing slightly. The shadows of Yoxtl's ears detached and morphed into more birds, which flew up to join their fellow. All spun and drifted slightly, as though they were suspended by invisible string.

"Why don't they flap?" asked Doris. "They're so . . . *wooden*."

"*Shh*," said Gloria. "She's doing well."

"What *is* that?" Doris asked Bethany, but the woman didn't seem to hear. She stared at the birds, mouth a tight line, and what was left of Yoxtl's shadow began to change into the shape of a basket.

"Oh, I get it," said Doris. "See? That's a crib and the birds are a mobile! I'm right, aren't I? Bethany, am I right?"

"Why can't you ever shut up?" Bethany snapped. She got to her feet and stalked into the house.

Doris stared after her, mouth agape.

"Well, uh . . ." Yoxtl's tail swished. "At least she did well. Evelyn, why don't you go next?"

The girl picked at her long dark hair, eyes on her lap.

Gloria gave her a nudge. "Evelyn, it's your turn."

"My turn to what?"

Gloria pointed at the car. "Can you make the shadows move?"

"I don't want to." Her voice was barely a whisper.

Yoxtl crept forward until yit was nearly on her lap. She had the most power out of any of them. Yit had to get her to use it somehow. "It's not too difficult. Just give it a try."

She glanced briefly in yits direction, then back at Gloria, who gave her an encouraging smile. "You can do it," she said.

"I don't want to look at them."

"You don't have to," Yoxtl said.

Again, the flick of her eyes. "Okay."

Yoxtl returned to yits spot behind the light. Evelyn didn't look up from her lap. Her brow furrowed as she twisted her dark hair, but the shadow on the car remained unchanged.

"Remember, it helps to pick something that looks like—"

"Oh my God *what is that*?" Doris stared into the dark, eyes wide.

Yoxtl followed her gaze. A tall figure emerged from the shadows. No—*figures*. All around, the night came to life with them. They had hollow eyes. Their arms were unnaturally long—fingers too—and their nails tapered to sharp points.

"They can't hurt you." Gloria spoke as though saying the words would make it true. She wrenched her eyes away from the things and put her hands on Evelyn's slender shoulders. "I think that's good enough, Evelyn. You can stop moving the shadows now."

Evelyn cocked her head as though confused. "They move themselves."

Josh whimpered. The one closest to him took a swipe and he yelped.

"It hurt him!" Doris cried. "I saw it!"

There was no mark that Yoxtl could see. Probably just startled the man, but Gloria didn't seem to be taking chances.

"Into the house," she barked. "Now!"

"It's nothing to worry about," Yoxtl began, but then Doris screamed. Three of the things hovered over her. They spoke in low voices, though Yoxtl couldn't make out what they said. "They can't hurt you," yit reminded her, but she didn't seem to hear over the insidious whispers.

Gloria grabbed Doris' arm and forced her toward the house. "Go!" Then, to the shadow men, "Leave us alone!"

Make them stop! Josh wailed. He shook his head and rocked as the shadow men leered and raked their claws along his flesh.

Gloria gave no indication of having heard Josh, yet her soul twitched at his cry and as soon as Doris was safely inside, she returned for him. She swatted at the shadow men but they crowded about her in a rapidly shrinking circle of darkness. She fumbled through it and felt for Josh. He screamed at her touch and pulled away, soul vibrating.

Go away!

"It's just me." She grabbed his wrist and tried to pull him to his feet. Every tug seemed to jostle his soul.

Let go let go let go!

"Stop touching him," Yoxtl cautioned. A storm was brewing inside Josh at every contact.

Gloria continued to pull. "We have to get inside. *Come on!*" She gave one last forceful tug and Josh exploded.

The magical burst shredded the nearest shadow men and threw Gloria backward. She slammed against the side of the house. The remaining shadow men dissolved into darkness.

Gloria rolled over and struggled to draw breath. At last she gasped, inhaling dust that set her coughing. She groaned and clutched at her side.

Josh covered his head with his hands. His body shivered violently. *I want to go home. Please just let me go home.*

31

TURKISH DELIGHT

Nikolai drifted at the edge of consciousness, between sleep and true wakefulness. His dreams had been plagued by self-loathing, suicidal ideation, and unfortunate memories. Mother had been there. Or not there—she'd pulled away after the war, treating him with the same polite courtesy one might offer a stranger. At the time he'd been confused and angry. Not once had she offered gratitude for all he'd done! In retrospect, he couldn't see her reacting any other way, but back then he didn't have a good understanding of people. She'd survived the war and come out hollow, losing everything that mattered to her—including her perception of her eldest son. When he'd tried to read her mind, it had been a hazy, incomprehensible mess. He'd given her up and left to find the Academy on his own.

In the dream, he'd stayed and tried to reason with her, knowing he would fail. She exploded in a torrent of accusations—something she never would have done in real life—but the curse made it seem plausible. It dug its tendrils into his mind and poisoned him with Useless thoughts of how he'd hurt one of the only people he'd ever cared about, how she'd never be the same, how he should have killed himself to save the others. The last one didn't even make sense but filled him with immeasurable pain at the time. At some point he realized it was a dream and recognized the thoughts as curse-induced. The knowledge didn't lessen the pain, but it did help his rational mind cope. The curse would pass as it always did. He just had to hold out.

Sunlight tickled his face and he opened his eyes. Grasses undulated in the morning breeze, sun shining through the tips of the stalks. A conjured fire burned low within a magic circle. Something pressed against his back and Medea jerked upright beside him. She spun away and stared at him bleary-eyed, her hands poised to cast what was no doubt a deadly and painful spell.

"Good morning to you too."

Medea blinked and lowered her hands. "Ward woke me." Her version of an apology.

His sluggish, curse-hungover brain finally caught up with what he'd just seen. She'd slept next to him. But had it been intentional? A book lay on the ground—she could have drifted off while reading, though given her level of paranoia it seemed unlikely. Magic permeated the campsite. He tried to get a feel for it without casting Magic Sight but couldn't pick out individual spells.

"How many wards did you cast?"

"A lot. Can't be too careful, you know." Medea yawned and rolled her shoulders, making an annoyed face as she did so. "Ugh, I hate sleeping on the ground."

"I'm surprised you did. Given your response yesterday I'd have thought you'd find the car preferable."

"I considered it."

"Why didn't you?" Probably not the smartest move to ask her outright, but curiosity got the better of him. Had he succeeded despite the curse? The timing of its appearance was a clear indication he'd been doing well.

Medea stood and began plucking bits of grass from her clothes with painstaking slowness. It was a deliberate stall if he ever saw one. If she hadn't considered him a threat while under the effects of the curse, she'd just tell him so. Was she afraid to say how she felt? Or maybe confused, given the professional nature of their relationship.

"Well?"

"I don't know! It just felt *wrong* to leave you out here by yourself. You were crying and . . ." She shook her head and waved a hand. The magic fire vanished.

His jaw clenched. Pity. She'd stayed with him out of pity. No—concern. Aside from the recent foray into the mental hospital, Medea wasn't overly worried about the feelings of others. Every other time the curse had struck, she'd displayed nothing but disappointment and disgust. The fact that she'd stayed indicated a level of concern for him beyond anything she'd previously displayed. He *was* making progress.

He smiled. "Shall I summon breakfast while you remove the spells?"

She nodded and turned away, mumbling to herself while ticking off her fingers. The magic around them began to evaporate. After quadruple-checking to ensure all spells were removed, they ate a simple breakfast and drove back to the farmhouse.

Medea bustled toward the kitchen counter, where yesterday's bread was stacked. A few slices had toppled to the floor. "Help me throw this out."

She went to throw out yesterday's now-stale bread and frowned.

"What?" he asked. "Did you forget to catalogue it?"

"The stack isn't as neat as I left it."

"That's what happens when you leave out food in a rat-infested house."

She shuddered and sandwiched a loaf between her palms, as

though trying to avoid as much contact as possible, and marched it out of the kitchen for disposal.

The day passed far more pleasantly than the last, all things considered. Sometimes he could tell when the machines were on. Once Medea returned to the kitchen and hurriedly closed the door before glancing furtively in his direction. The thin wood wasn't enough to completely block out the mechanical whirring.

"That the washer or the dryer?"

She winced. "It doesn't *count* if you know. You're not even supposed to know if they're *on*."

"Maybe next time don't pick a two-bedroom shack with paper-thin walls for your experiments."

"No, no, we can make this work. Let's see . . ."

Her solution was to tear apart a tampon and twist the cotton into earplugs for him.

"I'm sorry," she said. "I know this doesn't help with your beige problem."

She didn't permit talking during the experiment itself anyway, so it wasn't that big of a loss, but they took breaks far more frequently and she permitted talking then. During the first break she slid into the seat across from him with a faint smile.

"I thought of something to keep you engaged," she said once he'd removed the earplugs. "You can teach me the current Turkish."

Not something he would've chosen, but it turned out to be rather insightful, as it challenged his mind and allowed him to show off an area in which his knowledge was superior. Medea proved an apt student, picking up the patterns exceptionally fast.

"I see. So they've excluded all the words with Arabic or Persian roots." She was at the counter, cutting up his most recent batch of bread loaves and inspecting each individual slice.

"All foreign words, I believe. It was rather jarring arriving in

Istanbul and finding out that only the old-timers could understand me."

"Who taught you Ottoman Turkish then?"

"My mother. She must have immigrated prior to the change—1930s I believe? When I found out the Academy was in Turkey, I thought I'd have a leg up on other students. Then I arrived and had to learn it all over again."

"You little shit." She winged a slice of bread at him. It landed flat and slid across the table, coming to rest a few inches from his hand. She made a derisive snort at her own bad throw. "When you arrived on my island you asked to hear my Turkish, *knowing* the language had changed, and laughed when I spoke Ottoman."

He picked up the bread with a grin. "What can I say? I wanted to be better than you at something. Do you know how many people took the time to learn *both* of the Academy languages? Just me. *And* I became fluent. When I moved to Haven, I spent weekends in Dublin, watching movies to pick up accents. I studied idioms and colloquialisms. Give me an Irishman, Englishman, American, or Turk, and I can convince each I'm one of them. And then there you were, all-knowing in magic and claiming to be fluent in *every* language. I got competitive."

"There's an understatement. Give me that!" She strode over and yanked the bread from his hand. "I haven't logged it yet. And what's this about 'both' Academy languages? Are there only two now?"

"Yeah, Turkish and English. Why? Are they supposed to teach in *Latin*?" he teased.

"And Arabic and Greek and a host of other languages, though the first three are the most important. They're the languages of science. I can understand teaching Turkish so you can communicate with local Mundanes, but why English? It's the bastard child of several languages and not remotely academic."

"I asked the same thing. Apparently when the Collective started sticking their nose in everyone's business, they installed a British chancellor who wanted a universal Magi language. In true British fashion, he decided it would be English. Pretty pointless since most Magi don't attend the Academy anyway. Turkish was offered as a formality for anyone who wanted to learn it, but no one does. At the time I attended, only a couple professors taught classes in Turkish."

Medea frowned and her cutting slowed. He could almost see the wheels turning. Her oldest, most in-depth texts were in Latin, Greek, or Arabic. Many of them were translations themselves—copies of documents brought in from the East along the Silk Road, or from Africa, filtered through ports in Egypt. Even with her translation disks, she preferred to read original sources whenever possible.

He answered the unspoken question. "The Academy has been whittling down their library over the years. Why keep books even the staff can't read? And even if they could read them, they wouldn't be able to perform the magic. Some of the things I've seen you do—those were in our library, way in the back, under dozens of other books. And they're seen as myth. Gateways and teleportation—myth. Volume expansion—grossly limited. Summoning—conflated with conjuring. Do you think this has anything to do with magic dying? It's a sort of chicken-or-egg problem, isn't it? Which came first—the decline, or the culling of knowledge?"

"I don't know, but that's a very Eurocentric way to view things. The Academy used to be an institute for higher learning, optimally positioned to service Europe and the Middle East. But African and Asian countries have always done things differently. Magic is so often tied to the local religion or culture, and not every society fears it. They may have people practicing openly and taking on apprentices as needed, negating the need for centralized training. China had many Academies throughout its history, but most were eventually repurposed by Mundanes."

"What about the rest of the Americas?"

She gestured toward the small kitchen window. "It is as you see here. Colonizers destroyed or drove out the native people. Many were forced to convert to Christianity. Special schools were built with the sole purpose of indoctrinating children into European culture. Now their magic is gone or has dwindled to the point of statistical insignificance, and witch hunters kill off anyone daring enough to practice openly."

There was a thought. "When did you first notice magic declining?"

She paused and leaned against the counter, closing her eyes. Her lips moved as though recounting to herself. After a minute, she pushed away from the counter and resumed slicing bread.

"It's hard to say for certain because it was so slow in the beginning. I want to say I first noticed in the 1800s. It's gotten worse lately, especially in the big cities. Out here it's not so bad."

"America was colonized when, starting in the 1500s? And the Collective was founded in the mid-1600s after a century of witch hunts. Maybe *that* started the decline—fewer practitioners. The effects might not have been noticeable immediately." He stood and began to pace. There was something here, he could feel it. "Magi generate magic, don't they? Yoxtl told me that souls get more powerful over time, but much more so if they practice magic. If a bunch of Magi were killed at once, could that cause the dip?"

"If anything, there'd be a temporary bump in ambient magic when their souls dissipated. But long term . . ." She shook her head and began cutting the bread more vigorously, chopping more than slicing. "Fewer Magi means fewer people to train the next generation."

"And witch hunters preventing magic in the Americas and the

Collective restricting magic in Europe would only accelerate matters."

"I don't like that hypothesis."

He stopped pacing and frowned. "I thought it was rather good."

"It is. I just don't like it because it means I'm partly responsible."

He gave her a questioning look.

Medea sighed. "I've killed a lot of people. Mostly Magi. Especially in the last few centuries. Fucking Jacques." An overzealous cut sent a heel of bread spinning off the counter. She swore and retrieved it, brushing it off on her pants.

"Who's Jacques?"

"An asshole. Like you. Not like . . . I didn't mean . . ." She looked stricken.

He gave her a disarming laugh. "Go on then. What *did* you mean?"

She took a breath as if steadying herself. "Jacques was a manipulative liar who was very good at swaying public opinion. He was instrumental in the Collective's formation. Or rather, he hijacked the Collective shortly after its inception. He's the one who sent assassins to my island—fifty or so by my count. After I killed them, he told everyone it had only been a small, peaceful delegation. The number has increased in the retellings, but it hasn't come close to what I actually faced. If it had, people would have been less likely to buy the delegation lie. The damage was done, though, and I've faced countless attempts at retribution since."

Medea stared at the loaf of bread, now chopped to bits, and set down the knife. Her fists clenched against the counter. "Every one of us that dies is another one we can't get back. Most people these days are born below the threshold to cast spells, and it will only get worse as the ambient magic declines. I can't help but think . . .

If I hadn't killed so many . . ." She closed her eyes and rubbed the side of her face.

"It doesn't matter."

"What?" She looked at him with confusion.

"It can't be changed, so it doesn't *matter*. Focus on what you can do, not what you can't. The only way is forward."

Medea nodded, though she still looked distraught. She picked up the knife reflexively, saw the mangled bread before her, and set it down again. "It's not as easy as that, you know. I can't just turn it off. The guilt, the worry, the second-guessing of every decision I've ever made. Sometimes I wish I was as unfeeling as you." She hastily shot him an apologetic look. "I didn't mean—"

"I know what you meant. And it *is* easier. I don't worry about anything. I ruminate on problems and make decisions, and sometimes I get angry or annoyed, but I don't *worry*. At least I didn't before the curse. I don't know how you people can stand it."

"Neither do we. But then we have the highs to make up for the lows." She chuckled softly. "Better than the beige, I guess."

"I'm not so sure about that. I've seen how people tie themselves into knots inside their heads. I prefer being me."

She gathered up the bundle of sticks for the next part of the experiment and set them on the table with painstaking slowness. A contemplative #3 frown was written prominently on her face.

"Go on. I can tell you're dying to ask me something."

Her mouth opened, but it was a moment before she blurted out, "Do you ever feel bad about things you've done?"

"No."

"Never?"

"Never."

"Then how do you— How do you *not* feel remorse over a single thing you've done? Killing Petrov—"

"Seemed like a good idea at the time." He shrugged. "It turned out not to be."

For a moment she stared at him like he was one of her plant samples, one she debated on culling due to its undesirable characteristics. It stung, surprisingly. Most people's opinions didn't matter, but as someone he respected, Medea's ranked slightly higher than zero, and after last night he'd hoped for a little understanding. This was what he got for opening up.

"You asked me to be honest with you," he reminded her.

"I *know* that." She set down the last of the twigs. "And I've known people like you before. It's just . . . How do you *change*? How do you improve and make better choices if you can't look back and reflect on your actions?"

"I can do all that, I just don't feel one way or another about it. If a choice leads to a suboptimal outcome, I attempt to learn from it and do better, but it has nothing to do with how I *feel*. It's like a data point—immutable, but something I can use to inform my decisions going forward. And that's really all that matters—moving forward." He searched her face for acceptance, anything besides judgment, but her expression was unreadable.

They continued through the exercises—lighting the twig on fire, pushing the Bible across the table, creating an illusion of a black line, and boiling water. Medea took meticulous notes. Her face betrayed nothing of the results, though he suspected they were far better than yesterday. At least he hadn't accidentally set her shirt on fire.

By mid-afternoon, Medea had begun to wilt. He had no other way to describe it. She just became lethargic and quiet, until finally she declared them done for the day. Her moods had always seemed worse in the big cities, but perhaps here, working in such close proximity to the machines, was beginning to take a toll.

"Did you need to go upstairs and rest?"

She glanced at the ceiling with a #3. "Maybe. We need to figure out sleeping arrangements for tonight."

"I'll find a motel."

"There weren't any in the towns we passed."

"Then I'll find another place to sleep." It was still relatively early—time enough to check out the local bar.

Medea gave him a long look, then shook her head. Of course she wouldn't want to be reminded of his promiscuity. He should have lied, specified that he'd talk his way into someone's spare room. Then she surprised him by saying, "I can't believe how easy it is for you. 'I'll find another place to sleep.' Like it's nothing. You probably wouldn't even need telepathy, would you?" It was a stark reminder of just how difficult she was to read. Oh, he could decode her expressions well enough, but the emotions behind them remained elusive as ever.

"No, I wouldn't."

She shook her head again. "Sleep where you like. I'm more worried about where I'll bed down. I suppose I could hike a mile away and set up camp."

"Why can't you just take my room? If I'm not here, I mean."

She considered him a moment before replying. "I know you think I'm being silly, but I take security seriously. My room is no longer adequate as I cannot block the door, not even with my own body, now that there's a hole in the floor. Yours has a window right next to the chimney—easy for someone to scale."

How could anyone live with so many anxieties? It was a wonder she hadn't worried herself to death over the years. At least this one he could solve. "What about the sill that broke off your window? Surely that has nails sticking out of it. We can place it on the floor as a sort of caltrop."

"Maybe, but it's not wide enough."

"Go get it." He went upstairs to her window and stuck his head out. As he suspected, there were three slender boards framing the window. He grabbed one and worked his fingers underneath, rocking it back and forth until it came loose. The wood was so rotted it came off easily. He pried off the other two and brought them to his room, where he set them in a row below the window. Medea joined him a moment later with the broken sill. Laid together, the four pieces gave the window a foot-wide barrier. Sparsely nailed, yes, but better than nothing.

"How's that?" he asked.

"It'll do, I suppose."

"Alright. I'll see you in the morning." He was halfway down the stairs when she called his name. He stopped short and looked back to where she stood framed in the doorway of his room. "Yes?"

"If you can't—" She paused and took a breath. "If you can't find a place, you can stay here tonight. Downstairs. Or in my room. My old room, I mean."

He nodded, and left with a smile.

32

IMPULSE

Medea settled onto her makeshift pallet with the book. Nikolai expected her to sleep braced against the door. Instead, she'd wedged several pieces of wood into it and made up her pallet in a corner closer to the window. A pile of clothes against the door would serve as a decoy. She didn't expect him to attack—not really—but one couldn't be too careful when dealing with apprentices, and there was always a possibility of outside intruders.

The data from the experiment, at least from her cursory analysis, still seemed inconclusive, though he'd done better today. Hard to believe someone could perform better *with* added distractions, but it made sense given his explanation of the beige. It always took time to get to know her apprentices' idiosyncrasies. His newfound candidness would accelerate the process and allow her to customize his instruction.

Despite their rocky start, she was optimistic for the first time since Thomas. More than that, she couldn't have asked for a better apprentice to help with her experiments. He was good with people, *and* he felt at home in the Mundane world. Few of her apprentices did. It made him uniquely suited for the job. No doubt he could have easily secured them a new test site—though she didn't trust him not to cut corners. Or make stupidly impulsive decisions.

It didn't stop her from fantasizing about it. As she drifted to sleep, she dreamed of a responsible version of Nikolai, one she could trust to follow her instructions down to the letter. She sent him off to secure a new test site and collect numerous Magi so they could repeat the experiments. Once they'd found the reason for magic's decline (which somehow involved excessive summoning of bread), she sent him to sway the Collective to their cause, bringing a rebirth of magic in Europe. Then to the Academy, where Latin would be required once more. She was overseeing the reorganization of the Academy library, supplemented with copies of her most prized texts, when a noise brushed her consciousness.

Medea stared across the darkened room. A figure was making its way from the window toward the decoy bed she'd placed in front of the door. A *Mundane* figure. He moved with both the caution of one who did not wish to be heard and the stress of someone recently injured. Probably had stepped on one of the makeshift caltrops—thank you, Nikolai.

A Mundane she could easily handle. The problem, of course, was to do it without contaminating the site. There again, Nikolai had a point—she could simply cast spells they'd used during the experiments. As quietly as she could, she wriggled from her bedding and crept to the rotten boards under the window. She picked up a board and began twisting the nails free.

The man crouched over the faux bed with his back to her. She held a nail between her fingers, raised it level with his cervical vertebrae, and shot it across the room. It was more forceful than sliding a Bible across a table, but then she'd already pushed Nikolai through a window, so it wasn't all *that* different.

The nail pierced the man's spinal cord and he dropped like a stone. She approached and rolled him over. His eyes were wide but narrowed at the sight of her. His hands clutched the manacles of a witch hunter.

Damnit, she should have known something was off when she found toppled bread in the kitchen. They must have broken in last night too. But how had they known to search here?

A commotion sounded downstairs, followed by a gunshot. Her door opened a crack, impeded by the body of the paralyzed witch hunter. A hand grasped the wood and began to force the door open. Medea waited patiently, nails raised, until a male face came into view. She smirked as the man looked up, then launched the nails at his eyes. He screamed and clawed at his weeping sockets. Not for the first time, she was disappointed that eyeballs didn't pop when punctured. They looked like they should, and it would be so much more satisfying if they did. Alas.

She crossed the room and kicked the back of the man's knee. He stumbled and fell over his paralyzed partner. Before he could get back up, she grabbed the manacles and cuffed the two men together, ankle to wrist. Two down, and one of them would be alive long enough to question.

In the hallway she peered downstairs. A witch hunter with a rifle guarded the front door.

He spotted her and bellowed, "Stop right there! On your knees. Hands in the air."

She cast the illusion of a thick black line over his eyes and sidestepped. The gun boomed and the wall behind where she'd been standing splintered. She started downstairs, offhandedly hurling the man out the front door with a telekinetic shove, and peered into the kitchen.

Nikolai faced off against two witch hunters. One held a club and the other a knife. Nikolai himself had only a towel and a Bible. Despite this and several red gashes on his arms, he was smiling. When life was beige, combat probably added a bit of color.

The man with the knife lunged. Nikolai brought up the Bible like a shield. The knifeman faltered, clearly hesitant to damage the holy scripture, and changed his trajectory mid-strike. Nikolai took the opportunity to snap at his eyes with the towel.

The man hollered and stepped back, momentarily blinded, and Nikolai tackled him with the ferocity of a jaguar. They toppled to the floor in a flurry of fists.

The second man cracked his club over Nikolai's back. Nikolai merely grunted as he worked to pry the knife away from his target. He didn't seem to care about any incidental cuts. When it became clear he couldn't pry apart the man's fingers, he sank his teeth into the man's flesh.

"What the fuck?" screamed the knifeman, panic in his voice. "Get him off me!"

"I'm *trying*!" said the other, taking aim at Nikolai's head.

Men. Too busy killing each other to notice little old her.

Several beakers of water sat on the table in preparation for the morning's experiments. Medea grabbed one, willed the water to instaboil, and flung the contents at the man with the club. He dropped his weapon with a clatter and fumbled to remove his soaked shirt. She took a second beaker and strode over to where Nikolai had the knifeman pinned, then casually tipped the contents over the witch hunter's head.

He shrieked and clawed at his face. Nikolai lurched back from the hissing stream and took the knife, though he made no attempt to use it—simply watched as though mesmerized.

"Well?" she said. "What are you waiting for?"

Nikolai grinned up at her and slashed his blade across the witch hunter's throat. Of course he'd choose the messiest way to incapacitate someone.

"You get to clean that up," she said.

He stepped away from the spreading pool of blood and drove his knife up through the chin of the second man.

"What are you doing? That blade isn't long enough to reach his brain."

Nikolai mumbled something about micromanaging and pulled the blade free. He plunged it into the man's eye. "Happy now?"

"Quite. Where's your knife?"

"Around here somewhere. I had it, but *this* fucker knocked it out of my hand." He tugged the knife free of the witch hunter and shoved him out of the way while glancing about the kitchen. "Ah, there it is." He walked over to the sink and stooped to retrieve a knife wedged between the base of the cabinets and the floor. His gaze slid past her and he jerked his chin. "Incoming."

She turned to find the illusion-blinded witch hunter. He appeared to have lost his gun but seemed dead set on attacking anyway. He grabbed her roughly and fumbled his way toward her throat, then began to squeeze.

Nikolai hadn't seen Medea so calm since the beginning of their trip. She was downright *serene*. As she lifted a hand to the man's mouth, he couldn't help but be reminded of the day she scarred his face. She'd been deadly calm then, too, and when her hand came away he half expected to see a sealed mouth and nose.

The man's eyes bulged and he began to claw at this throat. Red-faced, he reached inside his mouth as though trying to remove something. With every second that passed he became more frantic, until at last he dropped to his knees and collapsed.

"What did you do to him?"

"Summoned a few loaves of bread into his nasal passages and trachea."

Okay now *that* was the sexiest thing he'd ever heard. She'd killed a man with bread. Bread! God, he wanted to take her right now, against the counter, blood of slain enemies pooling at their feet.

"Did you cast any spells when you were in town?" She was frowning at the corpse.

"Pardon?"

"I asked if you cast any spells when you were in town. They knew we were here somehow."

"Are you implying they're witch hunters? They're too weak for that." He didn't point out the obvious—that they hadn't blocked any of her spells. She might take offense and, besides, it was Medea. She probably had workarounds for that sort of thing.

She still gave him a funny look. "What else would they be?"

"Burglars."

She gestured to their surroundings. "Here? I may be out of touch, but even I know a building such as this should hold little of value. They also carry manacles, meaning their goal was to take us alive." She pointed to something on the floor. Handcuffs, which meant police. If they were here for the car, he'd never hear the end of it. Omaha was several hours away though. It had to be something more local. Better keep her on the witch hunter track.

"Maybe they saw us summoning food in the field the other night."

"Do you seek to avoid lying with a deflection?"

He tried for humor. "Why not? You do." She almost laughed. Almost. Then her face turned grave.

"Truth now. Did you cast any spells in town, or do magic of any kind?"

"No spells." The first part came out easily; the second took all his willpower. "But I did use telepathy to convince the clerk I'd paid. And I may have been a bit flagrant about it."

"How flagrant?"

"The shop owner pulled a gun on me."

She placed a hand to her face and inhaled deeply.

"That doesn't mean that's why they're here. I had a date with his daughter."

She shot him an exasperated look. "Come with me."

He followed her upstairs to where she'd handcuffed two men together. One was dead. One had nails embedded in his eyes—not as good as the bread killing, but still very entertaining. A shame he hadn't been there to see it. She nudged the man with her foot. "You—what brought you here?"

The man spat in their direction.

"Always with the spitting," Nikolai muttered.

"It's the Mundane version of cursing. They may not know why, but it spreads microorganisms that can make a person—"

"Medea, focus." He knelt and roughly shoved the blind man out of the way, grasped the dead man by the hair, and lifted his head up. "This is the shopkeeper who pulled a gun on me." He dropped the head with a thud. "Personal vendetta then. They're not cops, or they'd be in uniform with batons and pistols."

"Then why the manacles?"

"Those are handcuffs. They probably wanted to rough me up."

Medea didn't look convinced. "Hold him." Nikolai held the man down while she searched his pockets. She came away with a small pocket Bible and a flask. She unscrewed the lid and sniffed, then watched the man closely. "No alcohol in the flask."

His face lit up. "It's only water, miss, if you'd like a drink."

She rolled her eyes. "Definitely witch hunters. This is holy water. They think it has an effect on us." She tossed the flask aside in disgust and stood, but her glare was centered on Nikolai. He quickly rose to his feet.

"I'm sorry. You use illusions to pay all the time. I didn't consider using telepathy might jeopardize the test site."

The proactive apology seemed to take the wind out of her sails, but then she straightened. "Yesterday you said you didn't feel regret. Which means you're just telling me what I want to hear."

"In a way, yes, but 'sorry' is shorthand, isn't it? Like 'bless you' is shorthand for 'I'm socially obliged to acknowledge your sneeze.'"

"And what does it mean in this case? To you specifically?"

He considered a moment. It was a fine line to walk, but Medea wanted honesty. "I guess it's an acknowledgment that something I did bothered you, regardless of how I feel about it. At the time I wasn't thinking about the site getting found out, or even making myself a target of witch hunters. I was just—"

"Entertaining yourself?"

"Yes. I *have* been more careful since then." He waggled the blade. "Notice I didn't use magic to fight them. I did that, not because I don't think your fixation on this place isn't silly—I still don't understand why it's such a big deal—but because I respect you enough to jump through your arbitrary hoops to stay on your good side. And before you detail everything you went through to obtain this place, I already know you struggle with this kind of thing. I just can't fathom why that should matter, especially when you could simply have asked me to do it."

"No, I couldn't. You cut too many corners. How could I possibly trust you with something as important as this? Your impulsivity doesn't affect only *you*." She gestured to the bodies.

"Who cares about them? They attacked us."

"Not them. *Me*. This place. Witch hunting is a profession passed down through families or specific churches. Thanks to your indiscretion, they know we're here. Others will come."

"Not if I can help it."

She shook her head. "This is getting too complicated. Too

many setbacks. I'll have to find a new place and a new assistant." Her voice was resigned. People gave up so easily.

"Have faith in me." He offered her a smile. "If there's one thing I do well, it's making death look like an accident."

CLACKITY CLACK, GRANDMOTHER'S BACK

Evelyn gripped the armrests of the chair, skin whitening around her knuckles. Grandmother paced the motel room, heels clacking on the carpet. CLACK. CLACK. CLACK. Grandmother put her yellowed fingers to her mouth and took a drag on her cigarette.

"I don't like you being here. Not one bit. These girls are nothing but trouble. And that boy"—she flung up her hands—"Lord have mercy! At least you're not trapped with him. Rapists. Every one of them!"

Evelyn stared at the bed to avoid looking at Grandmother, but the woman always seemed to hover at the edge of her vision. Even if Evelyn left the room, the clacking and taunting would follow.

CLACK. CLACK. CLACK.

"You shouldn't be here." Grandmother laughed haughtily. "Not that you belong at home either. Nobody wants you there. Good-for-nothing girl. You should be married by now. What's wrong with you? You're pretty enough, if you'd just brush that dreadful hair of yours and take a bath once in a while. You smell.

Boys don't like girls that smell. Look at those clothes! Awful. Just awful." She tsked, a rasping sound like old metal creaking.

The door swung open. Doris entered with a peal of laughter and a boy on her arm. The boy barely had a chance to kick the door shut behind him, so insistent was Doris in tugging him toward the bed. She kissed him, her face melding to his, while his hand massaged one of her breasts.

Grandmother watched them with disdain. "Disgraceful! I told you that little harlot was a bad influence. Look at her!"

They made their way to the bed, discarding coats and kicking off shoes, Doris giggling all the way. She made it look enjoyable. Must be nice to be held like that. Caressed gently. Not like how it had been for her, crushing weight and alcohol and the stench of sweat. The boy unbuttoned Doris' blouse and began kissing her breasts. Evelyn felt her face flush.

"You like watching them, don't you? Little pervert. I knew you were rotten the day you were born. Gary should have done away with you as a baby. Drowned you like a sack of kittens."

The boy jerked upright and stared at Evelyn. "Who is *that*?"

Doris followed his gaze. "Oh, don't worry about her. She gets like that sometimes."

"See?" said Grandmother. "Even he knows there's something wrong with you."

The boy reached for his clothes. "I, uh, have to go."

"Don't worry about her, honey. She's not all there." Doris rubbed his crotch and pulled him into a kiss.

He returned the kiss, but his eyes kept straying back to Evelyn. After a moment he broke away. "I can't. I'm sorry, this is just too weird."

Doris grabbed his hand. "Don't go! Look, I'll take care of it." She hopped from the bed and stripped the comforter off the second mattress, then tossed it over Evelyn. The world disappeared. "All better! Where were we?" The bed creaked and the sound of kissing resumed.

CLACK. CLACK. CLACK.

"Disgraceful!"

CLACK. CLACK.

More kissing.

CLACK. CLACK. CLACK.

The bed began to creak and Doris moaned.

"I hope she gets syphilis and *dies*. You probably have it already, slut that you are, sleeping with all those men. How could you let them do that to you? No one will want to marry you now. Nice boys don't like whores."

"I didn't want them to," Evelyn said.

"Did she just talk?"

"Don't lie to me!" Grandma snapped. "You seduced them. I know you did. You enjoyed every minute of it. Filthy slut!"

"No, no, I didn't. I'm a good girl, I swear!"

"That's it, I'm out of here."

"Don't—"

She could only make out snippets of what the others were saying through Grandmother's shrill voice and relentless clacking.

"If you were a good girl, you wouldn't have run away when we tried to help you. Lord, how we tried to help you!"

"—crazy too?"

"But you preferred living on the streets. You liked being a filthy, godless WHORE."

"I—wait—"

There was a loud bang and then Doris' face appeared, blotchy with hatred and inches from her own. She shouted words, but Grandmother was louder. Grandmother was always louder.

Evelyn covered her ears, but there was no drowning out the dual tirades. "Leave me alone. Just leave me ALONE!" She bolted for the door and ran outside, surprised to see it was already evening. Light spilled from the office window. Someone leaned against the side of the building. There was a brief orange glow as they took a drag from their cigarette. Across the street she could hear music and laughter. A bar.

"Don't even think of going over there!" Grandmother shrieked.

Evelyn took off across the parking lot. Grandmother's heels kept pace.

"Get back here, Evelyn. I'm not through with you!"

"I said leave me alone!"

The person with the cigarette approached. A kindly old man. "Are you alright, miss?"

"No, I'm—" But his face began to melt upward. It dripped away like wax, revealing a demon with piercing orange eyes that burned with smoke.

They'd found her again. Come to drag her down to hell for her sins.

Evelyn screamed and ran toward the street.

Gloria ladled soup into a tin mug and set it in front of Josh. She'd given up on bowls—he had trouble using a spoon and preferred to use the bowl like a cup anyway, though it still resulted in some spillage. At least the mug had a large handle. Hopefully it would give him some added stability.

"Be careful, it's hot."

Josh rested his chin on his arms and watched the steam swirl above the rim. Yoxtl perched on a shelf above what passed for the kitchen. She filled a bowl for herself and stood eating with her back to the spirit so she could pretend it wasn't there.

She'd waited until the others left to grill Yoxtl.

"You said the shadows couldn't hurt us!"

"They *can't*," it had proclaimed.

"Oh yeah? Then how do you explain this?"

She'd pointed at Josh's shirt. It was torn in four parallel lines, as though he'd been raked by some animal. She reached for the fabric and Josh cried out.

"It's okay. I just want to take a look." She gently lifted the edge of the shirt. The skin was puffy and red underneath.

Yoxtl's foxish face had been unreadable. When it finally spoke, it said the same damned thing. "Illusions can't hurt you. They can make you feel things, but they can't leave a mark. Whatever Evelyn conjured, they weren't simple illusions."

"Whatever she conjured? You mean you don't *know*? How the hell are you qualified to teach us?"

"I *am*. I just didn't expect her to progress so quickly. Usually humans take longer to—"

"Heal it."

She swore she could see the spirit wince. "Such magic is not to be used on something so minor."

That was a lie if she'd ever heard one. "Where's Nikolai? He said he'd come check on us."

"Nikolai entrusted this training to me."

"His trust was clearly misplaced. Give me one good reason we should stay."

Yoxtl's ears twitched. "Because society wants nothing to do with you. Or him." It nodded to Josh. "And because if you don't learn to control your magic—if *all* of you don't learn to control it —you're a danger to yourself and others. Look at what Evelyn did today."

True, all of it, and yet . . . "You did nothing to help us when the shadow men attacked. You don't heal us or conjure food. I'll admit we need training, but that doesn't mean we need *you*."

Yoxtl made more excuses, but she barely heard them, turning

her mind to their predicament. As she ladled her own soup, she considered how much money they had left and whether it would be enough to travel someplace else. No, and anyhow it would be best to stay here in case Nikolai came back. She'd have to find work. Maybe she could find something for Josh too. He could follow simple instructions. The problem would be getting Evelyn away from Bethany and Doris before they inevitably took off on their own. She had no doubt Bethany would insist on taking Evelyn just to spite Gloria, then dump her in a facility at the first sign of trouble. At least Yoxtl could watch Evelyn while she and Josh worked. It was probably the only thing the spirit was good at.

Gloria blew on her soup and was about to take a bite when Yoxtl jumped down from the shelf and bounded toward the door, tail twitching.

"Someone's coming."

She sighed, set the bowl down, and joined Yoxtl at the door. There were headlights in the distance. A moment later she could make out the sound of a car traveling too fast over the uneven dirt. Goddamn Doris! One of these days she was going to wreck the Suburban. There was another thought—if Bethany and Doris left the group, they'd try to take the car, leaving the rest of them stranded. She'd have to get Yoxtl to steal the keys.

"I sense Doris and Evelyn, but no Bethany."

Gloria frowned. They never came back before morning. Had something happened to Bethany? She felt a momentary thrill at the idea, then a stab of guilt.

The Suburban lurched to a halt in front of the house and Doris got out.

"What happened?" Gloria asked. "Where's Bethany?"

Doris opened the passenger-side door and pulled the seat forward. "Come on, Evelyn," she said cheerily. "Time to go!"

Evelyn stepped out cautiously and Doris steered her toward the house.

"Look, Evelyn, soup! Yum yum." Doris plopped her down across from Josh and slid Gloria's soup toward her. She brought a spoonful to Evelyn's mouth.

Gloria strode forward. "What the hell happened?"

"Can't you see I'm busy? Mmm! Isn't that good?"

"Out with it!"

"Here you go. Take the spoon, dear. That's it."

Gloria waited in seething silence as Doris carefully handed the spoon off to Evelyn and walked back outside. At the Suburban she bent beside the mirror and reapplied lipstick.

"Evelyn got out of her room, that's all. Bethany wanted me to bring her back."

"Just like that?"

"Just like that. And since you've taken an interest in her, well, we thought it would be best if she stayed here from now on."

"What aren't you telling me?"

Doris arched an eyebrow. "Whatever do you mean?"

"Come off it. You've never cared about Evelyn before, and now you show up and start doting on her like a child?"

"For your information, I've *always* cared about her. In fact, *I'm* the one who takes care of her when we stay at the hotel."

"And then you let her get out."

"I seem to recall you had the same problem with Josh. Are you saying you don't care about him?"

Gloria flinched. Doris offered a sickly-sweet smile. "I just needed a little break is all."

"Of course you do." Yoxtl appeared on the hood of the Suburban, gave her a wink, then gazed at Doris with warm amber eyes. "Evelyn can't have been easy to look after. I bet Bethany refused to help you at all. She probably blames you for what happened today."

"She does! Can you *believe* that? *I'm* the one who has to share a room with her. I get no sleep. No time to myself. It's enough to drive a person mad! And then she has the gall to blame *me* for what happened! If she'd just taken a turn with Evelyn—"

"What *did* happen?" Gloria tried to keep the accusation from her voice. "Evelyn have one of her hallucinations in public?" Yoxtl shot her a look and she belatedly added, "If so, that's not *your* fault. Bethany should have been helping. I didn't realize she wasn't, or I would have asked you to leave Evelyn here earlier."

"Pfft." Doris rolled her eyes. "But of course she'd never agree to that either. Or she didn't before today."

"What changed?" asked Yoxtl.

"It was like I said—Evelyn got loose. Only she was having one of her episodes—raving to herself and crying and the like. I saw her bump into some guy. He must've tried talking to her, but she screamed and the next thing I knew she was headed for the intersection. She ran right out in front of a truck!"

"Oh my gosh!" Gloria exclaimed. "Was anyone hurt?"

"I don't think so. The truck just *stopped*. There was this loud crunch and I saw the back tires lift up a bit. I ran over to Evelyn— thought for sure she was dead—but she was just standing there in the road, arms over her head. Wasn't a scratch on her. But the front of the truck was caved in, like it'd hit an invisible tree."

Gloria exchanged a look with Yoxtl. This was bad. Nikolai had warned them to keep a low profile. That it was dangerous to do magic in public. "What happened next?"

"I grabbed Evelyn by the arm and got her out of there! Drug her right to Bethany's room and told her what happened. And she blamed me. Can you believe that? As if *I* can control when Evelyn has an episode!"

For once, she agreed with Bethany. Gloria swallowed the urge to scream at Doris and forced a smile. "Well, it's good that you've brought her here. At least now if she runs off she won't get into trouble."

"Yeah . . ." Doris sighed. "Some night this has turned out to be. Now none of the guys at the bar are gonna want to go out."

"You can't stay in town any longer," said Yoxtl. "Any of you. It's not safe."

Doris gaped at Yoxtl.

"It was never the plan to have you stay in town, and this is why. You're too exposed. We need to return immediately and get Bethany."

"Are you out of your mind? I'm not staying here! It's filthy and small and—"

"It would be a lot nicer if you helped me fix up the place," Gloria interjected. "I think we should hold off magic lessons for now, at least until we get this place in order."

But Doris was already stalking around the car. "To hell with this! I didn't bust out of one nuthouse to join another."

Gloria climbed into the passenger side and yanked the keys away from Doris.

"What are you doing? Give those back!"

"If you're done with this group, fine, but you are *not* leaving us stranded."

"I would have come back in the morning."

"Please. You and Bethany would be on the road at first light, going God knows where. The car was enchanted to keep us warm. It's *supposed* to stay here. You've monopolized it long enough. You want to leave? Take the bus."

Doris glared at her. "Fine. But take me back to the hotel. I'm not spending the night in this shithole."

"Move over. I'm driving." Gloria got out of the car. Her eyes sought Yoxtl's. "Watch over Evelyn and Josh. I'll be back as soon as I can."

"This is a mistake. If Bethany and Doris leave, they'll be in danger."

"It's their decision, and it's not my problem." She turned away and walked around the hood to the driver's side.

Yoxtl appeared on the roof like the Cheshire cat, one paw on the door. "I know you dislike them, but do you really wish them harm?"

"They're doing more harm than good here."

"You didn't answer my question."

She thought back to the pang of guilt at the idea that Bethany might be hurt. "No, I don't wish them harm." She sighed. "Not serious harm anyway."

"Then convince them to stay." Yoxtl's amber eyes were pleading.

"I'll try. I can't imagine either of them listening to me, but I'll try."

"That's all I ask." Yoxtl removed its paw.

She slid into the Suburban. Doris stared resolutely out the window, refusing to look at her. This was going to be a long night.

3 4

RITUALS

"Where are we going?" Medea asked.

Nikolai shot her a smile. "It's a surprise."

Her expression didn't change. "I don't like surprises."

He squinted at the road, pulling over when he spotted a familiar patch of trees. He'd driven this road so many times in the past week that he knew it well. Not that there were many landmarks to be had—trees tended to stick out. These trees were clustered near a river, providing a picturesque view. This was their last night here and he wanted it to be memorable.

He parked the car and got out, shooting Lance at a fence post barring their way. The wood splintered and the post went flying into the darkness. He conjured a light in his hand and motioned Medea over. She wore a frown, one he didn't recognize, but it was somewhere between #2 and #3, so nothing to be overly concerned about.

"Why are we here?"

"Because you've gone without proper magic for nearly a week and I thought we could have a bit of fun. Come on, cast something. We're well away from the test site."

Medea looked at him and then the tree line. She swung her hand upward, as though throwing a ball. Light blazed from her hand and shot straight up, a hundred feet or more. It exploded like a firework into dazzling blue. He thought the light would disperse, but it stayed, illuminating the surrounding landscape like moonlight. She walked toward the trees, waving her hand to part the grass before her like some modern-day Moses.

At the riverbed she called twigs and dried wood from nearby and lit a bonfire. She levitated a large boulder next to it, altering the shape until it was smooth like a bench. She plopped down and patted the spot beside her with a smile. All week he'd gradually chipped away at the boundaries between them. Nice to see his work paying off. He stretched out beside her and let the warmth of the fire tickle his toes.

"Thank you," she said. "I'll admit I haven't felt myself this week. Magic is such a part of me, to live without it . . . ." She shook her head.

"I know what you mean."

"At least you've been casting *some* spells at the test site, minimal as they've been."

"That wasn't what I was referring to. At the Academy, and for most of my life since then, I've had to hold back my telepathy. People don't like it when you read their minds. Sometimes I wish I could live in a big city—you know, if the Mundane technology weren't a problem—and spend all my time around Mundanes. I can be myself more when I'm around them. Part of that is simply the power dynamic, of course, but they've never treated me ill for using my natural abilities."

"That's because they didn't know you were using magic on them. They'd feel differently if they knew the truth."

"But they don't, so it amounts to the same thing. I do better with them. I always know what to say. Mind you, I've learned to read Magi the old-fashioned way, but I can still be wrong." He turned to look at her. "Like I was wrong about you."

Medea rolled her eyes. "I have no idea *why*. All the signs were there."

"Maybe so, but I'd never met someone like you before. The idea that someone could say what they mean all day every day . . . Do you have any idea how rare that is? Nobody does that. They think they do, but they don't. I like that about you. We may not always see eye to eye, but I always know what I'm getting."

Her face flushed red, whether from the warmth of the fire or the unexpected compliment he couldn't be sure. She swiftly turned the conversation to something safer. "How have you found your telepathy training thus far? Has it been satisfactory?"

"Yes. With Mundanes, I can get them to do just about anything I want—though there are exceptions." Like the owner of the Chevy. The man had resisted most of his efforts. He'd have to figure out how to get around that, whether by logic or pure willpower. "And, of course, it's made getting laid a lot easier," he laughed, then broke off when he saw Medea's face.

Figures she'd judge him for his promiscuity despite asking for honesty. He was letting the mask slip far too often around her. He quickly tried to salvage things.

"When we get back, I'll start writing down some of my methods for you to put in the library. See if we can't make your telepathy section more robust."

"I would appreciate that." Her voice was flat.

Goddamnit, she was still angry. What the hell did he have to do to get in her good books? "You said you studied with the people here. What was their magic like?" He was really taking a bullet by asking that. Once she got rolling, they'd be here all night, but lecturing was her favorite pastime.

"Nature based, mostly. They could grow fruit from bare twigs and coax a full cornstalk from a kernel in a matter of minutes."

Dear god, it was the Aztecs all over again. "What is it with the American natives and corn?"

"It was important to them, important to the survival of their people." She looked at him pointedly. "Every culture, every person, has things that they value."

"Uh, okay."

Her face was unreadable. It was like she'd gone blank. Too many of her expressions tonight hadn't fit into any of the standard categories.

"What do you value?" she asked.

Power. Himself. He couldn't say that though. She was searching for something, but he had no idea what. "A moment, please."

"Take your time." She leaned back on her arms, long blonde hair flowing free, pert breasts tilting up. She'd struck a similar pose the day they met in Petrov's shop. Back then he'd thought she was trying to appear seductive, but he now doubted she realized how alluring the pose was.

What the hell could he say that was both true and acceptable? She'd know immediately if he was lying. Medea might not catch all his lies, but she could ferret out this kind with startling precision. He had to dig deeper.

What did he value? Himself, obviously, because everything started and ended with him. Everyone thought the world revolved around themselves, even though they'd deny it wholeheartedly if you brought it up. He embraced it. Every man was an island. Self-contained. You made bridges with other people, but that was only to obtain things you needed. It was a matter of self-preservation. Power was like that too—a means to an end. With enough power, you could fortify your island against outside influence. At the heart of it all was the self.

"Autonomy."

Medea gave a little half snort. "Me too." She hunched forward, propping her elbows on her knees, and stared at the fire.

"And I value you." She probably thought it was a line—and it was, though that didn't make it any less true. Yes, he longed to have sex with her—success would stroke his ego on so many levels—but even without it he enjoyed her company, frustrating as it could be.

Medea sat up, face still unreadable. "Come, I want to show you something."

She led him away from the fire. Her spell still hung overhead, bathing the trees in pale blue. She hugged his coat against her slender body, her breath visible in the chill air. As they walked, she examined the trees, as though searching for something. At last she came to one she seemed to recognize, patting the bark and leaning against it to look out over the river.

"I thought I recalled this place. There used to be a village here." She pointed across the water and an illusion took shape. Dwellings and people appeared on the opposite bank. Like the images she'd conjured when they'd first arrived at the farmhouse, these were blurry, the humans faceless, as if she couldn't quite recall how everything was supposed to look.

He stepped closer, ostensibly to get a better view, allowing his chest to brush against her back. She didn't pull away.

"I trained with the Pawnee. Trading spells and languages with one of their medicine men, though I daresay he picked up English faster than I did Pawnee. My head was overflowing with languages at that point." She chuckled softly.

His efforts had finally paid off. Medea was opening up. As he always did when pursuing a woman, he encouraged her to keep talking. "What did you learn?"

"Not much new, sadly. Their magic was similar to the tribes I had already visited in the East. Different variations, but nature magic is all the same once you truly understand it. On a cellular level, growing squash isn't all that different from growing corn."

She moved her shoulders as if uncomfortable, then continued. "One morning, the camp was abuzz with news that a warrior had been charged with performing the Morning Star ritual."

"Charged? By who?"

"By their deity, in a dream. Who's to say if it was just a dream, or if it really was a visitation by a spirit, though knowing what I do about spirits, the latter is entirely possible. The men left. When they returned, they brought a girl from an enemy village. She was held in one of the dwellings, kept separate from the rest of the tribe. I gathered that the ritual would take place in five days, but they refused to tell me what it entailed, and as an outsider, I was not permitted to witness it."

"But you saw it anyway."

"Yes. You can imagine what I thought. What I suspected. I concealed myself and followed the men when they took her from the dwelling. They led her to a scaffold, where they strung her up naked and spread-eagled." Medea's fist clenched and unclenched at her side. "I don't interfere with the politics of mortals, but there are some things, some lines, that can't be crossed. I revealed myself and demanded to know their intent. My mentor—he cried when he told me. Many of them did, but they felt duty bound to perform the ritual, and it wasn't cause for interference, especially not when it held such cultural significance. I—" Medea shook her head and clutched her coat in a death grip. "I stood by and observed."

He placed a hand on her shoulder, expecting to find it trembling, but she stood as though made of iron. She spoke again, voice monotone.

"When the Morning Star appeared, they burned the girl's armpits and groin with torches. She thrashed and screamed until a man put an arrow through her heart, while others struck her from behind with clubs. The rest of the men shot her with arrows, symbolically mating with her, while my mentor cut open the wound on her chest. They lay the body face down in a nearby field, allowing the blood to fertilize the ground."

An image of the girl, still strung up, appeared in front of them. Unlike the rest of Medea's illusions, this one was crystal clear. The girl's face was a mask of pain streaked with tears. Her torso bristled with arrow shafts, blood oozing from the wounds. Even the scent of burning flesh tinged the air. The grotesque tableau was forever etched in Medea's memory. No wonder she'd been so uncomfortable at this location—it reminded her of *that*. Still, there was no reason not to take advantage of the situation. He could play consoling.

"You did the right thing. Who knows how they would have taken it had you intervened."

She chuckled sadly. "That's just it—I found out years later that the ritual wasn't common practice. It's not easy, coming into a place where you know absolutely nothing and trying to extrapolate what the people are like. I had limited time, and much of that was spent learning the language. The Pawnee nation was vast. I just happened to stumble on a group that still practiced the ritual. Most didn't, and many argued against it. I recall reading a newspaper article on a man who demanded the release of a Comanche girl. When he couldn't sway his people, he cut her down and let her ride away on his horse. Had I known there'd been dissenters . . ." She took a shuddering breath and the illusion vanished.

He gave her shoulder a squeeze. "You didn't know. And more importantly, there's nothing you can do about it now."

"I used to intervene, long ago. With my power, I thought I could do good in the world, right all the wrongs. It never turned out that way. People complained about my methods, that they hadn't wanted my help, or that I'd helped them wrong and made things worse. There always seemed to be other forces at play that I'd failed to consider. Politics. Human nature. Government systems. Problems always seem easy to fix from the outside, but that's because you don't live in the thick of it. You don't see how everything connects, and when you pull on one thread, it can unravel the whole garment. I've seen it time and again when nations colonized people they knew nothing about.

"That's why I stopped intervening. I realized I didn't have the knowledge to combat things at a systemic level. Even when I tried to understand, everything was so horribly complex and unfathomable it made my head spin. Ignorance is not bliss, it merely shields you from understanding the depth of your mistakes. Without knowledge, there can *be* no moral action. Apathy is the armor I wear to protect my soul. Easier to feel nothing at all than everything at once. I know that might seem jaded or craven, but it's allowed me to live this long, when so many others have been driven to despair over what could be and isn't. Immortality doesn't favor those who connect themselves with humanity."

"Sounds like it would suit me perfectly."

"Yes, it would."

She turned with a calculating expression and reached up. The coat opened, exposing the loose shirt underneath to the cold night air. Her nipples hardened and he wrenched his eyes up to her face. Her chill fingers brushed his cheek and he was suddenly very aware of his disfigurement. But there was no disgust on her face as she traced the line of his scars. Would she finally heal them? Make him immortal? He slid his hand down her back. She glanced aside as though surprised to find it there, then returned to studying his face. He pulled her close enough to feel just how ready he was.

A wave of desolation washed over him. Of course the magical

libido killer would hit now. If Petrov weren't already dead, he'd kill him. He slumped against the tree, already wilting. Medea frowned. How she must hate him for ruining the moment. Thomas never would have had this problem. He was nothing. Just an ugly, cursed boy.

Just like that, the dark thoughts receded. Impossible. The curse might be sporadic, but it never faded that quickly. The only explanation was that Medea had intervened, which was even less likely. But then love was the one thing capable of making her break a self-imposed rule.

"Did you remove my curse?" He kept his tone carefully neutral.

"No. I subdued it for a time—an hour, maybe two. I know it's selfish, but I need your mind clear tonight. I want you to feel everything I do." He'd expected her to look abashed, but her eyes confidently sought his.

He smirked. "Only an hour or two? I can last all night if you want."

She blinked at him in surprise. "Well, *I* can't."

His breath quickened as her fingers caressed his lips. She gently lifted his arms above his head, standing on tippy-toes to do so, nipples grazing his chest. He couldn't wait to tear off her shirt and see what lay beneath, but she was a present he'd only just now earned and he wanted to savor every second of unwrapping.

He bent to kiss her, but his lips refused to part and something constricted his wrists—vines. Pain lanced through his gut. He gritted his teeth and waited for the flood of adrenaline. This was even better than he'd anticipated. Pain went hand in hand with pleasure, but too few women were willing to indulge that partic- ular side of him. Medea was a master healer though, and she knew him well enough to cater to his tastes. She'd fuck him up, he'd fuck her bloody, and she'd heal them both. It was the perfect partnership. He sought her eyes, but she was staring across the river again.

"I should've known when they cried that they knew what they were doing was wrong. They cried because they knew they were taking the life of an innocent." Her gaze snapped to his, but it held no affection, only contempt. "I'll shed no tears for you."

BRANKS

Gloria pulled up to the hotel. The Suburban hadn't even come to a complete stop when Doris started to get out. Gloria grabbed her arm.

"Pack your stuff and meet me back here. I'm going to talk to Bethany."

"Don't tell me what to do." Doris yanked her arm free and stormed toward her room.

Gloria shook her head and killed the engine. Great, just great. Part of her wanted to pack up and leave too. If it hadn't been for Josh and Evelyn, she would have, but she couldn't leave them on their own. She pocketed the keys and made her way to Bethany's room.

It was nearly ten and the hotel was quiet. Her breath came out in little white puffs. Gloria knocked gently on Bethany's door and thrust her chilly hands back into her coat. She should've thought to wear gloves. The door cracked and she hurried inside, as much to get out of the cold as to get this over with. Bethany would never agree to leave with her, but she had to at least try. If Bethany's decision got her into trouble, it would be her own fault.

The room was dark, and she didn't see Bethany anywhere.

Before she could even say hello, someone grabbed her arms and flung her face first against the bed.

"What the hell?"

"Quiet!" The man's voice was dark and gravelly.

She could feel someone binding her wrists and ankles. "Let me—*AH*!"

The man yanked her up by the hair while the second person tied a gag around her mouth. They fished around in her pockets and removed the key to the Suburban. The man thrust her head back down.

"Where's the other one?" he said.

"I saw her go into a different room. Looked like the one from the bar who tried to lead me into temptation." He nudged Gloria in the back. "*This* one I haven't seen before."

"There's no telling how many of them there are."

"Could be a whole coven!" said an enthusiastic younger voice.

"Don't get ahead of yourself, sonny. We must proceed with caution. Ralph, go talk to her. Act interested. See if you can find out how many there are and where they're holed up."

"Yes, sir."

Gloria heard the door open and close.

"What do you want?" she tried to ask, but it came out muffled by the gag. Who were these people? Where was Bethany? Did they have her too? She tried to scream Bethany's name through the gag. "ET-AH-NEE!"

"I said quiet!"

Someone punched the side of her face. Stars blossomed across her field of vision. Gloria waited in silence, brain scrabbling to figure a way out. From the voices, there were at least four of them. Her eyes slowly adjusted to the dimness. She could just make out two figures across the room, one seated and the other standing. The seated figure resolved into Bethany—at least she thought it was Bethany. There was the outline of her bushy hair. But her face looked wrong.

"Ralph's coming back."

"Anyone with him?"

"No."

The door opened. Gloria tried to twist and see but the man held her firmly against the bed.

"I don't have much time. She's packing up. I've offered them a place to stay. She didn't want that one or the one who did magic to come, but I insisted. They're staying in some shack west of here."

"Good. Tell her this one wants more time to pack and to go on ahead. We'll follow you. She say how many there were?"

"Four. She's coming." The door closed again.

So Doris had neglected to mention Josh. What would they do when they found him? What would they do with all of them?

"Quick, get her out of the chair. We need to be prepared to move."

A light clicked on beside the bed and Gloria found herself yanked to her feet. She could finally make out Bethany properly, handcuffed to a chair. The side of her face was puffy and blood dribbled from a split lip. There was no gag, so maybe they'd been interrogating her. A man held a knife to Bethany's throat while another undid her cuffs, pulled her arms behind her back, and replaced the handcuffs. He held out the second pair of cuffs to the man holding Gloria.

"Save 'em. We only have so many and this one's bound good."

The men waited until they saw Doris leave with Ralph, then hustled them toward the Suburban. Halfway across the parking lot Gloria tried to make a break for it, but they kicked the back of her leg and she fell painfully on the asphalt.

"Try that again and I'll take your eye," said the eldest man. He looked to be in his sixties, with the weathered face of someone who'd spent a lifetime working in the sun. He tossed the car keys to a middle-aged man who got into the driver's seat. The youngest —just a kid, fourteen at most—sat shotgun and addressed the driver as "Pa." Another middle-aged man, who resembled the driver enough that they could have been brothers, held Gloria and Bethany on the floor of the Suburban at knifepoint while the old guy climbed into the back seat.

They followed Doris and Ralph at a distance, headlights off to avoid detection. She doubted it was necessary. Doris was probably too busy flirting with Ralph to notice they were being followed. Maybe Yoxtl would see them coming and have Josh and Evelyn hide. She glanced over at Bethany, registering the fear in her eyes.

The ride turned rough. Gloria felt every jiggle and bump through the floor of the car. She had to figure a way out of this. At five against five, their odds didn't seem so bad. The kidnappers had knives, but there were hammers at the house. If one of them could get loose and alert the others, they might have a chance. Then again, Josh probably wouldn't hurt a fly, and who knew if Evelyn would have the presence of mind to defend herself. They had to try.

If only her hands weren't bound behind her back! She tried to get Bethany's attention and indicate with her eyes and eyebrows that she intended to do something. Bethany gave a slight shake of her head. She looked terrified.

"Stop here and kill the engine," said the eldest man. "We don't want to get too close. Isaac, you stay here with Peter. Watch these two. Make sure they stay quiet until we have the others sorted."

The driver and the eldest man got out. In the distance, Gloria could just make out Doris calling Evelyn.

"Who's that?"

Josh uncovered his head and looked toward the unfamiliar male voice. A flashlight blinded him. He held up a hand to shield his eyes. Two figures stood in the doorway.

"Oh, don't worry about *him*," Doris' voice tittered. "He's just a halfwit mute Gloria likes to keep around."

Josh's gut clenched. Doris was never nice to him, but she'd never been this outright mean. She was acting more like Bethany.

Yoxtl bounded forward. "Where's Gloria?"

Doris walked past Yoxtl and took Evelyn by the arm. "Time to go, dear."

"Where are we going?" Evelyn asked. "I thought we were supposed to stay here now."

"This is no place for a lady," said the man. "I've got a nice house where you all can stay."

"Evelyn, stop. What do you think you're doing, Doris? Who is this?" asked Yoxtl.

"I'm supposed to stay," said Evelyn. "Yoxtl said—"

Doris laughed loudly.

"What's she talking about?" asked the man.

"Oh, nothing, nothing at all," said Doris, smiling benignly at the man. She turned back to Evelyn and lowered her voice to a whisper. "Hush now and let me do the talking. I don't need you ruining this for me."

Josh wanted to tell Doris to leave Evelyn alone, tell Evelyn she should stay, but he couldn't, and getting in the way of white folks was just asking for trouble. He stared at his lap, thumb running over the rough edge of his checker.

Suddenly Yoxtl's body began to stretch and change. It grew into a towering black wolfish creature that took up half the cabin.

The creature opened its mouth to reveal teeth red with blood. "LEAVE HERE NOW OR FACE YOUR DEATH."

The man yelped and took a step back. He fumbled at his shirt collar and pulled out a crucifix on a chain. He held it out in front of him and bellowed, "I need help in here!"

Doris stared at the man. "Who are you—" Before she could finish, two men with knives barged into the cabin. They slashed at Yoxtl's new form but their blades simply whistled through thin air. The man who'd arrived with Doris grabbed her from behind and put a knife to her throat.

"Call the beast off."

"What? I don't understand. Who *are* you people?"

"Banish the demon."

"You think *I'm* controlling that thing?" Doris laughed. "*You* banish it."

He pressed the blade into her throat and she cried out.

"Okay, okay! Yoxtl, you heard the man. Stop."

"I said LEAVE!" the beast roared.

"I told you. No one listens to me."

"It's just a phantom," said an older-looking man. "If it could hurt us, it already would have."

Yoxtl continued to bellow commands, but the men just raised their voices and spoke over the racket. The walls seemed to close in on Josh. Everything was too loud, too emotional. He felt like his chest was constricting. The eldest man grabbed Evelyn, snicked handcuffs about her wrists, and shoved her toward the man he'd entered with. "Gag and blindfold this one." He pointed a knife at Josh. "What's this? I thought there were only four."

"Just some mute servant of theirs."

"LEEEEEAVE!"

"Have they cursed him? Why's he rocking and whining like that?"

"He's an imbecile."

"We ought to put him out of his misery then."

Josh covered his head. This could not be happening. This could *not* be happening. He wanted to shrink into a tiny ball and vanish.

"That's not up to us. The good Lord will decide what becomes of him. If he *is* cursed, dealing with this lot ought to break it."

"Should we leave him here then?"

"We can't chance it. Recall that it was a faithless slave who corrupted the women of Salem. And what do we have here? A male Negro with four of our women. More likely he's the devil in disguise, here to fornicate and corrupt. You there!" The man nudged Josh with his foot. Josh shrank back, expecting a boot to the ribs. "Get up."

Would they leave him alone if he obeyed? What choice did he have?

Yoxtl appeared at his knee, normal sized again. "Don't listen to them, Josh! You have more magic than you know. If you focus, you can fight back."

"I said, get—"

"—don't—"

"—hands off me!"

"—now!"

So many people and so many voices. They whirled together like a cloud of electricity and knives, alternately frying and carving into his brain. Pressure built inside him. His mind buzzed. Rough hands gripped his arm and his skin was on fire. It felt like they were pulling his arms out of their sockets. He had to get out of here. He had to get out of here. He had to—

A valve opened and the pressure poured out. The men's hands were gone, followed by a crash and confused shouts.

Josh shivered. He knew what he'd done—sent the men flying away from him. Except the house was small, so they hadn't gone far. He'd done the same thing the day the cops arrested him.

They'd been beating him something fierce, and the pressure just released. They hadn't been happy about that. One officer had started screaming at him and pulled a gun, but he'd seemed too scared to use it. What would these men do?

"Did you *feel* that?"

"Yeah." A spitting noise, followed by the sound of someone getting to their feet. "We might as well do it here. This one is too dangerous to move. Place is remote, no one for miles. Easy enough to dispose of the bodies once we're done. Take your girl out and bring the other two inside."

"Bodies?" Doris' voice was suddenly shrill. "What do you mean bodies? Ow! You're twisting my arm! You're not very nice, you know. Misleading a woman like this. It's ungentlemanly. Your mother would be *ashamed*."

"And go get the branks for that one!"

NOT HIS KINK

Blinding pain tore through Nikolai's abdomen. He'd once been boiled alive, and yet somehow that had been easier to endure, for it had been all of him, all at once. The isolation of this agony contrasted sharply with the rest of his healthy body, making it a thousand times more intense. He willed necrosis into the vines keeping him bound, but they morphed into something like wire and bit into his skin.

"You seem surprised," Medea said. "I'll admit you fooled me for a time. That night outside the Spotted Sow I thought you were different. A killer, yes, to be sure—who among us is not?—but no, men are all the same."

He tried to ask what she was talking about, but his sealed lips muffled the words.

"No talking your way out of this. Well do I know how you like to twist words, and I'll take no chances tonight. I should have killed you the second I found out you were a telepath. Did you know it was once customary to dispatch your kind? Men with your talent inevitably use it for ill. I suppose you think that preying on Mundanes makes what you do better?"

What the fuck was she talking about? He racked his brain.

Where had he gone wrong? She must have taken something out of context. Another wave of agony broke his concentration. Had he not been bound to the tree, he would have fallen to his knees.

"Would you like to know what I'm doing to you?" Medea's anger, usually hot, burned cold. She put a hand to his stomach. Despite the malice in the touch, his skin tingled at her proximity to his waistband. She smiled ruefully at the bulge in his trousers, then stood on her tiptoes, seductively close to his face, and whispered, "Enjoy it while it lasts. You won't have it for much longer."

She ripped open his shirt and raked her fingernails across his stomach. Jesus Christ, she was hot when she was killing him.

"I'm a fleshweaver—I can rearrange parts of the body any way I please or change them completely. It proved quite lucrative when I was young. For some reason, people are rarely satisfied with their bodies." Her hand traced the skin of his belly. It rippled in response.

"I designed this punishment for men just like you. Your digestive tract is detaching—that's what you're feeling. Your intestines are tearing themselves away from their connective tissue and moving elsewhere. When I'm through, your colon will be attached to your mouth, and your esophagus to your asshole. I'm going to cut off your manhood and shove it up your ass. You'll experience the pleasure of digesting that which matters most to you and shitting it out through your mouth." She leaned forward. "Because that's all that's ever come out of your mouth—shit."

Medea conjured a ball of fire in her hand and sent it drifting slowly toward him. She knew how to tease—he'd give her that. The warmth of it increased gradually until it became unbearable agony under his armpit. The hair and skin sizzled, momentarily displacing the pain in his gut. It would have been fascinating if she were doing it to anyone else. The fire dispersed and the internal rending returned with a vengeance.

He had to find out why she was mad and state his case, but she'd made that impossible. There was really only one option left to him, but she'd sworn she'd kill him if he ever tried that again. She hadn't left him much of a choice though.

The key would be to get into her head and *not* read her mind. He'd never tried it before. What was the point of entering a mind if you didn't want to read it? But it was the only way he could see using telepathy without her wanting to kill him over the violation in trust.

He ignored the pain and focused on Medea's mind. She had a barrier ready this time. Telepathic barriers differed from shields, taking on the properties of whatever material you imagined them to be. His own was like ice—thick enough that an attack would require significant telepathic force to penetrate, and she'd hear it coming. Other casters might choose something like fog, water, or stone.

Medea's barrier was solid, clear, and multifaceted. She'd definitely see an attack coming. He examined the barrier from a distance, contemplating its structure. It couldn't be glass. She'd never choose something so weak.

He suddenly recalled Medea on the beach, shifting the sand into a cubic, tetrahedral pattern. *The molecular structure of diamond,* she'd said. *See? This is what makes it so strong.*

No. She couldn't possibly have been that stupid. It had to be a trap.

But she *did* love sharing information, and she'd admitted no other Magi approached things on a molecular level.

He only had one shot at this. She'd kill him rather than allow him access to her mind.

He focused his will, imagining it as a shaft of pure light, and shot himself through the barrier.

Medea flinched and tried to fling him out, but he was ready this time, digging in with imaginary hooks. He could sense her panic, and oddly, a burning hatred for Yoxtl. The spirit must have taught him how to do this!

I just want to talk.

She clenched her fist, and he could feel something in his body tearing apart. "I told you I'd kill you if you ever tried that again."

Firstly, I don't respond well to threats. Secondly, you were already *killing me. Now you're doing it faster. It's not like you left me much of a choice. I have nothing to lose and everything to gain. You haven't even told me why you're doing this. Don't I have a right to know?*

Medea was a rational person at heart. As he'd hoped, his calm logic won him a momentary reprieve. She clutched her hands to her head and yelled at him to get out.

Not until you tell me why you're so upset.

Her mouth curled into a snarl. "You're using telepathy to control people."

Wasn't that the whole motherfucking point? *So you're training me how to do something, and then you're mad when I do it?* Was this about the car? *The guy with the car gave it up willingly, though I don't see how blackmail is all that different from subliminal coercion.*

"To hell with the car," she spat. "You're using telepathy to force women to sleep with you!" She conjured an arrow and shot it into his shoulder.

What the hell? *No, I'm not.*

"You've already admitted to it. 'I can get them to do just about anything I want now.' Or do you not consider Mundane women worthy of personhood?"

That's not what I meant. I was talking about people giving me money or car keys and such. And it doesn't work all the time anyway.

"You *said* telepathy made it easier for you to 'get laid.'"

Because it does. *I've always used it for that, just not in the way you think. I use it to gather information. More recently, I've been able to send subliminal messages. Like, 'I'm available' or 'I lick pussy.' I don't force them into anything. There's no game in that.*

"Game?!" She spawned another fireball and sent it winging toward his other armpit, no slow approach this time.

Not the word he would've chosen. Verbal communication allowed him to filter his thoughts into something more palatable, but telepathy was instantaneous, and he was finding it difficult to censor himself.

I. Am. Competitive—you know that. He cast about for an example she might understand. The burning flesh was horribly distracting. *Hypothetically speaking, if I used my powers to make you think I was your best apprentice, better than Thomas, do you think I'd be satisfied?*

That made her pause. "Of course not, because it wouldn't be true. I might not know it, but *you* would, and it would eat away at you. Nothing would change the fact, save you getting better. But I don't see what this has to do with—"

Sex is a competition. Me against other men. Who wins? Me. Because I'm better. I know it. Women know it. Don't you see? If I forced them, it would be an admission of my own defeat. They have to choose me or it doesn't count.

Medea was wavering. He could see it in the way she looked to the side, brow furrowed in concentration, but then she shook her head. "You're a liar. Always have been. That's why I sealed your mouth. I knew you'd try to talk me out of this."

Yet you didn't kill me instantly, which you could have. Search your heart. You know I'm not like that.

Medea's face hardened. "Do not mistake my brand of justice for hesitation. Search my heart, you say? All that matters is the mind, and mine sees a man who lies, who kills his own master over a minor inconvenience, who steals and cheats—"

I AM NOT A RAPIST.

"You expect me to believe that you, *you*, who take the easiest route to *everything*, don't take the easiest route to sex?"

Yes. The woman was unhinged, so stuck in her own reality that she couldn't see the forest for the trees.

"Bullshit! What's stopping you? You, who lust after every woman you see? All men are capable of it, and you have more power than most."

Is that what you think? How the hell had her world view gotten so skewed? *Wait a minute—is that why you barricaded your door? It was, wasn't it? You weren't afraid I'd come in there and kill you, you were afraid I'd rape you.*

All this time he thought they'd been getting close, that she knew him better than anyone, and yet this proved she didn't know him at all. His anger crystallized.

It's not my job to convince you that the lie you believe is wrong.

"Don't you *dare* use my words against me."

Why the hell not? You've already convinced yourself I'm guilty. Where's your evidence?

"It's right there in your head! I've seen your brain. You don't feel emotions like the rest of us. Hell, you probably don't feel anything at all. Look at you! The pain in your body would have a normal man screaming and begging for mercy by now, but you push it aside like it's nothing."

First of all, just because I'm not screaming and thrashing about doesn't mean I'm not in agony. I just don't think hollering is particularly Useful. Second, don't mistake my lack of empathy for a lack of morality. It's true—I don't feel like you do—but that doesn't mean there aren't lines I won't cross based on my own set of values. And unlike the rest of the world, MY morality isn't subject to the momentary whims of feelings.

"No, it's just subject to the whims of your cock."

She really thought rape was about sex? That if men were horny enough, they'd rape all the livelong day?

Rape has nothing to do with sexual desire. It's about power.

"And power is the thing you desire most. You think I don't know what the first thing out of your mouth would've been if you hadn't taken a minute to come up with 'autonomy'? How many women have you sought to overpower?"

None.

"Why not? What's stopping you?"

My mother!

He didn't register the thought until it was gone. Too late to call it back. He never got flustered. Why did Medea's constant prodding push him to the edge?

"Your mother?"

Yes, my mother. He didn't want to think about Mother, let alone discuss her.

"You don't strike me as the type of person who cares what anyone thinks."

Maybe you don't know me as well as you think you do. Mother was one of the only people I ever cared about. Her and Harper . . . and you, if it comes to that. She was beautiful. Stunning. Raven-black hair, bewitching blue eyes, body of a goddess. I saw how men coveted her. Heard what they said to her. Knew how much she hated it. God, how she'd hated it. *I saw, too, how the neighbors treated their wives. Slapped them around for saying the wrong thing. Father wasn't like that. It's why she chose him, even though he was a soldier, barely home often enough to knock her up before leaving again. But he was good to her when he* was *home. And that's what she taught me. "Be good to your woman, Kolya, and she will be good to you." She said it, not realizing that I considered her mine.*

"Yours?" Medea gave him a puzzled, somewhat repulsed look.

Not like that! Mine like Harper is mine. And you. *Someone I care about. Someone I'll slit a hundred throats to protect, because they're Useful to me in a way I can't quantify. Pushing me to be better, to do better.* Fuck, he wasn't making any sense. *The point is, Mother was my whole world, and I hers—or I was, until my brothers showed up. But for a time, it was just the two of us.*

"Where is she? You never speak of her."

Because she hated him now. Because he couldn't stand to see the disappointment in her eyes every time he looked at her. *We had a falling out after the war. She was angry about something I'd done.*

"What did you do?"

Harper knew better than to probe old wounds. Medea didn't. He had her attention though, and the pain had ceased completely. Truth—something Medea valued—was the only way out of this. It's not like he had to tell her everything.

I made a choice. My country abandoned us to the Nazis. It was either save my brothers or save Mother. I chose Mother. It wasn't even a choice, really. Mother was my world, and I was never particularly fond of my siblings. When the war was over, she only saw what she'd lost and blamed me for it. Blamed me *for keeping her alive instead of them.* The youngest two hadn't even been Useful. Mewling fucking babes. A constant drain on their limited resources. And he was supposed to prioritize *that*? Like hell. *When it was clear she'd never forgive me, I left. We haven't spoken since.*

Medea crossed her arms. "When you told me about your first experience with magic, you said you defended your mother from your abusive father. Now you tell me this."

Fuck. *I lied back then.* His thoughts came tumbling out. *You liked it when I saved Kate from those drunks, and so I constructed a story with a similar narrative. What I tell you now is the truth.*

"You could be lying though. Convenient how you always

seem to tell me exactly what I wish to hear. I can't *trust* you, Nikolai. Not with this story, and certainly not when you could be using telepathy to force women."

Then come inside my head and see for yourself. He surprised himself with the decision but immediately knew it was right. Medea would never take advantage. He knew it with the same certainty he knew the sun would rise in the morning. Trust went both ways, and it was his turn to trust her. He dispelled his hooks and eased out of her mind.

Medea took measured breaths, as she always did when upset and frantically processing something. "I don't want to. You know I don't want to."

He offered no argument, no solace. Merely gazed at her with a neutral expression.

"Goddamnit." She approached uncertainly and put a hand to his mouth. His lips parted.

He opened his mouth wide and flexed his jaw. His lips were tacky. "I . . . Look, I'm not saying I'm perfect. Will I lie to get in bed with a woman? Abso-fucking-lutely. But I never force them, and I always make sure they have a good time. It's *important* to me that they have a good time. I don't know if it's because I'm a telepath, but if the mind isn't into it, it ruins everything for me." He laughed. "My idea of hell is a faked orgasm. I don't understand why that appeals to anyone. Why strippers and prostitutes appeal to anyone. Sure, if that's all you can get, fine, but I've seen men take the illusion of attraction at face value. It's why I don't fuck little girls." There was no sport in it, none at all. "I prefer women who can tell good sex from bad. I know that's odd for someone my age, but there's more to it for me than just a body. I'll manipulate anyone, but with sex . . . The playing field has to be level. I don't know if I'm making any sense."

"You are. In a roundabout way." A wisp of a smile crossed her lips. "Do you know that you ramble when you're honest?"

"I do now. You really shouldn't tell things like that to people like me."

"I suppose not. But then I'm still reeling at the revelation that sex is merely an ego-boosting activity for you."

He smiled wryly. "What isn't?"

The vines about his arms loosened and he pulled himself free. His feet threatened to give out beneath him. He slumped against the tree and eased himself to the ground. Medea paced at a distance. Her healing magic tingled against his armpits, though it did nothing to conceal the smell of burnt hair and flesh that clung to his clothes. He waited until the pain of internal healing subsided, then stood and began to strip.

"Run back to the car and grab my change of clothes from the trunk." Without looking to see if she'd obey, he waded into the river and began to scrub himself clean. She returned a few minutes later with his clothes and made to put them beside the shore. "I have to dry off first. Put them by the fire."

Medea blanched.

"I'm not going to hurt you," he said a little too forcefully.

Her jaw clenched, but she returned to the fire, sitting on the rock with her back to the river. When he approached the fire, her whole body tensed. But why? It's not like he'd never stood behind her before. He often allowed her to walk first—it was a great way to circumspectly check out a woman's ass. The only difference now was his nakedness and the lack of her usual defensive enchantments. It had to be the latter. During their healing lessons they'd worked around naked bodies hundreds of times—granted, always with the genitalia covered—but . . .

"Does it really make you that uncomfortable to have a naked man standing behind you?"

"Just dry off and get dressed."

When she'd encountered him half-naked outside the bath-room, he'd read her body language as nervous desire. Even when she'd refused to fully heal him after his drowning—as Yoxtl had put it, carved off a bit of her soul to avoid touching his manhood —he'd taken it as a modesty thing, but her behavior tonight spoke of something much darker. No wonder so many of his attempts to seduce her had proven counterproductive.

"I'm reaching over to grab my pants." He went slowly, announcing each movement. She tensed every time. How the hell had she ever slept with Thomas? Or did Thomas do this to her? Maybe they fucked fully clothed. The guy had been Puritan, after all. His own chances seemed to diminish with each successive reach for clothing.

"It's safe to turn around now."

She turned hesitantly, as though worried he was lying—she'd done that when Yoxtl healed him too. When she saw him fully clothed, her body instantly relaxed.

He sat beside her and began pulling on his shoes. She believed him enough to let him live, but only barely. It was suddenly much more important that she know he was telling the truth. "We're going back to the farmhouse," he said. "I want you to pack up your things. We're leaving tonight."

AN ATTEMPT WAS MADE

Gloria sat up at Doris' shriek. Her captors said nothing as she wriggled onto the seat and stared out the car window.

"Get a good look," said the man. "You're next."

Ralph held Doris with her arms pinned behind her back while the older man tried to force a metal cage over her head. She thrashed and screamed until he slugged her in the gut. She doubled over, gasping. He grabbed her roughly by the chin and pinched her mouth open, then jammed the cage over her head. They forced Doris on her belly. She lay there, hem of her dress falling open like a wilted flower, and for a heartbeat Gloria thought they meant to rape her, but then one withdrew twine from his pocket and began to hog-tie Doris' limbs. When he was done he made a beckoning gesture at the car.

Gloria and Bethany were unceremoniously dragged from the vehicle and thrown beside Doris. The cage on her head looked like a medieval torture device. It probably *was* a medieval torture device. Doris gave a muffled sob.

The kid stood over them, a knife in his hand and a shit-eating grin on his face, while the others threw their meager possessions from the shack.

Yoxtl appeared in front of Gloria. "They're witch hunters. Here to convert and kill you. You have to get away!"

No shit, she wanted to say.

"I'm going to loosen your bindings and then distract the young one so you can run. Most of the others know my illusions can't hurt them. You won't have much time." Yoxtl slipped behind her and began tugging on the rope around her ankles.

Why wasn't it helping them with real magic? Screw illusions! It should be tossing the men in the air like Medea had, or conjuring a cyclone filled with lightning like Nikolai. *Anything* but this.

She felt the pressure on her ankles vanish. Yoxtl reappeared in front of her.

"I can't get your wrists without him seeing." At her puzzled expression, Yoxtl clarified, "I can only interact with things in a corporeal state. When I mess with something like a phone or a lock, it's only my paw that's solid and it's *inside* the thing so no one sees it. I'd have to work with the rope from the outside. He's bound to notice." Yoxtl glanced pleadingly at Bethany.

Bethany took the cue and began mumbling to Doris through her gag. Gloria couldn't make out the words, but the tone was clear enough—words of comfort. She shuffled closer to Doris, directly in front of Gloria, and laid her head on the woman's shoulder.

Gloria felt the weight of the spirit against her knees. To her chagrin, Yoxtl didn't cast a spell to untie the knot but instead started chewing apart the rope with its teeth. What the hell? Why was it wasting time like this? She wanted to scream at it to do magic.

Finally the rope parted and Yoxtl's weight disappeared. "Get ready to run," it said.

Yoxtl bounded off to the side and danced behind the kid with the knife. It raised a paw and slashed the boy's ankle. The kid yelped and spun.

"What was that?" he yelled, eyes wide and searching for his attacker.

Yoxtl reappeared at the edge of the shadows. The spirit's body began to morph into something that looked like a werewolf. It growled at the boy and bared its fangs. Needless to say, it now had the kid's full attention.

"Help, help! There's a monster over here!"

Gloria yanked off the gag and dashed around the side of the shack. There was a hammer here somewhere. She felt around in the dark until she grasped a smooth wooden handle.

Now what? She was one against five armed with knives. Could a hammer smash through Bethany's handcuffs? Somehow she doubted it, and she'd waste valuable time by trying. Her only chance was to get to town and maybe return with the cops, or split the group, allowing the others a chance to escape. Neither option seemed feasible. She swore internally and fled into the dark.

It wasn't long until she heard shouts behind her. Someone was yelling to ignore the monster and get the others inside.

"Spread out and find her!"

She quickened her pace, mindful that running might land her on the wrong end of a prairie dog hole. It was impossible to see where she was going in the dark, though she glanced behind her now and again to make sure she was heading away from the light of the cars. She judged she was moving somewhat northeast of the trail they'd cut through the grass with the Suburban.

In the distance she heard car doors slam. Shit. There was no way she could outrun a car.

Headlights swept the prairie far to the south. The second pair swept in her direction. Shit shit shit!

She flung herself to the ground. The grass was only a foot

high and didn't offer much cover, but it was better than nothing. Maybe they'd miss her at first glance and head the other—

A car horn blared and she heard the engine rev.

She leapt to her feet and sprinted across the plain. Behind her, two sets of horns blared.

Yoxtl appeared, running through the air alongside her. "Keep going! Medea has a gateway in this direction. You won't be able to pass through, but her wards will be enough to ensnare them."

What about me? she wanted to ask, but just then the earth gave way below her foot. Her ankle screamed as she slammed awkwardly to the ground. There were hoots from the nearest car. Her ankle erupted in fire as she tugged her foot free of the hole.

"Fuck, I think it's broken. You have to heal me, quick!"

"There's no time. You'll have to get up and walk. Hurry, they're almost here."

She couldn't imagine moving her foot, much less standing on it, but she tried nonetheless. The pain, already intense, shot up her leg and she crumpled, choking back a sob.

"I can't!" she cried.

"You must."

She reached for Yoxtl, intending to shake some sense into the beast, but her hands slid through its insubstantial glossy fur. "Help me, damn you!"

"I can't," Yoxtl said with a pained expression. "Truly, I wish I could, but I don't have the power. I— I'm sorry, Gloria, but that's the truth. I get my power when mortals die and leave their souls to me. No one has done that in a long time. I used the last of my magic to heal Josh's leg."

She had no idea what to say. The confession felt less like a betrayal and more like a confirmation of what she'd already known deep down—that they were well and truly on their own, and that if they were going to get out of this mess, it was up to her. She patted the ground until she found the hammer and gripped the handle tight.

A car halted in front of her, blinding her with its headlights. She felt the rumble of the other circling behind. Two men stepped from the first car. She couldn't see them clearly through the light —just their silhouettes. They reminded her of Evelyn's shadow men and the sudden longing for magic was a physical ache in her chest. Medea had tossed them all into the air as if it were nothing. If she had that kind of power, she could save them all.

Instead, she had a hammer.

She waited until they got close before taking a swing. Her ankle screamed at the subtle shift in weight but she gritted her teeth and managed to land a blow on the first man's arm. He cried out and leapt back, but then someone was grabbing her and yanking the hammer from her grasp.

"Let go of me! LET GO!"

She thrashed and spit like a cornered cat but it was four against one—they didn't even need their knives for this. Within seconds they had her pinned against the earth. The eldest man stood above her. He toyed with the knife in his hand.

"I told you if you tried that again, I'd take your eye." He straddled her and squatted over her chest. The weight of his knees dug into her arms as he brought the tip of the blade toward her face. She tried to pull away but he gripped her jaw with the strength of a vise.

She closed her eyes tight, like a child cowering under the covers to protect herself from monsters. As long as no flesh was exposed, she was safe. Except she wasn't a child, and the monsters were real.

When the tip pricked, her eyes flung open—or tried to. The pain wasn't as intense as she'd expected, certainly not enough to overshadow the burn of her ankle. It was more a distinct discomfort, like a large grain of sand in her eye. The world half blurred into a haze of red as blood poured from the wound and blocked her vision.

The man pulled back and held up something round. She couldn't focus well enough to see it, but knew what it was. The empty night sky swallowed her scream. How could she save the others when she couldn't even save herself?

38

VERIFICATION NEEDED

"This isn't the gateway." It wasn't even the right part of Omaha. Nikolai had driven them to some sort of nightclub. What was he playing at?

He killed the engine and threw his arm over the back of the seat, shifting to face her. "We're going in there. I don't want you to see how I operate, but I *need* you to see it. I don't want this thing hanging between us."

"That's really not necessary."

His face hardened. "Oh, it's necessary. After what you did to me, you don't get to decide what proof of my innocence is acceptable." He got out of the car, walking around it to open her door.

"I can't go in there like *this*." Medea gestured to her clothes. She still wore his too-large shirt and pants.

"Since when do you care what others think of your clothes?"

"I'll stand out. Besides, it'll be loud and crowded and—"

"Can you get into my head from there, and stay inside? Because that's what I need you to do. I know you don't want to. *I* don't want you to. I'd damn near rather be spit-roasted alive than have someone else traipsing around in my head, you understand that? Except that I value our relationship, and you're the only person on this planet I can trust not to go trespassing into other areas of my brain. Stick to the surface. And I don't want to hear any complaints about what you see there. Because remember— I'm sacrificing my own peace of mind for the sake of yours."

There was nothing she could say to that. He was right. As uncomfortable as it would be climbing into his skull, he was the one truly putting himself at risk. She nodded and closed her eyes. She willed herself out of her own mind and settled into his, perching as one might in a public outhouse—hovering, avoiding every surface for fear of picking up some pathogen.

"I can *feel* your disgust. Thanks for that." He slammed the car door and stalked off into the club.

The club was as crowded and noisy as she expected, but somehow far more manageable when viewed through Nikolai's eyes. He made his way to the bar and ordered a drink. Then he parked himself on a stool and watched the room, drink untouched.

It was disturbing to see him rapidly catalog the women, sorting them into categories depending on how willing they'd be to have sex with him. Body type didn't seem to factor into it, only willingness, though he seemed to have a fondness for large breasts. He surreptitiously observed them, asses too, though less frequently, and even once the ass of a man. His drink remained untouched.

WHY AREN'T YOU DRINKING?

Nikolai winced. "You're in my head. You don't need to yell."

I'M NOT YELLING.

"Yes, you are. And to answer your question, it makes my mask slip faster."

MASK?

"The persona I create to get close to people."

A man nearby chuckled. "Look at this guy over here, talking to himself!"

She was treated to a brief fantasy of him slitting the man's throat. Nikolai didn't reach for a blade, though. Instead, he aimed a thought at the man.

Give me your wallet. The man complied, placing his wallet into Nikolai's hand with a dazed expression. *Now go fuck yourself.* The man wandered off toward the club exit.

I DON'T UNDERSTAND HOW YOU EXPECT HIM TO COMPLY WITH THAT.

"Stop. Yelling. For the love of god, woman, you're giving me a headache. You're going to force me to drink just to shut you up. And I'm sure he'll figure it out. Now hush, I'm going to work."

He approached one woman after another, making small talk and asking them about the most inane things, swapping targets if he detected too much hesitation. It was difficult to see how he was making use of telepathy, as the thoughts were shooting out so fast. From what she could gather, he was collecting information based on their interests and using it to steer the conversation. He cared nothing for what they said, only how he could use it to ingratiate himself.

With chagrin, she realized he'd probably done the same thing to her.

Don't worry about that. I do it to everyone.

HOW CAN I NOT WORRY ABOUT THAT?

Because it's what people do. It doesn't have to be malicious. This is just how people connect.

THAT'S NOT TRUE CONNECTION. IT'S BASED ON LIES.

Throughout the exchange, Nikolai was still talking to his target—a brunette with an hourglass figure Nikolai greatly admired—*and* reading her mind. How the hell was he doing three things at once?

Because I'm only half listening to her. Anything I want to know I can just look up in her head.

IT'S DISHONEST. YOU DON'T CARE ABOUT ANYTHING

SHE HAS TO SAY. YOU'RE COMPLIMENTING HER ON THINGS YOU DON'T CARE ABOUT.

It's a business transaction. I make her feel good about herself, and if I do a good enough job, she'll let me fuck her tits. The last thought was accompanied with a visual.

NIKOLAI!

I said you don't get to complain about what's in my head. This is the real me. Nobody gets to see this. An internal grin. *You should feel honored.*

She realized he was having fun. Not just the act of selling himself to women, but the fact that she was witness to it.

Is it really that odd to take pride in one's work? Another grin. *You should stick around till later. I'm very good at what I do.* She suddenly saw herself from Nikolai's point of view. She was naked, or how he imagined her naked—with larger breasts and hips. He kissed one of them and tongued his way down her belly.

She recoiled, almost backing out of his head completely. The image vanished.

Sorry! Don't go. Goddamnit, this was a bad idea. I'm trying to keep things clean in here, but I haven't had sex in two days so it's hard. A smirk at the unintentional innuendo.

Two days? Was he really sleeping with a new woman every night?

Not every night. I went through the local ladies pretty fast. There aren't many near the farmhouse. I've been driving to Omaha every night since and working the clubs. It's a long drive but I don't need much sleep.

DO YOU HAVE ANY IDEA WHAT SYPHILIS DOES TO A PERSON? DO YOU USE PROTECTION?

Are we really *having this conversation?*

ANSWER THE QUESTION!

No, I don't.

How could he be so reckless and irresponsible? Just like a man to leave a path of wanton destruction behind him.

That's a little melodramatic. When I leave a woman, she remembers me fondly as the best lover she ever had. He smiled at the brunette, gently touching her arm as he whispered in her ear, "How about we get out of here?"

NOT IF YOU GET HER PREGNANT, SHE DOESN'T.

Can't women prevent that?

Was he really that naive? But then, if he'd started as a teenager, he would have been sleeping with other Magi at the Academy, girls with access to spells and potions.

MUNDANE WOMEN CAN'T. YOU'RE A TELEPATH. HAS NO WOMAN EVER WORRIED ABOUT THIS BEFORE SLEEPING WITH YOU?

Well, yeah, but people have irrational fears all the time. 'Maybe this boat will go down.' 'Maybe I'll fling myself off this bridge for no reason.' 'Maybe everyone hates me.'

And then it hit her—he didn't understand because he'd never lived with those things. All the little insecurities or fears that most people experienced were foreign to him. Sure, he might feel them during the malaise, but that would only reinforce that such things weren't to be taken seriously.

IT'S NOT IRRATIONAL.

But I thought . . . Can't women time their cycles or something?

THAT'S NOT EVEN CLOSE TO FOOLPROOF, AND SOME WOMEN DON'T HAVE REGULAR CYCLES.

His mind spun back through all the women he'd slept with on this trip, on his weekends before that. A parade of miserable women appeared with squalling babies in their arms. They stared at him accusingly. More than anything, that convinced her he'd been telling the truth before. He actually cared what the women thought, insomuch as it reflected poorly on their remembrance of him—a narcissistic view to be sure, but one that ensured he'd never take someone against their will. It was antithetical to his views.

Nikolai looked down at the brunette with new eyes. *I guess tonight is going to be a blow job. Are there infertility spells for men?*

YES, THOUGH MEN DON'T USUALLY THINK TO USE THEM.

You can leave now. Unless you want to see what comes next. Not that I'll get very far with her. Why would she want to sleep with a sorry sod like me? It was as though a bucket of cold water had doused his mind. He was sinking in a bottomless morass. Not only had he failed to win over Medea, she hated him. And why not? He was a worthless shit who couldn't keep it in his pants. He should've let her finish the job.

Nikolai sagged. The brunette looked up at him, concerned. "Are you alright?"

Medea fled his mind. She'd seen enough.

Nikolai stared morosely at the miniature pie. Medea had come into the club and dragged him away from the brunette with some lame excuse. Unable to drive the car herself, she led him by the hand to a nearby diner. She probably had the location of every damned diner in America memorized.

"Eat." Medea nudged his plate with a smile, as though by being unnaturally cheery she could drive back the malaise. That, or she enjoyed seeing him like this.

"You don't get to tell me to eat when you never eat yourself." He picked up his fork and knife and cut a square out of the pie, depositing it on the side of the plate.

Medea made a sour face. "Why must you do that?"

He picked at the pie. He'd already shared too much of himself tonight. Perhaps it was the malaise urging him to finish throwing himself off that cliff, for he found himself telling her.

"I was in Leningrad during the war." Just naming the city made him want to vomit. She wouldn't know the significance. His classmates would have, which was why he'd never told them, not even Harper, not even after endless remarks that Nikolai had no idea what it was like to live through the war. He'd told everyone he'd spent the war in Turkey with relatives—an obvious lie, but if you repeated something often enough, people took it as fact. Harper alone probably suspected he'd gone through more than he let on.

The civilians had tried to evacuate, but too late. Mother had gone into labor on the road. She handed him and his brothers off to a stranger and urged them to get to safety, but he wasn't about to leave her alone. Father was off fighting. With his brothers gone, it could be just the two of them again. Everyone was yelling and crying. Easy enough to double back in the chaos. But the little shits had followed him, even after he pelted them with rocks and told them to leave. Mother was so upset to see them back.

"We had no food. The Germans cut off our supply lines. There were bread rations, but it wasn't enough, especially once they started mixing in sawdust and who knows what else. Thoughts of food became all-consuming. When the rats were gone, we ate wallpaper glue. We boiled shoes to make soup . . ."

His hand began to shake. He set the fork down and hid his hands in his lap. Damn the curse for making him relive all this. Not just relive, but expose weakness. He hoped she was enjoying the show, though he dared not look at her face.

"It wasn't enough. I want to punch people who say they're 'starving' when they're only hungry. They don't know what hunger is. How consuming it is, not just your body, but your mind. You can't *think*." He shook his head. "So many people died that first winter. At first they tried to bury the bodies, but there were too many to keep up, and the labor required calories we didn't have. They were left in the snow until spring. You'd walk by and see . . . chunks taken out of them."

It felt good to tell her this, in a masochistic sort of way. The malaise clamored for him to continue debasing himself. He picked up his fork in defiance and broke open the flaky pie crust. A bouquet of rich cinnamon billowed out. Apple pie. Nothing more American than that. He took a bite, but the flavor died on his tongue. The malaise made everything taste like cardboard. He chewed mechanically and washed it down with water. Perhaps he could drown himself.

"Eight hundred and seventy-two days," he continued. "That's how long we were under siege. I am not a normal man. What troubles others usually doesn't trouble me. But this . . . Even I didn't come out unchanged. I couldn't see food wasted without going into a rage. I tried to fight it with logic. I could keep myself from diving into the trash after a discarded bit of food or prevent myself from punching the person who casually tossed it there, but I couldn't stop my stomach from growling at the smell of glue or the sight of a rat." Or bragging about how he used to catch them, as if that were a perfectly normal thing to brag about. He and mother had eaten better than most.

"When I arrived at the Academy, they always had food. I found it difficult to control myself. So I ate. Far more than was necessary. I went from gangly little boy to round little boy. I would have stuffed myself to death if I could, like a goldfish. And then they taught us how to summon food. You can't imagine how that was for me. Food, at my fingertips, any time I desired it." He laughed bitterly. "I locked myself in my room—my *shared* room —and spent all day summoning bread. Rye loaves and wheat loaves and loaves with nuts. I cast the spell until I ran out of mana, then I waited and cast it again. I had to see if it kept working. If it really was unlimited. What if it stopped? What if I was starving one day and I tried to summon bread and it didn't come? I had to know."

Medea shifted uncomfortably in her seat, biting her lip, as though she was dying to interject but knew it was impolite to do so.

"My roommate banged on the door the whole time. Eventually he had the sense to go get Harper. Not that I opened the door to him either. At least not right away. He told the others to leave, offered his own bed to my roommate, and sat by the door all night. Eventually I let him in. There I was, sitting on the bed, surrounded by a dragon's hoard of loaves. And that was *after* I'd hidden as much bread as I could. Harper never asked why. Just emptied out my trunk, loaded it with bread, and helped me haul it down to the kitchens. Trip after trip after trip. I was reluctant to let it all go. Harper told me to wrap up one loaf and keep it in my trunk. I still do that, you know—keep a loaf or three in my room. After that, I knew I had to work on my self-control. Every meal, I make a sacrifice." He pointed to the square of pie he'd separated out on his plate. "This is a promise to myself that there will always be more food. That nobody controls my destiny but me."

Medea waited a moment. When it was clear he'd finished speaking, she burst out, "No, I meant why are you cutting a square piece out of a round pie? A triangle is the most logical shape to use. You cut it out of the middle, for god's sake. Who *does* that?"

Had she not heard a single word he'd said? Here he was, pouring his heart out like he'd never done to anybody before, and her eyes were focused on the damned pie. Just like that, the malaise lifted. Apparently his quota for misery had been filled for the day.

"Oh, I'm sorry. Does this *bother* you?" He cut a second square, this time off-center from the middle.

Medea clutched the edge of the table in a death grip. "Stop that!"

He kept at it, cutting more mismatched pieces until she turned away with a harrumph. He took a bite of pie, savoring it almost as much as he savored annoying Medea. As glad as he was that she would remember none of his confession, it still irked him that she hadn't listened.

The waitress came by with the check and a reminder that they were closing soon. He thanked her and aimed a smile at Medea.

"I'm amazed you're still functional this late in the evening. Don't you turn into a prune if you don't bathe in the blood of newborns every day at five p.m.?"

Medea rolled her eyes. "One of your more disgusting guesses."

He suddenly had to know. She knew far too much about him, and yet she shared nothing of herself. It was rare that she spoke of her past, although given the events of the evening, she must've lived through even more than he'd thought.

"Why do you retire to your room so early?"

"Done with guesses already?" she teased.

"I want to know. I want to know about you."

"It should be fairly obvious. I read."

"Why don't you just read downstairs? In the common room. In the library. Anywhere."

Her lips pinched together. "I'm afraid if I tell you, you'll be hurt."

"Oh, *now* you're afraid I'll be hurt? Come on. Give me something. I've shared enough with you tonight."

"It's hard for me, having an apprentice in my home all day every day. As much as I enjoy teaching, it's tiresome. I have no time to myself. I need . . ." She took a breath, and then the words tumbled rapidly out. "I need time alone in a place where no one can talk to me or bother me or make any demands on me. Where I can just exist and not have to worry about anyone else."

"Is my presence really that offensive?"

"It's not you. It's everyone. Anyone. At some point I'm just . . . done with people for the day."

"If I avoided you after lessons were finished, would you stay downstairs?"

She scoffed. "Fat chance of that happening. It seems like every time I turned around this summer, there you were lounging about the common room, interrupting my reading. I couldn't even garden without you—"

"Forget about this summer. It's a . . . it's an invalid data point. If I left you alone after lessons, would you feel comfortable being downstairs?"

She shrugged. "Possibly. Usually it takes three years or so before apprentices stop pestering me every waking moment. By that point, they're usually planning to kill me."

"Well, you no longer have to worry about that from me. I promise to leave you to your reading. If I forget, you can just tell me to piss off. Much more straightforward. I'm surprised you don't do it already."

"I do have *some* manners," she said, before releasing a loud belch.

39

RESULTS

It was late and the night was chilly as they stepped out of the diner and made their way back to the car. Medea shivered. Before she even thought to ask, Nikolai was handing over his coat. She draped it over her shoulders. Mmm, still warm. He didn't seem at all bothered by the cold, and she thought again of how warm he must find her island to go shirtless so often. At least his constant desire to exercise and stay fit made sense now.

"You know," she said, "I can teach you a spell that will negate any extra calories you consume above a certain threshold. That way you could eat as much as you want."

"So you *were* listening."

"I'm sorry. I get so focused on . . . other things."

"Like whether or not my pie is cut symmetrically?"

"Yes. And anyway, I never know what to say to things like that. 'Sorry you starved and had a terrible childhood?' Who didn't? Everyone thinks their tragedy is the worst thing ever. I've seen so many horrific things in my lifetime—yours barely rates. But you can't tell people that. Or that their struggles don't matter in the grand scheme of things. They get upset. And saying 'sorry' implies a fault on my part, or that I feel something about it, which quite frankly, I don't. I have difficulty caring about things that do not impact me personally."

"But you *do* care. You cared about that sacrificed girl enough to remember her face."

Indeed, it had been pristinely preserved in her memory when most everything else Mundane had faded.

"Probably not in the way you think. She went through pain and it was awful, but what bothered me more was the injustice of the whole thing, how unnecessary it was. Societal systems, not any individual person, caused that pain. If I had taken her down, it would've accomplished nothing. Yes, I would've spared her, but in a few years another girl would've been taken. It wouldn't have ended the cycle. To make that change, people would have had to collectively decide that what they were doing was wrong. Which they did, eventually."

"I'd like to say that you could have spoken with the tribal leaders and persuaded them to stop, but I realize who I'm talking to."

She scoffed. "Indeed. I could have forced or frightened them into compliance, but that doesn't lead to prolonged change. And besides, it would be imposing my own morals on another culture. That's something I cannot do."

They'd reached the car and she made to get in. Nikolai stopped her with a touch to the shoulder, quickly withdrawn. "Wait. I need to know. What do you intend to do about the magic problem?"

"That depends on what the data suggests."

"You must have some idea by now."

He wanted answers. Of course he did, but science wasn't always neat or fast. It took time and you had to determine if the results were repeatable.

"This isn't something we can get the answer to overnight.

Science is precise, but it's slow and methodical. It takes time, especially if you want more accurate results."

He looked disappointed, but surely he should know this. An uneasy thought crept into her head. "Did you really read the science texts I gave you?"

Without hesitation, "Of course."

"I know your first instinct is to lie, so I will give you the opportunity to amend your answer. Truth now. Did you read the books?"

A pause. "I skimmed—just enough to get the gist of things in case you asked me any questions."

She closed her eyes and took a breath.

"I prefer getting my information from you. You're more concise. The older texts—they wax poetic about philosophy and so much stuff that doesn't matter. It doesn't make sense for me to read all that when I can just get the distilled version from you in a fraction of the time. I'm sorry. Well, not really, but, well, there it is."

He really didn't know what the hell to do with honesty. At least he was trying. And could she really fault him, given what she now knew about how his brain worked? Always she'd use the same methods with her students, the same methods that she'd grown up with and had worked for her. It never occurred to her to tailor instruction to the individual student. But Nikolai's mind was restless. It craved constant stimulation. For someone like that, sitting in the library drilling Latin out of ancient philosophical texts was probably torture. He'd always done best in their practical lessons. It's not like he wasn't capable of book learning, but when he did study on his own, he zeroed in on the information he needed and left the rest. Practical, concise—she could do that.

"Thank you for telling me the truth."

"You're welcome. Now can you tell me your preliminary guess regarding the results of our experiment?"

"I don't want you taking my words and spinning off ludicrous hypotheses—"

"I won't."

"Because *clearly* you're the epitome of foresight and restraint." He said nothing, merely gazed at her until she rolled her eyes and continued. "From what I saw, the results were inconclusive. Your first day was the worst. Half the appliances seemed to affect your ability to cast, yet when I repeated them two days hence, you performed fine."

"I was distracted that first day."

"Clearly. But I can't discount it entirely. There was some evidence to suggest that appliances might have impacted a few of your spells. I don't know enough about Mundane technology to determine what, if anything, those appliances have in common. In any case, you are a sample size of *one*. Hardly compelling. If we get a hundred Magi out here, then maybe we can decipher a real pattern, though my head hurts just thinking about the logistics."

"Then let me help. I can find people to participate. Find someone to run the whole experiment. You wouldn't have to do anything."

"You expect me to let someone *else* run the tests? Never. Why would I ever pass something this important off to—"

"Medea, you leak."

She felt herself flush and twisted, trying to look at the back of her pants. Not that she could see well from this angle. Hadn't she'd stopped menstruating? She turned back to him with a glare, expecting to be the butt of a joke.

"Not *that*. You leak magic. I noticed it the night we played Truth or Dare. You're so damned powerful I don't think you can help it. That's definitely more likely to contaminate the test site than any stray spell."

"Why didn't you tell me before now!" If it was true, the entire experiment was compromised.

"Because I only just remembered. Look, this is better for us anyway. You're terrible with people. You've been stressing the whole time about contaminating the site because it would be so hard for you to get a new one. So don't. Let me handle the people stuff. I can have a new site up and running in a few weeks. Multiple sites even. Won't that give us more data points? What I need from you are the logistics of the experiment—lay it all out for me and I'll implement it."

Ludicrous. Turn her experiment over to someone else? To him and *then* someone else? How could she trust him with something this important, let alone a third party? The whole idea was—

"Don't respond now. Just think on it. What I really want to know is what you plan to do once we have the results?"

The abrupt change in topic threw her. "What do you mean?"

"What will we do with the data?"

She hadn't really thought that far ahead. The action, of course, would have to be informed by the cause of the magical decline. "Take our findings to the Collective, I suppose?"

He scoffed. "And you think they'll do anything about it? The Collective is a useless bureaucracy. What I mean is, what will *you* do about it? If you don't interfere with mortals, and the cause of the decline is Mundane machines . . ." He left the rest hanging.

She didn't know. She'd intentionally avoided thinking about it, for that very reason. "Let's hope it's not."

"But if it is?"

"I don't know."

"What do you mean, you don't know?"

"I'll seek an audience with the Collective—"

"Even if you manage to convince them, they won't do anything. It's up to us."

His words were a poisonous cloud of gas, slowly suffocating her. The problem was too big, too abstract, too full of unknown variables. She couldn't answer. If they had been walking, she would have increased her pace, but he had her cornered against the car. She could get in, but then so would he, and there'd be no escape. The lack of response seemed to spur him on.

"Do you plan to stand by and let magic die out? You of all people? What will become of the world if you do? How can you possibly—"

"I said I don't know!" She was vaguely aware she was shaking. "Once I have answers, then . . . then I'll figure out what to do. Stop . . . stop *pestering* me about it."

"Okay." His face was unreadable. "When do you think we'll have answers?"

"I, uh, fuck." She was having trouble thinking through the fog. The question hung there in space, but she couldn't piece two and two together enough to answer it.

"We have to do more experiments, yes?"

She nodded.

"Let's say that takes a year. What about your stones—the ones collecting data on ambient magic—how long will those take?"

There, that was more concrete. She pushed through the fog. "About ten years. Twenty would be better"—he winced at that—"but I'm sure we can check them every five years to see if a pattern is developing."

"You should add some to your gardens, plus the Aztec temple, and any other places where there's a pocket of ambient magic. Then we can measure if there's any decline based on encroaching Mundane activity."

Good. That was good. She reached for her hip pouch, intending to jot it down in her notebook, and clutched empty air. Damn, it was back at home.

Magic burst forth beside them. Medea nearly crushed the roof of the car before she saw it was only Yoxtl. The spirit ignored her and directed its attention to Nikolai.

"The Magi—they've been attacked!"

Medea half regretted not smashing the car and Yoxtl with it. She knew it had been a mistake letting the Magi go with such a treacherous creature. If it couldn't keep them safe, it should never have accepted responsibility for their care. The spirit avoided her seething gaze and kept its attention firmly on Nikolai, who didn't seem the least bit surprised to hear the Magi had been taken by witch hunters.

"What do you expect me to do about it?" he said. "They're your responsibility now."

Yoxtl gaped. "You freed them from that place. They're Magi. I thought you'd care what happens to them."

"You thought wrong." Nikolai wore a thinly concealed smile. What was he up to?

Yoxtl made a disgusted noise and then meekly turned its amber gaze her way. "They took Gloria's eye."

"So grow it back," she snapped, surprised by her own vehemence but unable to offer the spirit a shred of sympathy. "I gave you plenty of magic last year. More than enough to help them out of their predicament. Don't tell me you've spent it already."

"There was an accident with Josh. I spent the last of your power healing him. Training hasn't gone so well."

Yoxtl began to describe what passed for its magical lessons and her stomach knotted. Josh had been injured. Gloria couldn't cast. Evelyn refused to participate and when she did, things went wrong. Why had she allowed Nikolai to talk her into letting the spirit take the Magi? Because she hadn't wanted the responsibility, her conscience nagged. Now they were at the mercy of witch hunters and it was her fault.

"Why didn't you just teach them to summon food?" asked Nikolai.

Yoxtl glared at him. "That's not how it's done." The spirit

turned back to her. "Please, Medea. I know you don't trust me, but—"

"You're right, I don't." Her anger at the deception came flooding back. How could she be so stupid? This whole thing had to be a ruse. "You taught them spells without teaching them how to control their magic first. Of course you were going to have issues! You probably allowed them to get captured as an excuse to get your claws back into Nikolai. Well, I won't have it!"

She willed ethereal chains to bind Yoxtl in place and began the chant for Banish. A thought pressed gently against her mind barrier. *Don't.* She shot a glance at Nikolai. His eyes remained fixed on Yoxtl, but a firm hand touched the small of her back. Did that mean he'd sent the message? It *sounded* like him.

"I might be willing to help," said Nikolai, "but you'll have to relinquish your claim to the Magi and ask nothing in return."

Yoxtl's fur bristled. "That's not what we agreed."

"I agreed to build you a following, and I've done that. It's not my problem if you can't hold on to them or keep them safe. I warned you this would happen. I'm more than happy to help, but you'll make no more demands on my time. Understood?"

So that was Nikolai's intent. Had he planned this all along?

Yoxtl looked from Nikolai's impassive face to her own and visibly deflated. It bared its teeth as it answered. "Agreed."

"Well, I don't." She ignored the flick Nikolai gave her back. Rude. "This is the problem with intervening. We thought we were doing a good thing by releasing them from the hospital, but now they're in a worse situation."

"I'm pretty sure Josh's situation at the hospital was worse," Nikolai remarked. "And *we* didn't think it was a good thing. *You* did. I told you Evelyn was probably better off where she was."

"That's my point! At the hospital they were alive. Perhaps not well treated, but alive. And now they've been thrust into a world they know nothing about, one with people who seek to kill them.

This is what happens when I help others—unforeseen consequences."

Nikolai shifted his gaze from her to Yoxtl. "Give us a moment."

She released the chains and Yoxtl vanished. She half hoped it would stay gone, but it reappeared on the other side of the street.

Nikolai stepped between them. "Unforeseen to *you*. *I* predicted all of this. Well, not the witch hunters, but definitely Yoxtl's failure."

"Then why the hell did you let them go!" she hissed.

"Because it was clear you didn't want to deal with them. The experiments were your priority. You cared a *little* bit, but not enough to do something *really* significant—just enough to assuage your conscience. That's the problem with philanthropy. No one's ever honest about why they do it. Help, *real* help, is a long, arduous process that takes time and resources. No one wants to commit to that. They just want a half second to feel good about themselves, or get in with god, or make themselves look decent. Think about those people in the diner who gave me their change. They didn't know me. They didn't know what supposed charity I ran, only that it would look good that they gave money. I could set up a donation bucket in any city for some fabricated cause and people would give without bothering to look into where the money went. It's not about how the money is spent, it's about how they *feel* when they give, and as long as I maintained that illusion, they'd be satisfied to keep giving. Do some people really care? Sure, but there are fewer than you'd think, and you'd never know it because they don't take credit. If you *really* want to help people, you need to *commit*." He paused to let her absorb his words.

"If what you say is true"—and she knew it was, as much as she hated to admit it to herself—"then why did you agree to save the Magi? Even if we do, they're in the same position as before. No protection, no one decent to train them—"

"I'll train them."

She frowned. "When would you even have time?"

"In the afternoon, when you're indisposed. Or you could give me a couple extra days off a week."

"At that rate your apprenticeship will take twenty years. And afternoons are for practice." The bigger question was why.

As if sensing her unease, he shifted his body and tone to be more relaxed and pensive. "When I sought this apprenticeship, I didn't realize how much I'd be giving up. It's clear you thrive in solitude, but I don't. I miss spending time in Haven, running my little dueling club. After spending time in this country, it's clear to me that it could benefit from a more organized approach to magic."

Of course. "Placing yourself at the top, I assume?"

"Is that so bad? I have the chance to build something from the ground up. These Magi are the perfect test case. They're a small enough group that I can start over again if something goes awry, but I don't anticipate that happening. *You* may not be willing to commit, but I look after my investments."

"What you're suggesting . . . It's going to take so much time away from your studies."

"I think you'll find it more useful than you realize. Nothing cements a concept better than having to explain it to someone else, and I've always performed better when juggling multiple projects simultaneously. Think of how much more time you'll have alone!"

That *was* a selling point, but this wasn't about her. It was his education that would suffer. How could she consent to such lax hours?

"I need this," he said quietly.

He did, didn't he? Unlike her, Nikolai needed people. He fed off the interactions and subtle manipulations. The past year he'd excelled, and while he claimed that practical lessons were enough to alleviate the beige, in retrospect she could see how he itched for more. If he was willing to extend his apprenticeship for this, why not allow it? Just because she'd always trained a certain way didn't mean she couldn't change her methods. She'd already done it for him once.

She took a steadying breath and straightened. "Very well. As long as you use your time judiciously and do not neglect your studies."

Nikolai smiled. "Let's go rescue some Magi."

40

24TH STREET

Nikolai set out for the 24th Street gateway at a leisurely pace. He'd told Yoxtl to get in the back seat. Medea's animosity toward the spirit hadn't diminished. At least now he knew why—she believed Yoxtl had entered her mind and taught him to do the same, or worried it might. Her thoughts on the matter had been tinged with fear, and fear made people irrational. He mulled over whether to dissuade her of the idea of Yoxtl's intrusion.

Medea sat tensely in the front seat, hands gripping the top of her legs. Since he'd relieved her of the burden of what to do with the Magi long term, she'd been remarkably anxious to get to them. She leaned forward as though willing the car to speed up.

"Why aren't you driving faster? It's like you're taking your time."

"I am. Nothing unifies people like shared trauma."

She rubbed her forehead. "I'm going to pretend you didn't say that."

"You wanted to know the real me. Well, this is it. Don't worry," he added at her look, "I'm not going to let them die. I'm just saying it's not a bad thing if they get a little hurt." He turned to Yoxtl. "You've had nothing but petty infighting this week, am I right?"

The spirit hung its head. "Bethany's the main culprit. She took Doris and Evelyn to a hotel, and she constantly belittles Josh. He's tried to leave a few times. Gloria's been looking after him, but they don't communicate well and I can't always help."

Medea harrumphed.

"If we swoop in and save them, nothing will change. The group needs to be unified if they're to succeed, and nothing unites people like facing a common enemy."

"What exactly are you suggesting?" asked Medea.

"That we help them help themselves. Once we're through the gateway, I can use telepathy to walk them through a counterattack."

"Can you reach that far?"

"We'll see. If not, I can get closer, but they need to fight for themselves."

"You're playing with their lives," Yoxtl complained.

"What's the matter? Afraid they'll die before they've sworn their souls to you?"

"Despite what you think, *mortal*, I care about my charges."

"Cease your bickering," said Medea. "I'm not opposed to letting apprentices fend for themselves—it's a good way to learn —but they've not had proper training. It's risky."

"Not if we're close enough to intervene if things go wrong." He didn't mind playing the savior, but it had to be him, not Medea.

"We need a plan of action." She turned to Yoxtl. "Tell me about each Magi. Who did you sense was the strongest?"

"Evelyn, by far, but she has no focus. Next are Doris and Josh —they're about the same, though Josh has been skittish since his injury. Next is Bethany, followed by Gloria. Don't count on Gloria to perform any magic."

"Who among them has the will to kill?"

"Bethany. Possibly Gloria, but she'd be more likely to do it in defense."

"The best defense is a good offense," he and Medea said together.

He looked askance at her. "That's not what you said the first year you trained me."

"In this case it's true. They've not had time to craft unbreakable defenses. Besides, I was trying to broaden your skills. You didn't exactly need help pursuing offensive magic."

"Fair enough." He grinned. "You bring out the best in me, you know that?"

She rolled her eyes but there was a hint of a smile on her lips. "Kicking and screaming, but yes."

"I hate to interrupt," said Yoxtl, "but the Magi still need help."

"Tell me about the lessons again. In detail this time. I need to know every spell you taught and how each Magi fared. Leave nothing out."

As Yoxtl described its training, Medea pinched the tips of her fingers, her brow furrowed in concentration. After interjecting with about a million clarifying questions, she launched into an attack plan based on the location, items at hand, spells learned, and the Magis' various strengths.

"Any weapons?" Nikolai asked.

"Only knives. But they put some sort of contraption on Doris' head."

Medea waved a hand. "That's just a branks." Then, at his blank look, "Scold's bridle? No? Did they not teach you— Never mind. It's a cage with a bar on the inside that goes inside the mouth like a bit so the person is unable to talk. They were popular in New England for women who got out of line, though they fell out of favor when—"

"Focus, Medea."

"Right. Yoxtl, you go on ahead and assist however you can. Tell them we should be along shortly." Once the spirit vanished from the back seat she muttered, "I still don't trust that thing."

Should he tell her? The wedge it had created was between her and Yoxtl, not him, but he planned to keep the spirit around. Most of his time would be spent on the island and he needed someone to keep an eye on the Magi. Even if Medea didn't directly interact with Yoxtl, she would forever be suspicious and resentful of his continued relationship.

"Time for a little Truth or Dare."

She gave him an incredulous look. *"Now?"*

"Yes. I choose truth."

"You told me you were going to tell me the truth from now on."

"Indeed I did, but we both know it requires a conscious effort on my part. This ensures that if you really need an honest answer on something, you'll get one."

"And what do I really need an honest answer on?"

"Yoxtl."

Medea leaned back with a calculating frown.

"I saw what you believe, back when you had me tied to that tree. So ask and I'll give you an honest answer."

She pursed her lips and inhaled. "Did Yoxtl teach you how to break into my mind?"

"No, you did." He ignored her shocked expression and continued. "On the beach with your focus exercise. The molecular structure of diamond."

She slumped in her seat and put a palm to her face, no doubt berating herself.

"I've stayed out since, just so you know."

"I know. Or I guess I don't *know*, but I appreciate how you've sent me messages externally. What the *hell*?" She sat up suddenly and squinted down the darkened street.

There were far more cars parked on the block than he'd seen the last time they were here, and even a few motorbikes. A makeshift shantytown seemed to have sprung up at the mouth of one of the alleys. People, bundled against the cold, slept in chairs or on mattresses laid on the sidewalk. Medea ducked to the floor with a, "Shit shit shit!"

"Isn't that the gateway alley?"

"Yes. Have they seen us yet? Can you turn around?"

They'd definitely been spotted. Several children pointed at the Chevy and took off running to rouse the adults. People wriggled out of sleeping bags or stood up from their chairs and stretched. Heads poked out of windows, car doors opened, and people began trickling from the buildings onto the street.

"Yes, they've spotted us, but no one looks upset. If anything, they look interested."

"Fuck! I *knew* I shouldn't have healed him. They always talk."

"Who? The cabbie?"

"Yes," she hissed. "I agreed to heal his mother. He's gone and told the whole neighborhood. They'll have brought out anyone a doctor couldn't fix."

"So?"

"So?! We have to save the Magi!"

"Yeah, but this will only take you a few minutes and they'd be forever in your debt."

She looked as though she'd rather drink poison. "I don't *want* them in my debt. I don't want them knowing about me or healing or magic."

"Why not? Isn't that a *good* thing, what with magic dying out?"

"I— No— It's not about magic. I'm fine with them knowing it exists. What I *don't* want is them banging on my door every time one of them gets injured, leaving offerings, erecting bloody statues."

A thought occurred to him and he laughed. "Is this the *real* reason you don't interfere with mortals? You don't like the attention?"

"Of course I don't!"

"Well, too bad. You told Arthur you were going to heal his mother. You have to at *least* do that, though I suggest you heal them all if you don't want this friendly crowd to get hostile."

"We don't have time!" Medea shrank further to the floor as he pulled to the curb. "I'll have to abandon this gateway. I can't come back here again, not after this." She made it sound like the end of the world rather than a minor inconvenience. He could leave her to sort through things in her own time while he dealt with the Magi, but . . .

"I dare you to face the crowd."

She looked up with a puzzled expression.

"I know this makes you uncomfortable, so let's make it a dare. I'll stay with you the entire time. If you get overwhelmed, just give me a signal and I'll cut things short gracefully."

After a long moment, she gave a weak nod and he came around to open her door. She regarded his extended hand as one might a gallows, but she took it and clung to his arm like a life raft as he led her through the rapidly growing crowd. No one asked any questions or blocked their way. They were curious, yes, but highly skeptical, though many had brought their ailing relatives just in case.

Arthur emerged from the alley and grinned. "Glad to see you made it back."

Medea regained some of her usual composure and stormed toward the cabbie. "I told you I don't like drawing attention to myself!" She magically shoved him back into the alley, which was now crowded with chairs and a few makeshift tents. "What the hell do you think you're doing, inviting everyone here?"

"I didn't invite nobody. Just told my family what you did—"

"And they told others!"

Arthur gestured to the street. "They're curious is all. Most of them think I'm a fool."

"But when they see your mother restored, they'll know you were telling the truth." She squeezed her eyes shut. "I can't heal her. Not anymore. It's too risky."

"We had a deal!"

"Don't you understand? If I heal her now, everything changes, everyone loses. Warlords will invade and demand the source of your power. They'll torture you to get information, and when they don't hear what they like, they'll slaughter your people! Everything you hold dear will be ruined!"

Arthur looked at her as though she'd lost her mind. Medea continued to rant, voice rising to a shout, words becoming ever more antiquated. She wasn't making any sense. Worse, she didn't realize it. Worried faces peeked around the corner of the building.

Nikolai had known her long enough to sense the shape of her fear. It wasn't just the crowd, it was what it represented—interference, and all that it brought—only she wasn't giving the man any context with which to understand her concerns. He suspected her anxiety about reaching the Magi in time was only making things worse.

He turned to a little girl standing at the mouth of the alley. "You. Find the ten sickest people and bring them here. The ones the doctors can't cure, who'll die without medical intervention. Quick, go." The girl darted away. "Medea. *MEDEA.*"

She paused mid-rant and shot him a glare.

"He doesn't understand. You have to give him some context."

Her eyes darted back and forth. Frown #3 creased her brow. At last she turned back and said, "Politics. You lectured me about them—how that man—whatever his name was—was a casualty of forces more powerful at play."

Arthur nodded.

"It's the same with this. Every time I've done a mass healing or tried to better the lives of mortals, someone more powerful comes along and tries to turn it to their advantage, usually at the expense of those I sought to help. Can you imagine what would happen to your people if word of this got out? If the rest of Omaha learned there was a woman here who could cure any ill?"

Nikolai watched Arthur's mind turn it over. He didn't know about the gateway, but he understood that the location was important somehow, which meant that others might try to take it. He scoffed internally—whites had been fleeing the upper 24th Street neighborhood since the end of World War II. With them had gone any government interest in maintaining public infrastructure. It would be just like them to come back for something like this. They'd buy up the block, the street, the neighborhood, and try to force them out by any means necessary. Let them come. Tensions were high, but they'd always been that way in Omaha. If they had magic on their side . . . A world of possibilities unfurled, and Arthur straightened.

"With all due respect, ma'am, it's not your decision to make."

She flinched, then coolly remarked, "You speak for everyone here then?"

"I speak for my family, and I ask that you do what you promised. Heal my mother. As for the others who've brought family here—the call is up to them, but I'm sure many will feel the same way. There aren't a lot of options here. The People's Hospital—*our* hospital—closed four years ago. There are a few Negro doctors, all private practice with limited resources. I understand you don't want to make waves, but that's life for us. We're *always* treading water in this city. Least you can do is help us save a few who'd die otherwise. Though I will say this—teaching us magic would go a lot further in keeping our community safe than simply going on your way and doing nothin'."

"I can't— You don't—"

"We'd be happy to," Nikolai interjected, ignoring Medea's shocked expression. "We've already located a few people with magical aptitude here in Omaha and have begun their training. I'd like to return and search for others, but I'm afraid you've caught us at a bad time. Our fledgling students are under attack and we must go to their aid."

"What?!" A woman's voice resounded from the mouth of the alley like a whip crack. He turned to see Josh's mother storming toward them.

He threw on a smile. "Mrs. Jones! So pleasant to see you again."

"You said you'd keep my son safe!"

"Indeed I did, which is why I'm afraid we must hurry along. I've sent for the ten sickest people as that's all we have time for today, but I'm surprised to see you here. I thought you fit as a fiddle."

"I'm here with my mother. And because I heard there were magicians coming and knew it had to be you. Where is Josh? Who's attacking him?"

"Witch hunters," said Medea. "They're a bit of a problem here in the Americas."

"But nothing to worry about, I assure you," Nikolai countered.

Arthur exchanged a look with Mrs. Jones. "Which is it then? You in a hurry to save your students or is it nothing to worry about?"

"Both." Medea responded before he could. "While I prefer to arrive before any significant damage has been done, it's true that I can heal just about anything save irreparable brain damage. Nikolai here worries over nothing. It's part of his *charm*." She put an odd inflection on the last word and threw a look in his direction. "But this is getting overcomplicated. You"—she jabbed a finger at Arthur—"where is your mother?"

He blinked at her. "Uh, right this way." He gestured deeper into the alley.

Mrs. Jones stepped up to Nikolai. "I'm coming with you."

"No, you're not," Medea said flatly over her shoulder. "I'll not have strangers traipsing through my home."

Mrs. Jones glared at her with pursed lips. Her expression rivaled some of Medea's best.

"I apologize," said Nikolai. "She's very particular and not the least bit polite. Do you happen to have a map of Nebraska? I can show you where they're staying and you can meet us there."

"If you're trying to get rid of me—"

"Oh, I'd never want to be rid of a woman as beautiful as you." He gave her his most disarming smile.

She gaped. "Are you getting *fresh* with me?"

"That depends on whether or not you enjoy it."

"I . . . What . . . I'm old enough to be your *mother*!"

"You don't look a day over twenty-five." He had the pleasure of watching a number of emotions flit through her mind—involuntary delight at the flattery, guilt over her reaction, shock and disbelief that he would try this *now* of all times, and to a married woman twice his age. But he'd achieved the overall effect he desired, which was to break the tension somewhat. His confidence and calm under pressure often eased the minds of those around him, and he hoped that would be the case here. He could have used telepathy, but it was so much more *fun* this way.

"There's something wrong with you."

"Oh, I'm wrong in all the best possible ways."

Mrs. Jones blinked and shook her head, then glanced at Medea. "That woman is right. You *don't* worry about anything." She unconsciously traced the scar she'd gained back at the hospital.

"Life was meant to be lived. We must seize opportunities as they appear lest they pass us by. Now, let's get you that map."

* * *

Bonnie Jones coolly observed the fake doctor's proffered arm. It felt like he was playing with her. Perhaps he was. She couldn't afford to anger him and risk losing Josh, but neither could she stoop to taking his arm. She walked past him to the sidewalk and called out, "Anyone got a map?"

Someone did, and a minute later it was laid out on the hood of the nearest car.

"Where is Josh?" she demanded.

The fake doctor strode over and gazed down. Heavens, she hadn't even gotten his *name*. Feather-something, though that was probably an alias.

"It's Nikolai Fedorov, but you can just call me Nikolai."

Her insides turned to ice. She'd forgotten he could read minds.

He gave her a smile and pointed to the northern border, up near Valentine. "Here."

"That's over three hundred miles away!"

"Yes, but it won't take me but a minute to get there. My mentor has a way to travel rapidly between locations."

Despite what she'd already seen, it seemed far-fetched. Magician he might be, but he was still a con man. She had to go with them and make sure Josh was okay.

"I'd happily take you with me," he said. "Unfortunately, it's not my call to make. My mentor is exceedingly private and paranoid about attacks. *She's* the one you have to convince. You're welcome to make your case to her." She got the vague impression he was issuing a challenge. "Now if you'll excuse me." He hurried away, leaving her to ponder her next move.

"Everything alright, dear?" Her husband's familiar voice gave her strength. She picked up the map and turned to him.

"No. Josh is in trouble. Gather everyone you can and meet me in Valentine."

"Valentine! What's he doing all the way up there? What's going on?"

"I don't have time to explain. I need to talk to someone before I lose my chance. Just *go*. I'll see you there!" She rushed back into the alley.

The witch, a white woman, would have been easy to pick out even if she hadn't been surrounded by Black folk. She wore a man's shirt and pants, several sizes too big, with the sleeves and legs cut off unevenly. Her lank blonde hair looked as though it hadn't been brushed in days. She stood before an elderly man with her eyes closed, a severe expression on her face. Bonnie half wondered if the woman was touched. She *had* been in a mental hospital, after all.

The witch's eyes snapped open, and she bellowed, "Next!"

Bonnie steeled herself and approached. "I'm coming with you to get Josh."

The witch didn't spare her a glance. A middle-aged man approached with a wheezing older woman.

"Just stay there!" called the witch. She closed her eyes again and frowned. A second later the older woman gasped.

"Praise Jesus! I can breathe again!" She hugged the man beside her and then took several steps toward the witch, who jerked backward with a furtive glance.

"It's fine. You can go."

"Thank you. *Thank you!*"

"You can thank me by clearing the alley for the next person."

The healed woman looked surprised, then indignant, but it was clear she wasn't about to complain and risk angering the witch, so she turned heel and made her way back with her escort.

Bonnie cleared her throat. "I said—"

"I heard you. Must I repeat myself? I don't want people traipsing through my home. Now stop pestering me. The sooner I finish here, the sooner I can go save your son."

Her temper flared. "My son wouldn't *need* saving if you and Nikolai had stayed with him!"

"True. But I fail to see how that has any bearing on your request."

This woman! "Does my son's life mean so little to you?"

"Of course it means little to me." She flung a hand out, and the next person in line jerked forward twenty feet and stopped before her. The witch ignored the man's fearful expression and traced a finger along his spine. "I'm immortal. *Every* life means little to me. Better?" she asked the man. He nodded and she shot him backward. "If it's any conciliation, Josh's life means slightly more, given that he is Magi and I invested considerable time repairing his brain."

Bonnie realized she'd mistaken the witch to be a young woman—she certainly looked it—and therefore naive about the workings of the world. There was something indescribably *foreign* about her. She had to find something in common. Something the woman could empathize with.

"Do you have children?"

The witch scoffed and closed her eyes again, presumably focusing on the next person.

Immortal, and yet childless. She was completely unaware of how having a child changes things. It was both a blessing and a curse. The most love you'd ever feel, yet it cursed you to forever watch your heart walk around outside your body.

"Josh is my everything," Bonnie said simply. "I promise not to get in the way or disturb your things. I just have to get to my son."

"We're already going to rescue him. There's no reason you have to be there."

"I may not have magic, but you know how they say, if you want something done right, do it yourself? You're so precious about your things that you won't even let me into your home. Take that feeling and magnify it by a thousand and you'll get a fraction of how I feel about my son. I can't *trust* anyone but myself with this."

The witch opened her eyes but refused to meet her gaze. After a pause, "Fine." She grabbed Bonnie roughly by the hand and tugged her toward the back of the alley.

"What're you—?" Before she knew what was happening, the witch had opened a door in the brick wall and thrust her through it. Bonnie staggered onto sand. Light blazed all around her, so bright she had to shield her eyes. It took her a moment to realize it was *daylight*. Where in the world *was* she?

"Walk up the path from the beach and follow it to the house. We'll meet you there." The witch paused. "Feel free to read the books, but mark not the pages!"

Bonnie spun, trying to catch sight of the witch, but she was gone. All that remained was an empty archway with the ocean beyond.

INTERVENTION

"Did you really just push Josh's mom through the gateway?" Nikolai asked.

"You've already cost us enough time. I don't need to waste any more giving her a private escort. Besides, with any luck we'll be done by the time she arrives at the house. Though I'm resetting my wards just in case." Medea reopened the portal and they entered the circular gateway room. Without pause, she removed the peg from Omaha and reinserted it higher on the map.

He opened the door and stepped onto grass, conjuring a ball of light in his hand. Aside from a flat stone marking the location, the spot looked like any other. There was magic though—not as strong as Medea's island or the Aztec temple, but it was there. He couldn't tell if it was her wards or if that's why she'd chosen this place. He reached out with his telepathy, further and further, until he could just make out the shape of Doris' mind. He slid into her brain, unnoticed, the overwhelming discomfort and fear of her predicament masking his presence.

The Milky Way stretched out in a band above her, partially obscured by three men. She lay on a table, far too short to accommodate a grown woman, and her lower legs dangled uncomfortably over the side. They'd stripped off her dress and undergarments. A few places on her upper body wept blood—a beauty mark here, a birthmark there, a scar she'd gotten on her elbow as a child. Goose bumps dotted her bare skin and her teeth chattered against the iron bar in her mouth. She hated the branks —not just the discomfort of it and how it caused her to salivate and drool from the corners of her mouth, but the humiliation of wearing the thing, though that paled in comparison to what she endured now.

Two middle-aged men held her down on the table while a third, the eldest, pored over her naked body with a flashlight. Without warning, he grabbed her left breast. Through the branks, Doris mumbled, "No no no." The man drove a needle into her areola. Doris screamed and tried to move, but the two holding her did their job well. Blood welled beside her nipple and dribbled down the side of her breast.

The older witch hunter released her left breast and probed the right. Doris tensed in anticipation of pain but he'd already moved on, flashlight scanning toward her belly. He ran his finger along the inside of her navel, then continued his search down her left leg. Finding nothing of interest, he gripped her inner thigh and began to spread her legs. Doris panicked, thrashing so badly that one of the men holding her gripped her throat and growled, "Hold still." What the hell were they looking for?

"I've found them," Nikolai said to Medea. "They've got Doris naked on a table and they're poking her with needles."

Medea scoffed. "Devil's mark. They'll jab everything from moles to birthmarks, looking for a spot that feels no pain. Gives unsavory men an excuse to strip and examine women in private places. The belief is that magic is gained via sexual congress with the devil, and that he hides his marks well."

"Excuse me." He turned his attention back to the Magi.

Doris. It's me, Nikolai. Relief buffeted him. Always Magi had reacted to his telepathic touch with fear or revulsion. Even Harper, who'd given him access at times, had merely tolerated the invasion. Doris greeted his entry with open arms. The welcome made him giddy. *This* was how it was supposed to be.

Say nothing. The next time he pokes you, don't react. He's looking for a spot that doesn't feel pain. Give him that, and he'll put you back with the others.

I don't want him to put me back! Do you see *what he's done?! They're poking me, hurting me, they've stripped me—*

He bombarded her mind with a sense of calm. *I know, and I'll get you out of there, but I'm still a ways off. I need you to buy me some time.* He wasn't sure if a telepathic command would help in this case, but he tried it anyway. *Ignore the pain.*

Easy for you to say! It hurts. *I never know when it's coming and I can't even bite my lip.*

Dig your fingernails into your palms to displace the pain. And laugh.

Laugh?

It'll unnerve them and mask your pain. I need to check in with the others. Do as I say and everything will be fine.

He left her mind and searched for the others, careful to avoid touching any of the witch hunters lest he tip them off. Evelyn's mind was the most memorable, and he found her next. She was inside the house, handcuffed to a chair and kept apart from the others, who were bound on the floor. Josh huddled in a corner, twirling his checker and rocking. Bethany stared vacantly ahead, her face blemished with little red dots—freckles pricked by the witch hunter's needle. Someone had taken a knife to her bushy hair, cutting it off in chunks and leaving bloody spots on her scalp.

Beside her sat Gloria. One eye socket was empty and crusted with dried blood. Though he could see no bloody spots, her clothes were as disheveled as Bethany's, hinting she'd been through a similar examination.

Two witch hunters guarded them—a young teenager and a man in his early twenties.

Muffled laughter came from the doorway and Doris appeared, dress on but askew. She'd gone limp, forcing two of the witch hunters to carry her. One was clearly disturbed by the change in her attitude. They dumped her on the floor beside Bethany, who gave her a sympathetic look and scooted closer. She pressed her body against Doris—the closest she could get to a hug.

The teen witch hunter kicked Bethany's leg. "Stop that!" She sat up with a glare.

"Which one do you want next, Pa?" said the man who'd just relinquished Doris. "The Negro?"

The old man peered inside the cabin and took in Josh's odd behavior. "No. Boy might give us some trouble. We'll save him for last." He nodded at Evelyn. "We'll start with confessions."

The youngster watched eagerly as the men hauled Evelyn's chair into the center of the room. The elder approached and looked down on her with feigned kindness.

"Tell me, young lady, did you fornicate with that man in the corner?" His question confused Evelyn, and Nikolai was treated to a flutter of disjointed memories from her time of forced prostitution.

"I don't remember. There were so many. Day after day they brought them to me."

"Why didn't you fight back?"

Her voice began to quaver. "I tried. I swear I tried! I screamed inside and tried to fight back but I couldn't move. Grandmother says I must have wanted it."

That's bullshit. Your grandmother is a bitch and that wasn't your fault.

"No, no, Grandmother was right! I should have fought harder.

I should have been able to move if I really wanted to. And now I'm ruined. No man will want me and Christ will never accept me into Heaven." She bowed her head and sobbed.

The elder witch hunter looked around at his fellows. "Take note," he said with a commanding voice, gaze lingering on the teenager. "This is why we do what we do. This poor girl has been corrupted." He crouched and gently lifted Evelyn's chin. "You *are* ruined, but your soul may yet be saved. Confess your sins and repent so that you may enter the Kingdom of Heaven."

"What's going on?" Medea's voice obscured whatever Evelyn said next. He sensed her pacing beside him.

"They're trying to get Evelyn to confess."

"Have her summon the shadows."

This man seeks to harm you. Protect yourself! Call the shadows!

Evelyn was reciting religious gibberish for the witch hunter. She paused and cocked her head. "The voices are telling me to call the shadow people."

"Don't listen to them, child! That's the devil trying to lead you astray." The witch hunter pulled a flask from his breast pocket and doused Evelyn over the head with what could only be holy water. His palm slapped her forehead and he roared for Satan to be expelled. Great, just great.

"Forget Evelyn," he told Medea.

"Try Josh next. Remind him to focus. The constraints *must* be tight or he'll injure them all."

He suspected the man might be even more difficult to reach if the storm was raging in his mind. Gloria seemed calm under pressure so he tried her next, allowing her to feel the intrusion.

This is Nikolai. Don't speak aloud, I can hear your thoughts. I'm on my way there, but I'm not sure I'll make it before they start executions. I need you to buy me time. I'm going to have Yoxtl slip you a dagger. As soon as the witch hunters are distracted, I need you to attack. These are the best places to stab. Thanks to the past year of anatomy lessons, he had intimate knowledge of the body's major blood vessels. He sent her images of how to access the femoral, carotid, and axillary arteries, as well as the spinal cord. *I'll let Doris and Bethany know. Wait for the distraction and watch each other's backs. Yoxtl!* He threw the thought wide.

About time you showed up. I've been trying to speak with Evelyn but they've got her convinced I'm a demon.

Never mind that. Can you steal a dagger and get it to Gloria?

I have to be corporeal to interact with stuff. They'll see me.

Look around for anything sharp then. Something that can be used to stab. He sought Doris.

Oh thank goodness you're back!

You did wonderfully. I'm going to have Josh make a distraction. Yoxtl's going to get Gloria a weapon, but I need you to keep the witch hunters off of her. He leapt from Doris to Bethany and relayed the plan.

Through Bethany's eyes, he spotted Yoxtl in the doorway with a wooden spoon. The handle had been snapped to create a sharp point. Perfect. Bethany started yelling at the witch hunters to leave Evelyn alone, allowing Yoxtl to creep across the shack and plant the spoon behind Gloria.

Once you've undone Gloria's bindings, he told Yoxtl, *I need you to try Evelyn again. Make yourself look like Jesus Christ or something. If that doesn't work, try appearing as her grandmother and yelling at her.*

Do I have to yell? Can't I be a nice grandma?

She'll never believe that. He sent Yoxtl an image of what he'd witnessed in Evelyn's mind.

THAT'S what she's used to? Poor thing. No wonder she can't focus on anything.

Use it if you have to. I'm going to work on Josh now. Be ready. He steadied himself and plunged into Josh's roiling mind.

It was as if every discomfort, humiliation, fear, and insult over the past week had coalesced into a massive storm. Everyone hated him. He wanted to go home. He'd embarrassed himself again. The bed was damp and itchy and cold. He'd shown his ability, and now these strange men wanted him dead. They'd tortured the others. Would they do that to him? Oh God, how he wanted to go home!

Josh! The storm snatched Nikolai's thought away and carried it into oblivion. He tried again, sending thoughts of reassurance and stability, but nothing seemed to breach the abyss of Josh's misery. He pulled away and spoke to Medea.

"I can't reach Josh. His mind is like a storm. That's the only way I can describe it. Like there's so many thoughts at once they all become background noise—but it's a roar."

Medea looked up from the book that she'd pulled from god knew where and pinched the tips of her fingers. "Can you . . . Can you show me?"

He nodded, and felt the familiar presence of her mind nestled in his. He reached for Josh again, not knowing if she'd be able to see what he saw, but willing it to be so. "You see that?"

"The shape is familiar." Medea reached through him, the warmth of her magic tickling his soul, and began relaxing Josh's body. She lowered his heart rate and respiration, unclenched his muscles, and dulled sensations to a tolerable level. "I can't do the next part. Send him some sort of calming image—nothing static. Something repeatable, like the patterns we use during the focus exercise."

He chose a single spinning checker as his image and sent it to Josh. Then another, lining it next to the first. As he did with the focus exercise, he stacked more and more, alternating the colors, until he had several neat rows of spinning checkers and he felt Josh's attention shift.

Josh?

Help.

That's what I'm trying to do, but I need your help as well. Before he could elaborate, Medea barged in.

YOU NEED TO GROW CORN. FOCUS YOUR MAGIC ON EVERY CORN KERNEL IN THE VICINITY OF THE SHACK, BUT ADD THIS ONE EXCLUSION—NOTHING ON OR NEAR THE WOMEN. DO YOU UNDERSTAND? NOTHING!

I can't! People will get hurt.

THAT'S THE POI—

What she means, said Nikolai, shoving Medea out of his mind, *is that we need your help. Growing corn will create a diversion. Think of it! The men won't know what happened. They'll look around for the source.*

I can't. Someone will get hurt.

Don't worry, we'll make sure it doesn't get out of control.

"What are you telling him?" asked Medea.

"Will you shut up and let me handle it?"

Medea harrumphed and crossed her arms.

I know you don't want to hurt anyone. On the off chance someone gets injured, we can help them.

Yoxtl healed me and my leg still hurts.

Yoxtl's not a proper healer. Medea is. Remember how she healed the ice pick in your skull?

It was the wrong thing to say. Josh's anxiety shot up at the mention of the ice pick.

You're all better now! My point is that Medea—

"Make sure you reiterate that he needs to exclude the Magi from his focus."

—can heal anything. But we need that diversion. I need you to focus on all the corn—

"Are you listening? He needs to exclude—"

"Would you stop interrupting me? I'm telling him now." *Sorry about that. As I was saying, you need to focus on all the corn*

EXCEPT the corn on or near the Magi. Got it? Just to be extra safe. Also, you want to grow it as fast as possible, okay?

What are Magi?

You and the women. Focus on all the corn EXCEPT the stuff on or near you, Bethany, Doris, Gloria, and Evelyn.

Josh briefly considered leaving Bethany out of the lineup and immediately felt guilty about it.

Don't worry. When this is all over, I'll have a little chat with Bethany and Doris.

After this I want to go home.

SHARED TRAUMA

Gloria clutched the spoon shard tight in her hand. The ropes around her wrists slackened and fell away. Could she really do this? Fear clutched at her heart. These men were serious. They'd taken her *eye*. She had no doubt they'd take the other if she crossed them again, but then what would they do to all of them if she didn't act?

"It'll be alright," said Yoxtl. "Nikolai and Medea are close."

If they were close, why weren't they helping? They had to be far enough away that they wouldn't get there in time—that, or Yoxtl was lying again, like it had about its powers. She clenched the spoon harder and took a breath.

What would the distraction be? Nikolai said to wait for it but hadn't told her what it was. She tried to figure out who she would kill first. Kill— God, could she really kill someone? Hurt, sure, but kill? One of them was just a boy. She felt her gaze drawn to Josh. No longer huddled in a ball, he sat and stared resolutely at his lap with a furrowed brow.

Without warning, spears of green erupted from the floor. They shot upward with impossible speed and thumped into the ceiling. Dust and dirt rained down and the witch hunters cried out in confusion. Gloria heard a scream but there was no time to think—she had to act.

Bethany and Doris had already leapt to their feet. Yoxtl had untied their feet, but their wrists were still cuffed. Doris slammed her cage into the face of the nearest man. He yelled and clutched his nose.

You can do this. Nikolai's presence strengthened her resolve.

She sprinted toward the closest witch hunter and drove the wooden spoon into his neck. It felt as though some invisible force guided her hand. She wrenched the spoon sideways as she pulled it out.

It'll bleed more that way, remarked Nikolai.

What she saw next almost caused her to drop the spoon. The boy writhed on the ground, a cornstalk erupting from the seat of his pants. His mouth opened in a wordless scream and leaves burst from his mouth. They gushed forward like unnatural green vomit, a thick stalk growing in their wake. The stalks grew from both ends until he looked like a skewered pig ready to roast over a fire.

He must have eaten corn the past few meals.

She shuddered and something urged her to look away.

A witch hunter had grabbed Doris by the cage. He shook her like a rag doll while Bethany screamed and kicked at his shins. Gloria strode forward and drove her spoon into the base of his skull.

The man dropped like a stone. She bent to retrieve the spoon but it was slick with blood—when had it become covered with blood?—and wedged firmly between bone.

Leave it. Behind you.

She spun, expecting to find Nikolai just over her shoulder. Instead she found Ralph, the witch hunter who'd flirted with Doris. He slashed at her with his knife. She jerked backward and tripped over the man she'd just paralyzed.

Ralph lunged for her but cornstalks grew between them, thicker and tougher than normal. He tried to push his way through the plants. Gloria stepped out of reach of his grasping hands. Doris approached, flinty eyes locked on Ralph. Roots snaked from the base of the stalks and wound up his legs. He cried out and slashed at them with his knife, but they only grew back.

Doris paused beside the paralyzed witch hunter and kicked at his pockets until Gloria heard the clink of keys.

Gloria fished them out and uncuffed Doris. "Sorry, I don't see the key to the cage."

Ralph was trapped in his own cage now, one made of corn. Doris knelt to grab the fallen witch hunter's knife and approached him with serene purpose. Gloria didn't want to watch. She put her back to them and uncuffed Bethany.

Bethany tore out her gag and spat, then took a great gulp of air. "There's a wall between us and the last guy."

Indeed there was. The shack had become of forest of cornstalks. Josh still sat in the corner, seemingly observing his navel.

"Josh!" Gloria called. "JOSH! You can stop growing the corn now."

Josh finally looked up and glanced around the room. He saw the dead boy, gave an inhuman wail, and began beating his fists against his own head.

"What on earth is wrong with him?" said Bethany. "This isn't over yet!"

Gloria's stomach twisted. "I think he feels guilty about the boy."

Bethany's face softened. "Oh."

Doris grabbed them both and pointed through the wall of cornstalks to the door—the last witch hunter was getting away with Evelyn.

Gloria and Bethany exchanged grim looks and began slamming into the corn wall with their shoulders while Doris hacked at the plants with her knife as though it were a miniature machete. The barrier that had done so well at keeping the witch hunters at bay now worked against them. Every passing second felt like an eternity, with Evelyn and the witch hunter getting farther and farther away.

"Don't hack, saw," she told Doris. "Here, let me." She took the knife and sawed at the stalk. It was tough going without a serrated edge and she switched to piercing. Once a stalk was weakened she moved to another while Bethany and Doris snapped the first. Eventually they'd broken enough that they were able to climb their way through to freedom.

***

Evelyn stumbled through the grass, pulled along by the man beside her. He'd tried to take one of the cars, but the black fox had appeared and locked the doors. He tried his key to no avail until the shouts from the shack forced them to flee.

He spoke to her as they ran, words of comfort and absolution. Christ would forgive her for her sins if only she would confess to them, that she had to *confess*. But she was unsure what more he wanted to hear. She'd already repeated the myriad of sins Grandmother lobbed against her, but these were unsatisfactory somehow. What more had she done? She didn't know. The past few years had been a confusing mess. It was hard to hear herself think over the whispers of ghosts and demons. This man promised salvation. If only she could remember and confess, she could be rid of them all.

Even now, the fox thing ran doggedly beside them. It told her to call the shadows, but she would not be fooled. Her grandmother lived there sometimes, hovering at the edge of her vision. Calling the shadows meant calling ghosts. Or worse —demons.

"I have to save you," the man said. "My boys can't have died in vain."

Evelyn nodded, unsure what to say. She'd learned it was better to say nothing. The demons enjoyed making her look a fool.

"I can't save you unless you confess your sins."

"I've already told you the sins I know, though I'm sure there are more."

"What about witchcraft? You haven't confessed to that."

"I told them I wouldn't participate. Magic is evil."

He jerked her arm. "Don't lie to me! My grandson saw you stop a car in its tracks!"

"I did?"

His look darkened, and she could feel herself getting smaller.

"Please forgive me! If I did magic then, I didn't mean to, I swear!"

His scowl softened and he beamed at her. "Good girl." His teeth glinted like knives in the moonlight, unnaturally white, and for a second she wondered if she'd made the right decision going with him. Something at the back of her mind urged her not to trust him, that he would hurt her, but didn't she deserve pain? That's what Grandmother always said.

The others called for her in the distance. She didn't like Doris, but Gloria had always been nice. Gloria kept Doris from hanging things on her when she was catatonic. Sometimes she came over and just talked. Told her stories about her time in the WAC. It helped pass the time. Most people assumed she couldn't hear anything when she was still and mute, or that she didn't care. She should've stayed with Gloria at the shack, but Bethany had said that the Negro, like all of his kind, wasn't to be trusted, and that Gloria was a sexual deviant who would do unnatural things to her if she stayed. But then Bethany had made her bunk with Doris, a flagrant sinner of the worst kind who brought boys back to their hotel room and made her watch. Evelyn shivered, and the man put a calloused hand on her shoulder.

"I won't let them get you." For the first time, she noticed the blade in his hand.

Grandmother stepped into view, her face solemn. "He's going to kill you."

"I know," Evelyn whispered. "It's no more than what I deserve."

"Indeed," said the man.

"If you let him, it's the same as suicide. You'll go to hell."

Evelyn looked at the man. "This will absolve me of all my sins, won't it?"

"Yes."

"No." A divine figure emerged from the darkness. He wore robes of purest white and the sun blazed behind him, lighting up his shoulder-length brown hair like a halo. Kind eyes watched her above the characteristic beard and mustache. His skin was darker than what she'd thought, but she would have recognized him anywhere.

Jesus spoke again. "Death is not the answer, my child. Did I not say if you do not forgive, neither will your Father in heaven forgive your trespasses? This man cannot absolve your sins. *You* must forgive yourself."

"I . . . I *can't*!"

"You must," said the man, who didn't seem to notice the apparition.

Jesus held out a hand in supplication. "Death is not the way. To live is harder, but necessary, for that is the only way to do good in the world. Whoever sows generously will also reap generously, for God loves a cheerful giver. God is able to bless you abundantly, so that in all things at all times, having all that you need, you will abound in every good work. Forgive yourself, and do good deeds—*that* is the way to absolution."

Pain lanced her shoulder. The man had stabbed at her and missed.

Jesus smiled. "You see how I deflect his blows. But you must save yourself."

The man raised his knife again. Gloria leapt from the shadows, and he redirected his blow toward her arm. Bethany and Doris were there, too, Doris with her own knife. The man whirled in a circle, blade whipping past each of them, forcing them to step back or be cut.

Doris lunged at him with a muffled scream. He slammed an open palm against her cage. It rattled against her face with a sickening crunch. Blood leaked from her mouth and nose. The man sliced across her stomach but Doris didn't seem to notice. She fell to her knees and clutched her head.

Gloria dove for Doris' knife. The man kicked it aside and slashed at her face. She lurched back with a cry, arms up to cover her face.

"I'll have your other eye!" he bellowed.

"The hell you will," she spat back.

He slashed at Gloria's arms. Bethany punched him in the back. He swung an elbow back and caught her on the jaw. She spat blood and lurched away from the fight.

"Bethany!" Gloria yelled, but the woman had already melted into the darkness, heading back toward the cabin and the cars.

The man laughed. "See? You witches always turn on one another. Backstabbing bitches."

He slashed at Gloria with renewed ferocity. She danced away, arms up, but he was relentless. Soon her sleeves were stained red.

"Stop." Evelyn's words disappeared into the night like so many shadows. She turned to Jesus. "Please make them stop!"

He smiled benignly. "Does not God help those who help themselves? This man lied to you and led you astray. He means to kill you all."

Doris was a sinner. Did she deserve this?

"Doris will repent in her own way. God has blessed you with a gift, Evelyn—each of you—but you must work together, help one another, to reap the benefits."

This wasn't right. Magic was the devil's work.

Jesus arched a brow. "And what would you call what I did—turning water to wine, healing the sick, feeding the multitude?"

She swallowed. "Miracles."

"Miracles are simply magic sanctioned by God."

Gloria made another try for Doris' knife. The man blocked her and thrust his blade into her flank. Evelyn screamed. Gloria clutched her side and met her eyes. "Get out of here," she murmured, then toppled to the ground.

The man straddled her fallen body and put his blade to her face. Gloria barely had time to scream before he'd dug out her other eye and cast it into the darkness.

"Only you can save her, Evelyn. Call the shadows and punish this man as God punished the Egyptians."

"I can't control them."

"You *can*. Focus on what you wish them to do."

Evelyn tried to remember how she'd done it before. Ghosts often hovered at the edge of her vision. She normally avoided looking at them for fear of calling Grandmother, but when Yoxtl had asked her to call the shadows, she had invited them to step forth.

She did so again. It was easy, far easier than she thought it would be. The shadow men came forward in twos and threes.

"Good. Will them to circle the man and shield the others."

Three of the shadows darted toward the man, who scoffed. "The power of God protects me. Your devil tricks can't—"

They grasped him by the arms and pulled him away from Gloria, who vanished under a blanket of night. "What?" he cried. *"How?"*

Shadows encircled the man. They knocked his blade away, but Evelyn didn't have it in her to command them to do more. He was a godly man, even if he was misguided. He'd only done what he thought was righteous.

He shouted at her from inside the circle, first pleading with her not to give in to witchcraft, then railing at her for doing so. He called her a harlot and a sinner who would burn in hell. Was she? She had only been trying to help her friends. Jesus had told her to help.

And then Grandmother appeared.

"What do you think you're doing, Evelyn? This man was trying to help you! Do you really think you're blessed by God? *You?*" Grandmother cackled.

Focus!

But she couldn't focus, not with Grandmother lending fuel to the righteous man's fire. Her shadows quavered and the man tore himself free. He charged at her. Calloused hands encircled her throat. All the while, Grandmother laughed.

"Now you'll get what you deserve, you filthy whore!"

Another voice—quieter, as though from the bottom of a well—told her she didn't deserve this, that she should fight back. Evelyn kicked out feebly but the man seemed made of stone. Her fingernails scraped uselessly against his hands. Stars appeared at the edge of her vision, and then someone was screaming.

"YOU LEAVE HER THE FUCK ALONE!"

Gloria was there, fumbling blindly at the man's shoulder and driving a knife into his back. Again and again the blade sliced through the air. Long after he'd fallen. Long after he'd ceased to move. Blood leaked from Gloria's empty eye sockets, streaking her cheeks like red war paint. The man's white shirt soaked through until Evelyn could no longer make out individual wounds.

Bethany appeared from the shadows with Josh and a hammer in each hand. "Oh shit," she murmured.

Evelyn found her voice. "Gloria, I think he's dead."

Gloria's arm slackened but didn't stop. Evelyn approached and touched her shoulder. The reflexive stabbing ceased.

Evelyn knelt down and gently took the blade, tossing it into the grass behind them. "It's okay, now. We're safe." She put a reassuring arm around Gloria.

The woman sagged and began to weep.

UNITY

Nikolai opened his eyes and looked at Medea. She was sitting cross-legged beside him, hands picking at the grass. His feet ached from standing still for so long.

"It's done." The easy part anyway. The next part would be much more difficult.

Medea looked up. "Injuries?"

"Some of it I can handle—cuts and bruises, a few broken bones—but Gloria lost her eyes, Doris' mouth is severely mangled, and both suffered stab wounds. I'm going to need your help."

"But of course." Medea stood and brushed off her pants.

"You mistake my meaning. I need you to stay here."

"What? Why?"

"Two reasons. One, I don't need your magic upstaging mine. And two, I'm going to manipulate them and I don't need you contradicting me."

"So you're going to lie to them. Why do you need to do any of that?"

"I need to bind them together. A shared traumatic experience goes a long way toward that, but they're still going to be divided. They're too different, and their interests don't align, not yet. I need to make them a unit and I don't want you interfering."

"I understand. I won't."

"No, you won't because you're staying here."

She opened her mouth to protest, but he cut her off.

"You have the worst poker face in history. I don't need you making shocked and horrified faces on the sidelines."

"I've seen you work before."

"Not like this you haven't. You won't like it. Please. Trust me." He hoped like hell she would. He could always start over with a fresh batch of Magi, but this group was primed perfectly.

"How am I supposed to help you with healing from here?"

It wasn't an agreement, but it was a start. He smiled and tapped the side of his temple.

She made a face like he'd asked her to eat lumpy mashed potatoes. *"Really?"*

"Think of it as another lesson. What better way to teach me healing than to guide me through the process mind-to-mind?"

After a pensive pause, Medea settled into his head and he struck out toward the Magi. He reached out to Evelyn's mind again.

Blood leaked from the wound in Gloria's side.

"Lie back," said Evelyn, tilting the larger woman into the grass. She didn't like that they were so near the dead man but feared moving Gloria would aggravate her injury.

Bethany rifled through the man's pockets until she found the key to Doris' cage. She pried the cage open and Doris gave a bloodcurdling scream. The metal bar had mangled the inside of her mouth when the man had slammed the cage against her face. She leaned forward to spit out several teeth and a good deal of blood, though her jaw hung oddly and her lips were torn, so she dribbled more than spit. She took a ragged breath and sobbed. Bethany wrapped an arm around her.

Gloria's face was a ghostly mask, pale and clammy. Evelyn pressed her fists tight against the wound to stanch the bleeding. Josh tried to take off his shirt and hand it to her, but his fingers fumbled at the buttons and he gave up in frustration. Instead, he began collecting handfuls of grass. He knelt beside Gloria and tapped Evelyn's hands.

"What? Oh. Oh yes, go ahead." She moved her hands out of the way and let Josh press the grass against Gloria's side.

Hurry up and get there. I want to see how bad the injury is. He could feel the urgency in Medea's command. Thankfully she seemed to have ceased telepathically shouting. Maybe it had something to do with her comfort on the topic. She was all business now.

Nikolai jogged the last quarter mile, just enough to get his heart rate up and make it look as though he'd run the whole way. "There you are!" he called when he got into sight.

"Hurry," said Evelyn, "Gloria's bleeding really bad."

She was not, in fact, bleeding all that much, but he supposed it looked like a lot to someone inexperienced with such things.

Wrong. The bleeding's internal. See how her abdomen distends? Place your hands over the wound.

He did as Medea asked.

Nicked her small intestine, which makes sepsis a risk. You remember the cleansing spell?

In answer, he muttered, *"Tathir,"* and gestured over the area of concern. Deeper in the body, he sensed Medea's careful knitting of flesh. He enjoyed working with her like this. It felt right. He repressed a satisfied smile, careful to maintain his outward mask of concern for the Magi.

Once finished with Gloria's stabbing, he cast two globes of

light and handed them to Evelyn and Josh, bidding them follow as he went about healing the others. He offered each Magi words of comfort and an acknowledgment of the trials they had overcome. Doris' stomach wound was shallow, her jaw cracked, and her teeth needed to be reimplanted—all things he could handle. He did the best he could with her mouth, though his healing was not yet good enough to avoid leaving scars. He hoped Medea would interject with some wisdom that would aid in the fixing of his face.

Your wounds were different, she remarked. *This is a simple healing of an injury. Your face required a complete rebuild. Once they're settled and we're back on the island, I'll teach you to heal wounds without scarring.*

He tried to hide his disappointment, but it was impossible, joined as they were at the moment.

You'll get there eventually. Her statement lacked conviction.

He moved on to Bethany, who had a broken nose and dozens of smaller injuries all over her body. Evelyn leaned forward as he worked, breathless and full of wonder. Her spirituality, already renewed by her conversation with Yoxtl's Jesus, was strengthened all the more by the sight of his healing. To his amusement she thought him holy, at the very least a saint, perhaps even a reincarnation of Christ.

Josh followed reluctantly, arms at his sides, light globe dangling precariously from one hand. It illuminated the patch of ground at his feet but nothing more. He stooped to pick up something in the grass and walked over to where Gloria lay. He cupped his hands and held them over her face.

"What?" she said. "Who's there?"

Doris knelt beside her. "It's Josh. He has your eye. I, uh, think he's trying to hand it to you."

Gloria took a shuddering breath. Her fingers clenched the grass beside her, as though she clung to the earth itself.

"It's okay. Nikolai'll fix you up right good. You didn't see it, but he put my teeth back in."

Josh turned and offered the eye to Doris.

"Oh! Uh, no, you hold on to it for now." She offered a weak smile. Josh sat back, cupping the eye gently in his hands.

Nikolai had been saving Gloria's eyes for last, wanting her to be conscious. It was important that all of them witness what he could do.

GRANDIOSE AS EVER. He sensed Medea's amusement, though he winced at the return of her yelling.

He finished with Bethany and approached the others. "Let me see about that eye."

Doris helped Gloria sit upright. He motioned for Evelyn to bring the light closer and took the eyeball from Josh. A moment later it was restored to its rightful place. Gloria exhaled and slumped forward, trembling. "I thought I'd never see again."

"I'm not done yet."

"But I don't have my other eye."

He smiled and tugged at his cuffs. "Thankfully, I don't need it. Now hold still."

Eye regeneration wasn't something he'd practiced, but the anatomy was simple enough and he could use her other eye as a model. He worked slowly and carefully, taking his time to get it perfect.

NIKOLAI, YOU'RE—

I know.

BUT—

Trust me.

Medea didn't nag further, but her desire to intervene was an increasing pressure in the back of his mind. When he was sure he'd done everything correctly, he double-checked his work and connected the eye to the optic nerve. Gloria took a shuddering sob and burst into tears. Evelyn hugged her, and Doris too. Bethany watched with a wistful smile. Josh, who'd been standing aside, strode forward and thrust his light globe into Gloria's face.

"We don't need it anymore!" said Doris.

"It's okay. I can see." Gloria waved the globe aside, but Josh simply brought it back. "Really now, cut it out!"

Josh gestured again with the globe, trying in his own way to call attention to the thing everyone except Gloria could see but hadn't mentioned—that while her original eye was a warm brown, the new one was bright blue.

"He's trying to tell you that your eyes are different colors," said Nikolai.

"What?"

Nikolai shrugged. "Sometimes that happens."

I TRIED TO WARN YOU.

I did it on purpose. Every time she looks in the mirror she'll remember the cost of dealing with witch hunters, and who gave back her sight. The rest will be reminded as well.

"Does anyone have a mirror?" asked Gloria.

"I do, in my bag back at the car." Doris helped Gloria up and the two of them struck out for the house. The rest followed suit. Josh rapidly walked ahead of the others, suddenly full of energy.

I'LL MEET YOU THERE.

Not yet.

He felt Medea's annoyance.

I'm not done. Summon a meal or something.

I'M NOT HUNGRY. Despite the protest, he sensed her summon a kebab. His stomach growled.

He reached the house. Josh had vanished inside. Evelyn and Bethany sorted through their belongings. The witch hunters had thrown everything into a pile next to the cars. Doris opened the white car and fished a mirror out of her bag for Gloria, then checked her own reflection in the side mirror. Doris gasped and touched her face.

"What?" asked Gloria. "What is it?"

Doris didn't answer immediately. She dove for her bag and dug around in it further, eventually pulling out a much larger magnifying mirror, suitable for putting on makeup. She sagged against the car and stared at her face.

"No. No no no no no." Doris choked back a sob. "I'm *hideous*!"

Gloria gave her a sympathetic look. "It's really not that bad. The scarring is minimal. You can probably cover it with foundation."

I'LL FIX THE SCARS WHEN I ARRIVE.

Leave them. They'll serve the same purpose as Gloria's eye.

IS THIS BECAUSE I SAID YOU COULDN'T APPLY WHAT I TEACH YOU ABOUT SCARS TO YOUR OWN FACE?

Doris is an impulsive woman who needs a stark and constant reminder of what happens when she errs. Looking at Gloria will do nothing for her. It needs to be personal.

He felt her bemusement. *SO WHEN I SCAR YOUR FACE FOR THE SAME REASON IT'S TERRIBLE, BUT WHEN YOU DO IT, IT'S FINE.*

I didn't scar her face. The witch hunters did that.

YOU KNOW WHAT I MEAN.

He wanted to argue that he'd learned his lesson, that his facial scars were no longer necessary, but the Magi needed attention. They were picking through their belongings, sorting them into piles. Evelyn stacked the bowl and cutlery and moved to set them on the table.

"No!" shouted Doris. Evelyn looked at her, confused. "Just . . . not there. I don't want to see that thing ever again, let alone eat there."

Gloria patted her shoulder, then walked to the table and flipped it over and gripped one of the legs. "I say we use it for firewood. Bethany, you still have those hammers?"

Bethany knelt and picked up the hammers, offering one to Doris first, who shook her head, then to Gloria, who took it. The two women set to work dismantling the table. The thing was remarkably sturdy, given its age, but soon succumbed to their efforts. They piled the legs and boards beside the house.

"We'll have to get a new table," Bethany said once they were finished, "and some other decent furnishings. Perhaps a rug for the floor."

"First, we have to fix up the building," Gloria reminded her.

Bethany nodded. Her fingers ran over what remained of her hair, tentatively touching the uneven ends. She glanced at Nikolai. "It'll be easier, now that he's here."

"Indeed it will." He approached the building and pretended to observe it. *Can you expand this place like you did with your home?*

I NEED BUILDING MATERIALS TO MAKE FRAMES FOR THE ROOMS, BUT YES.

"We'll have to build this place out. Rooms can be expanded magically, just like bags, but we need a framework." He spoke to Gloria but pitched his voice to carry. "You'll be working with Medea once she arrives. I'd like you to draw up plans for what you want—how many bedrooms, bathrooms, etcetera, with room for expansion—I'd like to turn this into a whole campus. There's never been a magical school in America before. This will be the first. A grand place for a grand people, and as the founding students, you'll have a hand in customizing your quarters. I'll get you Josh's specifics. Evelyn!" He waved her over. "Tell Gloria what you want."

As he expected, Doris and Bethany rushed forward to tell Gloria what they wanted. He held out an arm to bar them.

"Not you two." He kept his voice casual so as not to give away the game too early.

Doris looked, if anything, even more excited. "I knew it!

We'll get our own house, won't we? That's it, isn't it? Ooooh, I can't wait!"

"I'm afraid not. Your days of learning magic are over. You and Bethany are no longer welcome here."

Bethany's face crumpled. Doris just looked confused.

"What? What are you talking about?"

Time to let it sink in. He hardened his voice. "Back at Shady River Hospital, I told you what it was like, what you'd be up against, and what you needed to do in order to survive. I told you to stick together, protect one another, that being a Magi is more important than things like age or sex or color or creed. Not everyone is worthy of joining the Magi community." He locked eyes with Bethany. "Some are unable to put past prejudices aside." Now Doris. "Others disregard the safety of their fellow Magi and cast magic in public."

"That wasn't *me*! It was Evelyn who—"

He closed the gap to Doris in two strides and she flinched as though he might slap her.

"You *knew* Evelyn was prone to psychosis and that her magic was unstable. Yet you split the group and stayed in a location guaranteed to bring the witch hunters to our door."

"We had to split up," protested Bethany. "This place is tiny. You couldn't expect us to sleep in a one-room house with a . . . a *man*. It's not proper. Besides, if Yoxtl had done a better job teaching us, Evelyn would be able to control her magic."

"As much as I hate to agree with Bethany," said Gloria, "she's right about Yoxtl. You said it was a god with the power to heal us, but when I needed it most, Yoxtl told me it didn't have any magic left."

The spirit was nowhere to be seen, but Nikolai had no doubt it was still around. Time to bring them to heel, Yoxtl included.

"Yoxtl is my familiar. It was here to observe you on my behalf."

Medea reeled at the lie, though she stayed blessedly quiet in his mind. Yoxtl appeared beside him as though on cue. It looked resigned to the fate he'd appointed. He gestured magnanimously toward the spirit.

"This week was a test to see which of you were ready to join my community. While you may have come together in the end to face your foes, two of you have failed on every other account." He looked to Bethany and Doris. "You're not fit to be Magi."

Bethany seemed to shrink in on herself as the reality of her situation came crashing down, but Doris shrieked and grabbed him by the lapels. "Please don't send us away! We can do better! I know we can."

He observed her coolly. "You haven't done anything to show me you're ready for this kind of power. Again and again you've put yourselves first at the expense of the group."

"That's not true," said Bethany. "We tried to keep Evelyn safe."

"Bullshit!" he snapped, startling her with the ferocity behind the word. "You weren't trying to save Evelyn from Josh or Gloria or anyone else. You wanted control. Because as long as you have control, as long as you put down others and *their* supposed sins, you don't have to confront *yours*. And we both know yours are far greater than those of anyone else here."

HOW DO YOU EVEN KNOW *THAT? YOU WEREN'T ABLE TO USE TELEPATHY ON HER AT THE HOSPITAL.*

I'm speculating based on her file and Yoxtl's observations. It doesn't matter though. People love twisting things to fit them. That's why horoscopes work. See how the blood drains from her face? That means I'm on the right track.

"Everything had to be perfect," he continued. "Perfect hair, perfect nails. Perfect home, perfect husband. But not everything was perfect, was it? Some things in life are messy. They can't *be* controlled. And when you can't control things, well, there's no place in your life for that."

Bethany looked as though she'd been stabbed, and Medea marveled at his ability to injure a person so thoroughly with mere words. He didn't need telepathy to make Bethany feel this way and he enjoyed the sport of manipulating her without it.

YOU DON'T HAVE TO FUCKING GLOAT.

Doris approached Bethany and took her arm. They clung together, two leaves about to be carried away on the wind.

"There's no place in my community for such people. Pack your bags. In a few days you'll be on a bus back to Omaha. You can return to your husband, if he'll have you. See how much control you'll have then." He turned away and strode toward the house.

THAT'S IT? WHAT HAPPENED TO UNIFYING THE GROUP?

I am. Look at Gloria.

Gloria watched Doris; her face was pinched as though she'd eaten something unpleasant.

LOOKS LIKE SHE'S TRYING TO HOLD IN FLATULENCE.

She's conflicted. Even though she dislikes them, she knows they need this. Not just the training, but the protection from witch hunters. Eventually she'll request that I give them a second chance. The request will reinforce my position and put Bethany and Doris in Gloria's debt.

YOU'RE MAKING MY HEAD HURT. Her bafflement was palpable. *AND THIS WILL MAKE THEM GET ALONG?*

Not completely. They won't like it, but they'll acquiesce long enough for me to acclimate them to a new way of thinking. It'll be even better once Josh's family arrives. Speaking of which, can you bring Mrs. Jones now?

WHO?

Josh's mother. The woman in your home.

OH SHIT, I FORGOT ALL ABOUT HER.

I'm surprised, given she might be touching all your books.

SOMEHOW I TRUST HER MORE WITH THEM THAN I DO YOU. I WAS LOOKING THROUGH THE WATER BREATHING SPELLS THE OTHER DAY AND FOUND JAM OR SOMETHING STICKING THE PAGES TOGETHER.

I have no idea what you're talking about.

REQUESTS

J osh waited in the house with the dead boy. He'd didn't look at the body—one glance had been enough to sear the image into his brain, and he couldn't stop thinking about it.

At first he'd been upset. Nikolai had said they wouldn't let his magic get out of control, but it had. Now he was optimistic. Nikolai could heal! And not like Yoxtl, who'd left his leg feeling sore all week. Nikolai had grown a whole new eye for Gloria. Someone who could do that could heal anything. He'd rushed back to the house and anxiously waited for Nikolai to come undo the damage Josh had caused.

There were multiple bodies. Thankfully, most of them were shielded from view by numerous cornstalks jutting through the floor. All but the boy. He was painfully aware of how close the boy was.

Josh retrieved his blanket and covered the boy. There. Now he just looked to be sleeping. Once healed, he'd push back the cover and yawn, thinking he'd just woken from a bad dream. He was only a few years younger than Josh. Did he have any family besides these evil men? If not, maybe Gloria could adopt him.

Then Josh would have someone closer to his age to play with. He'd always got along better with younger kids—at least when he was little, back when his differences weren't so different. Now kids ignored or made fun of him.

He heard Nikolai speaking with the women outside, about how he was going to start a school. Josh had mixed feelings about that. He wanted to go home, but Nikolai and Yoxtl were the only ones to ever understand him, and with Nikolai back, everything might be okay. He was getting rid of Bethany and Doris for being mean.

He looked down at the boy. He'd also been mean, but he probably didn't know any better, not if his family was like that. Gloria could teach him to be nice, though. And Nikolai could help Josh talk to the boy. He'd finally have a friend.

Nikolai appeared in the doorway. He waved a hand and the stalks of corn began to buckle and wilt. A sickly smell filled the house, like trash left too long on a hot summer day. With another wave of his hand, Nikolai sent a gust of wind to push the putrid plants out the door until only the bodies remained. One by one, he floated each of the dead men out.

At last the boy lifted into the air. Cornstalks still protruded from both ends of his body, making it tilt oddly in the air and difficult to maneuver. One of the stalks caught the door frame on the way out. Nikolai made a sound that could have been an irritated grunt or a stifled laugh. Josh suspected the former, as there was nothing funny about the situation. Nikolai tried again and slid the corn-impaled body through the doorway.

Josh followed them outside. Nikolai had stacked the dead neatly in the trunk of the men's car. With growing alarm, he began to suspect Nikolai had forgotten to heal the boy. Josh reached out and tugged Nikolai's sleeve.

"What is it?"

When are you going to heal the boy?

Nikolai gazed at him curiously. "He's dead."

You said Medea could heal anything.

"He's *dead*, which means his soul has passed on. Even if Medea heals the wounds, the body would remain an empty shell."

Josh felt as though he'd tipped headfirst down a long, dark well. He'd only done magic because Nikolai promised no one would get hurt. He'd promised! The betrayal stabbed at Josh. He'd had acted based on a lie, and now he was guilty of murder. *Murder!* No matter what the boy had done, he didn't deserve to die.

"I'm sorry, Josh. I didn't know it would happen, truly I didn't. Medea gave me the tactics, I simply relayed them and did my best to guide you through."

Josh barely comprehended Nikolai's words. Already he was moving away, striding through the grass. He had no idea where he was going; he just knew he had to get away. A hundred tiny hurts swirled around his mind—the lies and death, the discomfort he'd experienced all week, the indifference the others showed him, the ache for some sense of normalcy and predictability. Compounded as they were, he couldn't parse out the thoughts individually, but their weight bore down on him and drove him forward.

No matter what, he was going home.

Bonnie Jones sat in the plush armchair and glared at the fireplace. She'd followed the road from the beach to a dilapidated cottage and knocked. After waiting for some time, knocking and waiting again, she tentatively opened the door. The room inside was small and cluttered with boots and dried plants, but there'd been an open door straight ahead that led to a much larger area. She'd walked in and stood dumbstruck by the two-story house magically contained within the small dwelling she'd seen outside.

"Josh?" she'd called. "Nikolai? Hello?"

Awe quickly turned to chagrin when no one appeared. She waited as long as she dared before trying the doors downstairs. All but a bathroom were locked. Either she'd missed Nikolai, or he'd intentionally gone on without her. She wanted to scream and beat on the doors. Instead, Bonnie forced herself to sit and wait.

After what seemed like an eternity, she heard a door behind her open, and the blonde witch strode into the room. Without so much as a glance in Bonnie's direction, she said, "I have to change," and climbed the circular iron staircase. It was all Bonnie could do not to yell at the uncaring woman's back.

The witch reappeared a moment later wearing some sort of renaissance costume. She ran her hands down the red dress with a smile. "Soooo much better."

"Where's Josh?"

The witch waved a hand as she walked down the stairs. "He's fine. Nikolai handled it. I'm told Josh performed admirably, all things considered."

"Performed?"

"Nikolai reached them with telepathy and instructed them on how to fight back. Not to worry, the attackers are dead."

Bonnie's stomach twisted. She reluctantly followed the woman into a circular room decorated with maps. "Dead?"

"I know," said the witch with a touch of resignation. "I can't fault them, of course. Leaving one alive for questioning would have been risky. Nikolai will root out any others in the area, and I'll place protection enchantments around the property. They'll be safe enough."

She opened a door and Bonnie blinked. Light spilled from the doorway onto knee-high grass. The sky was dark. Bonnie stepped onto the plain and looked back. There was no arch this time, only a door-shaped opening showing the circular room they'd just left. The power this woman wielded—and the way she spoke about *death* . . . Her poor baby Josh. What had she gotten him into? She could see the allure of magic, but not if the cost of using it was to lose one's humanity.

The circular room vanished. Bonnie was startled to see the witch already making her way through the grass, a pale blue orb hovering before her to light the way, and rushed to catch up. She wanted to ask what they planned to do with her son—surely they didn't need him and would allow him to leave—but feared showing her hand. Better to find Josh first and then come up with a way to extricate him. She berated herself for letting Josh go. Why hadn't she properly vetted these people first? The con man must have cast a spell on her.

She was so lost in her thoughts, eyes on the ground to watch her steps through the darkness, that she didn't notice Josh until she heard his familiar wail. She looked up to see him barreling toward her. Josh slammed into her and she had to brace herself to keep from falling. He pressed his face against her shoulder and pushed as though he could bury himself in her flesh. The intensity of it was startling. He normally avoided hugs, except from her mother, who could somehow always coax one out of him. It reminded her of when he was young and headbutted her in the stomach. He'd always been a plump boy, but now he was taller than her and every push threatened to knock her over.

"Josh. *Josh!* You're pushing me too hard."

He broke off and stood looking down, his breath coming fast. Pale blue light reflected off his moistened cheeks. It was clear he'd been crying.

"What's the matter, baby? Are you hurt? Can you show me where?"

He grabbed her hand and tried to pull her through the grass back the way she'd come. She had to use her full weight to keep from being yanked.

Bonnie looked to the witch. "Can you reopen the portal?"

"Nikolai wanted to speak with you."

No going back that way then. Thankfully her husband should be on the way to meet them. "Which way is Valentine?"

The woman shrugged. "There's a town that way." She pointed vaguely behind them. "But as I said, Nikolai wanted to speak with you. The Magi had a vehicle. I'm sure someone could transport you to Valentine."

Bonnie nodded and turned to Josh, who was still attempting to pull her across the field. "Josh. *Joshua Edwin Jones!* I need you to stop that and look at me. Look at me, son."

He did neither.

She leaned in close and whispered urgently, "I'll get you out of here. Papa is coming to pick us up, but I need to talk to Nikolai and get us a ride into town. Okay? I need you to come with me. I promise we'll get you out of here."

Josh released her arm. The sudden lack of counterweight made her stumble. Josh stared at the ground for a moment then started back the way he'd come.

Bonnie fretted about him as they walked. Had they really just let him run off by himself? What if he hadn't wandered into them? Or had Nikolai let Josh go, knowing the direction he took would lead to their meeting? Why was Josh so desperate to get away? Was it because he missed them? Missed his routine? Or because he'd been treated badly? She hated not knowing. It frightened her to think what might've happened to her son in the hands of these people. He'd already been lobotomized. The magicians saved him, but that did not make them trustworthy, especially not the woman, who seemed so distant and callous.

They arrived at a tiny house that looked like the kind settlers had used. Bonnie squashed her initial discomfort—she'd already seen what these people could do with the inside of such a small dwelling.

Responding to her thoughts, the witch said, "We plan to fix it up like I did with my home."

Nikolai emerged from the house with a brunette white woman wearing overalls and strode over with a smile. "Mrs. Jones! So good to see you! This is Gloria." He gestured to the woman at his side, who held out a hand. As Bonnie shook it and exchanged pleasantries, Nikolai turned to the witch. "Gloria has several ideas about how to expand the place but needs to know exactly what you need for the magic to work."

The witch reached for a pouch on her hip and pulled out a sheaf of paper and pen. "Yes, yes, you can get acquainted later," she interrupted, grabbing Gloria's shirt cuff and leading her back into the house.

Bonnie stared at the witch.

"Uh, sorry about her," said Nikolai. "She's always like that. Josh, I need a moment alone with your mother. Can you go help the ladies sort through their belongings?" After Josh had ambled away, he led Bonnie over to a car and paused with an apprehensive and apologetic look. "I need to show you something. I know you're concerned about leaving Josh with us. I'll admit things did not go well this week. We didn't anticipate an attack so soon, before the students were ready to defend themselves. I had someone watching over them who alerted me to the danger immediately, but as you saw it still took us some time to get here. Everyone's okay, but it's clear either Medea or I need to be on-site until the proper protection enchantments are in place."

"That all sounds fine and dandy, Mr. Fedorov, but Josh belongs at home. He *wants* to go home."

"Josh is scared of his own power, but running away before he's learned to control it only puts others at risk. I hate to show you this, but you need to understand. This is what Josh did. This is what he's running from."

Nikolai opened the trunk of the car. There was the body of a white boy inside. His face was frozen in a silent scream, lifeless eyes staring vacantly upward. A thick plant stalk protruded from his open mouth. His neck bulged unnaturally and she wondered for a moment how deep down the stalk had been shoved. She wanted to step back from it, to run away screaming, grab Josh and go, but her feet stayed frozen in place.

"One of the beginner spells we teach is how to create food," Nikolai explained. "Josh was taught how to make a corn kernel grow faster so that food could be harvested immediately. He was very good at it."

Bonnie stared at the bulge in the boy's neck with dawning horror. Dear God, if anyone found out about this, Josh would be lynched.

"When the group was attacked, Josh sprouted the corn scattered on the floor of the house to form barriers between the Magi and their assailants. It was a brilliant move. Unfortunately, because Josh lacks control, he accidentally targeted corn in the digestive system of this boy. Don't worry about the authorities or anyone else. Trust me, I have ways to ensure this goes away quietly. What concerns me more than this"—Nikolai gestured to the body—"is that Josh didn't seem bothered by it at all. Like he didn't understand the gravity of what he'd *done*. I had to explain to him that death can't be fixed. That's why he ran away. He was devastated to learn what he'd done was permanent." There was no mistaking the grave concern on Nikolai's face.

Bonnie attempted to find her voice. "If he'd been properly supervised, this never would've happened."

"If he'd been properly supervised, he never would've been arrested or given a lobotomy either."

She felt herself flush. "My mother watches him just fine—"

"Your mother is getting old, and as much as I regret to remind you, she won't be around forever. Magic gets stronger over time. Josh needs to learn to control it before someone else gets hurt. He doesn't yet understand the boundaries. I told him I could heal things, and so naturally he assumed I could heal the dead back to life. Misconceptions are fixable. We *can* teach him, but it will take time."

"What if . . ." She paused and took a breath. "What if he can't learn?"

Nikolai cracked a smile. "I promise you he can. I'm sure my mentor has a spell or two that could counteract the worst of his magic if it comes to that, but it won't."

"Is there . . . is there a way to cut him off from doing magic?"

Anger flashed across Nikolai's face, so potent with malice that she shrank back. "I'll not amputate your son's magic to placate your fear. You want me to take away his only path to autonomy and independence?"

"What? No! I . . . Do you really think he can become independent?"

Nikolai's expression softened. "Magic makes the impossible possible. You should have an inkling of that, having traversed Medea's home. I'm confident that Josh will come into his own, but I need your help convincing him to stay. He's terrified that he might hurt someone, rightly so, but running away won't help. I need you to convince him to give it a try, even just for a year."

Bonnie wasn't so sure she was convinced herself, but a year wasn't so long, and she knew where Josh was. They could check on him regularly, though Josh wouldn't be able to tell them if he was being mistreated. All she had was this man's word.

"In Europe, most Magi live separate from the Mundane, to protect their magic from technological interference. I don't intend to follow that precedent here. You're more than welcome to have a family member stay with Josh, as long as they understand they won't have access to electricity and whatnot. We have other ways of making life comfortable."

Mother would do it. She knew that immediately. And Josh adored his grandma. It might work.

"You're wrong about one thing, though," Nikolai said with a smile. "You *can* talk to Josh. Would you like to?"

She wanted nothing more.

DEMANDS

Josh got excited when he saw his mother walking back with Nikolai. Finally they could go. He went to grab her hand and lead her away, but she resisted his tug and said, "We need to talk. Nikolai has offered to interpret."

Josh sagged. He didn't like this. Didn't like all the stalling. Why couldn't they just go?

Mama gripped his hands and held them to her lips. He hated the soft tickle of her breath.

"Josh, I . . ." She paused as though to collect herself. "Is there anything you want to tell me?"

I want to go home.

"He says he wants to go home," said Nikolai.

"How have they been treating you?"

Bad.

"He says two of the others haven't been very kind to him," said Nikolai. "I've already been informed of this and have taken steps to rectify the problem."

That's not what I said.

It was close enough to what you felt. "Bad" doesn't give your mother much to go on.

"Have they hurt you at all?"

Josh held out his leg. *It still hurts. Yoxtl didn't heal it right.*

That was just a training injury. She means has anyone in the group physically harmed you.

Oh. Then no.

"He says no."

"Then why did he stick out his leg?"

"He misunderstood the question. He sustained a minor injury—"

It wasn't minor!

"—during training, but no one has harmed him."

Mama didn't look convinced. "Are injuries common during training?"

"We do our best to prevent them, but they're bound to happen. Better to happen when we have experienced casters present who can ensure things don't get out of hand. A Magi left to their own devices is far more dangerous. It's no surprise that each of these Magi ended up in a mental institution. Doris and Evelyn made objects fly, and Bethany is rumored to have killed someone."

There was a pregnant pause before his mother spoke again, and something had changed in her tone. "I saw what you did to that white boy."

Josh yanked his hands away. He didn't want to talk about this, didn't want to be reminded of what he'd done, he just needed to get out of here. He tried to walk away but Nikolai blocked him.

"Wait," Nikolai said. "Your mother's trying to talk to you. At least hear her out."

NO!

"What's he saying?" asked his mother desperately.

"He doesn't want to think about what he's done. The thoughts are overwhelming to him. He just wants to escape."

"Josh, listen to me. You can't run away from your own conscience. You can't run away from God's judgment."

Josh sank to the ground and covered his head. She was right, he couldn't. That made it even worse. He ran his hands over his shorn scalp—a poor substitute for his checker. It was gone again, lost or taken by the witch hunters, he didn't know which, but it had come back to him before. That was magic too, wasn't it? He rubbed his fingers together and imagined how the little ridges felt on his skin. And then he *did* feel them. Just like that, he'd called the checker to his hand. He bowed over it, caressed it, and began to rock.

Mama knelt beside him and placed a hand on his shoulder. He tried to shrug it off but she held it firmly in place.

"Mrs. Jones, if you'd kindly remove your hand. It bothers him."

"What? I . . . Oh. Yes, of course."

Josh felt a sudden swelling of gratitude for Nikolai.

"I know you don't want to think about what you've done," Mama continued. "It's a horrible thing. So we have to make sure it doesn't happen again, do you understand? You have to learn to control your powers."

If I hadn't had lessons, if I hadn't learned that spell, if I hadn't come here in the first place or been lied to, I never would've done that.

No, you'd just be stuck in a jail cell or lobotomized, came Nikolai's thought sharply.

I don't want to be here.

"He says he doesn't want to be here."

Josh felt a flush of irritation that Nikolai had only repeated the last part.

"Your father's on the way here with family," said Mama. "Nikolai would like you to stay at least a year. Long enough for you to get your powers under control."

Josh shook his head vehemently.

"I'm going to talk to Grandma and see if she can stay here with you. Would you like that?"

I want to go home. Tell her.

Come on, Josh. Give me a year. I promise I'm a much better teacher than Yoxtl.

Tell her! If you don't tell her, if you try to make me stay, I'm just going to leave again.

"What's he saying?"

"He's just reiterating that he wants to leave. A moment, please."

If you leave now you'll be a danger to your family. Not just from accidental spellcasting but from witch hunters. They don't know how to tell who has magic and who doesn't, so they'll kill all of you. Besides, I hear you're pretty good at magic. Wouldn't it be nice to show up those other two? Nikolai glanced meaningfully at Bethany and Doris, who were sulkily going through their things.

Maybe.

"Nikolai tells me that with magic you might be able to do things on your own. Think about it! You could dress yourself, tie your own shoelaces—"

He didn't hear the rest of what she said. Those things would be helpful, but there was something he needed far more, something he'd never had.

I want to be able to talk. I'm sick of people ignoring me and pretending like I don't exist, like I don't hear everything they say about me. Give me a way to communicate, and I'll do it.

Medea jotted down the last note on building modification and slid the pad back into her hip pouch. She'd expected Gloria to be hesitant in her requests—unlike men, women generally avoided overstepping on things they knew little about. But Gloria had made requests for a building that was grand, almost fanciful, as though anxious to put Medea's limits to the test. Her face had lit up as she described various rooms. Now that the pen and paper were away, the woman seemed to sag.

"Can you really do all this stuff?"

"Rooms aren't a problem, nor light. Plumbing is more complicated. The important thing is to get the framework in place. What troubles you?"

"This was a nice distraction, but now that we're done . . ." Gloria shook her head and wrapped her arms around her middle.

"You can't stop thinking about what happened."

"Yes. Yes! I'm sore. There's all these little pains where they, where they . . ." Gloria swallowed. "They were *monsters*."

"No, they were people. There are no greater evils than those people inflict on one another, especially when they believe themselves in the right."

Gloria said nothing for a moment and Medea turned to leave.

"How common are they?" Gloria finally said. "Witch hunters, I mean."

"In America, quite common. There has been no one to stop their spread. Since the events in Salem, they have gotten better at operating in secret, picking off Magi one by one. Any hint of magic can bring you to their attention—not a problem for a talented caster, but those are few and far between these days." She scoffed. "Even Nikolai had trouble with them of late."

"About that . . ." Nikolai appeared in the doorway and nodded back outside. "I'd like a word."

Medea felt herself flush. Now that she thought on it, mentioning his failure probably undermined his authority. Well, it was his own damn fault for getting himself into trouble with witch hunters in the first place. It wasn't her fault for mentioning it. How was she supposed to know he didn't want it talked about? He should have said something.

She followed him away from the house. The sky was starting to lighten, though the sun had yet to appear over the horizon. Nikolai led her to the vehicles, parked in a line on a slightly worn path through the grass. He leaned against the first car.

Before he could chastise her, she spoke. "I didn't say anything that wasn't true. You *did* have trouble with them! Gods know why when you handled yourself fine before, but it's not like you told me not to mention it. I can't be expected to keep track of—"

"Would you say these witch hunters were on par with the others you've faced?"

"I . . . What?"

"When you came up with the plan to combat these witch hunters, I noticed you didn't include anything about anti-magic capabilities. Why would you? It's not as though these Magi know any real spells. Magical attacks would be irrelevant." He turned and opened the trunk, exposing a cramped pile of bodies. "See anything wrong here?"

She did a quick scan. "If you want their deaths to look like an accident, you may want to move them soon before rigor sets in. Though I'm not sure there's any disguising that boy."

"Anything else?"

What was he getting at? "No."

He closed the trunk. "I think it's time for another game of Truth or Dare. It occurs to me that you may have thought I was lying when I described my first encounter with witch hunters. Ask me again."

The implication was absurd, but his face showed no hint of humor. "Truth: Did they have anti-magic capabilities?"

"Yes. They could block magic. Every spell I threw at them failed. If these witch hunters were like those I faced in North Carolina, there's no way Josh could have killed the boy like that, from the inside out. The only thing that worked was manipulating objects around them with telekinesis. Any direct hit . . ." He paused, considering, then shook his head. "I'm not sure how to explain it. It wasn't a shield. It's like the spells were absorbed. And I couldn't get into their minds. This lot"—he nodded to the trunk—"I didn't try until the very end, and it was easy. I altered the last man's aim to make it less lethal. I couldn't even get *inside* the group in North Carolina."

Could it be? Always witch hunters had used the tools of the Mundane—iron manacles, holy water, ropes and chains. They *hated* magic, and now they were using it? It made no sense. They had to be captured, interrogated—

"Don't get excited. My first priority is to get my pouch back, which means I need *you* to stay here with the Magi while I'm gone."

"What?!" He couldn't be serious.

"I shouldn't be more than a few days. Start work on the house, teach them some magic, analyze your experimental data."

"Don't be foolish. They almost managed to capture you last time. I should be the one to go."

A shadow flitted across his face. "No. I wouldn't want you to *interfere* where my curse is concerned."

"I can kill the witch hunters and let you know if I see your pouch."

"After what you told Yoxtl about allowing apprentices to fight their own battles? I don't think so. Besides, you'd probably blast it to smithereens while vaporizing a witch hunter."

"I would *not*," she said indignantly, and he gave her a look. "Okay, maybe I would, but I don't see why you can't just go back into the jungle and collect more Frog's Fancy."

"I already told you, the grove burned."

She waved a hand. "Then postpone until the Magi are set up properly. It's not like your curse struck all that often on this trip."

Curious, that. She'd thought for certain it would hit during the lobotomy or while they were saving the Magi from the witch hunters. "You don't care enough about the Magi for it to trigger, do you?"

He looked momentarily surprised, then glanced over her shoulder and back. He replied in Latin. "Don't say that kind of thing out loud. Not in English. Of course I don't, but they don't need to know that. I can't control how I prioritize things. The more time and effort I put into this settlement, the more important it will become. I'll need my pouch soon. The last thing I need is to appear weak in front of these people." He glanced up again. "It's getting light. We need to dispose of these bodies before Josh's family arrives."

"How do you plan to dispose of them? I don't want anything leading the authorities here."

"I'm going to make it look like they had an accident. A fiery crash, perhaps the result of reckless, drunk driving. Speaking of which . . ." He grinned and held out a key. "I dare you to drive."

Thanks for reading!

You can get a bonus epilogue with Yoxtl, Nikolai, and Medea at **valneil.com/bonus-content**.

If you enjoyed this book, please leave a review on any and all storefronts, and shout about it on social media. Nothing makes an author look more conceited or desperate than constantly pushing their own work, but nothing sells a book faster than readers recommending it to one another. For those of you who have already done so, I am eternally grateful.

AUTHOR NOTES

Medea's Expressions (According to Nikolai)

Frowns

1. That's just her face
2. Reading or concentrating
3. Confused by what you just said
4. Accusing
5. Concentrating, but not happy about it—probably disagrees with what you just said and is currently thinking of a reply

Glares

1. Mildly irritated
2. Moderately irritated—you might get hit
3. Angry but holding back
4. Furious
5. Someone's gonna die

Fun fact: The word "micromanage" (used in *Impulse*) wasn't coined until the seventies, but my editor and I agreed it was too funny to take out.

Not-so-fun fact: Homosexuality was known as "sociopathic personality disturbance" in the 1950s.

Kolya is the diminutive of Nikolai. Like Bill is short for William and, for some fucking reason, Dick is short for Richard. Nikolai's mother called him Kolya.

The painting in Nikolai's room is *Ixion Thrown into Hades*. The first time I saw an image of this painting it struck me as being Nikolai's vibe. He'd love Roberto Ferri's work, but that's too recent. I'm not familiar enough with art to have a painting in mind for the reclining nude woman.

Morning Star Ritual: I stumbled across this while researching Nebraska's Indigenous people and debated on whether to include it. Indigenous Americans have been shafted every which way throughout history and it seems unkind to bring up an embarrassing and localized custom. The Pawnee nation was huge, spanning most of Nebraska and half of Kansas, and this ritual is not representative of most of them (maize was a far more common sacrifice).

Reading about it fucked me up though, and I couldn't get it out of my head. I pulled up my map of Nebraska and looked at where the farmhouse was in relation to where the rituals took place. They were nearly on top of each other. That cinched it. I'm writing dark fantasy, after all.

Medea's views, while critical of what happened to Indigenous peoples, are still that of a white European looking at things from the outside. I hope to have better representation later in the series, including Indigenous characters. The Magi are settling along Nebraska's northern border, which is right next to current-day reservations.

Will Brown's story is real. During World War I, there were major labor shortages. Black people migrated en masse from rural areas in the South to more industrialized cities for work, leading to friction when whites returned home from war. There were race riots all over the country in 1919, known as Red Summer, and Will Brown was tortured and murdered by a mob during that time. It's terrible history everyone should know. You can read more about it at northomahahistory.com/2019/02/19/the-lynching-of-will-brown/.

North 24th Street in Omaha is a product of redlining. Redlining is a discriminatory practice used to box minorities (usually Black people) into specific areas of a city, often by denying loans or refusing to rent to them. Whites would then move away from these areas (known as "white flight"). Cities would then stop investing in infrastructure, leading to a steady decline in services. You can read more about it at wikipedia.org/wiki/Redlining.

The mental hospital is fictional and segregated. There were several Black-operated hospitals created in Omaha over the years, but they all closed by 1957. Even today (2022), the redlined areas of Omaha remain a "healthcare desert" with little in the way of services compared to the rest of the city. Josh's run-in with the police was necessary to get him into the hospital, as he wouldn't have been brought there voluntarily. Most of my Black author friends are older women who told me that disabled family members were usually kept at home and not talked about much, thanks to lack of resources, mistrust of the medical community, and the societal shame associated with disability.

I could not find out for certain if a real mental hospital would be racially segregated in Omaha at that time, but it seemed likely, so I went with it. In truth, I was so focused on trying to find this out that I completely flubbed the first draft, making the hospital racially but not sexually segregated. It wasn't until I stumbled across *Behind Locked Doors: Human Warehouse: 1950 Insane Asylum and Memoir of a Man's Registered Nurse Training* by Robert Higgins—which gives a detailed account of the boring nitty-gritty of everyday hospital life—that I realized my error, which was obvious in hindsight. Men and women were housed in separate wards and, while female nurses could treat male patients, male nurses could not treat female patients. I had to rewrite the majority of character introductions and make up the mingling in the cafeteria. In reality, that would have been separate too.

It goes without saying that mental healthcare was pretty shit in the 1950s. Lobotomies were finally going out of fashion, but electro-convulsive therapy (ECT), hydrotherapy, and insulin shock therapy were still in, and psychotherapy (talk therapy) was just gaining popularity. Chlorpromazine, the first real antipsychotic medication, was developed in France and approved for treating schizophrenia in the United States by 1954. Prior to that, there really wasn't any way to treat psychosis.

ECT was used broadly, both as a treatment and as anesthesia. One of the mistakes I made in my first draft was giving Josh a chemical restraint (injection) for the lobotomy scene. They didn't have that back then, or if they did, it was not utilized. Patients were knocked out with the ECT machine.

Josh: I wanted this series to have more than one autistic. Functioning labels are frowned upon within the autistic community, but it's safe to say that some of us pass more easily than others. Medea reflects much of my own experience. She's viewed as eccentric or odd and she's often misunderstood, but she speaks well, self-accommodates, and her stims are fairly inconspicuous. I wanted an autistic who showed the other side of the coin—

someone who could not hide in plain sight, whose differences were so obvious that neurotypicals immediately marked them as *other*. Autistics often struggle to be understood, but it's far worse for nonspeaking autistics, who are assumed to have an intellectual disability and are infantilized. BIPOC (Black, Indigenous, and people of color) autistics are less likely to be diagnosed and even more likely to be victims of violence.

Intersectionality was important to me with Josh because the disabled and autistic communities share many of the same concerns as the Black Lives Matter movement. Autistics are still legally shocked, excluded, and restrained, both in health care and in schools. I have a friend whose son attended Guiding Hands school, where an autistic child was killed with prone restraint (wikipedia.org/wiki/Death_of_Max_Benson). Max Benson was white, but his story will be all too familiar to Black people. The media reported Max as "violent" (he got frustrated and kicked a wall) and nonverbal (parents say he was speaking), and they exaggerated his size to make it seem like he was dangerous and had to be restrained.

My friend was horrified. This was considered a good school for disabled children, and it wasn't until the story broke that she found out how often her own son had been restrained (hint: a LOT). As a parent of an autistic son who doesn't pass as well as I do, I worry about how he might be treated, particularly as he gets older.

I originally had a prone restraint scene with Josh, which I removed after George Floyd was killed (wikipedi-a.org/wiki/George_Floyd). I had to rewrite the mental hospital sequence anyway, and even though restraint is absolutely the lived experience of many Black and disabled people, I didn't want to be seen as cashing in. George Floyd's case was nothing new to anyone paying attention to the treatment of Black people in the United States, but it received an unprecedented amount of media attention, due to white folks being stuck at home doomscrolling during the pandemic. Even my apathetic and conservative relatives suddenly wanted to learn more about race.

My goal for Josh going forward is to show how accommodations can massively change the autistic experience. Right now he's constantly stressed, infantilized, dismissed, and ignored. He can communicate with Yoxtl and Nikolai, but none of the other Magi can properly interpret his body language.

I employed a sensitivity reader for the Black experience. Sensitivity reading is not the terrible thing some people make it out to be. The biggest issue is that no one person has the lived experience of *everything* and it costs a pretty penny, so you kinda have to pick the topic that needs it the most. Josh is Black *and* disabled *and* nonspeaking *and* autistic. Evelyn is schizophrenic and deeply religious. Gloria is a lesbian. Doris is bipolar. Bethany we're not getting into yet. All the Magi have PTSD on some level. As an autistic, I have my toes in the disabled and nonspeaking autistic communities. I based many of Josh's outward behaviors on how my son would react. I generally get queer characters right, and I have bipolar relatives.

So I picked Blackness, as that is the furthest removed from my own experience, has the most page space out of the above categories, and was the topic I worried most about getting wrong. Sensitivity readers can't possibly cover everything—they can only tackle what they know, and mine was younger, female, bisexual, and abled. Because of this, I also had Black beta readers who could offer feedback on other aspects, like accuracy for the time period and being disabled while Black, autistic, and nonspeaking.

Found a typo? Report it here: https://forms.gle/L3QBaFZp38QTCjXN9

goodreads.com/valneil

bookbub.com/authors/val-neil

patreon.com/ValNeil

twitter.com/ValNeilAuthor

facebook.com/valneilauthor

www.ingramcontent.com/pod-product-compliance
Lightning Source LLC
Chambersburg PA
CBHW060936190726
48286CB00005B/1300